HOMICIDE
A LA HOPKINS

❖ ❖ ❖

Hearing his name, Lloyd Hopkins swiveled and looked at the officers, who turned around and backed into a crowd of plainclothesmen. Again standing on his tiptoes for sight of Kapek, he saw the crowd part and create a space. A second later two M.E. assistants carrying a sheet-covered stretcher walked through it, and when he saw blood seeping through the white cotton, he walked over and yanked the sheet off.

Lloyd ignored the stretcher-bearers' shocked exclamations and stared at the corpse of a middle-aged white man. His chest and stomach bore three large cavities circumscribed by burned and shredded tissue, obvious high-velocity exit wounds.

Shot in the back.

.45-caliber quality holes.

Them.

SUICIDE HILL

ALSO BY
JAMES ELLROY

BROWN'S REQUIEM
CLANDESTINE
*BLOOD ON THE MOON**
*BECAUSE THE NIGHT**
*THE BLACK DAHLIA**

*Published by
THE MYSTERIOUS PRESS

Suicide Hill

JAMES ELLROY

THE MYSTERIOUS PRESS • New York

To Meg Ruley

MYSTERIOUS PRESS EDITION

Copyright © 1986 by James Ellroy
All rights reserved.

Mysterious Press books are published in association with
Warner Books, Inc.
666 Fifth Avenue
New York, N.Y. 10103

A Warner Communications Company

Printed in the United States of America

Originally published in hardcover by The Mysterious Press.
First Mysterious Press Paperback Printing: April, 1987

Reissued: January, 1989

10 9 8 7 6 5

You're alone and you know a few things.
The stars are pinholes; slits in the hangman's mask

Them, rats, snakes;
the chased and chasers—

Thomas Lux

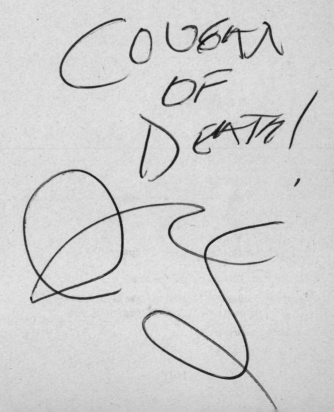

Psychiatric Evaluation Memorandum

From: Alan D. Kurland, M.D., Psychiatrist, Personnel
        Division;
To: Deputy Chief T. R. Braverton, Commander, Detective
      Division;
      Captain John A. McManus, Robbery-Homicide
      Division;
Subject: Hopkins, Lloyd W., Sergeant, Robbery-Homicide
           Division.

Gentlemen:

As requested, I evaluated Sergeant Hopkins at my private
office, in a series of five one-hour counseling sessions, con-
ducted from 6 November to 10 November 1984. I found him
to be a physically healthy and mentally alert man of genius-
level intelligence. He was a willing, almost eager, participant
in these sessions, belying your initial fears about his cooperation. His response to intimate questions and "attack" queries
was unwaveringly honest and candid.

Evaluation: Sergeant Hopkins is a violence-prone obsessive-
compulsive personality, this personality disorder chiefly mani-
festing itself in acts of excessive physical force throughout his
nineteen-year career as a policeman. Following secondarily
but directly in this overall behavior pattern is a strong sexual
drive, which he rationalizes as a "counterbalancing effort"
aimed at allaying his violent impulses. Intellectually, both of
these drives have been justified by the exigencies of "the Job"
and by his desire to uphold his reputation as a uniquely
brilliant and celebrated homicide detective; in reality both
derive from a strident pragmatism of the type seen in emotion-

ally arrested sociopathic personalities—quite simply, a preadolescent selfishness.

Symptomatically, Sergeant Hopkins, a self-described "hot-dog cop" and admitted sybarite, has followed both his violent impulses and his sexual desires with the heedless fervor of a true sociopath. However, throughout the years he has felt deep guilt over his outbursts of violence and extramarital womanizing. This awareness has been gradual, resulting in both the resistance to eschew old behavior patterns and the desire to abandon them and thus gain peace of mind. This emotional dilemma is the salient fact of his neuroses, yet it is unlikely that it alone, by its long-term nature, could have produced Sergeant Hopkins' current state of near nervous collapse.

Hopkins himself attributes his present state of extreme anxiety, despondency, episodes of weeping and highly uncharacteristic doubts about his abilities as a policeman to his participation in two disturbing homicide investigations.

In January of 1983, Sergeant Hopkins was involved in the "Hollywood Slaughterer" case, a case that remains officially unsolved, although Hopkins claims that he and another officer killed the perpetrator, a psychopath believed to have murdered three people in the Hollywood area. Sergeant Hopkins (who estimated the Hollywood Slaughterer's victims to include an additional sixteen young women) was intimately involved with the psychopath's third victim, a woman named Joan Pratt. Feeling responsible for Miss Pratt's death, and the death of another woman named Sherry Lynn Shroeder, who was connected to the Havilland/Goff series of killings (May 1984), Hopkins has transferred that sense of guilt to twin obsessions of "protecting" innocent women and "getting back" his estranged wife and three daughters, currently residing in San Francisco. These obsessions, which represent delusional thinking of the type common to emotionally disturbed superior intellects, were at the core of the professional blunders which led to Sergeant Hopkins' present suspension from duty.

On October 17 of this year, Sergeant Hopkins had succeeded in locating a third Havilland/Goff suspect, Richard

Oldfield, in New Orleans. Believing Oldfield to be armed and dangerous, he requested officers from the New Orleans P.D. to aid him in the arrest. Told to remain at a safe distance while the team of N.O.P.D. plainclothesmen apprehended the suspect, Hopkins disobeyed that order and kicked down Oldfield's door, hesitating when he saw that Oldfield was with a partially clothed woman. After screaming at the woman to get dressed and get out, Hopkins fired at Oldfield, missing him and allowing him to escape out the back way while he attempted to comfort the woman. The New Orleans officers apprehended Oldfield some minutes later. Two plainclothesmen were injured, one seriously, while making the arrest. Sergeant Hopkins said that his episodes of weeping began shortly after this incident.

At Oldfield's arraignment, Sergeant Hopkins was caught prevaricating on the witness stand by Oldfield's attorney. During our second session, he admitted that he faked evidence to obtain an extradition warrant for Oldfield, and that the reason for his courtroom lies was a desire to protect a woman involved in the Havilland/Goff/Oldfield case—a woman he was intimately involved with during the investigation. Sergeant Hopkins became verbally abusive at this point, bragging that he would never relinquish the woman's name to the district attorney or any police agency.

Conclusions: Sergeant Hopkins, forty-two, is experiencing cumulative stress reaction, severe type; is suffering severe nervous exhaustion, exacerbated by an intransigent determination to solve his problems himself—a resolve that implicitly reinforces his personality disorder and makes continued counseling untenable. As of this date I deem it impossible for Sergeant Hopkins to conduct homicide investigations without exploiting them in some social or sexual context. It is highly improbable that he can effectively supervise other officers; it is equally improbable that, given his grandiose self-image, he would ever submit to the performing of nonfield duties. His emotional stability is seriously impaired; his stress instincts disturbed to the point where his armed presence makes him at best ineffective, at worst highly dangerous as a Robbery/Homicide detective. It is my opinion that Sergeant Hopkins should be given early retirement and a full pension, the result of a service-connected disability, and that the administrative processes involving his separation from the L.A.P.D. should be expedited with all due speed.

> Sincerely,
> Alan D. Kurland, M.D.
> Psychiatrist

1

The sheriff's transport bus pulled out of the gate of Malibu Fire Camp #7, its cargo sixteen inmates awaiting release, work furlough and sentence modification, its destination the L.A. County Main Jail. Fifteen of the men shouted joyous obscenities, pounded the windows and rattled their leg manacles. The sixteenth, left unencumbered by iron as a nod to his status as a "Class A" fire fighter, sat up front with the driver/deputy and stared at a photo cube containing a snapshot of a woman in punk-rock attire.

The deputy shifted into second and nudged the man. "You got a hard-on for Cyndi Lauper?"

Duane Rice said, "No, Officer. Do you?"

The deputy smiled. "No, but then I don't carry her picture around with me."

Thinking, fall back—he's just a dumb cop making conversation—Rice said, "My girlfriend. She's a singer. She was singing backup for a lounge act in Vegas when I took this picture."

"What's her name?"

"Vandy."

"Vandy? She got one name, like 'Cher'?"

Rice looked at the driver, then around at the denim-clad inmates, most of whom would be back in the slam in a month or two tops. He remembered a ditty from the jive-rhyming poet who'd bunked below him: "L.A.—come on vacation, go home on probation." Knowing he could outthink, outgame and outmaneuver any cop, judge or P.O. he got hit with and that his destiny was the dead opposite of every man in the bus, he said, "No, Anne Atwater Vanderlinden. I made her shorten it. Her full name was too long. No marquee value."

"She do everything you tell her to?"

Rice then gave the deputy a mirror-perfected "That's right."

"Just asking," the deputy said. "Chicks like that are hard to come by these days."

With banter effectively shitcanned, Rice leaned back and stared out the window, taking cursory notice of Pacific Coast Highway and winter deserted beaches, but *feeling* the hum of the bus's engine and the distance it was racking up between his six months of digging firebreaks and breathing flames and watching mentally impoverished lowlifes get fucked up on raisinjack, and his coming two weeks of time at the New County, where his sentence reduction for bravery as an inmate fireman would get him a job as a blue trusty, with unlimited contact visits. He looked at the plastic band on his right wrist: name, eight-digit booking number, the California Penal Code abbreviation for grand theft auto and his release date— 11/30/84. The last three numbers made him think of Vandy. In reflex, he fondled the photo cube.

The bus hit East L.A. and the Main County Jail an hour later. Rice walked toward the receiving area beside the driver/deputy, who unholstered his service revolver and used it as a pointer to steer the inmates to the electric doors. Once they were inside, with the doors shut behind them, the driver handed his gun to the deputy inside the Plexiglas control booth and said, "Homeboy here is going to trusty classification. He's Cyndi Lauper's boyfriend, so no skin search; Cyndi wouldn't want us looking up his boodie. The other guys are roll-up's for work furlough and weekend release. Full processing, available modules."

The control booth officer pointed at Rice and spoke into a desk-mounted microphone. "Walk, Blue. Number four, fourth tank on your right."

Rice complied. Placing the photo cube in his flapped breast pocket, he walked down the corridor, working his gait into a modified jailhouse strut that allowed him to keep his dignity *and* look like he fit in. With the correct walk accomplished, he made his eyes burn into his brain a scene that he would never again relinquish himself to:

Prisoners packed like sardines into holding tanks fronted by floor-to-ceiling cadmium-steel bars; shouted and muffled conversations bursting from within their confines, the word "fuck" predominating. Trusties wearing slit-bottomed khakis listlessly pushing brooms down the corridor, a group of them standing outside the fruit tank, cooing at the drag queens inside. The screech and clang of barred doors jerking open and shut. Business as usual for institutionalized bulls and cons who didn't know they'd be shit out of luck without each other. Death.

The door to #4 slid open. Rice did a quick pivot and walked in, his eyes settling on the only other inmate in the tank, a burly biker type sitting on the commode reading a paperback western. When the door slammed shut, the man looked up and said, "Yo, fish. You going to classification?"

Rice decided to be civil.

"I guess so. I was hoping for a blue trusty gig, but the bulls have obviously got other ideas."

The biker laid his book on the floor and scratched his razor stubble. "Obviously, huh? Just be glad you ain't big like me. I'm going to Trash and Freight sure as shit. I'll be hauling laundry bags with niggers while you're pushing a broom somewhere. What you in for?"

Rice leaned against the bars. "G.T.A. I got sentenced to a bullet, did six months at fire camp and got a modification."

The biker looked at Rice with eyes both wary and eager for information. Deciding to dig for his own information, Rice said, "You know a guy named Stan Klein? White guy about forty? He would have hit here about six and a half, seven months ago. Popped for possession and sale of cocaine, lowered to some kind of misdemeanor. He's probably out by now."

The biker stood up, stretched, and scratched his stomach.

Rice saw that he was at least six-three, and felt a warning light flash in his head. "He a friend of yours?"

Rice caught a belated recognition of the intelligence in his eyes. Too smart to bullshit. "Not really."

"Not really?" The big man boomed the words. "Not really? *Obviously* you think I'm stupid. *Obviously* you think I don't know how to put two and two together or count. *Obviously* you think I don't know that this guy Klein ratted on you, made a deal with the fuzz and walked around the same time you got busted. *Obviously* you do not know that you are in the presence of a superior jailhouse intellect that does not enjoy being gamed."

Rice swallowed dry, holding eye contact with the big man, waiting for his right shoulder to drop. When the biker took a step backward and laughed, Rice stepped back and forced a smile. "I'm used to dealing with dumbfucks," he said. "After a while you start gearing your thinking to their level."

The biker chuckled. "This guy Klein fuck your woman?"

Rice saw everything go red. He forgot his teacher's warnings about never initiating an attack and he forgot the ritual shouts as he swung up and out with his right leg and felt the biker's jaw crack under his foot. Blood sprayed the air as the big man crashed into the bars; shouts rose from the adjoining tanks. Rice kicked again as the biker hit the floor; through his red curtain he heard a rib cage snap. The shouts grew louder as the electric door slammed open. Rice swiveled to see a half dozen billy clubs arcing toward him. Brief thoughts of Vandy kept him from attacking. Then everything went dark red and black.

Module 2700 of the Los Angeles Main County Jail is known as the Ding Tank. Comprised of three tiers of one-man security cells linked together by narrow catwalks and stairways, it is the facility for nonviolent prisoners too mentally disturbed to exist in the general inmate population: droolers, babblers, public masturbators, Jesus shriekers and mind-blown acidhead mystics awaiting lunacy hearings and eventual shipment to Camarillo and county-sponsored board-and-care homes. Although the "ding" inmates are kept nominally placid through the forced ingestion of high-powered tranquilizers, at night, when their dosages wear down, they spring verbally to life and create a din heard throughout the entire jail. When he returned to consciousness in a cell smack in the middle of Tier #2, Module 2700, Duane Rice thought he was dead and in hell.

It took him long moments to discover that he wasn't; that the tortured shouts and weeping noises were not blows causing the aches and throbs all over his torso. As full consciousness dawned, the pain started for real and it *all* came back, drowning out a nearby voice screaming, "Ronald Reagan sucks cock!" Reflexively, Rice ran his hands over his face and neck. No blood; no lumps; no bruises. Only a swelling around his carotid artery. Choked out and thrown in with the dings, but spared the ass-kicking the jailers usually gave brawlers. Why?

Rice took a quick inventory of his person, satisfying himself that his genitals were unharmed and that no ribs were broken. Taking off his shirt, he probed the welts and bruises on his torso. Painful, but probably no internal damage.

It was then that he remembered the photo cube and felt his first burst of panic, grabbing the shirt off the floor, slamming the wall when plastic shards fell from the wad of denim. His fists were honing in on the cell bars when the intact photo of Anne Atwater Vanderlinden dropped out of the right pocket and landed faceup on his mattress. Vandy. Safe. Rice spoke the words out loud, and the Ding Tank cacophony receded to a hush.

Her hush.

Rice sat down on the edge of the mattress and moved his eyes back and forth between the photograph and the scratched-on graffiti that covered the cells walls. Obscenities and Black Power slogans took up most of the print space, but near the wadded-up rags that served as a pillow laboriously carved declarations of love took over: Tyrone and Lucy; Big Phil & Lil Nancy; Raul y Inez por vida. Running his fingers

over the words, Rice held the aches in his body to a low ebb by
concentrating on the story of Duane and Vandy.

He was working as pit boss at a Midas Muffler franchise in
the Valley, pilfering parts from the warehouse and selling
them to Louie Calderon at half pop, twenty-six and on Y.A.
parole for vehicular manslaughter, going nowhere and waiting
for something to happen. Louie threw a party at his pad in
Silverlake, promising three-to-one women, and invited him.
Vandy was there. He and Louie stood by the door and criti-
qued the arriving females, concluding that for pure sex the
skinny girl in the threadbare preppy clothes was near the
bottom of the list, but that she had *something*. When Louie
fumbled for words to explain it, Rice said, "Charisma." Louie
snapped his fingers and agreed, then pointed out her shabby
threads and runny nose and said, "Snowbird. I never seen her
before. She just sees the open door and walks in, maybe she
thinks she can glom some blow. Maybe she got charisma, but
she got no fucking control."

Louie's last word held. Rice walked over to the girl, who
smiled at him, her face alive with little tics. Her instant
vulnerability ate him up. It was over as soon as it started.

They talked for twelve hours straight. He told her about
growing up in the projects in Hawaiian Gardens, his
boozehound parents and how they drove to the liquor store one
night and never returned, his ability with cars and how his
parents' weakness had given him a resolve never to touch
booze or dope. She scoffed at this, saying that she and her
brother were dopers because their parents were so uptight and
controlled. Their rapport wavered until he told her the *full*
truth about his manslaughter bust, wrapping up both their
defiances with a bright red ribbon.

When he was twenty-two, he had a job tuning sports cars at
a Maserati dealership in Beverly Hills. The other mechanics
were loadies who were always ragging him about his disdain
for dope. One night they fashioned a speedball out of phar-
macy meth and Percodan and slipped it into his coffee, right

before he went out to test the idle on a customer's Ferrari. The speedball kicked in as he was driving down Doheny. He immediately realized what was happening and pulled to the curb, determined to wait the high out and do some serious ass-kicking.

Then it got really bad. He started hallucinating and thought he saw the dope-slippers walking across the street a half block down. He gunned the engine, speed-shifted into second and plowed into them at seventy. The front bumper was torn off, the grille caved in, and a severed arm flew across the windshield. He downshifted, turned the corner onto Wilshire, got out and ran like hell, an incredible adrenaline jolt obliterating the dope rush. By the time he had run out of Beverly Hills, he felt in control. He knew that he had gotten his revenge, and now he had to play the game with the law and get off cheap.

A two-hour steam bath at the Hollywood Y sweated the rest of the speedball out of his system. He took a cab to the Beverly Hills police station, gouged his arm with a penknife to induce crocodile tears and turned himself in. He was charged with two counts of third-degree manslaughter and hit and run. Bail was set at $20,000, and arraignment was set for the following morning.

At arraignment, he learned that the two people he had killed were not the dope-slipping mechanics, but a solid-citizen husband and wife. He pleaded guilty anyway, expecting a deuce maximum, back on the street in eighteen months tops.

The judge, a kindly-looking old geezer, gave him a ten-minute lecture, five years state time suspended and his sentence: one thousand hours of picking up paper refuse from the gutters of Doheny Avenue between Beverly Boulevard on the north and Pico Boulevard on the south. After courtroom spectators applauded the decree, the judge asked him if he had anything to say. He said, "Yes," then went on to tell the judge that his mother sucked giant donkey dicks in a Tijuana whorehouse and that his wife turned tricks with the gorillas in the Griffith Park Zoo. The judge recanted his sentence suspension and hit him with five years in the California Youth Authority

Facility at Soledad—the "Baby Joint" and "Gladiator School."

When Rice finished his story, Anne Vanderlinden doubled over with laughter and launched *her* rap, chain-smoking two full packs, until all the guests had either split or were coupled off in Louie's upstairs bedrooms. She told him about growing up rich in Grosse Pointe, Michigan, and her hard-ass tax lawyer father, Valium addict mother and religious crackpot brother, who got bombed on acid and stared at the sun seeking mystical synergy until he went totally blind. She told him how she dropped out of college because it was boring and how she blew her $50,000 trust fund on coke and friends, and how she liked blow, but wasn't strung out. Rice found her use of street argot naive, but pretty well done. Knowing she was on the skids and probably sleeping around for a place to stay, he steered her talk away from the present and into the future. *What did she really want to do*?

Anne Vanderlinden's little facial tics exploded as she tripped over words to explain her love of music and her plans to spotlight her singing and dancing talents in a series of rock videos: one for punk, one for ballads, one for disco. Rice watched her features contort as she spoke, wanting to grab her head and smooth her face until she was perfectly soft and pretty. Finally he clutched her lank blond hair and drew it back into a bun that tightened the skin around her eyes and cheeks, whispering, "Babe, you won't have shit until you quit sticking that garbage up your nose, and you find someone to look after you."

She fell sobbing into his arms. Later, after they made love, she told him it was the first time she'd cried since her brother went blind.

It was over the next few weeks, after Anne Atwater Vanderlinden had moved in with him and become Vandy, that he figured it out: you don't wait for things to happen—you make them happen. If your woman wants to become a rock star, you regulate her coke use and buy her a sexy wardrobe and cultivate music business connections who can do her some good. Vandy could sing and dance as well as a half dozen female rock stars he knew of, and she was too good to go the tried-and-untrue route of demo tapes, backup gigs and lackluster club dates. She had an ace in the hole. She had him.

And *he* had a chump change job at Midas Muffler, a parole officer who looked at him like he was something that crawled out from under a rock and an overpriced apartment with world-class cockroaches. With his debits cataloged, Rice figured out his credits: he was a great mechanic, he knew how to deactivate automobile alarm systems and bore steering columns for a forty-second start, any car, anywhere, anytime; he knew enough industrial chemistry to compound corrosive solutions that would eat the serial numbers off engine blocks. He had solid Soledad connections who would fix him up with good fences. He would *make* it happen: become a world-class car thief, set up Vandy's career and get out clean.

For a year and a half, it worked.

With three strategically located storage garages rented, and armed with a battery-powered ignition drill, he stole late model Japanese imports and sold them at two-thirds their resale value to a buddy he'd known in the joint, supervising the engine block dips that rendered the cars untraceable, rotating his rip-off territory throughout L.A. and Ventura counties to avoid the scrutiny of individual auto theft details. In two months he had the down payment for a classy West L.A. condo. In three months he had Vandy primed for stardom with a health food diet, daily aerobics, coke as an occasional reward and three-walk-in closets stuffed with designer threads. In four months he had the feedback of two high-priced voice teachers: Vandy was a weak, near tone-deaf soprano with virtually no range. She had a decent vibrato growl that could be jazzed up with a good amplifier, and gave great microphone head. She had the haunted sex look of a punk-rock star—and very limited talent.

Rice accepted the appraisals—they made him love Vandy more. He altered his game plan for crashing the L.A. rock music scene and took Vandy to Vegas, where he dug up three out-of-work musicians and paid them two bills a week to serve as her backup group. Next he bribed the owner of a slot machine arcade/bar/convenience store into featuring Vandy and the Vandals as his lounge act.

Four shows a night, seven days a week, Vandy's vibrato growled the punk lyrics of the group's drummer. She drew wolf whistles when she sang and wild applause when she humped the air and sucked the microphone. After a month of watching his woman perform, Rice knew she was *ready*.

Back in L.A., armed with professional photographs, bribed press raves and a doctored demo tape, he tried to find Vandy an agent. One brick wall after another greeted him. When he got past secretaries, he got straight brush-offs and "I'll call yous"; and when he got past them and whipped out Vandy's photos, he got comments like "interesting," "nice bod" and "foxy chick." Finally, in the Sunset Strip office of an agent named Jeffrey Jason Rifkin, his frustration came to a head. When Rifkin handed back the photos and said, "Cute, but I have enough clients right now," Rice called his fists and took a bead on the man's head. Then inspiration struck, and he said, "Jew boy, how'd you like a brand-new silver gray Mercedes 450 SL absolutely *free*?"

A week later, after he picked up his car, Rifkin told Rice that he could introduce him to a lot of people who might help Vandy's career, and that her idea of showcasting her talent via a series of rock videos was an excellent "high-exposure breakthrough strategy," albeit expensive: $150–200 K minimum. *He* would do what he could with *his* contacts, but in the meantime he also knew a lot of people who would pay hard cash for discount Benzs and other status cars—people in the "Industry."

Rice smiled. Use and be used—an arrangement he could trust. He and Vandy went Hollywood.

Rifkin was partially good to his word. He never procured any recording or club gigs, but he did introduce them to a large crowd of semisuccessful TV actors, directors, coke dealers and lower-echelon movie executives, many of whom were interested in high-line cars with Mexican license plates at tremendous discounts. Over the next year, paperwork aided by an Ensenada D.M.V. employed cousin of his old Soledad buddy Chula Medina, Rice stole 206 high-liners, banking close to a hundred fifty thou toward the production of Vandy's rock videos. And then just as he was about to drill the column of a chocolate-brown Benz ragtop, four L.A.P.D. auto theft dicks drew down on him with shotguns, and one of them whispered, "Freeze or die, motherfucker."

Out on $16,000 bail, his show biz attorney gave him the word: for the right amount of cash, his bank account would not be seized, and he would get a year county time. If the money were *not* paid, it would be a parole violation and probable indictments on at least another fifteen counts of grant theft auto. The L.A.P.D. had an informant by the balls, and they were squeezing him hard. He could only buy the judge if he acted now. If he were quickly sentenced, the L.A.P.D. would most likely drop its investigation.

Rice agreed. The decision cost him an even $100,000. His attorney's fees cost him an additional forty. Ten K for Vandy and bribe money his lawyer slipped to an L.A.P.D. records clerk to learn the identity of the informant had eaten up the rest of his bank account, and had not yielded the name of the snitch. Rice suspected the reason for this was that the shyster pocketed the bread because he knew that the snitch was Stan Klein, a coke dealer/entrepreneur in the Hollywood crowd they ran with. When he learned Klein had been popped for conspiracy to sell dangerous drugs and that it was later dropped to a misdemeanor, he became the number one suspect. But he had to be sure, and the decision to be sure had cost him his last dime and gotten him zilch.

And two weeks away from the release date he'd eaten smoke, fire and bullshit to earn, he'd fucked it up and probably earned himself a first-degree assault charge and *at least* another ninety days of county time.

And Vandy hadn't written to him or visited him in a month.

"On your feet, Blue. Wristband count."

Rice jerked his head in the direction of the words. "I won't let you medicate me," he said. "I'll fight you and the whole L.A. County Sheriff's Department before I let you zone me out on that Prolixin shit."

"Nobody wants to medicate you, Blue," the voice said. "A few of L.A. County's finest might wanta shake your hand, but that's about it. Besides, I can *sell* that goose juice on the street, make a few bucks *and* serve law and order by keeping the Negro element sedated. Let's try this again: wristband count. Walk over to the bars, stick your right wrist out to me, tell me your name and booking number."

Rice got up, walked to the front of the cell and stuck his right arm through the bars. The owner of the voice come into focus on the catwalk, a pudgy deputy with thin gray hair blown out in a razor cut. His name tag read: *G. Meyers*.

"Rice, Duane Richard, 19842040. When do I get arraigned on the new charge?"

Deputy G. Meyers laughed. "What new charge? That scumbag you wasted was in for assault on a police officer with a half dozen priors, and you carried three L.A. County firemen to safety during the Agoura fire. Are you fucking serious? The watch commander read your record, then scumbag's, and made scumbag a deal: he presses charges on you, then the county presses charges on him for grabbing your shlong. Not wanting a fruit jacket, he agreed. He gets to spend the rest of his sentence in the hospital ward, and you get to serve as blue trusty here in the Rubber Ramada, where hopefully you will not get the urge to whip any more ass. Where did you learn that kung fu shit?"

Rice kicked the news around in his head, sizing up the man who'd delivered it. Friendly and harmless, he decided; probably close to retirement, with no good guys/bad guys left in him. "Soledad," he said. "There was a Jap corrections officer who taught classes. He gave us a lot of spiritual stuff along with it, but nobody listened. The warden finally got wise to the fact that he was teaching violent junior criminals to be better violent junior criminals, and stopped it. What's a ding trusty do?"

Meyers took a key from his Sam Browne belt and unlocked the cell. "Come on, we'll go down to my office. I've got a bottle. We'll belt a few and I'll tell you about the job."

"I don't drink."

"Yeah? What the fuck kind of criminal are you?"

"The smart kind. You booze on duty?"

Meyers laughed and tapped his badge. "Turned my papers in yesterday. Twenty years and nine days on the job, iron-clad civil service pension. I'm only sticking around until they rotate in a new man to fill my spot. Ten days from now I am adios, motherfucker, so till then I'm playing catch-up."

As Gordon Meyers explained it, the job was simple. Sleep all day while the dings were dinged out on their "medication," eat leftovers from the officers' dining room, have free run of his collection of *Playboy* and *Penthouse*, be cool with the daywatch jailer. At night, his duties began: feed the dings their one meal per day, move them out of their cells one at a time and mop the floors, get them to the showers once a week.

The most important thing was to keep them reasonably quiet at night, Meyers emphasized. He would be using his on-duty time to read the classified ads and write out job applications, and he did not want the dings dinging his concentration. Talk softly to them if they started to scream, and if that failed, scream back and make them scared of you. If worse came to worse, give them a spritz of the fire hose. And any ding who smeared shit on his cell walls got five whacks in the ass with the lead-filled "ding-donger" Meyers carried. Rice promised to do a good job, and decided to wait five days before manipulating the fat-mouthed cop for favors.

The job *was* simple.

Rice slept six hours a day, ate the high-quality institutional fare the jailers ate, and did a minimum of one thousand push-ups daily. At night, he would bring the dings their chow, G.I. their cells and stroll the catwalk exchanging words with them through the bars. He found that if he kept up a continuous line of cell-to-cell communication, the dings screamed less and he thought of Vandy less. After a few days he got to know some of the guys and tailored his spiels to fit their individual boogeymen.

A-14 was a black guy popped for getting dogs out of the Lincoln Heights Shelter and cooking them up for Rastafarian feasts. The bulls had shaved off his dreadlocks before they threw him in the tank, and he was afraid that demons could enter his brain through his bald head. Rice told him that dreadlocks were "out," and brought him a copy of *Ebony* that featured ads for various Afro wigs. He pointed out that the Reverend Jesse Jackson was sporting a modified Afro and getting a lot of pussy. The man nodded along, grabbed the magazine and from then on would yell "Afro wig!" when Rice strolled by his cell.

C-11 was an old man who wanted to get off the streets and back to Camarillo. Rice falsely reported him as a shit-smearer for three nights running, and gave him three fake beatings, thumping the ding-donger into the mattress and screaming himself. On the third night, Meyers got tired of the noise and turned the old man over to the head jailer of the hospital ward, who said the geezer was Camarillo quail for sure.

The tattooed man in C-3 was the hardest to deal with, because the white trash he grew up with in Hawaiian Gardens all had tattoos, and Rice early on figured tattooing as the mark of the world's ultimate losers. C-3, a youth awaiting a conservatorship hearing, had his entire torso adorned with snarling jungle cats, and was trying to tattoo his arms with a piece of mattress spring and the ink off newspapers soaked in toilet water. He had managed to gouge the first two letters of "Mom" when Rice caught him and took his spring away. He started bawling then, and Rice screamed at him to quit marking himself like a lowlife sleazebag. Finally the young man quieted down. Every time he walked by the cell, Rice would roust him for tattooing tools. After a few times, the youth snapped into a frisking position when he heard him coming.

Around midnight, when the dings began falling asleep, Rice

joined Gordon Meyers in his office and listened to *his* dinged-out ramblings. Biting his cheeks to keep from laughing, Rice nodded along as Meyers told him of the crime scams he'd dreamed up in his sixteen years working the tank.

A couple were almost smart, like a plan to capitalize on his locksmith expertise—getting a job as a bank guard and pilfering safe-deposit box valuables to local beat cops who frequented the bank, staying above suspicion by not leaving the bank and letting the beat cops do the fencing; but most were Twilight Zone material: prostitution rings of women prisoners bused around to construction sights, where they would dispense blowjobs to horny workers in exchange for sentence reductions; marijuana farms staffed by inmate "harvesters," who would cultivate tons of weed and load it into the sheriff's helicopters that would drop it off into the backyards of high-ranking police "pushers"; porno films featuring male and female inmates, directed by Meyers himself, to be screened on the exclusive "all-cop" cable network he planned to set up.

Meyers rambled on for three nights. Rice moved his plan up a day and started telling him about Vandy, about how she hadn't written to him or visited him in weeks. Meyers sympathized, and mentioned that he was the one who made sure his photo of her wasn't destroyed when the bulls choked him out. After thanking him for that, Rice made his pitch: Could he use the phone to make calls to get a line on her? Meyers said no and told him to write her name, date of birth, physical description and last known address on a piece of paper. Rice did it, then sat there gouging his fingernails into his palms to keep from hitting the dinged-out deputy.

"I'll handle it," Gordon Meyers said. "I've got clout."

Over the next forty-eight hours Rice concentrated on *not* clouting the dings or the inanimate objects in the tank. He upped his push-up count to two thousand a day; he laid a barrage of brownnosing on the daywatch jailer, hoping for at least a phone call to Louie Calderon, who could probably be persuaded to check around for Vandy. He stayed away from Gordon Meyers, busying himself with long stints of pacing the catwalks. And then, just after midnight when the ding noise subsided, Meyers' voice came over the tank's P.A. system: "Duane Rice, roll it to the office. Your attorney is here."

Rice walked into the office, figuring Meyers was fried and wanted to bullshit. And there *she* was, dressed in pink cords and a kelly green sweater, an outfit he'd told her never to wear. "Told you I had clout," Meyers said as he closed the door on them.

Rice watched Vandy put her hands on her hips and pivot to face him, a seduction pose he'd devised for her lounge act. He was starting toward her when he caught his first glimpse of her face. His world crashed when he saw the hollows in her cheeks and the blue-black circles under her eyes. Strung out. He grabbed her and held her until she said, "Stop, Duane, that hurts." Then he put his hands on her shoulders, pushed her out to arm's length and whispered, "Why, babe? We had a good deal going."

Vandy twisted free of his grasp. "These cops came by the condo and told me you were really sick, so I came. Then your friend tells me you're *not* really sick, you just wanted to see me. That's not fair, Duane. I was going to taper off and be totally clean by the time you got out. It's not fair, so don't be mad at me."

Rice stared at the wall clock to avoid Vandy's coke-stressed face. "Where have you been? Why haven't you been to see me?"

Vandy took her purse off Meyers' desk and dug through it for cigarettes and a lighter. Rice watched her hands tremble as she lit up. Exhaling a lungful of smoke, she said, "I didn't come to see you at camp because it was too depressing, and you know I hate to write."

Rice caught *his* hands shaking and jammed them into his pants pockets. "Yeah, but what have you been *doing*, besides sticking shit up your nose?"

Vandy cocked one hip in his direction, another move he'd taught her. "Making friends. Cultivating the right people, like you told me I should do. Hanging out."

"Friends? You mean *men*?"

Vandy flushed, then said, "Just friends. People. What about *your* friends? That guy Gordon is looney tunes. When he brought me up from the parking lot, he told me he was going to organize this hit squad of Doberman pinschers. What kind of friends have *you* been making?"

Rice felt his anger ease; the fire in Vandy's eyes was hope. "Gordon's not a bad guy, he's just been hanging around wackos too long. Listen, are you okay on bread? Have you got any of the money I gave you left?"

"I'm okay."

Vandy lowered her eyes; Rice saw the fire die. "You holding out on me, babe? Ten K wouldn't have lasted you this long if you were on a coke run. You feel like telling me about these fr—"

Vandy threw her purse at the wall and shrieked, "Don't be so jealous of me! You told me I should get in with people in the Industry, and that's what I've been doing! I hate you when you're this way!"

Rice reached out for her wrist, but she batted his hand and moved backward until she bumped the wall and there was no place to go except forward into his arms. With her elbows pressed into herself, she let him embrace her and stroke her hair. "Easy, babe," he cooed, "easy. I'll be out in a few days, and I'll get working on your videos again. I'll make it happen. *We'll* make it happen."

Wanting to see Vandy's face, Rice dropped his arms and stepped back. When she brought her eyes up to him, he saw that she looked like the old Anne Atwater Vanderlinden, not the woman he molded and loved. "How, Duane?" she said. "You can't steal cars anymore. Another job at Midas Muffler?"

Rice let the ugly words hang there between them. Vandy walked past him and picked her purse up off the floor, then turned around and said, "This whole thing wasn't fair. I've been making friends who can help me, and I deserve to do a

little blow if I want to. Your control trip is really uptight.
Uptight people don't make it in the Industry."

There was a rapping at the door, and Meyers poked his head
in and said, "I hate to break this up, but the watch commander
is walking, and I don't think he'll buy Vandy here as an
attorney."

Rice nodded, then walked to Vandy and tilted her chin up so
that their eyes locked. "Go back to the pad, babe. Try to stay
clean, and I'll see you on the thirtieth." He bent over and
kissed the part in her hair. Vandy stood still and mute with her
eyes closed. "And don't ever underestimate me," Rice said.

Meyers was waiting for him on the catwalk, tapping a billy
club against his leg. "Listen. A-8 is acting up. He shit on his
mattress and smeared food on the walls. You go give him a few
whacks with the ding-donger while I escort your girl downstairs. When you get him pacified, come back to the office and
we'll bat the breeze."

Rice grabbed the billy club and strode down the catwalk,
pushing images of Vandy's decay out of his mind by concentrating on the jumble of ding noises, wishing the babbles and
shouts would engulf him to the point where all his senses were
numbed. Slapping the ding-donger harder and harder into his
palm, he turned into the open front of A-8, wondering why the
light was off. He was about to call out for Meyers to hit the
electricity when the door slid shut behind him.

The darkness deepened, and the ding noise grew still, then
fired up again. Rice yelled, "Unlock A-8, Gordon, goddammit!" then squinted around the cell. As his eyes became
accustomed to the dark, he saw that it was empty. He smashed
the billy club into the bars full force; once, twice, three times,
hoping to scare the dings into temporary quiet. The crash of
metal on metal assailed him, and the force of the blows sent
shock waves through his entire body. A hush came over the
tank, followed by Meyers' mocking laugh and the words "Told
you I had clout."

When the meaning clicked fully in, Rice began smashing
the club into the wall, four shots at a time, hearing hellish

whispers in the wake of the noise: "It's real pharmaceutical blow, baby"; "Duane wouldn't want me to"; "Come on sweetie, party hearty." When the voices degenerated into giggles, he slammed the ding-donger harder and harder, until the wood casing cracked and the dings screamed along in cadence with his blows. Then sections of plaster exploded in his eyes and into his mouth, and his head started to reel. He surrendered himself to the asphyxiation and fell backward into total silence.

A severed arm spraying blood across a windshield; the steam room at the Hollywood Y. Rice came to with a ringing in his ears and a hazy red curtain in front of his eyes, snapping immediately to the bandage at the crook of his elbow and the wall-to-wall padding that surrounded him. Goose-juiced because he had destroyed A-8, because Gordon had—

Rice held his breath until he passed out, his last half-conscious thought to kill the dope with sleep and get even.

He slept; wakened; slept. Stumbling trips to the toilet, untouched trays of food and a thickening razor stubble marked his drifting in and out of consciousness. Dimly, he knew his kick-out date was coming and the bulls were leaving him alone because they were afraid of him. But Vandy . . .

No. Again and again he plunged into self-asphyxiation.

Finally hunger jerked him fully awake. He counted twelve trays of stale sandwiches, and figured his Prolixin jolt had lasted four days, leaving him three days from the streets. Ravenous, he ate until he threw up. That night a Mexican deputy came by his cell to bring him a fresh tray, and told him he was in Hospital Isolation, between the Ding and the High-Power tanks, and that his release date was two days away. The jailer was wearing a paper party hat. Rice asked him why. "The nightwatch ding jailer just retired," he said. "The watch commander threw him a party."

Rice nodded. *It couldn't have happened.* Vandy would never let a wimp like Gordon Meyers touch her. But when the jailer walked away, the doubts came back. He tried to force sleep, but it wouldn't come. The edge of his vision started to go red.

Hours of push-ups and leg lifts produced an exhaustion that felt pure and nonchemical. Rice drifted off again, then awakened to muffled voices coming from somewhere outside his cell.

He followed the sound to a grated ventilator shaft next to the toilet. Peering through the grates, he saw two pairs of denim-clad legs facing each other. The white stripes along the pants seams was a dead giveaway—he was looking into a High-Power Tank cell.

Laughter; then a deep voice taking over, his words echoing clearly through the shaft.

"I heard a dream score the other day, from this black guy on the Folsom chain. He and his partner were gonna do it, then he got violated on a liquor store heist. He was one smart nigger. He had it documented, the whole shot."

A different, softer voice: "Smart nigger is a contradiction in terms."

"Bullshit. Dig this: three-man stick-up gang, a bonaroo kidnap angle, an ace fucking safeguard.

"Here's the play: two guys hold the *girlfriend* of a *married* bank manager, at her pad, while the outside man calls the manager at *his* crib and has him call his chick, who of course is scared fucking shitless. The outside man calls back and gives him the drill: 'Meet me a half block from the bank an hour before opening, or your bitch gets killed and everyone knows you've been cheating on your wife.'

"Now, dig: the phone booth the outside man's been calling from is down the street from the manager's pad, so he can make sure the fuzz ain't been called. He trails the manager to the bank—still no fuzz—walks in with him, hits only the cashboxes, because the vault has gotta be time-locked, walks out, takes the manager out to his car, slugs him and ties him up, calls the inside men at the chick's pad, they tie *her* up, split, then meet later and divvy up the bread. Is that not fucking brilliant?"

The soft-voiced man snorted: "Yeah, but how the fuck are you supposed to find happily married bank managers with girlfriends on the side? You gonna put an ad in the paper: 'Armed robber seeks cooperative pussy-hound bank managers to aid him in career advancement? Send résumé to blah, blah, blah?' Typical nigger bullshit and jive."

"Wrong, bro," the deep-voiced man said. "I don't know how he got the info, but the black guy had two jobs cased—righteous rogue bank managers, girlfriends, the whole shot."

"And I suppose he gave you the skinny?"

"Yeah, he did, and I believe him. He got ten to life as a habitual offender, why not share the wealth, he's looking at a dime minimum. One chick lives in Encino, on the corner of Kling and Valley View, in a pink apartment house; the other, Christine something, lives in Studio City, a house on the corner of Hildebrand and Gage. I told you: one smart fucking nigger."

"I still don't believe it."

"If Bo Derek offered you a headjob, you'd think she was a drag queen. You're just a terminal fucking skeptic."

Rice listened as the conversation deteriorated into the usual jailhouse shtick of sports and sex. When the talk died altogether, he lay down with his head next to the ventilator shaft and once more fell asleep.

Vandy took over his dreams, short-take images of her laughing, moving around in bed. Then she was there with the Vandals, vibrato growling their closing number: "Gotta get down in the prison of your love. Get down, get down, gonna drown, gonna come so good, so hard, burn my body in your prison yard, prison of your love!"

Rice awakened for the final time in L.A. County Jail stint just as Vandy and the Vandals brought "Prison of Your Love" to its off-key crescendo. Coward, he said to himself. Coward. Using sleep the way a junkie uses smack. Maybe she fucked him and maybe she didn't; when you look into her eyes, you'll know. *So stay awake and fight.*

He stood up and looked around the cell, his eyes catching a

wad of newspaper beside the toilet and a book of matches on top of the sink. Thinking, *let them know,* he struck a match on the ventilator grate, then lit the newspaper and watched it fireball. When it started to burn his hand, he dropped it into the toilet and listened to the sizzle and hiss of newsprint. Satisfied with the way the ink was running, he turned his attention to the floor-to-wall-to-ceiling padding.

Gouging was the only way.

Rice dug his fingernails into a seam of wall padding and pulled outward. Naugahyde, foam and a layer of webbed cotton were revealed. He poked a finger into the hole and felt metal in back of the webbing. Spring reinforcement. He gouged his way to it, then twisted the nearest piece of metal back and forth until it broke off in his hand.

It took him hours to hone his tool on the ventilator shaft grates. When the spring was razor sharp, he pressed it into a sodden ball of newspaper and darkened the tip. Flexing his left biceps into a hard surface, he thought of Hawaiian Gardens and Vandy. Then he marked himself with his past and future, so the whole world would know. The words were *Death Before Dishonor.*

2

Bobby "Boogaloo" Garcia watched his kid brother Joe loosen his clerical collar and do air guitar riffs in front of the bedroom mirror. He felt his own priest outfit constrict his body and said, "I can't take none of your rock and roll rap today, *pindejo*. I quit fighting 'cause niggers kept knocking me out in the third round, and you'll never make it as a musician 'cause you got no drive and no talent. But we both got a job to do, and we're behind for the month. So let's *do* it."

Joe cut off the music in his head; his lyrics put to an old Fats Domino tune, "Suicide Hill" substituted for "Blueberry Hill." Leave it to Bobby to puncture both their balloons with one shot, so he wouldn't have a good comeback. "Tomorrow's December first. The Christmas rush and the rainy season. We'll double up on Bibles and prayer kits, *and* siding jobs." Bobby's jaw clenched at the last words, and Joe added, "And we'll give some money to Saint Sebastian's. A tithe. We'll find some suckers with bucks, and rip them off and give the *dinero* to earthquake re—"

Bobby stopped him with a slow finger across the throat. "Not earthquake relief, *puto*! It's a scam! You don't do penance for one scam by giving bucks to another one!"

"But Henderson gave two grand to that priest from the archdiocese for earthquake relief. He—"

Bobby shook his head. "A scam within a scam within a scam, *pindejo*. He gave the priest a check for two K and got a receipt for three. That priest has got a brother in the D.A.'s office. The Fraud Division. Need I say fucking more?"

Joe tightened his collar, feeling his nice guy/musician self slip back into Father Hernandez, the phone scam padre. He grabbed a stack of Naugahyde-bound Bibles off the floor and carried them out to the car, wondering for the ten millionth time how Bobby could love hating his brother and his job and his *life* as much as he did.

Bobby and Joe worked for Henderson Enterprises, Inc., purveyors of aluminum siding and Bibles in Spanish. The scam originated in a phone room, where salesmen pitched rustproof patios and eternal salvation through Jesus to unsophisticated and semi-impoverished Angelenos, offering them free gas coupons as a come-on to get the "field representatives" out to their homes, where he signed them up for "lifetime protection guarantees," which in reality meant a new siding job or Bible on a "regular installation basis"—meaning debilitating permanent monthly payments to whoever was gullible enough to sign on the dotted line.

Which was where Bobby and Joe, as Father Gonzalez and Father Hernandez, L.A.-based "free-lance" priests, came in. They were the "heavy closers"—psychological intimidation specialists who sized up weaknesses on the follow-up calls and *made* the sucker sign, setting in motion a string of kickbacks originating in the main office of U.S. Aluminum, Inc., and its subsidiary company, the Truth and Light Publishing House.

With the trunk of their '77 Camaro stuffed with Bibles, siding samples and wall hangings of Jesus, the Garcias drove to a "close" in El Monte on the Pomona Freeway. Joe was at the wheel, humming Springsteen under his breath so his brother wouldn't hear; Bobby threw short punches toward the windshield and stared out at the dark clouds that were forming, hoping for thundershowers to spook their closees into buying. When raindrops spattered the glass in front of him, he closed his eyes and thought of how everything important in his life happened when it was raining.

Like the time he sparred with Little Red Lopez and knocked him through the ropes with a perfect right cross. Red said his timing was off because bad weather made his old knife scars ache.

Like the time Joe and his garage band won the "Battle of the Bands" at El Monte Legion Stadium. He played adoring older brother and glommed a groupie who gave him head in his car while he smoked weed and kept the wipers going so he could eyeball prowling fuzz.

Like the righteous burglaries he and Joe pulled in West L.A. during the '77-'78 floods, when the L.A.P.D. and C.H.P. were all evacuating hillsides and mopping blood off the freeways.

Like the time he felt guilty about treating Joe like dirt, and agreed to rip off the guitars and amplifiers from the J. Geils bass player's pad in Benedict Canyon. Halfway down to Sunset with the loot, the car fishtails and sideswipes a sheriff's nark ark. Joe freaks at the badge and cocked magnum in his face and starts blabbing how a hitchhiker left the stuff in the trunk. No way, Jose, the cop said. Bingo: nine months in the laundry at Wayside.

Like the times when they were kids, and Joe got terrified of thunder and woke him up and made him promise always to protect him.

Bobby switched to left jabs aimed at the wiper blades, pulling his fist back a split second before it hit the glass, watching Joe flinch out of the corner of his eye. "I always carried you, ain't I? Like I promised to when we were kids?"

Joe kept his eyes on the road, but clenched his elbows to his side, like he always did when Bobby started talking scary. "Sure, Bobby, that's true."

"And you've always watchdogged me when I got off too deep into my weird shit. Ain't that true?"

Joe saw what was coming and swallowed so his voice would be steady. "That's true."

"You've got to say it."

Tightening his hands on the wheel, Joe fought an image of their last B&E, of the woman with her skirt up over her head, Bobby with his knife at her throat as he raped her. "Y-you'd be . . . you'd hurt people."

"What kind of people?"

Joe stared straight ahead. The sky was getting darker and taillights began flashing on. Concentrating on their reflections off the wet pavement gave him a moment to think up a new answer that would satisfy Bobby's weirdness and let him keep a piece of his pride. He was about to speak when a station wagon swerved in front of them.

Joe flinched backward and Bobby grabbed the wheel out of his hands and yanked it hard right. The car lurched forward, missing the station wagon's rear bumper by inches. Bobby jammed his foot onto the accelerator, looked over his shoulder, saw a tight passing space and jerked the car across four lanes and down a darkened off-ramp. He slowly applied the brake, and when they came to a stop at the flooded intersection, Joe was brushing tears from his eyes.

"Say it," Bobby said.

Joe screamed the words, his voice breaking: "You're a rape-o! You're a mind fuck! You're on a wacko guilt trip, and I'm not kicking out any more of *my* money for *your* penance!" He swung the car out into the stream of traffic, punching the gas, doing a deft brody that set off a chain of honks from cut-off motorists. Bobby cracked the passenger window for air, then said softly, "I just want you to know how things are. How they're always gonna be. I owe you for getting us out of burglary. Too many women out there; too many chances to pull weird shit. But you owe me your guts, 'cause without me you ain't got any. We gotta remember that stuff."

Knowing Bobby was trying to get at something, Joe pressed the edge that his tears always gave him. "You sent that woman five K, right? The money orders were cashed, so you know she got them. You sent her a note, so even though the signatures on the checks were false, she knew it was *you*. You haven't done it again, so why are you rehashing all this old stuff? We've got a good deal with Hendy, but you keep talking it down like it's nothing."

Bobby popped short left-right combos until his arms ached and his tunic was soaked with sweat. "I'm just getting itchy, little brother," he said at last. "Like something has gotta happen real soon. Take surface streets, I gotta cool out before the close."

They cruised east on Valley Boulevard, Joe driving slowly in the middle lane, so he could scope out the scene on both sides of the street. The rain died to a drizzle, and Bobby took a hand squeeze from the glove compartment and started a long set of grip builders, dangling his right arm out the window to get a good extension. When Joe saw that the streets were nothing but used-car lots, liquor stores, burrito stands and boredom, he tried to think up some more lyrics to "Suicide Hill." When words wouldn't come, he slumped down in his seat and let the story take over.

Suicide Hill was a long cement embankment that led down to a deep sewage sluice in back of the Sepulveda V.A. Hospital. The hill and the scrubland that surrounded it were encircled by high barbed-wire fencing that was cut through in dozens of places by the gang members who used it as a meeting place and fuck turf.

The hill itself was used to test courage. Steep, and slick from spilled oil, it served as the ultimate motorcycle gauntlet. Riders would start at the top and try to coast down, slowly picking up speed, then popping the bike into first and hurdling the sewage sluice, which was thirteen feet across and rife with garbage, industrial chemicals and a thirty-year accumulation of sharp objects thrown in to inflict pain. Gang rivalries were settled by two riders starting off on top of the hill at the same time, each armed with a bicycle chain, the object to knock the opponent into the muck while hurdling it himself. Scores of bodies were rumored to be decomposing in the sluice. Suicide Hill was considered a bad motherfucker and a destroyer of good men.

So was the man it was named after.

Fritz "Suicide" Hill and the V.A. Hospital dated back to the days immediately following World War II, when scores of returning G.I.s necessitated the creation of veterans' domiciles. Rumor had it that Fritz was housed at the brand-new institution for shell shock, and after his recovery was assigned to a domicile ward to ease his emotional readjustment. Fritz had other ideas. He pitched a tent in the scrubland by the embankment and started an L.A. chapter of the Hell's Angels, then embarked on a career as a motorcycle highwayman, shaking down motorists all over Southern California, always returning to his encampment by the Sepulveda Wash. That part of the legend Joe accepted as fact.

The rest was a mixture of bullshit and tall tales, and the part that Joe wanted to put into his song. Suicide Hill sliced the guy who sliced the Black Dahlia; he masterminded a plot to break Caryl Chessman out of death row; he tommy-gunned niggers from a freeway overpass during the Watts Riot. He turned Leary on to acid and kicked Charlie Manson's ass. The cops wouldn't fuck with him because he knew where the bodies were buried. Even legendary hot dogs like John St. John, Colin Forbes and Crazy Lloyd Hopkins shit shotgun shells when Suicide Hill made the scene.

The most popular ending of the legend had Fritz Hill dying of cancer from all the chemicals he'd sucked in during his many dunks in the Sepulveda Wash. When he saw the end coming, he hauled his 1800 C.C. Vincent Black Shadow up to the roof of the hospital and popped a wheelie over the edge in second gear, flying some five hundred yards before he crashed into the scrubland, igniting a funeral pyre that could be seen all over L.A. Joe knew that the whole story, rebop, truth and all, was the story of everything he and Bobby had ever done, but all he had so far was "and death was a thrill on Suicide Hill"—and those ten bars were enough for a plagiarism beef.

Bobby nudged him out of his reverie. "Hang a right. The pad should be on the next block."

Joe complied, pulling onto a street of identical tract houses, all of them painted pink, peach or electric blue. Bobby scanned addresses, then pointed to the curb and shook his head. "Jesus Christ, Father Hernandez. Another *stone* wacko."

"*Qué*, Father Gonzalez?"

Joe set the brake and got out of the car, then looked over at the front lawn of the closee's pad and answered his own question. "Wacko's not the word, Padre."

The walkway of the peach-colored house was lined with Day-Glo plaster statues of Jesus and his disciples. On one side of the lawn a plastic Saint Francis stood guard over a flock of Walt Disney squeeze toys. On the other side, stuffed teddy bears and pandas were arranged around a papier-mâché nativity scene. Joe walked over and checked out the manger. A Donald Duck doll was wrapped in swaddling clothes. Minnie Mouse and Snoopy leaned against the crib, sheepherder staffs pinned to their sides. The whole collage was sopping wet from the rain. "Holy fuck," he whispered.

Bobby cuffed him on the back of the head. "This is too fucking sad. Anybody this fucking crazy has gotta be a rollover. Let's just get a signature and split." He shoved a turquoise Bible and matching siding sample at Joe, then stared at the opposite side of the lawn. His eyes caught a toppled Jesus statue and a Kermit the Frog puppet going sixty-nine. He grabbed Joe's arm and pushed him up the walkway. "Five minutes in and out. No rosaries, no bullshit."

Before Joe could respond, a fat white woman in a rumpled housedress opened the door and stood on the porch in front of them. Grateful that she wasn't Mexican, Bobby said, "I'm Father Gonzalez, and this is Father Hernandez. We're the field priests from the Henderson Company. We brought you your siding sample and Bible. The workmen will be out to put up your patio next week." He reached into his breast pocket for a blank contract. "All we need is your signature. If you sign today, you get our November bonus, the Henderson Prayer Service: millions of Catholics worldwide will pray for you everyday for the rest of your life."

The woman reached into the pockets of her dress and pulled out rosary beads and a wad of one-dollar bills. She bit at her lip and said, "The phone man said I got to give to earthquake relief to get prayed for. He said to give you the money to give to him, and you'd pray for my husband, too. He's got the cancer powerful bad." Joe was reaching for the money when he saw Bobby smile; the slow smile he used to flash just before a fight he knew he was going to lose. He dropped his hand and stood off to one side as the veins in his brother's forehead started to twitch and spit bubbles popped from his mouth. The woman stammered, "He-he's sick powerful bad," and Bobby ran back to the car and began hurling Bibles and siding samples out into the street, covering the pavement with pastel Naugahyde and aluminum. When there were no more phone scam products left to throw, he tore off his priest jacket and his cassock and dropped them into the gutter, followed by the money in his pants pockets. Joe stood on the porch beside the shock-stilled woman, watching the last five years of his life go up in smoke, knowing that what made it so bad was that Bobby believed in God worse than any of the people he hurt.

3

Three weeks into his suspension from duty, Lloyd Hopkins flew to San Francisco and kept his family under a rolling stakeout. He rented a room at a Holiday Inn on the edge of Chinatown and a late-model Ford, and watched from a distance as his wife made her rounds of the city as an antique broker and met her lover for drinks, dinner and overnight visits at her Pacific Heights apartment; from a further distance he followed his daughters to school, on errands and out on dates. After a week of loose surveillance, he knew that he had gleaned no information and gained no special insights that would make his job easier. All he could do was let them find him, and see where it went from there.

He decided to let the girls make the discovery, and drove to their school and parked across the street. At 12:30, classes adjourned for an hour, and Anne and Caroline always ate with friends under the big oak tree in the school's backyard, while Penny skipped lunch and brooded by herself on the steps. If he stood by the car, big and familiar in his favorite herringbone jacket, then sooner or later they would notice him, and he would be able to read their faces and know what to do.

At precisely 12:30, the school's back door opened, and the first wave of students exited and jockeyed for positions under the oak tree. Lloyd got out and leaned against the hood of his car. Anne and Caroline appeared moments later, chattering and making faces as they examined the contents of their lunch sacks. They found spaces on the grass and began eating, Caroline making her usual liverwurst face as she unwrapped her first sandwich. Penny walked out then, peering around before disappearing into a swarm of children. Lloyd felt tears in his eyes, but kept them on his daughters anyway, waiting for the moment of recognition.

"Loitering in the vicinity of school yards, huh? Let's see your I.D., pervert!"

Lloyd did a slow turn, savoring the sound of Penny's voice and the anticipation of their identical gray eyes meeting. Penny foiled his plan by jumping into his arms and burying her head in his chest. Lloyd held his youngest daughter and dried his eyes on her Dodgers cap. When she started growling and nudging his shoulders like a cat, he growled back and said, "Who's the pervert? And what's with this feline stuff? The last I heard you were a penguin."

Penny stepped back. Lloyd saw that the color in her eyes had deepened, gaining a hint of Janice's hazel. "Penguins are passé. You've lost weight, Daddy. What are you doing in Frisco? This skulking-around scene wasn't too subtle, you know."

Lloyd laughed. "Do the others know I'm here?"

Penny shook her head. "No, they're not too subtle either. I figured it out two days ago. This friend of mine said there was this big man in a tweed jacket checking out the school yard. He said the guy looked like a nark or a perv. I said, 'That sounds like my dad.' I kept peeking outside during classes until I saw you." She stood on her tiptoes and poked Lloyd's necktie. "Speaking of which, my dummy sisters just figured it out."

Looking over his shoulder, Lloyd saw Caroline and Anne staring at him. Even from a distance he could see shock and anger on their faces. He waved, and Anne dropped her lunch sack and grabbed her sister's arm. Together they ran toward the school's back door.

Lloyd looked at Penny. "They're pissed. Why? The last time I came up we got along great."

Penny leaned against the car. "It's cumulative, Daddy. We're the geniuses, they're the plodders. They resent me because I'm the youngest, the smartest, and have the biggest breasts. They—"

"No, goddammit! What really?"

"Don't yell. I'm serious, Annie and Liney have gone très Frisco. They want Mom to divorce you and marry Roger. Mom and Roger are on the rocks, so they're scared. Daddy, are you in trouble in the Department?"

Realizing that his two older daughters weren't going to join him, Lloyd put an arm around his youngest and drew her close. "Yeah. I blew an extradition bust and fucked up at the guy's arraignment. I've been suspended from duty until the first of the year. I'm not sure what's going to happen, but I'm sure I'm finished in Robbery/Homicide. I might get transferred to a uniformed division until my twenty years come up, I might get my choice of flake assignments. I just don't fucking know."

Penny burrowed deeper into her father. "And you're scared?"

"Yeah, I'm scared."

"And you still want all of us back?"

"More than ever."

"Want some advice?"

"Yeah."

"Exploit this rocky period Mom and Roger are going through. Work fast, because they're going away this weekend, and they have this tendency to patch things up during long motel idylls."

Lloyd laughed. "I've been observing you lately. Don't you ever eat lunch?"

Penny laughed back. "The school serves nothing but health food, and Mom's sandwiches suck. I hit a burger joint on the way home."

"Come on, we'll get a pizza and conspire against your mother."

After a long lunch, Lloyd dropped Penny back at school and drove to Janice's apartment. There was a note on the door:

"Roger—running late, make yourself at home. Should ret. around 3:30." He checked his watch—3:10—and picked the lock with a credit card and let himself in. When he saw the state of the living room, he realized Janice's success, not her lover, was his chief competition.

Every piece of furniture was a frail-looking antique, the type he had told her never to buy for the house because he was afraid it wouldn't support his 225 pounds; every framed painting was the German Expressionist stuff he despised. The rugs were light blue Persian, the kind Janice had always wanted, but was certain he'd ruin with coffee stains. Everything was tasteful, expensive, and a testament to her freedom as a single woman.

Lloyd sat down carefully in a cherrywood armchair and stretched his legs so that his feet rested on polished hardwood, not pale carpeting. He tried to kill time imagining what Janice would be wearing, but kept picturing her nude. When that led to thoughts of Roger, he let his eyes scan the room for something of or by himself. Seeing nothing, he fought an impulse to check out Janice's bedroom. Then he heard a key in the lock and felt himself start to shiver.

Janice saw him immediately and didn't register an ounce of surprise. "Hello, Lloyd," she said. "Liney called me at the office and told me you were in town. I expected you to come by, but I didn't expect you to break in."

Lloyd stood up. A red wool suit and a new shorter hairdo. He hadn't been close. "Cops have criminal tendencies. You look wonderful, Jan."

Janice sighed and let her purse drop to the floor. "No, I don't. I'm forty-two, and I'm putting on weight."

"I'm forty-two and losing weight."

"So I can see. So much for the amen—"

Lloyd took two steps forward; Janice one. They embraced hands to shoulders, keeping a space between them. Lloyd broke it off first, so the contact wouldn't make him want more. He took a step backward and said, "You know why I'm here."

Janice pointed to a Louis XIV sofa. "Yes, of course." When

Lloyd sat down, she took a chair across from him and said, "I know what you want, and I'm glad that you want it, but I don't know what *I* want. And I may never know. That's as honest an answer as I can give you."

Lloyd felt threads of their past unraveling. Not knowing whether to press or retreat, he said, "You've made a good life for yourself here. This pad, your business, the life you've set up for the girls."

"I also have a lover, Lloyd."

"Yeah, Roger the on-and-off lodger. How's that going?"

Janice laughed. "You're such a riot when you try to act civilized. I read about you in the L.A. papers a couple of weeks ago. Some man you captured in New Orleans."

"Some man whose capture I fucked up in New Orleans, some man whose arraignment I almost blew in L.A."

Janice smoothed the hem of her skirt and leaned forward. "I've never heard you admit to making mistakes before. As a cop, I mean."

Lloyd leaned back. The sofa creaked against his weight and combined with Janice's words to form an accusation. "I never made them before!"

"Don't shout, I wasn't accusing you of anything. What did the man do?"

The creaking grew; for a split second Lloyd thought he could feel the floor start to tremble. "The *man*? He beat a woman to death during a snuff film. Roger ever take out any scumbags like that?"

Janice started to flush at the cheeks; Lloyd grabbed the arms of the sofa to keep from going to her. "Roger doesn't take out scumbags," she said. "He doesn't break into my apartment or carry a gun or beat up on people. Lloyd, I'm a middle-aged woman. I was in love with your intensity for a long, long time, but I can't handle it anymore. Maybe it isn't a nice thing to say, but Roger is a comfortable, no-fireworks lover for a middle-aged antique broker who put in nineteen years as wife to a hot-dog cop. Lloyd, do you know what I'm saying?"

The perfect softness of the indictment rang in Lloyd's ears.

"I've made amends as best I could," he said, consciously holding his voice at a whisper. "I've tried to admit the things I did wrong with you and the girls."

Janice's whisper was softer: "And your admissions were excessive and hurt me. You told me things that you shouldn't ever, *ever* tell any woman that you claim to love."

"I *do* love you, goddammit!"

"I know. And I love you, and even if I stay with Roger and divorce you and marry him, I'll always love you, and Roger will never own me the way you have. But I'm too tired for the kind of love you have to give."

Lloyd stood up and walked to the door, averting his eyes from Janice and groping for threads of hope. "The girls? Would you consider how they feel about me?"

"If they were younger, yes. But now they're practically grown up, and I can't let them influence me."

Lloyd turned around and looked at his wife. "You're not yielding on this an inch, are you?"

"I yielded too long and too much."

"And you still don't know what you want?"

Janice stared at the light blue Persian carpet she had coveted since the day of her wedding. "Yes ... I ... still don't know."

"Then I guess I'll just have to outyield you," Lloyd said.

4

She was gone, and she'd taken everything that could be converted into quick cash with her.

Duane Rice walked through the condo he'd shared with Vandy, keeping a running tab on the missing items and the risks he'd taken to earn them. TV console, state-of-the-art stereo system and four rooms' worth of expensive high-tech furniture—gone. Four walk-in closets full of clothes, three for her, one for him—gone. Paintings that Vandy insisted gave the pad class—gone. The down payment and maintenance costs on a flop that he now couldn't live in—adios, motherfucker. Add on the empty carport in back of the building and total it up: two hundred Class A felonies committed in the jurisdictions of the most trigger-happy police departments in the country. Sold down the river by a worthless—

When he couldn't finish the thought, Rice knew that the game wasn't over. He pissed on the living room carpet and kicked the front door off its hinges. Then he went looking for felony number 201 and the means to get back his woman.

The Pico bus dropped him on Lincoln Avenue, a stone's throw from Venice Ghosttown and the likelihood of a shitload of customized taco wagons without alarm systems. On Lincoln and Ocean Park he spotted a hardware store and went in and boosted a large chisel, rattail file and pair of pliers. Exiting the store, he smiled and looked at his watch: two hours and ten minutes out of the rock and back on the roll.

Rice waited for dusk at a burrito stand on the edge of Ghosttown, drinking coffee and eyeballing the East Venice

spectacle of overage hippies, overage hookers, overage low-
riders and underage cops trying to look cool. He watched
horny businessmen in company cars prowl for poontang, tried
to guess which hooker they'd hit on and wondered why he had
to love a woman before he could fuck her; he watched an aged
love child with an amplifier strapped to his back strum a guitar
for chump change and suck on a short dog of T-bird. The
scene filled him with disgust, and when twilight hit, he felt his
disgust turn to high-octane fuel and walked into Ghosttown.

Stucco walk-back apartment buildings, white wood frame
houses spray-painted with gang graffiti, vacant lots covered
with garbage. Emaciated dogs looking for someone to bite.
The cars either abandoned jig rigs or welfare wagons in mint
condition, but nothing exceptional. Rice walked west toward
the beach, grateful that the cold weather had the locals
indoors, seeing nothing that Louie Calderon would pay more
than five bills for out of friendship. He kept walking, and was
almost out of Ghosttown when automotive perfection hit him
right between the eyes.

It was a '54 Chevy convertible, candy-apple sapphire blue
with a canary yellow top, smoked windshield and full continental kit. If the interior was cherry and the engine was in
good shape, he was home.

Rice walked up to the driver's-side door and pretended to
admire the car while he got out his chisel and pliers. He
counted slowly to ten, and when he could feel no suspicion
coming down on him, jammed the chisel into the space
between the door-lock and chassis and yanked outward. The
door snapped open, no alarm went off. Rice saw that the dash
was a restored '54 original and felt underneath it for the
ignition wires. Pay dirt! He took his pliers and twisted the two
wires together. The engine came to life, and he drove the car
away.

Two hours later, with the Chevy safely stashed, Rice walked
in the door of Louie Calderon's auto body shop and tapped
Louie on the shoulder. Louie looked up from the tool kit he

was digging through and said, "Duane the Brain! When'd you get out?" Rice ignored the oil-covered hand he offered and placed an arm over Louie's shoulders. "Today." He looked around and saw two mechanics staring at them. "Let's go up to your office."

"Business?"

"Business."

They walked through the shop and up to the office that adjoined the second story of Louie's house. When they were seated across the paper-cluttered desk from each other, Rice said, "Now resting in your hot roller garage out by Suicide Hill is a mint '54 Chevy ragtop. Continental kit, 326 supercharged, full leather tuck and roll, hand-rubbed sapphire blue metal flake paint job. Intact, I'd say it's worth twelve K. Parts, close to ten. The *upholstery* is worth at least two."

Louie opened the refrigerator next to his desk and pulled out a can of Coors. He popped the top and said, "You're crazy. With your record, you have got to be the primo auto theft suspect in L.A. County. You bought your way out of what? A hundred counts? That kind of shit only happens once. Next time, they fuck you for the ones they got you on *and* the ones you got away with. How'd you get in my garage?"

Rice cracked his knuckles. "I cut a hole in the door with a chisel and unlocked it from the inside. Nobody saw me, and I covered up the hole with some wood I found. And I'm not planning on making a career of it. I just did it for a quick stake."

"Nice sled, huh?"

"Primo. If you weren't a Mexican, I'd call it a bonaroo taco wagon."

Louie laughed. "All Chicanos with ambition are honorary Anglos. How much you want?"

"Two grand and a couple of favors."

"What kind of favors?"

"When I was at fire camp, I heard you had a message service. You know, twenty-four-hour, bootleg number, tap-proof. That true?"

"*Es la verdad.* Two hundred scoots a month, but be cool who you give the number to, I don't want no shitbirds giving me grief at four in the morning. What else you want? Let me guess . . . Let's see . . . A car!"

"How'd you guess? I don't care what it looks like, all I want is something with legit registration that runs. Deal?"

Louie walked to the back wall and lifted up a framed *Playboy* centerfold, then twirled the dial of the safe and opened it. He pulled out two bank packets and tossed them to Rice. "Deal. The car is ugly, but it runs. Remember this number: 628-1192. Got it?"

Rice said, "Got it," and stuck the money in his pocket. "I also heard you were dealing guns."

Louie's eyes became cold brown slits. "You wanta tell me who told you that?"

"Sure. A guy at the County. Big blond guy on the Quentin chain."

"Randy Simpson, fat-mouthed motherfucker. Yeah, I've been trying to deal guns, but I can't find no shooters who want my product. I bought these big, heavy-ass army .45 automatics from this strung-out quartermaster lieutenant. He threw in these tranquilizer dart guns, too. A bullshit deal. The shooters want the lightweight Italian pieces, and *nobody* wants the dart guns. I gave my son one of the dart jobs, took the firing pin out so he couldn't hurt himself. Why? You going cowboy, Duane-o?"

Rice shook his head. "I don't know. I heard about a deal, but it might not float. I'll have to check it out."

"What *are* you gonna do for a living?"

"I . . . I don't know. Work on making a few scores, then work on Vandy's career. She split, but I—"

Rice stopped when he saw Louie's face cloud over. He shook his head to blot out the sound of Vandy's "But Duane wouldn't want me to," then said, "What is it? Don't hold back on me."

Louie drained his beer in one gulp. "I was going to tell you, I was just waiting for the right time. A friend of mine saw Vandy, sometime last week. She was walking out of this outcall service place on the Strip, you know, by the All-American Burger. He said at first he didn't recognize her with all this makeup on, but then he was sure. I'm sorry, man."

Rice stood up. Louie saw the look in his eyes and said, "Maybe it don't mean that."

"It means I have to find her," Rice said. "Go get me my car."

Duane Rice drove his "new" '69 Pontiac to the east end of the Sunset Strip, hugging the right-hand lane in order to check out the hookers clustered by bus benches, searching for Vandy's aristocratic features wasted by makeup and dope. Every face he saw burned itself into his brain, where it was superimposed against a reflex image of Gordon Meyers and preppy Anne Atwater Vanderlinden. But none of the faces was *her*, and when he saw three solid blocks of massage parlors, fuck pads and outcall services looming in front of him, he gnawed his lips until he tasted blood.

Rice parked in the All-American Burger lot and walked slowly west on the south side of Sunset. All the streetwalkers now were black, so he kept his eyes glued to the shabby storefronts and their flashing neon signs. He passed Wet Teenagers Outcall and Soul Sisters Mud Wrestling; New Yokohama Oriental Massage and the 4-H Club—"Hot, Handsome, Horny and Hung." After a block, the obscenities blurred together so that he couldn't read individual names, and he stared at front doors waiting for *her* to come out.

When he saw that guilty-looking men were the only ones entering and leaving, he started to see red and walked to a curbside bus bench and braced his hands against it in an isometric press. With his eyes closed, he forced himself to think. Finally he remembered the snapshot of Vandy he'd carried through jail. He reached for his wallet and pulled it from its plastic holder, then turned around and again confronted the flashing beacons. Nuclear Nookie Outcall; Wet and Woolly Massage; Satan's House of Sin. This time the words didn't blur. He pulled out a handful of Louie Calderon's twenties and walked through the nearest door. A bored black man behind a desk looked up as he entered and said, "Yeah?"

Rice held the photo of Vandy and a double saw under the man's nose. "Have you seen this woman?"

The man put down his copy of the *Watchtower*, grabbed the twenty and looked at the snapshot. "No, too good-lookin' for this jive place. If you want to pork this kinda chick, I can fix you up with a cut-rate version gives mean head."

Rice breathed out slowly; the red trapdoor behind his eyes eased shut. "No thanks, I want *her*. Got any ideas?"

The man stuck the twenty in his shirt pocket. "I don't know what places got what quality pussy, but I know this jive place ain't got nothin' but woof-woofs. You just keep walkin' and whippin' out that green, maybe you find her."

Rice took the man's advice and walked east. He showed the snapshot to every doorman and bouncer at every sex joint on the row, handing out over three hundred dollars, getting nothing but negative head shakes and a consensus that Vandy was too foxy to be doing either Strip outcall or street hooking. After four straight hours of breathing nothing but sleaze, he got coffee at the All-American Burger and sat down at an outside table to think.

He came up with facts that he trusted. Louie and his friends were solid; if one of them saw Vandy out here in whore makeup, it was probably true—without him to look after her she was a stone self-destructor. None of the massage and outcall slimebags he'd talked to had I.D.'d her—and it was to their financial advantage to do so. Louie's friend had seen her sometime last week, probably right after she visited him and cleaned out the pad. It all felt right.

Rice looked at his watch: 3:30, the whores thinning out as the traffic on Sunset dwindled. The only hookers still working were black, and unlikely to have info on Vandy—she avoided *all* jigs like the plague. Draining his coffee, he stood up and started for the car. Then he saw an incredible redhead walk over to the curb and stick out her thumb.

Rice moved fast, running to his car and pulling up in front

of the girl, cutting off a slow-trawling Mercedes. The redhead looked in the passenger window distastefully, then back at the status car. Rice yelled, "A c-note for ten minutes," and the girl hesitated, then opened the door and got in. Rice handed her a wad of twenties as the driver of the Mercedes accelerated and flipped them the bird.

The redhead stuffed the money into her purse and poked a finger at the tufts of foam sticking out of the seat. "This car sucks. Can we go to a motel or something?"

Rice turned around the corner, then pulled over to the curb and flicked on the dashboard light. "I don't want to get laid, I just had a feeling you could help me find this woman." He handed her the photo of Vandy and watched as she examined it, then shook her head.

"No, never. Your chick?"

"That's right."

"She a working girl?"

Rice swallowed a wave of anger. "Yeah. I've heard she's been doing outcall around here, but nobody recognizes her, and I believe them."

The redhead scrutinized the snapshot, then said, "She's real cute. Too classy for most of the places around here."

"What do you mean, 'most'?"

"Well, there's this high-line place a couple of blocks from here, off the Strip. They run only really foxy chicks, to these movies and rock big shots. I worked out of there for a week or so, then I quit. Too much of a drug scene. I'm into health food."

Rice felt his skin prickle. "What's the name of the place?"

"Silver Foxes. No 'outcall,' just 'Silver Foxes.' "

"What's the address?"

"Gardner, just off the Strip. Lavender building, you can't miss it. But they only send chicks out on referrals, you know, it's real exclusive."

"Phone number?"

The girl hesitated. Rice dug in his pocket for more money, then handed it to her. "Tell me, goddammit."

She grabbed the door handle. "You won't tell where you got it?"

"No."

"658-4371." The girl darted out of the car. Rice watched her counting her money as she walked back to the Strip.

It took him less than ten minutes to find the lavender apartment building. It stood just south of Sunset in the glow of a streetlamp, a plain Spanish-style four-flat with no lights burning.

Rice parked and walked across the lawn to the cement porch. Four doors were recessed in the entranceway, illuminated only by mailbox lights. He squinted and saw that three of the apartments belonged to individuals, while the last box was embossed with a raised metal insignia of a fox in a mink coat winking seductively. There was a buzzer beneath the words "Silver Foxes." Rice pressed it three times and heard its echo. No lights went on and no sounds of movement answered the buzzing. He reached into the mailbox and found it empty, then stood back on the lawn so he could eyeball the whole building. Still nothing but darkness and silence.

Rice drove to a pay phone and dialed 658-4371. A recorded woman's voice answered: "Hi, this is Silver Foxes, foxes of every persuasion for every occasion. If you're already registered with us, leave your code number and let us know what you want; we'll get back to you soon. If you're a new friend, let us know who you know, and give us their code numbers and your phone number. We'll get in touch soon."

There was an interval of soft disco music, then a beep. Rice slammed down the receiver and drove back to outcall row.

Only the dregs of the hookers were still out, garishly made-up junkies who stepped into the street and lifted their skirts as cars passed by. Rice sat at a table inside the All-American Burger and drank coffee while he scanned women on both sides of Sunset. Every face he glimpsed looked ravaged; every body bloated or emaciated. Toward dawn, the neon lights on the outcall offices and massage parlors started going off. When street-sweeping machines pushed the few remaining hookers back onto the sidewalk, he took it as his cue to leave and check out business.

Rice drove across Laurel Canyon, coming down into the Valley just as full daylight hit. When he reached Ventura Boulevard, he recalled verbatim the facts he'd heard through the ventilator shaft: "Kling and Valley View, pink apartment house"; "Christine something, Studio City, house on the corner of Hildebrand and Gage." Truth, half-truth or bullshit?

At Hildebrand and Gage he got his first validation. The mailbox of the northeast corner house was tagged with the name "Christine Confrey." That fact gave him a feeling of destiny that built up harder and harder as he drove west to Encino. When he got to Kling and Valley View and saw a faded pink apartment house on the corner, with an out-of-place Cadillac parked in front, the feeling exploded. Rice kept it at a low roar by calculating odds: five to one that the info was correct, making the heists possible.

Checking the mailboxes of the six-unit building, he saw that only one single woman lived there—Sally Issler in #2. He found a door designated 2 on the ground-floor street side, with a high hedge fronting the apartment's large picture window. Rice squatted behind the hedge, waiting for the owner of the Caddy to cut the odds down to zero.

He waited an hour and a half before a door opened and two voices, one male, one female, gave him pay dirt:

"My wife gets back tomorrow. No overnighters for a while."

"Matinees? You know, like the song—'Afternoon Delight'?"

The man laughed. "We can hit Hot Tub Fever during your lunch hour."

"Sounds good, but I read in *Cosmo* that those hot tub places all have herpes germs in the water."

"Don't believe everything you read. Call me at the bank?"

"Yeah."

Rice heard sounds of kissing, followed by a door slamming. He counted to ten, then stood up and peered around the hedge.

The Cadillac was just taking off. He ran for his car and pursued it.

It led him to a Bank of America branch on Woodman and Ventura. Rice sized up the man who got out. Tall, broad-hipped, sunken-chested. A wimp whose sex appeal was his money.

The man walked up to the front doors. Rice followed from a safe distance, passing him as he stepped inside. When the manager locked the doors behind him, Rice counted to ten, then peered through the plate-glass window and smiled.

The manager was alone inside the bank, and the surveillance cameras were fixed-focused at the floor. The tellers stations were visible from the street only if a passerby was willing to stand on his tiptoes and crane his neck.

Rice watched the manager walk directly to the teller area and take a key from his pocket, then open drawers and transfer cash to his briefcase, leaving pieces of paper in the money's place—probably doctored tally slips. The odds zoomed to perfection. Rice ran to his car, then drove to a pay phone and called Louie Calderon at his message drop number.

"Speak."

"Louie, it's Duane."

"Already? Don't tell me, the car broke down and you're pissed."

"Nothing like that."

"Another favor?"

"Yeah. I want three .45s and one of those dart guns. You've got darts, too?"

"Yeah. Before we go any further, I don't wanna know what you got in mind. You got that?"

"Right. Silencers?"

"I can get them, but they cut down the range to practically zilch."

"They'll never be fired; it's just an extra precaution."

"Mr. Smooth. Seven bills for the whole shot. Deal?"

"Deal. One more thing. I need two men, smart, with balls,

who want to make money. No niggers, no dopers, no trashy
gangster types, nobody with robbery convictions."

Louie whistled, then laughed. "You want a lot, you know
that? Well, today's your lucky day. I know two Chicano
dudes, brothers, who're looking for work. Smart—one righteous vato, one tagalong. Pulled hundreds of burglaries, only
got popped once. *Righteous burglars, righteous con men.*
They just hung up this phone rip-off gig and they're hurtin' for
cash."

"You vouch for them?"

"I fenced their stuff for seven or eight years. When they got
busted, they didn't snitch me off. What more you want?"

"Any strong-arm experience?"

"No, but one of them is downright mean, and I'll bet he'd
dig it. Used to fight welterweight, ten, twelve years ago. All
the top locals stomped on him."

"Can you set up a meet?"

"Sure. But I'm tellin' them and I'm tellin' you: I don't want
to know nothin' about your plans. *Comprende?*"

"*Comprende.*"

"Good. I'll call Bobby and set it up. When you meet him,
tell him how you saw him knock Little Red Lopez through the
ropes with a right cross. He'll eat it up."

The phone went dead. Rice walked back to his car. When he
stuck the key in the ignition, he was trembling. It felt good.

5

Even as the dream unfolded, he knew that it was *just* a dream, one of the stock nightmares that owned him, and if he didn't panic, it would run its course and he would wake up safe.

Sometime back in '67 or '68, when he was working Hollywood Patrol, he and his partner Flanders got an unknown trouble call directing their unit to an old house in a cul-de-sac off the Cahuenga Pass, a block of ramshackle pads rented out dirt cheap because noise from the freeway overpass made living there intolerable.

When no one answered their knocks and shouted "Police officers, open up!" he and Flanders kicked in the door, only to be driven back outside by the stench of stale cordite and decomposing flesh. While Flanders radioed for backup units, he drew his service revolver and prowled the pad, discovering the five headless bodies, brain-spattered walls, expended shotgun rounds and the note taped to the TV set: "I keep hearing these voices thru the freeway noise telling Peg and the kids about me and Billy. It's a lie, but they won't believe it was just one time when we was drunk, and that don't count. This way nobody's going to know except Billy, and he don't care."

The man who wrote the note was slumped by the TV set. He had jammed the sawed-off .10 gauge into his crotch and blown himself in two. The shotgun lay beside him in a pile of congealed viscera.

Then the dream speeded up, and he wasn't sure if it was happening or not.

Flanders came back inside and yelled, "Backup, detectives and M.E. on their way, Hoppy." He saw him reach for a cigarette to kill the awful stink, and was about to scream about gas escaping from stiffs, but *knew* Flanders would call it college boy bullshit. He ran toward him anyway, just as the match was struck and the little boy's stomach exploded and Flanders ran out the door with his face on fire. Then *he* was screaming, and ambulances were screaming, and he knew it wasn't a dream, it was the telephone.

Lloyd rolled over and reached for it, surprised to find that he had fallen asleep fully clothed. "Yes? Who is it?"

A familiar voice came on the line. "Dutch, Lloyd. You all right?"

"You woke me up."

"Sorry, kid."

"Don't be; you did me a favor."

"What do you mean?"

"Never mind. What is it, Dutch?"

When there was a long silence on the L.A. end of the line, Lloyd tensed and shook off the last remnants of sleep. He heard the bustle of Hollywood Station going on in the background, and pictured his best friend getting up the guts to tell him something very bad.

"Goddammit, Dutch, tell me!"

Dutch Peltz said, "So far it's just a rumor, but it's an informed rumor, and I credit it. That shrink you saw last month recommended you be given early retirement. You know, emotional disability incurred in the line of service, full pension, that kind of thing. I've heard that Braverton and McManus are behind it, and that if you don't accept the plan, you'll be given a trial board for dereliction of duty. Lloyd, they mean it. If the trial board finds you guilty, you'll be kicked off the Department."

A kaleidoscope of memories flashed in front of Lloyd's eyes, and for long moments he didn't know if he was back in a dream or not. "No, Dutch. They wouldn't do that to me."

"Lloyd, it's true. I've also heard that Fred Gaffaney has got a file on you. Nasty stuff, some sex shit you pulled when you worked Venice Vice."

"That was fifteen fucking years ago, and I wasn't the only one!"

Dutch said, "Sssh, sssh. I'm just telling you. I don't know if Gaffaney is in with Braverton and McManus on this, but I know it's all coming down bad for you. Retire, Lloyd. With your master's, you can teach anywhere. You can do consulting work. You can—"

Lloyd screamed, "No!" and picked up the phone, then saw the framed photograph of his family on the nightstand and put it back down. "No. *No. No.* If they want me out, they'll have to fight me for it."

"Think of Janice and the girls, Lloyd. Think of the time you'd have to spend with them."

"You're talking shit, Dutch. Without the Job, there's nothing. Even Janice knows that. So fuck 'em all except six, and save *them* for the pallbearers. See you in L.A., Captain Peltz."

Dutch's voice was soft and hoarse. "Until then, Sergeant Hopkins."

Lloyd hung up and walked into the bathroom, cursing when he saw the daintily wrapped soap bars and his disposable razor crusted with shaving cream. Muttering "Fuck it," he soaked a washcloth in cold sink water and wiped his face, then straightened his necktie, wondering why he always wore one, even when he didn't have to. When he looked in the mirror, the answer came to him, and he prepared to do battle with the institution that had given him all of his nightmares and most of his dreams.

At a stand of pay phones in the lobby, Lloyd found a copy of the San Francisco yellow pages and leafed through the "A's" until he hit "Attorneys." Dismissing the shysters who had full-page ads mentioning their low rates and drunk-driving experience, he got out a pencil and notepad and started jotting down names and addresses at random, filling up half a page before he noticed *Brewer, Cafferty and Brown* at an address on Montgomery that was probably only a half dozen blocks from where he was standing. Again muttering "Fuck it," he smoothed his necktie and walked there, jamming his hands into his pockets to keep from running.

The waiting room of Brewer, Cafferty and Brown was furnished in the old-line California style of leather armchairs and brass floor lamps; the photographs on the walls blew the sense of tradition apart. Lloyd walked in and knew immediately that chance had directed him to either *the* best or *the* worst law firm ever to be considered by a defendant in an interdepartmental police trial.

Bobby Seale, Huey P. Newton and Eldridge Cleaver glared down at him, giving the clenched-fist salute; a group photo of the United Bay Area Gay Collective beamed down. Hanging over the reception desk was a purple wall tapestry with "Power to the People!" embroidered in the center, and beside it there was a photographic blowup of dozens of Oriental men in karate stances. Lloyd examined the picture, figuring it for an outtake from a martial arts movie. He was wrong; it was the Boat People's Political Action Army. Sitting down to wait for someone to welcome him, he felt like he had been given the D.T.s without benefit of booze.

After a few minutes, a tall black woman in a tweed suit walked in and said, "Yes, may I help you?"

Lloyd stood up, noticing the woman catch sight of the .38 strapped to his belt. "I came to see an attorney," he said. "Your office was close to my hotel, so I came here."

"Then you don't have an appointment?"

The woman was staring openly at his gun. Lloyd took out his I.D. holder and badge and showed it to her. "I'm a Los Angeles police officer," he said. "I'm looking for an attorney to represent me at a police trial board. An out-of-town lawyer is probably a good idea. I've got forty thousand dollars in the bank, and I'll spend every dime to keep my job."

The woman smiled and walked back out of the room. Lloyd held eye contact with Huey Newton until she returned and said, "This way, please, Mr. Hopkins," and led him to an inner office. A pale man was sitting behind a desk reading a newspaper. "Mr. Brewer, Mr. Hopkins," the woman said, then exited and closed the door behind her.

Brewer looked up from his paper. "L.A.P.D., huh? Well, we know they didn't bring you up on charges of excessive force, because they don't recognize that concept." He stood up and extended his hand. Lloyd shook it, measuring the man's words, deciding his abrasiveness was a test. "I like your office," he said as he took a chair next to the desk. "Out of the low-rent district. You do a lot of oil-leasing contracts on the side, take down the pictures of the niggers when the fat cats come to call?"

Brewer filled a pipe with tobacco and tamped it down. "So much for light conversation. I don't have to agree with a client's ideology in order to represent him. Why are you getting a trial board?"

Lloyd forced himself to talk slowly. "The overall charge will probably be dereliction of duty. I'm currently on a six-week suspension, with pay. The specific charge or charges will have to do with a recent perjury I committed at a murder trial arraignment. I—"

Brewer jabbed the air with his pipe stem. "Why did you commit perjury? Is this a common practice of yours?"

"I lied to protect a woman innocently involved in the case," Lloyd said softly, "and I've lied previously only to circumvent probable-cause statutes in regard to hard felonies."

"I see. By any chance were you intimately involved with this woman?"

Lloyd grasped the arms of his chair. "That's none of your business, Counselor. Next question."

"Very well. Let's backtrack. Tell me about your career with the L.A.P.D."

Lloyd said, "Nineteen years on the Job, fourteen as a detective-sergeant, eleven in Robbery/Homicide Division. I've got a master's in criminology from Stanford, I'm considered the best homicide detective in the Department, I've earned more commendations than I can count, I've successfully investigated a number of highly publicized murder cases. My arrest record is legendary."

Brewer lit his pipe, then blew smoke at the ceiling. "Impressive, but what's more impressive is that someone with such an outstanding record should have incurred such departmental disfavor. I should think that one perjury slipup wouldn't have been sufficient to jeopardize your career. I know the L.A.P.D. looks after their own."

"There's other stuff. Minor fuckups over the years. The high brass sent me to a shrink. I shot my mouth off about things I shouldn't have."

"Why?"

"Because I wanted to get rid of it! Because I never thought they'd try to do this to me!"

"Please calm down, Sergeant. There are ways to get around one psychiatrist's report, usually by mitigating it with the report of a different analyst, one with a superior reputation."

Lloyd gripped the sides of the desk until he felt his hands go numb. "Counselor, this isn't a trial in a court of law, this is a kangaroo cop trial, and academic credentials don't mean shit. Saving my job is a long shot from the gate, and making a department employee look bad would only make the odds worse."

Brewer slid back in his chair and stared past Lloyd at the far wall. "Well . . . there are other approaches. You have a family?"

"Wife and three daughters. I'm separated from them."

"But you remain cordial?"

"Yes." Lloyd stared at the attorney, who kept his eyes fixed on a point just above his head and said, "Then we can exploit them as character witnesses, gain sympathy for you that way. You yourself present an interesting picture, one that can be used to advantage. Are you aware that your clothes don't fit? They're at least two sizes too large. We can portray you in court as a victim of your own conscientiousness, a man driven to radical weight loss by overzealous dedication to duty! If you were to lose even more weight, that sympathy factor would be increased. With the proper coaching your daughters would elicit the mo—"

"*Look at me*," Lloyd hissed, holding down a picture of his hands around Brewer's throat, squeezing until the lawyer's averted eyes popped out of his skull. "Look at me, you cocksucker."

Brewer closed his eyes. "Control your language, Sergeant. I want you to get used to wearing a penitent expression, one that wi—"

Lloyd stepped around the desk, grabbed Brewer by the arms and shoved him into a glass bookcase. The glass shattered; law texts spilled to the floor. Lloyd took hold of Brewer's neck with his left hand, and balled his right hand into a fist and aimed it at the lawyer's squeezed-shut eyes. Then he heard a scream, and his peripheral vision caught the receptionist with her hands clasped over her mouth. He pulled the punch at the last second, sending his fist through an unbroken pane of glass. Shoving Brewer aside, Lloyd held his bloody hand in front of him. "I . . . I'm sorry, goddamn you . . . I'm sorry."

6

Duane Rice looked at Bobby "Boogaloo" Garcia and knew two things: that, ex-welterweight or not, he could take him out easy; and that the little taco bender was incorrigibly *mean*. After a jailhouse handshake, Rice looked around his living room, saw quality stuff and pegged him as a non-doper who gangsterized because he was too lazy to work and in love with the game. Thinking, so far so good, he threw out a line to test his smarts: "I think I saw you fight once. You knocked Little Red Lopez through the ropes at the Olympic about ten, twelve years ago."

Bobby grinned and pointed to the couch; Rice sat down, seeing smarts up the wazoo and a big determination to milk the game. "Likable Louie must have told you that," Bobby said. "Told you I'd dig it. Louie's gotta be the dumbest smart guy I know, because only about six people in the world know about that, and I'm the only one cares, just like you're the only one gives a rat's ass about how you ragged that judge. Fucking Louie. How'd he manage to stay alive so long?"

"He can do things we can't do," Rice said, reaching into the back of his waistband and pulling out a silencer-fitted .45 automatic. "Like this." He worked the slide and ejected the clip, catching the chambered round as it popped into the air. "Dum dum. Likable Louie has stayed alive for so long because guys who can get nice things are likable. Right, Bobby?"

Laughing, Bobby held out his hands. Rice tossed the .45 up to him, and he grabbed it and did a series of quick draws aimed at the Roberto Duran poster above the fireplace. "Pow,

Roberto, pow! Pow! *No más! No más!*" Grinning from ear to ear, he handed the gun back butt first and slumped into a chair across from Rice. "Louie ain't likable, Duane. He's lovable. He's so lovable that I'd suck his daddy's dick just to see where he came from. How many of those you got?"

"Three," Rice said. "One for you, one for me, one for your brother. Is he coming?"

"Any minute. Wanta trade pedigrees?"

"Sure. The vehicular manslaughter conviction you already heard about, three years at Soledad because I lost my temper and reverted to my white trash origins; a bust on one count of G.T.A., a bullet in the County, reduced to six months. Y.A. parole and County probation, both of which I'm hanging up, because car thief/mechanic is what my P.O. calls a 'modus operandi—occupational stress combination.' In other words, he expects me to sling burgers at McDonald's for the minimum wage. No way."

Bobby nodded along, then flashed a grin and said, "How many cars you boost before you got busted?"

"Around three hundred. You and your brother did B&Es, right?"

"Right. At least four, five hundred jobs, with one bust, and that was a fluke."

"What did you do with the money? Louie pays a good percentage, and he said you guys aren't into dope."

Bobby cracked the knuckles of his right hand. "I *own* this house, man. Joe and I used to *own* a coin laundromat and a hot-dog stand, and I bankrolled a couple of fighters after I quit myself. What about *you*? Three hundred G.T.A.s and you drive up in an old nigger wagon looks like something the cat dragged in. What'd you do with *your* money?"

"I spent it," Rice said, boring his eyes into Bobby's, testing for real now, wondering if retreating was the smart thing to do. The two-way stare held until Bobby's eyelids started to twitch and he smiled/winced and said, "Shit, man, I like women as much as the next man."

Stalemate; Bobby had backed off, but returned with a good

shot, right on target. Rice tasted blood in his mouth, and felt his teeth involuntarily biting his cheeks. The bloody spittle lubed his voice so his next shot sounded strong to his own ears. "You think you can be cool with that gun? You think you can hold on to it and not shoot it?"

Three seconds into a new eyeball duel, the front door opened and Joe Garcia walked in carrying a bag of groceries. Rice broke the stare and stood up and stuck out his hand. Joe shifted the bag and grabbed the hand limply, then said, "Sorry I'm late," and reached into the bag and pulled out a can of beer. He tossed it at Bobby, who shook it up, then popped the top and let the foam shoot out and spray his face. Chugalugging half the can, he cocked a thumb and forefinger at the Roberto Duran poster and giggled, "Pow! Pow! *No más! No más!*" Rice watched Joe Garcia watch his older brother. He seemed wary and disgusted, a smart reaction for a tagalong criminal. Bobby killed his beer and plugged Roberto Duran a half dozen more times. Rice knew the charade was a machismo stunt to hide his fear. To hid his own contempt and relief, he watched Joe walk into the kitchen, then joined Bobby in laughing. When Joe returned looking outright scared and Bobby gazed over at him and wiped his lips, Rice said, "Let's talk business, gentlemen."

It took him half an hour to outline the plan exactly the way he'd heard it through the ventilator shaft, stressing that no one knew he'd heard it and that he'd cased the locations to a T, getting the facts validated straight down the line. He would be the "inside" man who actually hit the banks; they would be the "outside" men who held the two girlfriends captive at their pads and received the phone calls from the rogue bank managers. Gauging their reactions, Rice saw that Bobby wanted it for the money and the pure unadulterated thrill—every time he mentioned the kidnap angle the ex-welter popped his knuckles and licked his lips; he saw that Joe was afraid of the whole thing, but more afraid of putting the kibosh on his brother's glee. For a two-time-only deal, they were solid partners.

Finishing his pitch, Rice said, "A few other things: park your car on the nearest big street to the chicks' pads. That's Ventura for the Issler woman, Lankershim for Confrey. Wear gloves, but don't put on your ski masks until right before you go in the door. Carry briefcases and dress well so you'll blend in with the neighborhood. We meet at my place, Room 112 at the Bowl Motel on Highland up from the Boulevard, *one hour* after I call you at the girlfriends' pads. Tie the chicks up and tape their mouths, but make sure they can breathe. Questions?"

Bobby Garcia said, "Yeah. You said you been casing both gigs for three days. What do you mean by that?"

"We've got two on-the-sly romances going down," Rice said. "Hawley from the B. of A. and his bitch Issler; Eggers from Security Pacific and his babe Confrey. Both men open their banks early, by themselves, and pilfer from the tellers boxes, probably small amounts. Okay, three days now, I've seen them tap the tills before opening. I've watched the guards and tellers arrive, parked across the street with binoculars. At both banks the money at the tellers stations is left there overnight!"

Joe Garcia raised his hand. "Why are these banks so lax about their security?"

"Good question," Rice said. "I thought about that, then I did some more checking. First off, Hawley is a fuckup, too wimpy to run a tight ship. He's got nothing but party-hearty types working there, you know, everybody smokes dope on their lunch hour, young squares with no ambition, so they've got to get wasted to make it through the day. Also, the Security Pacific is only half a block from an L.A.P.D. substation—maybe Eggers thinks he's robbery-proof. Who knows? And who cares?"

Bobby held up his hands, then brought them together and began slowly cracking the knuckles on each finger. Finishing, he said, "Let's cut the shit and get to the cut. It's a righteous fucking plan, but how much are we gonna make?"

Rice said, "I'm guessing at least thirty K per bank minimum, sixty-forty split—sixty for me, forty for you guys to split."

Bobby snorted. Joe said, "That sounds fair to me, you did all the wo—"

"Shut up, *pindejo*!" Bobby yelled. Lowering his voice, he said to Rice, "I like you, Duane, but you're giving me the big one where it hurts the most. Fifty-fifty, or you go take a flying fuck at a rolling doughnut."

Rice faked a sheepish look; his split strategy had worked to perfection. "Deal," he said, sticking out his right hand for the brothers to grasp, wincing when Bobby slammed it with both callused palms, grinning when Joe's tagalong hands followed. "Day after tomorrow for Hawley and Issler. I'll meet you here tomorrow night at nine for a final briefing. If you need me for anything, call me at Louie's bootleg number."

The three men stood up and shook hands all around. Rice turned to walk out, and Bobby tapped him on the shoulder. "Ain't you forgetting something, Duane?"

Rice smiled and did a two-gun pirouette, drawing one .45 from his back waistband and another from his shoulder holster, flipping them up by the silencered barrels and catching them by the grips. "Be cool," he said as he handed the guns to Bobby.

Bobby "Boogaloo" Garcia grinned and emptied both .45s at his back living room wall, blowing Roberto Duran to shreds and the wall itself into a rubble heap of rotted wood, dust and plaster chips. Joe squinted through the gun smoke and saw that the shots had ripped apart the connecting door to his bedroom. Screaming, "You rape-o motherfucker, you wasted my albums!" he ran back to inspect the damage. Bobby bowed to Rice and said, "Never liked Roberto since Hearns kicked his ass. Silencers work good, Duane."

7

Deputy Chief Thad Braverton slammed down the phone and muttered, "Fuck," then buzzed his secretary. When she appeared in the doorway, he said, "Ring Captain McManus at Robbery/Homicide and have him come up immediately, then call Captain Gaffaney at Internal Affairs and have him come up in fifteen minutes, no sooner."

The woman nodded and about-faced into her vestibule. Braverton sent exasperated eyes heavenward and said, "Crazy Lloyd. Jesus fucking Christ."

McManus rapped on the doorjamb only moments later. Braverton took his eyes from the ceiling and said, "Sit down, John. Close the door behind you. Fred Gaffaney is joining us shortly, and I don't want him to hear any of this."

McManus nodded and eased the door shut, then sat down, waiting for the superior officer to speak first. Close to a minute passed before Braverton said, "Hopkins isn't accepting the retirement deal."

McManus shrugged. "I didn't think he would, sir. I also didn't know that you'd spoken to him."

"I haven't," Braverton said. "Someone leaked the word to him in Frisco. Hopkins went out looking for an attorney to represent him at his trial board and blundered into the office of the most prestigious left-wing firm in the city. He ended up shoving around the head shyster and punching out a bookcase."

McManus breathed out slowly. "Jesus fucking Christ."

"My initial reaction, too."

"Charges filed?"

Braverton shook his head. "S.F.P.D. talked the shyster out of it, applied pressure somehow. I just spoke to the station commander who caught the squeal. He said when the beef came in, Hopkins got a standing ovation from the detective squad."

McManus felt chills dance up his spine. "Typical. Have you decided what you're going to do?"

"No."

"Would you like my feedback?"

"Of course. You're his immediate supervisor, and, as cops go, an atypical thinker."

McManus didn't know if the chief's last remark was a compliment or a jibe; Braverton was a poker voice all the way. Trying hard to keep his own voice level, he said, "Sir, I've been Hopkins' supervisor since Gaffaney made captain and went to I.A.D., and I've handled him the way Fred and his previous bosses did. Let him pick his own shots, let him head up investigations that should have gone to field lieutenants, let him work without a partner. The results he's given me have been outstanding; his methods of obtaining them either dubious or outright illegal. For example: he solved Havilland-Goff brilliantly, but in the process shot it out with Goff in a crowded nightclub, then let him get away. Then he pulled at least two burglaries to obtain evidence. You know how I feel about violation of due process, sir. Hopkins is essentially a criminal. What sets him apart from a run-of-the-mill street thug is a one-seventy I.Q. and a badge. And he's slipping. That foul-up at Oldfield's arraignment is just the beginning. He's obsolescent. Cut him loose."

Braverton remained silent for long moments. McManus fidgeted, then said, "Sir, why have you called Gaffaney in? He was Hopkins' previous sup—"

Braverton cut him off. "I'll tell you after he's left. What you said makes perfect sense, John. You're probably the world's only liberal Irish cop. I th—"

The sound of a buzzer interrupted him. Braverton said,

"There he is," then pressed a button on his phone console. There was a tapping on the doorjamb. Braverton called out, "Enter!" and Captain Fred Gaffaney walked in and nodded briskly at both men. "Chief, Captain," he said.

Braverton pointed to a chair. McManus stood up and shook the I.A.D. adjutant's hand, feeling like he had stepped backward in time—Gaffaney's crew cut and bargain-basement blue suit always reminded him of his rookie days, when departmental regulations demanded such a visage. His bone-crusher handshake was another anachronism, and McManus sat down wondering what kind of game Braverton was playing.

Gaffaney settled into his chair and fingered his cross and flag lapel pin. Braverton looked straight at him and said, "Lloyd Hopkins is about to be brought up on a trial board. Dereliction of duty, maybe a criminal prosecution for perjury if he doesn't accept the retirement deal the Department is going to offer him. We're looking for backup dirt. What have *you* got on him?"

"Internal Affairs has a substantial file on Hopkins," Captain Fred Gaffaney said. "Notations covering his numerous insubordinations and illegal search and seizures. What are you using for ammo at the trial board?"

Braverton smiled. "The court transcript of his perjury, a psychiatrist's report that states, essentially, that he's a burnout. If need be, we may utilize his I.A.D. file. Your personal testimony might help."

Gaffaney's left hand jerked up to his lapel pin; McManus watched the witch hunter's eyes narrow as he said, "You mean as to the information in the file?"

"That's right."

"Of course I'll testify, Chief."

Braverton sighed. "Thanks, Fred, I knew I could count on you."

Gaffaney got to his feet, then said, "If there's nothing else, I have an interview in ten minutes." Braverton nodded dismissal, and McManus watched the crew-cut anachronism exit the office looking *strange*.

The chief's silent deadpan stare compounded the feeling of strangeness. Knowing he was being tested, McManus dropped his usual "sir" and said, "What was that all about?"

Braverton responded with an open-armed gesture that took in his whole office. "You may well be sitting in this chair one day. If you make it, you'll be dealing more with ambitious brass like Gaffaney than with street dicks like Crazy Lloyd."

McManus' whole being tingled; the testing was moving toward a veiled offer of patronage. "And, sir?"

"And I have a nominal regard for due process myself. Gaffaney is on the promotion list. He'll be a commander very shortly, and he'll probably take over I.A.D. when Stillwell retires. As far as that goes, he deserves the job; he's a good exec.

"But he's a born-again Christian loony, so far right that he scares *me*. He's been playing savior to some very well placed junior officers—field sergeants in Metro, I.A.D. dicks, uniformed officers in a half dozen divisions. Sergeants and lieutenants, all born-agains and all ambitious. He's offered them his patronage and promised to move *them* up as *he* moves up."

McManus whistled, then said, "What's his ultimate end?"

Braverton repeated his expansive gesture. "Chief of police, then politics? Who knows? The man is forty-nine years old, twenty-three years on the Job and fucked up on religion. My wife suggested male menopause. What do you—"

McManus raised a hand in interruption. "Sir, where did you get this information?"

"I was getting to that. Gaffaney has a son in the Department, Steve Gaffaney, a rookie working West L.A. Patrol. The kid has been pilfering from the station, clerical supplies, ammo, that kind of thing, for months. Finally the daywatch boss got pissed and called Intelligence Division, because if he initiated an investigation through I.A.D., Gaffaney senior would pick up on it. Intelligence checked the kid out and discovered that he had been suspended from high school for pilfering from lockers and that Captain Fred had bribed the principal of the school to erase all notations pertaining to disciplinary problems on the kid's record, and to improve his grades. Junior wouldn't have been admitted to the Academy with his real transcript."

McManus whispered, "And, sir?"

"And Intelligence did some more checking on Jesus Freak Fred and got wind of his little cross-and-flag coterie, which of course is perfectly kosher within departmental regulations."

"What's the upshot?"

"For now I'm going to sit on it. If the kid fucks up big or Captain Fred gets obstreperous, I'll lower the boom."

McManus smiled as the chief of detectives' machinations moved into out-and-out barter. "Sir, you still haven't told me where Hopkins fits in, and you want something."

Smiling back, Braverton said, "The Intelligence dicks said that Jesus Fred has got a shitload of personal dirt files on officers he hates and wants to curry favor with. He hates Hopkins' guts, and I know for a fact that he's privy to a lot of the sleazy stuff Lloyd has pulled over the years. That charade was to confirm that the files exist. His reaction proved that they do."

"And, sir?"

"And, John, what's *your* reaction to all this?"

"Cut Hopkins loose, blackmail Jesus Fred into retiring by threatening to expose the kid, fire the kid and stonewall the whole fucking mess."

Braverton gave his new protégé a round of applause. "Bravo, except your love of due process and lack of paranoia is appalling. First we have to neutralize Gaffaney's files, which may take awhile."

"Then?"

"First things first. Today is December sixth. On January first you will leave Robbery/Homicide and take over the Violent Crime Task Force in South Central L.A. I want a broad-minded man down there, someone who can deal rationally with blacks."

McManus' throat went dry; his first reaction was to offer

effusive thanks. Then respect for the barter game took over. "What's it going to cost me?"

Braverton's eyes clouded. "I want to ease Hopkins out," he said. "Hopefully without a trial board. I want you to call him back from San Francisco and give him some sort of assignment that does not involve homicide and will not insult his intelligence. I want him around Parker Center where I can talk to him. He's got to be cut loose, but I want it done gently."

McManus winced at the price of his high-visibility promotion. "You could have made it an order."

"Not my style," Braverton said. "Liberals should be adept at trading up, seeing as how they're handicapped from the gate."

The epiphany clicked into McManus' head and made him forget caution. "You love him."

"Yes. And I owe him, and you owe him. He got the Slaughterer and Havilland and Goff within fifteen months. Do you know the story on the Slaughterer?"

"No."

"Then you don't want to know. Will you do this for me?"

McManus felt old notions of duty crumble in the pit of his stomach. "Yes."

"Good. Do you have an appropriate assignment for him?"

"Not right now. But something should come up soon. It always does."

8

Duane Rice stood in a phone booth adjoining a 7-11 store in Encino. He was wearing a three-piece suit bought for ten dollars at a Hollywood thrift shop, and a curly-haired wig and beard/mustache combo purchased at Western Costume. His shoulder holster held a silencer-attached .45; his rear waistband a tranquilizer dart gun loaded with PCP darts. His hands were covered with surgical rubber gloves. He was ready.

At exactly 7:45 the phone rang. Rice picked up the receiver and said, "Yes?"

The gloating voice was unmistakably Bobby Garcia's: "Got her. Broke in the side door. Nobody saw us, nobody's gonna see us. She's scared shitless, but the kid is playing Mr. Nice Guy and sweet-talking her. Have lover boy call."

Rice said, "Right," then hung up and dialed the home number of Robert Hawley. The phone rang twice, then a female voice yawned, "Hello?"

"Robert Hawley, please," Rice said briskly.

The woman said, "One minute," then called out, "Bob! Telephone!" There was the sound of an extension being picked up, then a male voice calling, "I've got it, Doris. Go back to sleep." When he heard the original line go dead, Rice said, "Mr. Hawley?"

"Yes. Who is it?"

"It's a friend of Sally Issler."

"What the he—"

"*Listen to me* and be real, real cool and we won't kill her. *Are* you listening?"

"Yes, oh God . . . What do—"

Rice cut in, "What do you think we want, motherfucker! The same thing you rip off from your own fucking employer!" When he heard Hawley start to blubber, he lowered his voice. "You want to be cool or you want Sally-poo to die?"

"B-be cool," Hawley gasped.

"Then here's the pitch: One, I've got photographs of you pilfering the B. of A. tellers boxes, with the clock in the background, showing that you're on the job when you're not supposed to be, and some juicy infrared shots of you and Sally fucking. If you don't do what I want, my buddies chop Sally to pieces and the pictures go to your wife, the L.A.P.D., the bank and *Hustler* magazine. Dig me, dick breath?"

The gasp was now a whimper. "Yes. Yes. Yes."

"Good. Now, I want you to call Sally and have her introduce you to my colleagues. I'll call you back in exactly three minutes. There's a tap on your phone, so if you call the cops, another colleague will know and call Sally's roommates and tell them to do some chopping. Do you understand?"

"Y-yes."

Rice said, "Three minutes or chop, chop," then hung up. He watched the second hand on his Timex, pleased that his spontaneous bullshit about the photographs and phone tap had been so easy. When the hand made three sweeps, he again dialed Hawley's number.

"Yes?" A *groveling* whimper.

"You ready?"

"Yes."

"Good. I want you to get in your car and take your usual route to the bank. I've been tailing you for days, so I know the route. Park on the west side of Woodman a half block north of Ventura. I'll meet you there. You're being tailed, so don't fuck up. I'll see you there in twelve minutes."

Hawley's reply was a barely audible squeak. Rice hung up and walked very slowly to his Pontiac, forcing himself to count to fifty before he hit the ignition and eased the car into traffic. When he was six blocks from Hawley's house, he resumed counting, figuring that the bank manager would pass him in the opposite direction before he hit twenty-five. He was right; at twenty-two, Hawley's tan Cadillac approached at way over the speed limit, swerving so close to the double line that he pulled to the right to avoid a head-on. There were no cop cars anywhere. Nothing suspicious. Just business going down.

Rice cut over to side streets paralleling Ventura, pushing the car at forty-five, so that he wouldn't get stuck waiting for Hawley to arrive. At Woodman he turned right and parked immediately, a solid hundred and fifty yards from the spot where the bank man was to meet him. Just as he set the brake and grabbed a briefcase from the back seat, Hawley's Caddy hung an erratic turn off Ventura and slowed. Rice checked his fake mustache in the rearview mirror. Mr. Solid Citizen out for a stroll.

The bank man was acting like Mr. Solid Citizen on a trip to Panic City. Rice walked toward the bank parking lot, watching Hawley scrape bumpers as he parallel-parked his Caddy, plowing into the curb twice before squeezing into an easy space. When he finally got out and stood by the car, he was shaking from head to foot.

Rice approached, swinging the briefcase casually. Hawley frantically eyeballed the street. Their eyes locked for an instant, then Hawley turned around and checked out his blind side. Rice grinned at his protective image and came up on the bank manager and tapped him on the shoulder. "Bob, how nice to see you!"

Hawley did a jerky pivot. "Please, not now. I'm meeting someone."

Rice clapped Hawley on the back and spun him in the direction of the bank, keeping an arm around his shoulders as he hissed, "You're meeting *me*, dick breath. We're going straight to the tellers boxes, then straight back to your car." He dug his fingers into the bank man's collarbone and gouged in concert with sound effects: "Chop, chop, chop." Hawley winced with each syllable and let himself be propelled toward the bank.

At the front door, Hawley inserted keys into the three locks while Rice stood aside with one eye cocked in the direction of Ventura Boulevard. No patrol cars; no unmarked cruisers; nothing remotely off. The doors sprung open and they stepped inside. The bank man locked a central mechanism attached to the floor runner and looked up at the robber. "F-fast, please."

Rice pointed toward the teller area, then stepped back and let Hawley lead the way. When the manager's back was turned, he opened his briefcase and took out a pint bottle of bourbon and stuck it into his right front pants pocket. Hawley stepped over a low wooden partition and began unlocking and sliding open drawers. Rice glanced down and saw rows of folding green, then looked closer and saw that it was *off-green*—fancy traveler's checks done up in a Wild West motif. "The cash," he hissed. "Where's the fucking *money*?"

Hawley stammered, "T-t-time-locked. The vault. You said on the phone you wanted—"

Ignoring him, Rice opened the rest of the drawers himself, finding nothing but fat stacks of B. of A. "Greenbacks" in denominations of twenty, fifty and a hundred. Replaying his casing job in his mind, he snapped to what happened. Hawley was pilfering the traveler's checks. The paperwork he saw him doing was some sort of ass-covering. Seeing the banker outlined in red, he said, "*There's no cash in these drawers?*"

"N-nn-no."

"You've been ripping off *traveler's checks*?"

Shooting a panicky glance at the window, Hawley said, "Just for a while. I've got bad gambling debts, and I'm just trying to get even. Please don't kill me!"

Rice held the briefcase open, thinking of Chula Medina and twenty cents on the dollar tops. When Hawley started stuffing the rows of Greenbacks inside, he said, "Talk, dick breath. Give me a good line on your scam, and maybe I'll let you slide."

Hawley fumbled the packets into the briefcase, his eyes averted from Rice, his voice near cracking as he spoke. "The Greenbacks are tallied by the week. I've got duplicate bankbooks for two old lady customers—they're senile—and I transfer cash from their accounts to the bank and take it out in Greenbacks. I can't do it for much longer, it's wrong, and the paperwork juggling has got to come back on me." He opened the last drawer and transferred its contents to the briefcase, then held up supplicating hands and whispered, "Please, fast."

Rice took in the bank man's "scam," feeling it sink in as truth, knowing that Eggers' pilfer scene was probably something similar—he was a fool to think bank pros would leave cash out overnight. Noting wraparound tabs on the Greenbacks, he flashed a psycho killer smirk and held his jacket open to show off his .45. "I know about exploding ink packets, dick breath. You ink me and I'll come back and chop-chop your whole family."

Hawley shook his head and mashed his hands together. "We do ink only on cash, only on payroll days. *Please*."

He looked up doglike for instructions. Rice closed his briefcase and said, "Back to your car. Stay calm. Think about your golf game and you'll be cool."

Hawley moved toward the front doors in spastic steps; Rice was right behind. When they hit the street and the manager locked the door behind them, he threw his left arm over his shoulders and shifted the tranq gun from his waistband to his right jacket pocket.

They approached the Cadillac from the street. Rice pointed to the driver's-side door, and Hawley got in behind the wheel. Terror hit his face as he saw Rice reach into his waistband, and he squeezed his eyes shut and began murmuring the Lord's Prayer.

Rice shot him twice point-blank: once in the neck, once in the chest just below his left collar point. Hawley jerked backward in his seat, then bounced forward into the steering wheel. Rice watched him slump sideways, his eyes fluttering, his limbs going rubber. Within seconds he was sleeping the open-mouthed sleep of the junkie. Rice leaned into the car and poured the pint of whiskey over his chest and pants legs. *"Bon voyage,"* he said.

* * *

After driving to a pay phone and giving Bobby Garcia the all-clear and setting up plans for the split, Rice removed his facial disguise and hit the 405 Freeway to Redondo Beach, the briefcase full of bank checks on the seat beside him. He did another replay of the Eggers case job as he drove, remembering that he had only seen him rummage through the tellers boxes—he'd never seen him with money in hand. That heist had to be a cash rip, and that meant the Garcias couldn't know about the Greenback fuckup. Turning off the freeway onto Sepulveda, he beat time on the dashboard. The melody was a Vandy/Vandals tune; the words he murmured were, "Be home and be flush, Chula."

Chula Medina was at home.

After bolting the door behind him, Rice unceremoniously opened the briefcase and dumped the contents on the floor, then said, "Quarter on the dollar, cash. And fast."

Chula Medina smiled in answer, then sat down cross-legged beside the pile of bank checks. Rice watched him lick his lips as he counted. When he finished, he said, "Nice, but consecutive serial numbers and an off-brand check. These are gonna have to be frozen, then sent east. You've got sixty-four K here. My first, last, final and only offer is a dime on the dollar; here, now, cash, you walk out and we never met. Deal?"

Rice fingered his "Death Before Dishonor" tattoo and knew it was a fucking he had to take. "Deal. Put the money in the briefcase."

Chula got up, gave a courtly Latin bow and went into his bedroom. Rice had the briefcase held open when he returned. Chula dumped in a big handful of real U.S. currency, bowed again and pointed to the door. "*Vaya con Dios*, Duane."

Rice took the 405 to the Ventura to the Hollywood, wondering how the Garcias would react to the low numbers, and if Eggers could be intimidated into the vault for the real stuff. At Caheunga he exited the freeway, and within minutes he was at his new "home," the Bowl Motel, seventy scoots a week for a room with a sink, toilet, shower and hot plate. Too expensive

for dope fiends; too far up from the Boulevard for hookers; too
jig-free to interest the local fuzz. A good interim pad for a
rising young criminal. He parked in his space, grabbed the
briefcase and walked to his room, threading his way past
groups of beer-guzzling pensioners. Inside, he tossed the briefcase on the bed and flopped down beside it, grabbing the
snapshot of Vandy off the nightstand. "Coming home, babe;
coming home."

Ten minutes later the doorbell rang. Rice put the photo in
his shirt pocket, then walked over and squinted through the
peephole, seeing Joe and Bobby Garcia standing there looking
hungry: Joe itchy and anxious, like he couldn't believe what
he'd just done, but drooling for the payoff; Bobby in a gang-
stered-back thumbs-in-belt stance, drooling for *more*, the butt
of his .45 clearly outlined through his windbreaker.

Rice opened the door and pointed the brothers inside, then
bolted it shut behind them. He grabbed the briefcase and
dumped the money onto the bed and said, "Count it; it's a
little less than I figured." Bobby started to giggle while Joe
made a beeline for the cash and began separating it into piles.
Rice locked eyes with Bobby and said, "Tell me about it."

Bobby let his giggle die slowly; Rice saw that the ex-welter
was closer to stone loon than he thought—he couldn't play
anything straight.

"Went in easy like I told you," Bobby said. "Wham, blam,
thank you, ma'am. Kept our masks and gloves on, tied her up
good, taped her mouth shut. I think maybe she dug it. Her
nipples were all pointy." He went back to giggling, then
segued into sex noises while he jabbed his right forefinger into
a hole formed by his left thumb and pinky. When he started
making slurping sounds, Rice said, "Ease off on that, will
you?"

Bobby kiboshed the slurping and started fondling the religious medals that encircled his neck. "Okay, Duane-o. But she
was fine as wine, I'll tell you that. It go good for you?"

Rice watched Joe stack the loot according to denomination,
realizing that he liked the tagalong as much as he despised his

brother. Joe hummed as he counted, a tune that sounded like "Blueberry Hill." Listening to the humming made it easy to talk to Bobby without wanting to vomit. "Yeah, it was pie. Day after tomorrow for Confrey/Eggers. I've got a recon job for you guys in the meantime."

Bobby giggled and said, "Pie like in hairpie?" and Rice saw red. He was cocking his fists when Joe jumped up from the bed, frowned and said, "Sixty-four hundred on the nose. That's really sh—"

Bobby shoved his brother aside, moved to the bed and began recounting the money. Finishing, he spat on the pile of bills and turned to look up at Rice. "Slightly less than you figured, huh? Like twenty-five K less. Like Little Bro and me just risked ten to life for *three fucking grand*?" He paused, then whispered, "You holding out on us?"

Knowing that fire full was the only way out, Rice said, "I'll chalk that up to disappointment and a bad temper, but you say it again and I'll kill you."

Joe stood perfectly still; Bobby gripped the mattress with both hands, his jaw trembling, saliva starting to creep out the corners of his mouth. Seeing more fear than anger, Rice threw him back a chunk of his *cojones*. "Listen, man, I'm just as pissed about it as you. And it's my fault. I should have realized that the real money was left in the vault. But we're still on for the next—"

Bobby screamed, "You're fucking crazy! These bank fools are leaving out peanuts to pilfer, and I'm not risking my ass again for another three grand!"

Thinking, macho counterpunch, Rice smiled and said, "I'm going to make Eggers go into the vault for us. The same hostage plan, for twenty times the money. I'm going to intercept him in person as he enters the bank, then force him to call you guys for confirmation that you're holding his bitch. If he agrees to hit the vault, I'll tell him to sit tight at his desk with his hands in view, and I'll go across the street and keep him eyeball pinned. When the guard and tellers arrive and the real money comes out, Eggers grabs what he can carry on his person and goes across the street to meet me. He figures out a cool way to do this, or his bitch gets chopped. Then I walk him to his car and tranq him."

Grinning like a macho ghoul, Bobby said, "Suppose he don't agree?"

Rice moved to Joe and threw a rough arm around his shoulders. "Then I kill him then and there and take the teller box money. But he'll agree. He always wears a baggy suit. Lots of room, and I'll tell him c-notes only. You in, partners?"

Bobby whooped and jumped up and down, dunking imaginary baskets; Rice tightened his grip on Joe's shoulders. Joe twisted free and stared at him, and Rice snapped to the fact that he was the smarter of the two. Joe's eyes pleaded; Rice whispered, "Two more days and it's over." Joe looked at Bobby, who was throwing left-right body punches at his reflection in the wall mirror. Rice stuck two fingers into his mouth and forced out a loud, shrill whistle.

The noise brought the scene to a halt. Bobby leaned against the mirror and said in exaggerated barrioese, "Thirty-two hundred. Come up green, homeboy."

With an exaggerated shit-eating grin, Rice moved to the bed and began a slow-motion recount of the money, dividing it first in half and shoving that part under the pillow, then separating the remaining half into two portions. Finishing, he offered Joe the first handful of bills, Bobby the second. Both brothers jammed the cash into their front and back pants pockets, then stuffed the overflow into their windbreakers. When the last of the money was stashed, Rice gave them a slow eyeball and shook his head. His crime partners looked like two greedy greaseballs with elephantiasis; like a world-class dose of bad news.

Bobby cracked his knuckles; Joe looked at Rice and blurted, "What about the recon job, Duane? You gonna tell us now?"

Rice leaned back on the bed and shut his eyes, blotting out the bad news. "Yeah. I was thinking that maybe Hawley and Eggers know each other. Remember, we don't know who originally scoped out the heists, how he knew, who he knew, that kind of thing. I'll be watching the papers to see if they mention Hawley and Issler, and I want you guys to keep a loose tail on Eggers and Confrey, see if the cops or feds are nosing around. If they are, we have to call the heist off. I'll call you late tomorrow night. If there's no heat, we hit Friday morning."

Bobby popped his knuckles and said, "What kinda recon you gonna be doing?"

Rice opened his eyes, but kept them away from the brothers. "A little added terror angle, in case Eggers gets uppity. I'm going to trash his pad and steal some kitchen knives, then bring the knives with me when I brace him. That way, I can tell him you're gonna chop up his bitch with a knife with his prints on them. That and the fact that his pad's been violated ought to keep him docile."

Bobby whooped and jumped up and touched the ceiling; loose bills started to pop out of his pants pockets. Rice said, "What was your record as a fighter?"

"Eleven, sixteen and zero," Bobby said. "Never went the distance, knocked out or got knocked out. My tops was seven rounds with Harry "The Headhunter" Hungerford. Lost on cuts. Why you asking?"

"I was wondering how you survived this long."

Bobby giggled and shoved Joe in the direction of the door. "Clean living, anonymous good deeds and faith in Jesus, Duane-o," he said, kneading his brother's shoulders. "And a good watchdog. Don't you worry. I'll keep a good tail on Eggers and his mama." He unlocked the door and waggled his eyebrows on the way out. Rice could hear him giggle all the way back to the parking lot.

With the money under his pillow, Rice tried to sleep. Every time he was about to pass out, the staccato beat of the Vandals' gibberish number "Microwave Slave" took over, and Vandy jumped into his mind in the frumpy housedress she wore when she performed the tune. Finally, staying awake seemed like the easier thing to do. Opening his eyes, he saw the ugliness of the room merge with the ugliness of the music. The frayed cord on the hot plate; a line of dust under the dresser; grease spots all along the walls. A lingering echo of Bobby Garcia's psycho/buffoon act was the final straw. Rice packed the money and his shaving gear into the briefcase and went looking for a new pad.

He found a Holiday Inn on Sunset and La Brea and paid $480 for a week in advance. No grease spots, no dust, no senile boozehounds clogging up the parking lot. TV, a view, clean sheets and daily maid service.

After stashing the bulk of his loot, Rice drove up to the Boulevard and spent a K on clothes. At Pants West he bought six pairs of Levi cords and an assortment of underwear; at Miller's Outpost he purchased a half dozen plaid shirts. His last stop was the London Shop, where a salesman looked disapprovingly at his tattoo while fitting him for two sport jacket/slacks combos. He thought about buying a set of threads for Vandy, but finally axed the idea: after he got her off the coke, she'd be healthier and heavier and a couple of sizes bigger.

Now the only white-trash link to be severed was the car. After dropping off his clothes at the new pad and changing into a new shirt and pair of Levi's, Rice drove to a strip of South Western Avenue that he knew to be loaded with repo lots.

Two hours and six lots got him zilch—the cars looked shitty and none of the sales bosses would let him do under-the-hood checks. The seventh lot, a G.M. repo outlet on Twenty-eighth and Western, was where he hit pay dirt, a bored sales manager in a cubicle hung with master ignition keys telling him to grab a set of diagnostic tools and scope out any sled he wanted.

Rice did timing checks, battery checks, transmission checks and complete engine scrutinies on five domestics before he found what he wanted: a black '76 Trans Am with a four-speed and lots of muscle—good under the hood and even better looking—a car that would impress any crowd he and Vandy sought to crash.

The sales manager wanted four thou. Rice countered with twenty-five hundred cash. The sales manager said, "Feed me," and Rice handed it over, knowing the joker made him for a non—Boy Scout. After signing the purchase papers and pocketing the pink slip, Rice walked over to the street and saw an old wino sucking on a jug in the shade of his '69 Pontiac. He tossed him the keys to his former clunker and said, "Ride, daddy, ride," then strolled back to his sleek muscle car. When he got in and gunned the engine, the wino was peeling rubber down Western in the Pontiac, the bottle held to his lips.

Now Vandy.

Rice drove north to the Sunset Strip, savoring the feel of his Trans Am. He avoided putting the car through speed shifts and other hot-rod pyrotechnics; he was now technically a parole and probation absconder, and traffic tickets would mean a warrant check and instant disaster.

Street traffic on the Strip was light, sidewalk traffic lighter—schoolgirl hookers from Fairfax High turning a few extra bucks on their lunch hour, bouncers sweeping up in front of the massage parlors and outcall offices. Rice turned off Sunset at Gardner and parked. The lavender four-flat that housed Silver Foxes looked bland in the daylight, like just another Hollywood Spanish style. He walked over and rang the bell beneath the sexy fox emblem.

A young man in white dungarees and a Michael Jackson '84 Tour tank top opened the door and blocked the entranceway in a hands-on-hips pose. Rice sized up his muscles and figured him for a bodybuilder who couldn't lick a chicken; strictly adornment and a little jazz for the fag trade. "May I help you?" he asked.

Rice said, "Some friends in the Industry said this was the place to go for female companionship. I'm in town for a week or so, and I haven't got a lot of time to hit the party circuit. Normally paying for it isn't my style, but you were *very* highly recommended." He sighed, pleased with his performance—not a trace of Hawaiian Gardens and Soledad in his speech.

The youth flexed his biceps and imitated Rice's sigh. It came out a pout. "Everybody pays for it somehow, this is the herpes generation. Who were these people who recommended us?"

Rice pointed to the office he could glimpse past the youth's broad shoulders. "Jeffrey Jason Rifkin, the agent, and some buddies of his. I can't remember their names. Can we go inside?"

Nodding, the youth stepped aside just enough to let Rice squeeze through the door sideways. Their arms brushed, and Rice felt his stomach turn over when the kid let out a little grunt of pleasure.

The room was all white, furnished in Danish modern/High Tech—white walls and carpeting, metal tubular desk, bentwood chairs with white fabric backing. Scenes from rock videos were hung on the walls: Elvis Costello in fifties garb superimposed against an A-bomb mushroom cloud; Bruce Springsteen hopping a freight train; Diana Ross drenched to the bone at her Central Park concert. Rice sat down without being asked and watched the kid flip through a white Rolodex on the desk, moving his lips as he read. Thinking of him coupled obscenely with Bobby Garcia kept his revulsion down and gave him an edge of frost.

With a sighing pout, the kid looked up and said, "Yes, we've done business with Mr. Rifkin. In fact, we've sent over lots of foxes for his theme parties."

"Theme parties?" It was a reflex blurt, and Rice knew immediately that it was the wrong thing to say.

The youth hooded his eyes. "Yes, theme parties. Many of our foxes are aspiring actresses, and they enjoy theme parties because they get to act out more than they would on a straight assignment. You know, playing slave queens or topless cowgirls, that kind of thing. What do you do in the Industry?"

Rice said, "I'm a talent scout," and knew from the young man's puzzled expression that it was an outdated term. "I've been out of the Industry for a while," he added, "and Jeffrey

Jason is helping me get rolling again. It's a tough racket to get back into."

"Yes," the young man said, "it is. What kind of fox were you looking for?"

Rice stretched his legs and smoothed his shirt front, then said, "Listen, I'm very choosy about my women. If I describe exactly what I want, can you check out your files or whatever and take it from there?"

The young man said, "We can do better than that. We've got *au naturel* photographs of all our foxes." He dug into the top desk drawer, and pulled out a white plastic binder and handed it to Rice. "Take your time, sweetie; it's a fox hunter's candy store, and nobody's rushing you."

Rice opened the binder, feeling a crazo sensation of being ripped upward from the crotch. The first page was a spiel about rare breeds of foxes and fulfillment of fantasies, scripted on lavender paper; on the second page the women began. Posed nude in identical reclining postures, they were all outright beautiful or outright gutter sensual, superbly built in the skinny model and curvy wench modes. White, black, Oriental, and *latina*, they all fire-breathed *sex*.

Rice turned the pages slowly, noticing blank spots where other photos had once been pasted; he read the hype printed below each girl's first name and physical stats. "Aspiring actress" and "aspiring singer" were the usual subheadings, and next to them were lurid sex fantasies, supposedly written by the "foxes" themselves. The ridiculous accounts of three ways and four ways made him want to retch, and he flipped through to the end of the binder, looking only for the body he knew by heart. Not finding it, he glanced up at the young man and said, "Is this all your women?"

The youth nodded and flexed his biceps. "You're really hard to please. Those foxes are the *crème de la crème*."

Rice thought about mentioning former "foxes," then got an idea. "Listen, do you know most of the girls who work out of here?"

"Some. I've only been dispatching for a little over a week. Why?"

Rice said, "I was looking for a chick I saw walk out of here the last time I was in L.A. About five-six, one hundred ten, blond, skinny, classy features. Preppy clothes. Ring a bell?"

The young man shook his head. "No . . . I'm new on the job, and besides, the owners wouldn't let the foxes dress preppy— no sex appeal."

Another idea clicked into Rice's head. "Too bad. Listen, since I didn't see that particular girl, I'd like you to give me a recommendation. Brains turn me on. I want a smart chick— one I can talk to."

The young man smiled, picked up the binder and leafed through it, then handed it to Rice. "There," he said. "Rhonda. She's got a master's degree in economics, and she's really groovy. A real brain fox."

Rice studied the photograph. Rhonda was a tall buxom woman with a dark brown Afro; deeply tanned except for bikini white across her breasts and pelvis. She was described as an "aspiring stockbroker," and her fantasy was listed as "orgies with rich, intelligent, beautiful men on my own private island in the Adriatic." Rice thought she looked shrewd and probably didn't write the retarded fantasy blurb. Snapping the binder shut, he said, "Great. Can you send her over to the Holiday Inn on Sunset and La Brea, in an hour?"

The youth gave his sigh-pout. "I'll call her. Rhonda is three hundred dollars an hour, one hour minimum. All our foxes gratefully accept tips over that amount. Rhonda carries her own Visa, Mastercard and American Express receipts and imprinter for the basic fee, but please tip her with cash. What room number?"

"814."

"We require a friendship fee of one hundred dollars for first-time fox hunters."

"Like a hunting license?"

The youth giggled; Rice thought he sounded just like Bobby

"Boogaloo" Garcia. "That's cute. Yes, call it your deed to the happy hunting grounds. Cash, please, and your name."

Rice slipped a c-note from his shirt pocket and stuck it inside the binder. "Harry 'The Fox Hunter' Hungerford." The youth giggled as he wrote down the name, and Rice walked out wondering if the world was nothing but wimps, pimps, psychos and sex fiends.

Back at the Holiday Inn, he killed time by watching TV for word of the robbery. There was no mention of the heist or of a bank manager zoned on dust, let alone the hostage angle—the bank bigshots had probably stonewalled the media to save face. So far, so good—but his money was running out.

Just as the news brief ended, the door chimes rang. Rice grabbed a wad of twenties from the briefcase and stuck them under the mattress, then walked to the door and opened it.

The woman who stood on the other side in a green knit dress and fur coat was her photograph gone subtle. Expecting sleazy attire and makeup, Rice saw class that rivaled Vandy at her healthiest. No makeup on a face of classic beauty; large tortoiseshell glasses that set off that face and made it even *more* beautiful; a Rolex watch on her left wrist, an attaché case in her right hand. Rice's eyes prowled her body until he snapped to what he was doing and brought them back up to her face. Pissed at his lack of control, he said, "Hi, come in."

The woman entered, then did a slow model's turn as the door was shut, setting her attaché case on the floor, tossing her coat onto a chair. Rice sized up her moves. There was something non-whorish about her act.

Her voice was cool, almost mocking: "In olden times, fox hunting was the private sport of the landed gentry. Today, all natural-born aristocrats, busy men with taste and no time to waste, can enjoy that pleasure with Silver Foxes—the ultimate sensual therapy service for today's take-charge man."

Rice said, "Holy shit," and stepped backward, his heels bumping the attaché case and knocking it over. On impulse, he bent down and opened it up. Inside were three metal credit card imprinters, a stack of charge slips and a copy of *Wealth and Poverty* by George Gilder. The woman laughed as he snapped the case shut, then said, "I'm Rhonda. Most clients either love the intro or get embarrassed by it. You were incredulous. It was cute."

Rice flushed. The last time he'd been called "cute" was the sixth grade, when he nicknamed Hawaiian Gardens "Hawaiian Garbage." Carol Douglas shouted, "You're so cute, Duaney," and chased his ass the rest of the semester. "Cute, huh? Come to any conclusions?"

Rhonda took off her glasses and hooked them into her cleavage by a temple piece. "They're plate glass. I only wore them to look brainy. Yes, I've come to one conclusion—you don't want sex."

Rice sat down on the couch and motioned for Rhonda to join him. When she sat down an arm's length away, he said, "You're a smart lady. Is that a bogus Rolex?"

Rhonda flushed. "Yes. How did you know that?"

"I used to hang out in a Hollywood crowd. Everyone had fake Rolexes, and they used to talk about how their Rolex was real, but everyone else's was phony."

"Are you calling me a phony?"

"No, just seeing if you can level."

"Can you level? You don't look like any Hollywood type I've ever seen. What were *you* into?"

Rice laughed. "I was selling stolen cars. Want me to get to it?"

"If you want to. It's your money."

Rice said, "I'm looking for a woman. My girlfriend. A friend of a friend saw her up on the Strip near all the outcall joints. I was in jail for six months, and she was having a tough time, and I—"

Rhonda put a hand on his arm. "And you thought if she needed money badly, she'd turn tricks?"

Pulling his arm away, Rice said, "Yeah. She visited me in jail, and I could tell she was strung out on coke." He thought of Vandy and Gordon Meyers—"It's real pharmaceutical blow, baby"—"Duane wouldn't want me to." The words and a backup flash of Vandy's prep clothes hanging loose on her gaunt frame forced his words out in a tumble: "And I know she'd only do it if she was desperate, and not really like it, and she's a singer, and a lot of girls at Silver Foxes are aspiring singers, and maybe she thought she could help herself while I—"

Something strange and soft in Rhonda's eyes stopped him. He moved to the bed and dug under the mattress until his hands were full of money, then walked back and dumped the stash of twenties in her lap. "That's for starters," he said. "Find her and there's lots more."

Rhonda counted the money and folded it into a tight roll. "Six hundred. What's her name? Have you got a picture?"

Rice took the snapshot from his wallet and handed it to her. "Anne Vanderlinden. She also goes by 'Vandy.'"

Rhonda looked at the photo and said, "Foxy. Does she—"

Rice screamed, "Don't say that!" Catching himself, he lowered his voice. "She's not a fucking animal, she's my woman." Catching Rhonda's strange look again, he said, "Don't stare at me like that."

Rhonda said, "Sorry," then patted the couch. Rice sat down beside her. She put a tentative hand on his knee and asked, "What's your name?"

Rice brushed the hand away. "Duane Rice. Are you in?"

"Yes. Put some things together for me about you and Anne. Who she is, what she likes to do, that kind of thing. Was she in the Hollywood crowd with you?"

Rice stared at the wall and straightened out the story in his head, then said, "First off, I know she isn't working outcall on the Strip; I've already checked those places out. Second, she doesn't really have any friends in L.A. except me. The last time I saw her was in jail close to three weeks ago. She cleaned out the pad we had together. She—"

Rhonda squeezed his arm. "Tell me about the Hollywood crowd."

"I was getting to it. Vandy's a singer. Used to be lead singer

with a Vegas lounge group, Vandy and the Vandals. I was sort
of her manager. I did some favors for an agent named Jeffrey
Jason Rifkin, and he fixed us up with that Hollywood crowd. It
took me a while, but I finally figured out that those people
were all parasites who couldn't do Vandy a bit of good. But I
was unloading cars on them and making a lot of money. I had
plenty banked toward making Vandy's rock videos—"

"What?"

"Rock videos. That was my plan: get a stake together to
produce rock videos featuring Vandy. It was moving, but then
I got busted."

Rhonda said softly, "Look, Duane, I've been with Silver
Foxes for over a year, and I've never seen Vandy or heard of
her. But lots of outcall girls branch out into other scenes,
particularly around here, where there's all this movie and
music industry money. Especially girls like Vandy, budding
singers looking to get ahead, looking to meet people who can
help their careers. Do you follow me?"

Rice imitated Rhonda's soft voice. "I follow that you're
bracing me for something. Spit it out; I didn't give you that
money for bullshit."

Rhonda tucked the cash roll into her cleavage; Rice saw it
as her first whorish move. She said coldly, "Some girls quit
outcall because they get heavy into coke or they get offers to
live with men in the Industry. Most of these men expect their
girls to sexually service their friends, men who can do them
favors. The girls get room and board and coke, and if they're
very lucky, bit parts in movies and rock videos. There's an
Industry name for them: Coke Whores."

Coke Whores.

Rice forced the name on himself: tasting it, testing it. He
looked at Rhonda and thought about hitting her with "stockbroker groupie" and "moneyfucker," but couldn't do it. The
big question jumped into his mind and stuck like glue: Did it
happen with Meyers?

Rhonda was staring at him, giving out big sad doe eyes like
Carol Douglas back in Hawaiian Garbage. Rice kneaded his

tattooed biceps and said, "What do I get for that six hundred?"

"Three hundred," Rhonda said. "Silver Foxes gets three. I didn't want to tell you that, Duane."

"Anyone afraid of the truth is a chickenshit. You're into these 'scenes,' right?"

"On the edges of them, but I'm nobody's kept woman."

"I know. You're just working your way through college."

"Don't be ugly, I want to help you. Was this an A, B, C or D crowd you and Vandy hung out in?"

"What?"

Rhonda's voice revealed exasperation. "In the movie and music biz there are four crowds: A, B, C and D. The A's are the heavy, heavy hitters, B's below them, and so forth. D's are the nerds who are lucky to get work. I was just wondering if Vandy could have hooked up with someone she met in your crowd."

Rice shook his head. "No way. I kept her away from the men, and she doesn't trust women. What crowd are you in?"

Rhonda lowered her eyes at the jibe, then said, "Any crowd with money. If Vandy's in L.A. and into any Industry scenes, I'll find her. Can I call you here?"

Rice looked around his new home, wondering if his talk with the stockbroker/whore had skunked the place past crashing in. "No," he said. "I might split." He took a pad and pencil off the phone stand and wrote down Louie Calderon's bootleg number. "You can call me here and leave a message twenty-four hours a day. You locate Vandy, and you'll see lots of money."

Rhonda took the slip of paper, stood up and collected her attaché case and fur coat. Rice watched her walk toward the door. When her hand was on the knob, she turned around and said, "I'll be in touch."

Rice said, "Find her for me."

Rhonda traced a dollar sign in the air and closed the door behind her.

* * *

At dusk, Rice felt the skunk stench close in on the new pad. He knew it didn't come from Rhonda, or Psycho Bobby Garcia, or Hawley or anybody else. It came from being wrapped too tight in his own skull for too long, with no one to talk to except people he wanted to use. It was what it was like all the time before he met Vandy and started to make things happen.

He made the black '76 Trans Am happen.

First he fishtailed out of the Holiday Inn parking lot; then he cruised the Boulevard, idling the engine at stoplights, staying in second gear until he hit Western Avenue. On Western northbound he speed-shifted into third, sized up traffic and vowed not to touch the brake until he hit the Griffith Park Observatory.

So he tapped the horn as he clutched, weaved and shifted, and then Hollywood was behind him and the park road opened up. Then the whole world became a narrow strip of asphalt, headlight glow and a broken white line.

Seventy, eighty, eighty-five. At ninety, on the long upgrade approaching the Observatory, the Trans Am started to shimmy. Rice pulled to the side of the road and decelerated, catching a view of the L.A. Basin lit with neon. He thought immediately of Vandy and gauged distances, then turned around and drove toward the tiny pinpoints of light that he knew marked their old stomping grounds.

Their old condo was already up for sale, with a sign on the front lawn offering reasonable terms and fresh molding beside the door he'd kicked off. Splitsville, Cold City, *Nada*.

He drove to the 7-11 on Olympic and Bundy, where he used to send Vandy for frozen pizzas and his custom car magazines. A new night man behind the counter scoped him out like he was a shoplifter. The skunk odor came back, so he grabbed a West L.A. local paper and a candy bar and tossed the chump a dollar bill.

In the parking lot, he ate half the candy bar and looked at the front page. Vandalism at schools in the Pico-Robertson area; church bake-offs in Rancho Park; little theater on West-wood Boulevard. Then he turned the page, and everything went haywire.

The article was entitled, "Sheriff's Vet Heading Security at California Federal Branch," and beside it was a close-up photo of Gordon Meyers. Rice's hands started to shake. He placed the newspaper on the hood of the Trans Am and read: "California Federal Bank's District Personnel Supervisor Dennis J. Lafferty today announced that Gordon M. Meyers, forty-four, recently retired from the Los Angeles County Sheriff's Department, has taken over as head of security for the Pico-Westholme branch, replacing Thomas O. Burke, who died of a heart attack two weeks ago. Meyers, who served most of his duty time as a jailer in the Main County Jail's facility for emotionally disturbed prisoners, said: 'I'm going to make the most of this job. After a week on the job, Cal Federal already feels like home. It's great to be working with sane, noncriminal people.'"

Rice read the article three more times, then took his hands from the car's hood. They were still trembling, and he could see the blood vessels in his arms pulsate. A scream built up in his throat, then the "Death Before Dishonor" carved on his left biceps jumped out and calmed him. With his tremors now at a low idle, he drove to Pico and Westholme.

The bank was small, dark and still, a low-rent job for a low-rent ex-cop with wacko, low-rent criminal fantasies. Rice cruised by, once, twice, three times, each time forcing himself to say, "Duane wouldn't want me to," "Anyone afraid of the truth is a chickenshit," and "It happened." On the fourth circuit all that came out was, "It happened, it happened, *it happened*."

Now that he knew it himself, he parked the Trans Am and brainstormed. In and out in three minutes. A block from the 405 north and southbound, two minutes from the Santa Monica east/west, five from Wilshire. Fifty/twenty-five/twenty-five with the Garcias; then adios, greaseballs. The master keys at the repo lot for a foolproof getaway. *Make it happen.*

Rice sat back and made pictures of Vandy, of East Coast rock gigs, of New York crowds that didn't have letters in front of them and big houses in Connecticut. Then noises in his head bombarded the pictures: good metal-on-metal noises that he recognized as the clash of gears, high-powered engines igniting, double-aught loads snapping from breech to barrel.

9

Lloyd sat in the outer office of the Los Angeles F.B.I.'s Bank Robbery Unit, kneading his gauze-bandaged right hand and musing on his new lease on professional life. McManus had called him in Frisco with the word: his suspension was over, he was back on duty with a liaison gig with the feds; report tomorrow morning to Special Agent Kapek at the F.B.I. Central Office and don't fuck up. The "lease" was a phaseout, he decided; a stratagem to keep him occupied and docile while the high brass figured out a discreet way to give him the big one where it would do the most damage. On the flight down and cab ride over he had been exultantly happy, then a look at the clerk/receptionist's face when he flashed his badge brought it all to a crash. It had to be a shit assignment, or they would have given it to a field lieutenant. His glory days were dead.

A severe-looking woman poked her head out of the connecting door and said, "Sergeant Hopkins?"

Lloyd pushed himself out of his chair with both hands; his right hand throbbed. "Yes. To see Special Agent Kapek. Is he here yet?"

The woman walked toward him, holding a manila folder and a sheaf of loose pages. "He'll be here soon. He said you should please wait and read these reports."

Lloyd took the papers with his good hand and sat back down, dismissing the woman with a nod of the head. When he was alone again, he opened the folder, smiling when he saw that it contained a series of L.A.P.D. crime reports.

The first report was submitted by a West Valley Division daywatch patrol unit, and detailed events of Wednesday, 12/7/84, less than twenty-four hours before. While on routine patrol of Woodman Avenue, the officers of Unit Four–Charlie–Z came upon a middle-aged white male urinating in the open window of a 1983 Cadillac Seville. When they approached, they determined that the suspect was heavily under the influence of a narcotic substance, and cautiously advised him of his rights before arresting him for indecent exposure and public intoxication. The man screamed incoherently as he was handcuffed, but the officers were able to pick out the words "bank rob" and "ray gun."

At the West Valley Station booking area, the suspect was searched. His identification revealed him to be Robert Earle Hawley, forty-seven, the owner of the Cadillac Seville. Finding the name familiar, the booking officer checked with the daywatch commander and learned that security personnel at the Bank of America on Woodman and Ventura had entered the bank at opening time to find the cash boxes ransacked and the bank's manager, Robert Hawley, missing.

Hawley's booking was postponed. The F.B.I. Bank Robbery Unit was notified of the bank manager's incarceration, and a team of detectives drove him to U.S.C. County General Hospital for detoxification. After determining that Hawley was under the influence of "angel dust," a counterdose of Aretane was administered. When Hawley returned to a sober state, F.B.I. Special Agent Peter Kapek and a team of L.A.P.D. detectives again advised him of his right to remain silent and have an attorney present during questioning. Waiving those rights, Hawley gave the officers the following account of his morning's activities:

At 7:45 A.M. he received a phone call from an unknown man, directing him to call the home of his "girlfriend," Sally Issler. The man told Hawley (who is married) that Miss Issler would be killed if his demands were not met, and that he would call back in exactly three minutes. Hawley called Miss Issler. A man with a Mexican accent answered, then put Miss

Issler on the line. She screamed that she was being held captive by two men with guns and knives and to do whatever their friend said. Hawley said he would, then hung up. The man called back as he said he would, and told Hawley to meet him on Woodman near the bank in ten minutes, warning him that his phone was tapped, and any attempts to contact the police would result in Miss Issler's death. Hawley met the man near the bank, and described him as "white, late twenties, light brown hair, blue eyes, 5'11"– 6'1", 160 –170 pounds, with neatly trimmed beard and mustache, wearing three-piece tan suit." The man forced Hawley to open the bank and empty cashboxes containing approximately $60,000 in traveler's checks into a briefcase, then walked him back to his car, where he shot him twice with what looked like a "ray gun." Welts on Hawley's neck and collarbone and small metal darts still stuck to his clothing indicated that he was telling the truth. Officers were dispatched to the home of Miss Issler. They found her bound and gagged, but otherwise unharmed. She told them that her captors wore ski-masks that covered their faces, but were obviously Mexicans. They spoke fluent English with Mexican accents. One man, the "softer-spoken" of the two, was tall and slender; the other, who "talked dirty" to her, was short and muscular. She placed both men as being in their early thirties, and said they were both armed with army-issue .45 automatics with attached silencers.

Lloyd skimmed through the remaining reports, learning that Hawley was treated for toxic poisoning and was not charged with a wienie-wagger beef or with anything pertaining to the robbery, and that Sally Issler was treated for shock at a local hospital and then released. The disparate facts started to sink in, pointing to solid criminal brains. He was about to give the initial pages another go-round when he sensed someone watching him read. He looked up to see a tall man of about thirty hovering near the doorway. "Pete Kapek," the man said. "Nice caper, huh? You like it?"

Lloyd stood up. "Bank robbery's not my meat, but I'll take it." He walked over to the doorway. Kapek stuck out his right hand, then noticed the bandage and switched to his left. Lloyd said, "Lloyd Hopkins," and fumbled a handshake. Kapek said, "I've heard you're smart. What do you think, right off the top of your head?"

Lloyd walked into Kapek's office and went straight for the window and its view of downtown L.A. seven stories below. With his eyes on a stream of antlike people scuttling across Figueroa, he said, "Right off the top, why me? I'm a homicide dick. Two, what's with Hawley? Presumably, he was chosen because his affair with the Issler woman made him particularly vulnerable to a blackmail angle. Again presumably, his wife didn't know about Issler. Then why did he spill his guts so quickly?"

Kapek laughed. "It wasn't in the report, but the phone man told Hawley he had infrared fuck shots of him and Sally. He threatened exposure of the affair as well as Sally's murder. I sized up Hawley as a wimp and made him a deal. Talk, and we wouldn't press charges on him for flashing his shlong, and we'd keep the whole mess out of the media's clutches. You like it?"

Lloyd turned around and looked at Kapek, noticing acne scars that undercut his Fed image and made him seem more like a cop. "Yeah, I like it. Also right off the top of my head: one, we're dealing with brains. Stupider guys would have gone straight for Hawley's wife, right there at his pad, and kept *her* hostage, which might have driven Hawley to the cops from jump street. That's impressive. If the wrong guys got ahold of a family hostage idea and got away with it once, they'd keep going until someone was killed. As it stands, this is probably a one-shot deal, which leads us back to Issler. She been polygraphed?"

Kapek sat down and poked a pencil at the papers on his desk. "She's clean. No polygraph yet, but while she was at the hospital, I had a forensic team and latent prints team do a job on her apartment. They found jimmy marks on the side door, and rubber glove prints on all the surfaces the Mexicans would have touched. We got a bunch of viable latents, and the team stayed up half the night doing eliminations against Sally,

Hawley, and a list of friends and relatives that Sally gave us, working with D.M.V., armed forces and passport records. You know what we got? The above non-suspects, and one unaccounted-for set that later turned out to be some dipshit L.A.P.D. rookie who saw all the black-and-whites out front and thought he'd make the scene. The forensic guys got soil and mashed-up flower petals coming through the side door; the beaners trampled a flower garden on their way in. No, Sally baby was *not* in on it."

Lloyd said, "Shit. Competent print men?"

Kapek laughed. "The best. One guy is a real freak. He dusted the bedposts and logicked that Sally likes to get on top. You like it?"

"Only on Tuesdays. Let's get the obvious stuff out of the way. The phone man wore gloves and Hawley can't I.D. him from mug shots?"

"Right."

"No eyeball witnesses at either crime scene?"

"Right."

"The bank checks bug me. What can they yield cash—a quarter on the dollar?"

"If that. But they're *green*—and from a distance, you know, during a casing job, they might appear to be the real thing, which doesn't make our boys look too smart."

Lloyd nodded. "Employees and ex-employees, known associates of Issler and Hawley?"

"Being checked out. If we don't bust this thing in a week or so, I'll plant a man in the bank. Our approaches are narrowing down. You like it?"

Lloyd collected his thoughts by looking out the window at low-hanging clouds brushing the tops of skyscrapers. "No, I don't. One of the reports said Issler made the Mexicans as carrying army-issue .45s. That's a strange perception for a woman."

Kapek chuckled. "Sexist. Issler's father was a career officer. She knows her stuff. Those old heavy .45s are getting scarce, though. Maybe an approach."

Nodding silently, Lloyd watched dark clouds devour the restaurant atop the Occidental Building; for a moment he forgot that this "case" would probably be his last. Turning to look at Kapek, he said, "So we're stuck with figuring out where the robbers glommed onto Hawley and Issler, and if either of them have other bank manager friends in similarly vulnerable positions, which is a bitch of a fucking intelligence job."

Kapek slapped both thighs. "How about an ad in the singles tabloids—'Bank Managers involved in extramarital romances please come forward to act as decoy!' No, I've already questioned Hawley and Issler on that—zip. This is a one-shot deal, perpetrated by brainboys who can control themselves. Now the crunch question: what are you going to do about this thing?"

Lloyd cut off Kapek's eagerness with a chopped hand gesture. "No. First, how are we working this? I've been a supervisor and I've worked alone, but I've never worked an interagency gig with the Feds. I realize it's your investigation, but I want to know what I can ask for, who I can delegate and how much slack I've got on doing it my way."

Kapek muttered, "Your way," under his breath, then said out loud, "The investigation is structured *this way*. L.A.P.D. is handling the Issler assault-kidnap, with the squad lieutenant from West Valley dicks supervising. He knows you're the liaison; he'll give you any information or assistance you need. I've got three men checking out Issler's and Hawley's known associates, *and* the restaurants and motels they frequented, that kind of thing. They'll be compiling data on the people they come into contact with, checking them out with L.A.P.D. R&I, looking for connections. The traveler's checks are a long shot, but the serial numbers have been broadcast nationwide, and the West Valley cops have put out the word to their snitches. I want you as a floater between agencies. *You've* probably got snitches up the ying-yang, and I want you to utilize them. There is absolutely *nothing* in our computer or files on white/Mexican heist teams period, let alone ones given to kidnap-assaults. This caper sounds like street criminals graduating—more your beat than mine. You take it from there."

Lloyd breathed in the declaration of his second-banana status; it felt like a swarm of nasty little bureaucratic bees buzzing at his brain. His voice was tight and hoarse as he said, "Let's fucking *move*, then. You've got Hawley intimidated, so grab his credit card bills so we can see where he and Sally have been screwing. Don't trust his memory on it—subconsciously he'll be screwing *you*. Lean on him, polygraph him, rattle his skeletons. You like it?"

Kapek snickered, "Rubber hose him? Threaten him with an I.R.S. audit? He's got a son in college who's gay. Squeeze him by putting it on the six o'clock news? Ease off, Sergeant. The man is cooperating."

The buzzing grew deafening. Lloyd looked out the window, then jerked his eyes back when the notion of a seven-story jump to oblivion started feeling good. "I want to have a shot at Issler," he said. "I want to question her about her old boy-friends, and I want to put a tap on her home and work phones. I'll go easy on her."

Kapek stood up, put his hands on the desk and leaned forward so that his face was only a few feet from Lloyd's. "Unequivocally no. That order comes directly from your own immediate superior officer. Captain McManus told me person-ally to keep you away from her, and all other women involved in this investigation beyond the level of field interrogation. He told me that if you violate that order, he'll suspend you from duty immediately. He means it, and if you cross me on this, I'll report it to him in a hot flash."

Suddenly the bees did a kamikaze attack. Lloyd looked down at his bandaged hand and saw that he had gripped the window ledge so hard that blood was starting to seep through the gauze. He stared out the window at a dark mass of rain clouds. Seeing that the Occidental Building was now com-pletely eclipsed, he said, "It's your ball game, G-man. I'll call you every twenty-four unless something urgent comes up. Call me at home or Parker Center if you get anything. You like it?"

"I like it."

"What else did McManus tell you?"

"He implied that you have emotional problems pertaining to the pursuit of pussy. I told him that my wife's a black belt in karate, so I don't have those problems."

Lloyd laughed. "It's your ball game, but it's my last shot. I'm gonna nail these cocksuckers."

Kapek pointed to the door. "Roll, hot dog."

Lloyd rolled, first in a cab to Parker Center, where he formally reported back for duty, then in a '79 Matador to the West Valley Station, staying ahead of the northbound storm clouds that threatened to drench the L.A. basin to the bone.

In the empty West Valley squadroom, he read the reports filed by plainclothes officers who had canvassed the two crime scenes late the previous day. The Woodman and Ventura house-to-house was a total blank—three housewives had noticed Hawley passed out in his Cadillac, but no one had seen him in the company of another man. The canvass of Sally Issler's neighborhood was an even bigger zero—no male Mexicans, alone or traveling as a pair, were seen on the street, and no unknown or suspicious vehicles were parked on or near her apartment building.

Sally Issler's formal statement, made after she came out of her hospital-administered sedation, was more illuminating. Asked about the personalities of her two captors, she had stated that the "tall, slender" man seemed "passive for a criminal; soft-spoken, maybe even educated," and that the "short, muscular" man "came on like a sex freak, like one of those Mexicans who hit on every chick they meet." When asked exactly what the short man said, she refused to answer.

Lloyd called Telecredit and asked for lists of Robert Hawley's and Sally Issler's recent credit card transactions, emphasizing restaurant and bar bills and motel accommodations. The operator promised to phone him at Parker Center with the information.

Running down options in his mind, Lloyd left a note for the lieutenant handling the Issler investigation to call him at the Center, then wrote out a memo to be teletyped to all L.A.P.D. divisions for roll call: "All units be alert for two-man stickup team: male Mexicans, early thirties, one tall, slender and 'soft-spoken,' one short, muscular and a possible sex offender. Both armed with silencered, army-issue .45 autos. Also be alert for B. of A. Greenback traveler's checks, serial number and denominations in West Valley Div. 12/7/84 robbery bulletin. Direct *all* queries and field interrogation reports to Det. Sgt. Hopkins, Robbery/Homicide Div. x 4209.

On his way out, Lloyd left the memo with the watch commander, who assured him it would be transmitted in time for the nightwatch crime sheet. Then he rolled back to Parker Center, this time straight into the storm clouds.

He was skirting the east edge of Hollywood when the rain hit. Hawley, Issler and Mexican bandits rolled out of his mind, and Janice rolled in, freeze-framed as she looked the last time he saw her. After punching out the lawyer's bookcase, he had walked through Chinatown, pressing his bloody hand into his shirttail, numbed and directionless until it started to rain in buckets and he realized he was only a few blocks from Janice's apartment. He knocked on the door and Roger answered in a bathrobe, his yappy dachshund cowering in back of him.

Roger himself backed off as if fearing a blow. Lloyd walked past him into the kitchen, holding his hand tightly to avoid dripping blood on Janice's Persian carpet. The dog alternately yapped, growled and took a bead on his ankles as he wrapped a dish towel around his gashed knuckles.

Janice had walked in then, carrying a pitcher of frozen daiquiris. She jumped back at the sight of Lloyd, and the pitcher fell to the floor, banana and rum fizz flying in all directions. Lloyd held up his hand and said, "Oh shit, Jan," and the dachshund began lapping up the goo. Roger entered the kitchen as the dog began to reel from the booze. He tried to grab him, but slipped on banana residue and hit the floor ass first. The drunken hound lapped his face, and Janice laughed so hard she had to grab Lloyd for support. He held her with his good arm, and she burrowed into him until he could feel them melding into each other the way they used to. Then Roger broke the spell by blubbering about his robe being ruined, and Janice drew away from her husband and back to her lover. But a brush fire had been ignited. Lloyd whispered, "I love you," as he retreated from the kitchen. Janice formed "yes" with her lips and touched her hands to her breasts.

Back at his Parker Center cubicle, Lloyd let the brush fire smolder as he figured out "shitwork" logistics, first making notes for computer cross-checks, then writing an interdepartmental memo alerting Detective Division personnel to the case and its salient facts. The work forged the facts even deeper into his own mind, pushing back a notion to pad the job and thus postpone the inevitable.

The sense of inevitability dug in like spurs and drove him down to the fourth-floor computer room, where he had the programmer feed in queries on white/Mexican stickup teams and their current dispositions, male Mexicans with both armed robbery and sex offense convictions, and known and suspected gangland armorers. The results came back in twenty minutes—a printout of forty names and criminal records. The first two categories were washouts; the twelve white/Mexican heist teams all had at least two members currently in prison, and the nine Mexican armed robber/sex offenders were all men aged forty-eight to sixty-one.

Lloyd took the list of gun dealers up to his cubicle and read through the twenty-one names and criminal records, immediately dismissing the blacks—Latin and black hoodlums hated each other like poison. This eliminated thirteen names, and the printout showed that four of the eight men remaining were in county jail and state prison on various charges. He wrote down the four names that were left: Mark McGuire, Vincent Gisalfi, Luis Calderon and Leon Mazmanian, then called his most trusted snitch and gave him the names, an outline of the

Hawley/Issler case and the promise of a c-note for hard info. The shitwork completed, he looked out his window at the rain and wondered what Janice was doing. Then he balled his bad hand into a fist, checking the gauze for seepage. Seeing none, he pulled off the bandage and dressing and tossed it into the wastebasket.

10

Joe Garcia woke up on the morning of his second strong-arm assault and found himself eyeball to eyeball with another flattened .45 slug, this one mounted on mattress stuffing that had popped out of his Sealy Posturepedic while he slept. Rolling onto his back, he saw the lumber the workmen had stacked for the reconstruction of his bedroom wall and added the spent piece of metal to the ones he'd already dug out of his clothes and books and records. Eleven. Bobby had shot off both guns, a total of fourteen rounds. A stack of his sci-fi paperbacks, his Pendletons and all of his old Buddy Holly records got wasted, and three of the little cocksuckers were still hiding, waiting to tell him that even though he had almost two grand in his kick and Bobby was paying for the damage, he was thirty-one and going nowhere. Figure today's score as ten times the money in a ten times more dangerous plan, and he was going nowhere rich. Then Bobby would talk him into some sleazoid quick-bucks scam, and he'd be going nowhere broke. Pushing himself out of bed, Joe felt shivers at his back and nailed the source: two days ago he became a righteous hardball criminal. If he was going nowhere, at least he was doing it in style.

Then his eyes caught the silencered handgun on top of his dresser, and the source nailed him, turning his knees to rubber. He was an hour away from committing felonies that could send him to prison for the rest of his life or have him shot on sight. The one *good* line from his longtime "epic" song supplied the final nail and made his arms shake like Jell-O: " . . . and death was a thrill on Suicide Hill."

Joe fought the shakes by thinking of Bobby, knowing he'd get pissed or depressed or grateful if he kept running riffs on him. While he dressed he remembered growing up in Lincoln Heights and how Bobby held him when the old man came home juiced and looking for things to hit; how he tied him to his bed so he could go out and play without him; how all the neighbors despised their family because only two kids meant they were bad Catholics, and how Bobby beat up the kids who said they were really Jews in disguise.

Bobby saved his ass then, but when Father Chacon talked the old lady into trying for more rug rats against doctor's advice and she died in childbirth, Bobby kicked the shit out of him when he called the dippy old priest a *puto*.

And Bobby carried him through burglary and jail; and Bobby spit on his dreams; and he could split from him, but he had to stay in L.A. for the music biz, and if he stayed in L.A., Bobby would find him and Bobby would need him, because without him Bobby was a one-way ticket to the locked ward at Atascadero.

The rundown calmed Joe to the point where he could shave, and dress in his camouflage outfit of business suit and shiny black shoes. But when he stuck the .45 into his belt, the shakes returned. This time he fought them with pictures of 10K worth of guitars, amps and recording equipment. It worked until Bobby jumped into the doorway, his arms raised like the Wolfman, growling, "Let's go, *pindejo*. I'm hunnnnggry."

The brothers drove to their target.

At Studio and Gage they parked and fed two hours' worth of coins to the meter, then walked the three blocks north to Hildebrand. Street traffic was scarce, pedestrian traffic nonexistent. At 8:17 they came up on Christine Confrey's ranchstyle house, her red Toyota parked in the driveway. Bobby said, "Walk like you're the landlord"; Joe whispered, "Be ultra frosty." Bobby grinned. "Now, little brother."

They took the driveway straight to the back door. Joe looked for witnesses while Bobby took a metal ruler from his jacket pocket and slipped it between the door and doorjamb and pushed up. The catch snapped, and they entered into a tiny room filled with folding lawn chairs. Joe reset the latch and felt his sweat go ice-cold at the moment of B&E terror: if they were seen, it was over.

Bobby eyed the door to the house proper and picked a soiled towel up off the floor; Joe slipped a length of nylon cord from his back pocket, then watched his brother's lips do a silent countdown. At "5" they donned their ski masks and gloves; at "1" they *moved*, pushing through the door at a fast walk.

The connecting hallway was still. Joe heard music coming from a door at the far left end and took that side of the hall, knowing part of his watchdog job was to be the one who grabbed the girl. As the music grew louder, he pressed himself to the wall; when the music drowned out the slamming of his heart, he leaped through the open door and jumped on the woman who was standing with one foot on the bathtub ledge, poising a razor over her leg.

The woman screamed as Joe's arms went around her; the razor gouged a section of calf. Bobby elbowed his way into the bathroom and wrapped the towel over her head, stuffing a large wad of it into her mouth, stifling her screams. Joe fumbled her robe into her breasts so they wouldn't stick out, then circled the cord around her, pressing her arms to her sides. When he got it tied, he lifted her off the floor, kicking and flailing, still tightly grasping the razor. He whispered, "Sssh, sssh, sssh. We're not gonna hurt you. We just want money. *We just want money*."

Bobby got out his roll of tape and pulled a long piece loose, then withdrew the towel. The woman let out a short screech before he was able to loop the tape around her head and press it to her mouth. When he saw the terror in her eyes, his whole body started to twitch, and he whispered, "Get her fucking calmed down."

Joe loosened his grip on the woman as Bobby stumbled out

of the bathroom. With one hand he took out his .45 and held it in front of her; with the other he smoothed her disheveled hair. "Sssh. Sssh. We're not going to hurt you. This is a robbery. It's got to do with you and your boyfriend Eggers. You have to do two things: you have to *not* be scared, but you have to *act* scared when the phone rings and you talk to your boyfriend. My buddy's a crazy man, but I can control him. *Be cool and you won't get hurt.*"

Christine Confrey's tremors decelerated just a notch; Joe could feel her thinking. When she dropped the razor, he relaxed his grip and steered her into the hallway. Bobby was there, leaning against the wall, giving the thumbs-up sign. "The phone is gonna ring real soon," he giggled.

Joe nodded and moved Christine into the bedroom, motioning Bobby to stay out. He noticed the phone on a nightstand; it had the look of something about to explode. When it rang shrilly, he looked into his captive's eyes. "*Just be cool,*" he whispered, gently pulling the tape from her mouth.

He picked up the phone on the fifth ring and said, "Eggers?" getting a "Y-yes, Chrissy. P-please p-put her on." Nodding at Christine and holding up the .45 for her to see, he handed the receiver over.

She grasped it with shaking hands and tried to form words. Joe fought a desire to smooth her hair. Finally her voice caught: "John, there's these two men here. They've got guns and they say that all they want is money." She watched Joe stroke the barrel of his .45, and her voice accelerated: "Please, John, goddammit. Don't be fucking cheap — do whatever they tell you to do or they'll kill me. They—"

Joe grabbed the phone and put his free hand over Christine's mouth. He said, "Got it, Eggers?" and got "Yes, you animal" in return. Joe said, "Just do what our friend says," then hung up.

Christine Confrey twisted her head free and said, "Now what?" Joe thought of tire-squealing black-and-whites and shotgun-wielding fuzz. "Now we wait," he said. "An hour tops. Then we get another call, and we tape your mouth and you never see us again."

"You're a slimy piece of Mexican shit," Christine Confrey replied. Joe caught himself starting to nod in agreement, but said instead, "Be cool." His face began sweating beneath the ski mask. It felt like a shroud.

They waited in silence, Christine sitting on the bed, Joe standing by the bedroom door, looking at his watch and listening to Bobby giggle as he prowled the house. It felt like he had two senses, both of them working toward something bad. After thirty-two minutes of scoping out the Timex, Bobby's giggles exploded into a big burst of laughter. Then the door pushed open, and the ski-masked loony was there, a magazine in his hands, growling, "Check the skin book, homeboy. Righteous *hairpie*."

Christine pointed to the magazine Bobby was waving, hyperventilating, then getting out: "I-I-I was nineteen! I needed the money and I only kept it because John likes to see what I was like then and I—"

Joe moved to the bed and wrapped the discarded section of tape around Christine's mouth. Bobby was at his back, holding the copy of *Beaverooney* open, jabbing his right forefinger at the pictures inside. "Dig it, bro! Is this bitch fine as wine, or am I woofin'! Dig it!"

To placate Bobby, Joe glanced at the legs-apart nude spread. "Yeah, but just maintain. *Main-fucking-tain*."

Bobby shoved him aside and sat down on the edge of the bed. Christine strained against the cord and tape, kicking her legs in an effort to propel herself away, working her lips trying to scream. A stream of urine stained the front of her robe and trickled down her thighs. Bobby squealed, "Righteous," and grabbed both her ankles with his left hand and held them to the bed, while his right hand hovered over her pelvis in a parody of a shark about to attack. He grunted, "Duhn-duhn-duhn-duhn," and Joe recognized it as the theme from *Jaws*. Bobby's shark hand did slow figure eights; Bobby himself whispered, "We reconned you good, baby, but I didn't pick up on how fine you are. Fine as wine. I'm the Sharkman, baby. Duhn-duhn-duhn-duhn. I give righteous fin and even better snout."

Joe whimpered, "No, no, no," as Bobby stuck his tongue through the hole in his ski mask and lowered his head; when his mouth made contact with Christine's leg, he shrieked, "No, you fucking rape-o, no!"

The phone rang.

Bobby jerked his head up as Joe moved toward the nightstand. He pulled the .45 from his waistband and aimed it straight between his brother's eyes. "Let it ring, puto. The shark wants to give some snout, and no candy ass watchdog is gonna stop him."

Joe backed into the wall; the phone rang another six times, then stopped. Bobby giggled and started making slurping noises. Christine squeezed her eyes shut and tried to bring her hands together in prayer. Joe shut his own eyes, and when he heard Bobby titter, "Shark goin' down," he stumbled out of the bedroom, picturing tear gas and choppers and death.

Then there was a crashing sound from the rear of the house. Joe opened his eyes and saw Duane Rice running down the hallway holding a briefcase and the .45, no ski mask and no beard disguise on. The house went silent, then Bobby's "Sharkman, Sharkman," reverberated like thunder. Rice crashed into the bedroom, and Joe heard a sound he'd never heard before: Bobby squealing in terror.

He ran to the bedroom door and looked in. Rice had Bobby on the floor and was slamming punches at his midsection. Christine Confrey was still on the bed, trying to scream. Her robe was pulled up over her stomach and her panties were curled around her ankles. Joe ran to the bed and pulled down the robe, then grabbed Duane Rice's shoulders and screamed, "Don't! Don't! You'll kill him!"

Rice's head and fists jerked back at the same instant, and he twisted to look up at the voice. Joe said, "*Please,*" and Rice weaved to his feet and gasped, "Get the briefcase."

Bobby moaned and curled into a ball; Christine tried to

bury her head in the bed sheets. Rice felt the throbbing redness that was devouring him ease down. When Joe came back holding the briefcase, he pinned his shoulders to the wall and hissed, "You listen to this and we'll survive. Get psycho out of here and run herd on him like you never did before. Tie the woman up even better and don't let that piece of shit near her. If I find out he even *touched* her again, I'll kill him. Do you believe me?"

Joe nodded and said, "Yes." Rice released him, opened the briefcase and started extracting handfuls of money, dropping them on the bed. When the briefcase was half empty, he pointed to the pile and said, "Your share. I'll call you tonight. I trust you for some reason, so you take care of him."

Joe looked at the wads of cash covering the crumpled sheets and Christine Confrey's legs, then looked down at Bobby, slowly rising to his knees. He turned around for sight of Duane Rice, but he was already gone.

Rice forced himself to walk slowly to the Trans Am, parked a block from Christine Confrey's house. He swung the briefcase like Mr. Square Citizen and wondered how good a look the woman got at his face, and why for a split second *her* face looked just like Vandy's. Then he remembered how at their first meeting Joe Garcia had called his brother a rape-o and how it didn't register as anything but jive. Eggers was angel dust pie, but it was Bobby Boogaloo who put them inches away from the shithouse.

After stashing the briefcase in the trunk, Rice drove down Gage to Studio, and at the corner saw the Garcias' '77 Camaro parked at the curb. He pulled into a liquor store lot across the street to observe the brothers' getaway and see if the fuzz approached the Confrey pad. If no black-and-whites descended and Joe and the rape-o looked good, they were clear, and Pico and Westholme was still a possible.

He thought of the score, of the sheer audacity of trashing Eggers' sterile Colonial crib and the look on his face when he showed him the knives he'd stolen and said, "Christine Confrey, chop, chop. Your prints. *You know what I want.*" The look got better as the heist progressed, the bank man realizing there was no way out except to obey. Even though the take was probably only 12K tops, it was twice the amount of the first job—a good omen, and a better appetite whetter.

After ten minutes, no patrol cars or unmarked cruisers appeared, and he could see straight up Gage and tell that the house was still undisturbed. His hands throbbed from whomping Bobby Garcia, and he gripped the steering wheel to control the pain. After twenty minutes, the Garcias swung onto Studio Boulevard from a block east of Gage, walking two abreast with shopping bags partially shielding their faces. Bobby was limping, probably from abdominal pain, and Joe was talking him through the whole scene, more like a daddy than a kid brother. Rice smiled as they got in their Camaro and drove off. For a cowardly tagalong criminal, Joe Garcia had balls. If he could control the rape-o's balls for three hours, he'd make Pico and Westholme happen.

When he got "home" to the Holiday Inn, Rice changed from his bank robber suit into a new shirt-Levi combo and counted the proceeds of the Eggers/Confrey job. His half of the haphazardly split take came to $5,115.00. Fondling the money felt obscene, and he remembered what a soft-hearted old bull at Soledad told him: don't fuck whores, because then all women start looking like whores. He remembered Christine Confrey's terrified face and wondered if you loved a woman, then did all women start looking like her? Even though Christine and Vandy were physical opposites, their resemblance was weird.

Rice looked at the phone and flashed on an idea to call the fuzz and tip them to Christine, then double-flashed on it as suicide and dialed Louie Calderon's bootleg number.

Louie picked up on the first ring. "Talk to me."

"It's Duane. Got any messages for me?"

"Duane the Brain. How's it hangin'?"

"A hard yard. Any calls?"

"Yeah. If a nigger and a Mexican jump off the top of the

Occidental Building at the same time, who hits the ground first?"

"Jesus, Louie. Who?"

"The nigger, 'cause the Mexican's gotta stop on the way down and spray his name on the wall!" Louie went into a laughing attack, then recovered and said, "*I* thought it was funny, and I'm a fuckin' Mexican. Got a pencil?"

"I can remember it. Shoot."

"Okay. Call Rhonda—654-8996. Sexed-out voice, Duane, really fine."

Rice said, "Yeah" and hung up, then dialed Rhonda's number. After six rings, the hooking stockbroker's sleepy voice came on the line. "Yes?"

"It's Duane Rice. What have you got for me?"

"Brace yourself, Duane."

"Tell me!"

Rhonda let out a long breath, then said, "I found out that Anne did work Silver Foxes for a while, a few months ago. Now she's taken up with a man—a video entrepreneur. I'm pretty sure it's a coke whore scene. He's heavy into rock vid, and, well, I . . ."

Rice said, "Real slow now and you're a K richer. Name, address and phone number. Real slow."

"Can you pay me Monday or Tuesday? I'm going to the Springs for the weekend, and my car payment's due."

Rice screamed, "Tell me, goddammit, you fucking whore!"

Rhonda screamed back, "Stan Klein, Mount Olympus Estates, Number 14! You're a bigger whore than I am and I want my money!"

Klein the dope dealer who probably ratted him off on his G.T.A. bust—

Klein the lounge lizard who he always figured had the hots for Vandy and—

The hotel room reeled; adrenaline juiced through Rice like the shot of dope that had cost him three years of his life. The phone dropped to the floor, and through a long red tunnel Rhonda's voice echoed: "I'm sorry, Duane. I'm sorry. I'm really sorry." Everything went crazy, then a jolt of ice water made the room sizzle like a live wire.

You can't kill him.

You can't kill him because he's a known associate.

You can't kill him because Vandy's a known associate, and the cops will sweat her at Sybil Brand and the dykes will eat her up.

You can't kill him because then you and Vandy can't make the rock scene in the Big Apple and you'll never have the place in Connecticut, and—

It was enough ice-water fuel. Rice ran for the Trans Am, leaving the .45 under the pillow as added insurance. Rhonda's pleas were still coming out of the phone: "I'm sorry, goddammit, but I need money! You promised! You promised!"

Mount Olympus was an upscale tract of two-story Mediterranean villas situated off Fairfax in the lower part of the Hollywood Hills. Rice cruised the access road, looking for Stan Klein's red Porsche with the personalized plate "Stan Man." When all he saw were Benzes, Caddys and Audis, mostly color-coordinated to the houses, he pulled into the empty driveway of Number 14 and got out, grabbing a skinny-head screwdriver from the glove compartment.

The windows were too high to reach, but the door looked flimsy. Rice rang the bell, waited twenty seconds, then rang again. Hearing no sounds of movement inside, he inserted the screwdriver into the door runner just above the lock and yanked. The cheap plywood cracked, and the door opened.

He stepped inside and closed the door, making a mental note not to leave prints. The entrance foyer was dark, but off to his left he could see a big, high-ceilinged living room.

Rice walked in and gasped. Every inch of floor and wall space was covered with stereo and video equipment. V.C.R.s and Betamaxes were stacked along one wall floor to ceiling; home computer terminals, TV sets and giant cardboard boxes piled with Sony Walkmans were lined up on the floor. Three Pac-Man machines were propped by the doorway, and the rest of the room was taken up by mounds of small cardboard boxes. Threading his way into the maze, Rice grabbed a box at random. Rhonda the Fox and a naked man were on the cover, beneath the legend, 'Help me, Rhonda'—the Beach Boys. Private collector's item—available only thru Stan Man Enterprises, Box 8316, L.A., Calif 90036."

It all went red.

Rice tore through every box in the room; read every cover. Shitloads of naked women and oldies but goodies, but no Vandy. His frost was returning when he saw a phone and phone machine atop a color TV.

He punched the "Play Message" button and got: "Hi, this is Stan Klein on the line for Stan Man Enterprises. Annie and I are on a video shoot, but we'll be back Monday night. Talk to the beep. Bye!"

Rice pushed "Incoming." There was a tape hiss, followed by a beep and a male voice. "Stanley baby, it's Chick. Listen, Annie was great. Unbelievable skull. So listen, if you're free can we talk ad space like Tuesday? Call me." Beep. "Stan, this is Ward Carter. I . . . uh . . . want to thank you for the, uh, you know, Eskimo trade-off. Annie was fabulous. About the porn vid, it's strictly bootleg on the song rights, but I'm sure I can work out a deal with this man I know who's got a chain of X-rated motels. He's mob, and you know how those guys are into blondes, so maybe you could set up a party? Talk to you Mondayish."

The rest of the messages went unheard; a hideous wailing was drowning them out. Rice wondered where the sound was coming from. When his eyes started to burn, he knew he was weeping for the first time since the sixth grade in Hawaiian Garbage.

11

Lloyd was asleep in his Parker Center cubicle when the phone rang. Snapping awake, he pulled his legs off the desk and checked his watch: 2:40. Afternoon doze-offs: another sign of encroaching middle age. He grabbed the receiver and said, "Robbery/Homicide. Hopkins."

"Peter Kapek. We've got another one. I've got the manager; he's agreed to talk with no attorney. West L.A. Federal Building, fourth-floor interview rooms. Forty-five minutes?"

"Thirty and rolling," Lloyd said, and hung up.

He made the trip in thirty-five, lead-footing it Code Three all the way, then running upstairs to the F.B.I.'s Criminal Division offices. The receptionist looked at his badge and pointed him down a long corridor inset with Plexiglas cubicles on one side and listening rooms on the other. At the far end, he looked through the one-way glass and saw Peter Kapek and a middle-aged man in a tweed suit sitting at a metal table. The man appeared composed, Kapek harried as he jotted notes on a legal pad.

Lloyd stepped across the hall to the booth where a headset-wearing stenographer was transcribing the interrogation. He said, "L.A.P.D.," and the woman nodded and tore off the long roll of paper flowing out of her machine. "It's complete," she said. "You didn't miss that much."

Lloyd took the paper and pulled it taut, squinting to read the computer type:

14:45 hrs; 12/9/84, W.L.A. Fed. Crim. Div.

Present: SA Peter Kapek, John Brownell Eggers, W.M., D.O.B. 6/28/39, no wants; no warrants; no criminal record.

Re: Robbery at Security Pacific Bank, 7981 Lankershim Blvd., Van Nuys.

Subject waived attorney.

P.K.: Mr. Eggers, I want you to forget what you already told the L.A.P.D. officers at the station on the ride over. I want a chronological reconstruction of today's events. Take your time, and be as detailed as you like.

J.E.: Of course. I went to the bank early this morning—about 8:30—because I had some papers to go over. As I was about to unlock the door—

P.K.: Excuse me, Mr. Eggers. Was there anyone else there at the bank?

J.E.: No, there wasn't. The staff doesn't arrive until 9:15.

P.K.: Thank you. Please continue.

J.E.: A man approached me as I was about to unlock the doors. He was a white man, about thirty, about six feet, one seventy or so, medium brown hair, neatly trimmed mustache and beard. He was wearing a cheap tan three-piece suit and carrying a briefcase, and I didn't see him get in or out of a car. (*Long pause*)

The man showed me a gun in a shoulder holster and told me that *he* was the one who had broken into my home two nights before. I had already reported that to the police. He made me unlock the door, then he walked me to my desk. He told me that he wanted vault money, as much as I could carry outside on my person once the time lock went off at opening time. Then ... (*Pause*)

Then the man took out a knife that he had stolen from my kitchen. He told me that two accomplices of his were holding my wife and daughter hostage at our vacation house in Lake Arrowhead, and that if I didn't cooperate, they would be raped, then dismembered with a second knife of mine, one that he knew had my fingerprints on it. I said I would cooperate, and begged the man not to let his partners hurt my family.

P.K.: Go on, Mr. Eggers. Slowly, please.

J.E.: Thinking of my wife and daughter held hostage terrified me. The man told me to sit at my desk, facing the window, with my hands in my lap, and to remain that way until opening time. He said he would be across the street watching and waiting, and at 9:35, I should walk outside with the money, and he would find me. He said that if I called the police or I wasn't outside at the specified time, my wife and daughter would die—because his partners were going to kill them at exactly 9:40 unless he delivered the "all-clear." (*Pause*)

At 9:30, with money distributed to the tellers, I chitted for the contents of one station. I couldn't think straight, I just mumbled something about a cash draft, stuffed the money in my pockets and walked outside. When I was out of sight of the bank, the robber grabbed me and forced me to hand over the money. Then he led me to my car and made me sit down behind the driver's seat, and he shot me with this ray gun, and I blacked out. When I woke up, around one o'clock, I had an awful headache. I ran to a pay phone and called my wife in Arrowhead,

and she and Cathy were safe! No one had held them
captive! I had been had! The police were at the bank
because I had disappeared for hours, and the rest you
know.

P.K.: Backtracking, Mr. Eggers, could you
describe any distinctive mannerisms that the robber
had?

The computer roll ended. Lloyd handed it back to the steno
and walked across the hall and stared at the bank manager
through the one-way glass, wondering how much of his bullshit Peter Kapek bought. Thinking "Fuck it," he knocked on
the door and stood aside so that Eggers couldn't see him.

Kapek walked into the corridor seconds later, saw Lloyd and
smiled. "Is this bimbo slick as shit? You like him?"

Lloyd imitated the smile. "You charging him?"

"With what? Perjury? That's your scene. What we've got so
far is a pussy hound trying to protect his reputation. Except
for the Lake Arrowhead bullshit and no mention of his sweetie
pie, he's leveling. I'm going to goose him, then plea-bargain
him into cooperating by giving him immunity on the girlfriend
angle."

Lloyd shook his head. "Kapek, we can't do that. This makes
two in three days, and the M.O. is getting hairier. We need a
media alert on this. Have you hit him with Hawley and
Issler?"

"He doesn't know them. That I believe absolutely. This
whole shtick is beginning to get to me, Hopkins. You get
anything from your files? Your informers?"

Lloyd grabbed Kapek's arm and led him down the hall, out
of earshot of the steno booths. "Don't play this joker straight,"
he said. "He's slick, and he's got a lot of hardball in him, and
he'll tie us up for days trying to I.D. his girlfriend."

Kapek yanked his arm free. "He'll cooperate. As soon as I
say 'Getting any on the side?' he'll fold."

"Bullshit! You want a reconstruction on this? I buy the

stolen knives as our guys—Eggers isn't hip enough to come up with something like that. The robbery went down just like he called it. Our boys got stiffed on the traveler's checks, and they're pissed. Only Eggers came off the dust looking to save his ass. He made the call to Arrowhead from a pay phone, probably with a credit card, so there'd be a record, and he got detoxed from the dust before he hit the bank, so he'd be coherent. He should be zorched to the gills, but he's Mr. Lucidity. You mention adultery, and he'll shut up tighter than a crab's asshole."

"No, *he won't*."

Lloyd muttered, "Shit. That was gospel about his pad getting burgarlized?"

"All the way," Kapek said. "I read the crime report an hour ago—no witnesses, no prints—nothing."

"Eyeball witnesses at the bank?"

"Zero."

"Shit! Let's *lean* on Eggers."

"You're a black-glove cop, Hopkins. I'm not. Eggers is a big man, so the dust shot didn't hit him as hard as Hawley. We play it my way." He shook his head and started to walk away.

Lloyd stepped in front of him and made his voice placating. "Listen, trust me on something. Turn the heat up in the interview room, get him to take off his jacket. You'll see a spike mark or a Band-Aid at the crook of one of his elbows. My guess is that he hasn't even gone by the girlfriend's pad to see if she's okay. The cocksucker hit the family doctor for an antitoxin, then started covering his ass. You release him like everything's copasetic, he'll lead us straight to her."

Kapek smiled. "I like it. But if there's no track or Band-Aid, we play it my way." He walked to the front of the corridor and talked to the receptionist, then returned and winked. "You like it?"

Five minutes later, the corridor started heating up; ten minutes later, it was outright hot. Lloyd watched through the one-way glass as John Eggers fidgeted in his chair, then took off his jacket. Kapek aped his actions, then rolled up his sleeves. This time Eggers aped the F.B.I. man, and by squinting, Lloyd could see the small circular Band-Aid on the inside of his left elbow.

Kapek stood up and stretched, then walked past Eggers and stepped into the corridor. Seeing Lloyd, he closed the door and said, "You're good. I'm sending Slick home in a cab in five minutes. Tail him, but if he goes to his skirt, don't approach, call me." He drew a slow finger across his throat. "I mean that. Also, we should have another confab. Van Nuys Station at six?"

Lloyd said, "Be there or be square," then wiped a line of sweat from his forehead and walked downstairs. In the parking lot, he stood by the side-street entrance and waited for the arrival of the taxi. Shortly, a Yellow Cab pulled in and cruised up to the building's back entrance. John Eggers, his suit coat slung over one shoulder, walked outside and got in. When the taxi swung out onto Veteran Avenue, Lloyd counted to twenty-five and pursued.

He caught the cab at the on-ramp to the 405 northbound, and let a car get between them as they headed toward the Valley. At Ventura, the taxi exited and swung east, staying in the middle lane, the driver cruising so maddeningly slow that Lloyd wanted to ram him with his unmarked unit's snout and shove them all the way to Eggers' destination. Just when his frustration felt like it was about to peak, the cab lurched and hung a sharp left turn onto Gage Avenue and went north. Lloyd started to tingle. Too déclassé a neighborhood for a middle-aged bank exec; they were headed for the girlfriend's pad. When the cab drew to the curb at the corner of Hildebrand, he continued on, looking back through his side mirror.

Eggers got out and walked up the steps of a modest ranch-type house and let himself in. Lloyd parked and walked down the street to his target, eyeing the windows for good listening spots. Deciding to prowl the house's perimeter, he walked down the driveway with his ears perked for sounds of weeping and comforting. He was all the way around the back to the other side when he heard the sounds of pure hard female rage:

" . . . and it's all on you, you bastard! They were going to leave me alone until the bad one found that sleazy picture book that you're so fucking in love with!" The voice took on a baby talk tone: "Poor Johnny-poo got held up, and he's sooo afraid that the banky-poo and his wifey-poo are going to find out about his affair with Chrissy-poo. Awww. The mean old robber-poo shot Johnny-poo with dusty-poo, and he got his Brooksie-poo suit *allll* wrinkled. Awww." There was a sharp, flesh-on-flesh noise, then the woman's voice came out soft and dripping with contempt: "That man who robbed you is more of a fucking man than you'll ever be. Think about it, John. Next time you start talking about all the sacrifices you've made to be with me, think about that man beating up one of his partners to keep me from getting raped."

Eggers' retort was a beaten-dog grovel. "But you won't tell the police? Chrissy, my job—*our* future depends on keeping this quiet."

"No," the woman said, "I won't. I care about you too much to hurt you that way. But take this with you when you see your wife in Arrowhead tomorrow. He was sexy, and somewhere down the line when we're screwing, I'm going to be thinking of him, of the man who made you look weak and foolish. Now get out of my sight."

Lloyd leaned against the house and listened to the sound of an impotent, foot-stomping departure. When the door slammed, the woman's weeping took over, and he waited until the sobs trailed off before walking around to the front door. When he rang the bell, his hands were shaking. He looked at the name taped above the buzzer—Christine Confrey—and wondered what the woman with the volatile voice would look like.

The door swung open, and he saw. Chrissy Confrey was a small woman with a face of perfectly mismatched parts: high cheekbones, broad nose and pointed chin. Her hair was straight and long, and her tears had already dried. Lloyd winced at her handsomeness, and realized he didn't know how to play the interrogation. Holding out his badge, he said,

"L.A.P.D. I know all about it, Miss Confrey. Two Mexicans with ski masks, one soft-spoken, one the guy who tried to molest you, the white guy you were tell—"

Christine Confrey tried to push the door shut. Lloyd jammed his foot into the floor runner and wedged himself into the house, shouldering the door, and Christine behind it, aside, putting his hands up in a "no harm" pose. "I know what you've been through," he said. "And I don't want you to talk about it. All I want you to do is look at some photographs. Will you do that?"

Christine hissed, "Get out"; Lloyd stepped toward her. "You can give your statement to a woman officer, and I'll try to keep your relationship with Eggers out of it. This is the second one of these assaults, and I want you to look at some photos that the other victims probably didn't see. It won't take long."

Her face a hardening mask of hatred, Christine said, "Have John Eggers look at your pictures. This is his mess, not mine."

"I'm going to," Lloyd said, "but I need you, too. Victims tend to block out the looks of their assailants, and quick cross-check I.D.s can be very helpful. I know you got a good look at the man."

Christine's face mask stiffened to the point where Lloyd thought her features would crack. "You're the assailant. Peeping at windows. Get out!"

Lloyd leaned against the door and wondered what to do, watching Christine Confrey hold her ground in front of him, her feet dug like a frightened animal poised to attack. Strategies to cajole, retreat and press were roiling up in his brain, then blanking out as the violated woman held eye contact. Finally she did attack, rearing back her head and spitting. Lloyd wiped the wad of mucus from his shirt front and returned with an ice-voiced salvo: "Your way, huh? Okay, let's try this: unless we get these scumbags, this is going to happen over and over again. Your feelings and Eggers' job and marriage don't count. So you're going to look at mug shots of your sexy savior. I know he's a handsome fellow with his groovy beard and all th—"

Lloyd stopped when Christine's face registered befuddlement. A light flicked on in his head. The beard and mustache that Hawley and Eggers had described was a fake—one reason why Hawley hadn't been able to I.D. any of the mugs he viewed. Assuming it was only a three-man team, the white partner had probably called the Mexicans to inform them of his success with Eggers, and had gotten either a no answer or word of the impending molestation from the "soft-spoken" man. Panicking, the white robber had driven to the hostage pad, and had entered *without his disguise*.

Still staring at Christine, Lloyd said, "Get dressed. I'm taking you into custody as a material witness."

Christine Confrey broke the stare by spitting at Lloyd's feet, then walking toward the back of the house. When she returned to the living room five minutes later, she was wearing light makeup and a fresh skirt and blouse. As she locked the door, she said, "Don't touch me."

They drove in silence to the Van Nuys Station, Christine chain-smoking and staring out the window, Lloyd steering the cruiser in a circuitous route to give himself time to think. One train of thought dominated: since the L.A.P.D. and F.B.I. both kept their mug shots cross-filed according to M.O. and physical stats, Robert Hawley was probably only shown photographs of convicted armed robbers and men matching his "beard and mustache" description. Both Eggers and Confrey would have to view the entire white male age 25–40 file at Parker Center, but he now had less than two hours before he was to meet Kapek, and if Chrissy Confrey was to be tapped for maximum info during that time, he would have to shove mugs at her while the white robber's face was still fresh in her mind and let Kapek and the feds worry about her statement and known associates.

Thrilled with a solid lead all his own, Lloyd pulled into the station lot. Christine got out of the car without being directed, and walked ahead of him through the station's front doors, eyes downcast. Lloyd caught up with her and pointed her into the detectives' squad room; a plainclothes cop approached with a quizzical look. Lloyd said, "Please have a seat, Miss Confrey," then whispered to the plainclothesman, "Hopkins, Robbery/Homicide. The woman is an eyeball witness. I want to show her some mug books: white males with nonviolent felony convictions. It's a hunch I'm playing. Can you do that for me?"

The cop nodded and walked into the records booth adjoining the squad room. Lloyd saw that Christine had sat down in the assistant squad commander's chair and was helping herself to his cigarettes. He checked his watch, rankling that he had to have her out before Kapek arrived—kowtowing to a punk G-man ten years his junior. When the whole thing started to rankle, he walked over and said, "Are you going to cooperate?"

Christine blew smoke rings at him. "Of course, Officer."

The plainclothes cop came back with a stack of loose-leaf binders and placed them on the desk in front of Christine. Lloyd opened the top one and saw that the books displayed one man per page, with one close-up head shot, one full-body frontal and one full-body side shot. Below the black-and-white photos, the man's name, date of birth, arrest date and charge were typed, along with a five-digit file number.

Lloyd took a pencil from his pocket and poised it over the first sheet of mugs. "Study the pictures carefully," he said. "If you positively identify the man, tell me. I'll be studying you, and marking the ones you react to, so if you don't make an I.D., we can work up a composite from similar-looking men."

Christine put out her cigarette and lit another. "I only saw him for a second, and I only said he was sexy to hurt John."

"I realize that. Just look at the pictures carefully."

"And the papers and TV won't find out about John and me?"

Lloyd smiled and lied through his teeth. "That's right."

For an hour Christine smoked and looked at snapshots of white male felons. Lloyd sat beside her, reading her face for flashes of recognition. Twice she said, "Sort of, but not him"; three more times she held the binder up and gave it an extra close scrutiny, then shook her head. Lloyd marked the pages that drew her strongest reactions, and when Christine was finished with the last mug book, he wrote down the names and file numbers of the felons and went to the records booth to check their files on the off-chance that there might be some sort of connection to perk his mental juices.

He gave the five files cursory read-throughs, looking for the felons' current dispositions, known associates and brothers with criminal records, learning that George James Turney had been stabbed to death in a San Quentin race war six months previous and had two older brothers in their forties; that Thomas Lemuel Tucker was on federal parole in Alaska, and an orphan; that Alexander "Ramo" Ramondelli had a sister and was dying of cancer at Vacaville Prison Hospital; that Duane Richard Rice was an only child and was serving a year in the county jail for grand theft auto; that Paul Prescott Orchard had a mentally retarded younger brother and was a state parole absconder. The "known associates" were complete washouts—no familiar names, no sparks. It was time to write up a report to mollify Kapek, goose the media, chase snitch feedback and let the feds run with the ball.

Lloyd put the file numbers in a note to the squad lieutenant supervising the Issler assault, telling him to have a police artist utilize them with the assistance of a new eyeball witness the feds had. After dropping the memo off with the desk officer, he walked back to Christine and said, "Let's go. I'll drive you home."

They were walking out the door when Lloyd saw Peter Kapek striding up the steps toward them. He checked his watch: 5:30. The junior G-man had outfoxed him with an early arrival.

Kapek looked at Christine suspiciously; suddenly Lloyd felt sad for the bank manager's mistress. When Kapek started to fume silently for an explanation, Lloyd pulled him out of Christine's earshot. "I had to move fast or lose her. Call me at home and I'll tell you about it. If you don't like it, go fuck yourself and get me detached. She's your witness, but be good to her."

Kapek's fuming rendered him beet red. Lloyd nodded to Christine, then walked back into the station. The desk officer handed him a piece of paper. "Just got the call, from the switchboard at Parker Center. They didn't say who it's from. Sounds like a snitch to me."

Lloyd looked at the message. It said: Luis Calderon dealing army .45s. (Reliable info—call me for details.)

12

The restaurant was cool and dark; the Mexican music soft and harmless; the wraparound booth big and cushiony—a good, private place to talk crime plans. Sipping iced tea and waiting for the Garcias, Duane Rice felt his twenty-four hours of nonstop movement lose its frenzied edge. It was all going to happen; what he'd done since splitting Stan Klein's place proved he could do anything.

After trashing the pad for info on the "video shoot" Vandy and Klein were on, and getting zilch, he knew it was either tend to business or go gonzo, so he'd driven by the Pico-Westholme bank and memorized the floor plan, then cruised the side streets surrounding it for getaway vehicles. Around the corner on Graystone, he noticed an '81 Chevy Caprice parked in the driveway of a house whose screen door was spilling over with rubber-band-wrapped newspapers. He'd walked up and checked the name on the mailbox—Latham—then waited for the paper boy and handed him a spiel about being a friend of the Lathams', and by the way, when were they getting back? The kid said next Friday. Bingo. One vehicle down, one to go.

Then it was *think* or go gonzo, and he forced himself to remember small details all the way back to his kick-out from the slam. It took half an hour of brain-frying concentration, but finally he got it.

At the Burger King down the street from the Bowl Motel there was a fat slob security guard who bragged to the customers about his sixteen-hour shifts and all the money he was making, and how he was spending most of it on his '78 Malibu with a 327 and a B&M Hydrostick. It was never in the lot, but it had to be parked nearby. After a final recon of the Pico-Westholme area, he drove up to Hollywood and found the Malibu parked on De Longpre a half block from the Burger King. Two vehicles down—only the keys to go.

He drove to an art supply store and bought a large piece of molding wax, then cruised by the repo lot on South Western. It was closed up at nine o'clock, and there was no nightwatchman. A simple chisel pry, and he was inside the salesman's hut. There was an oversupply of master keys for *all* late-model Chevys, so he forgot about making wax impressions and glommed the keys outright. The two getaway vehicles were as good as his.

Next he called Rhonda, catching her on her way out the door to her weekend at "The Springs." She told him she didn't know where the video shoot that Vandy and Klein were on was, and that she didn't know whether Vandy performed in any of Klein's X-rated videos. She said she would talk to people in "The Springs" and leave a message if she got any hard info. She mentioned money several times, and he promised to call Silver Foxes Monday night to set up a meet.

Then came the tough part—manipulate the Garcia brothers: both of them for the Pico-Westholme heist; Joe for a watchdog. The heaviest gaming would be groveling to Bobby. Even though it was the right thing to do, it felt all wrong, and he was relieved when he called and got no answer.

Which left him at midnight with nothing to do and no one to do it with, and nowhere near sleep. The Holiday Inn was now total skunk city, so he moved back to the same room at the Bowl Motel, where the same grease spots and lines of dust greeted him, but did not ease him into sleep. Since he now had to stay awake to talk to Joe Garcia, it was either *move* or go gonzo.

So he *moved*, driving the Trans Am like a meek old man, going a weird kind of gonzo, where the superior type English he knew from police reports filled his head with thoughts he didn't want to say or even *think* out loud:

Unlike Stan Klein, Gordon Meyers is not a known associate. In the course of his career as Module 2700 night jailer, he incurred only mild resentment from the thousands of inmates he supervised, all of whom were mentally disturbed misdemeanants incapable of perpetrating armed robbery and murder;

Said unknown perpetrators were obviously seasoned bank robbers, most likely San Quentin or Folsom parolees, institutionalized and subconsciously desirous of committing felony acts in hopes of receiving ten-to-life habitual offender sentences.

The parole officer/cop/shrink rap kept eating at him; finally he started thinking of Vandy to hold it down. He thought of known associate Stan Klein, whom he couldn't touch, and got very calm, even cocky. Deciding to check out Stan Man's new scam, he started asking night clerks at "adult" motels if they had any good "fuck music." The first three clerks took his ten spot and said no; the fourth said yes and offered him a special "short timer" rate for private listening. Steeling himself, he accepted the offer.

The six cassettes stacked atop the V.C.R. in front of the sweat-stained bed all bore the "Stan Man" name and P.O. box. He loaded them into the machine and turned off the lights. Tremors and a flash thought hit him along with the "Stan Man" logo: he didn't want it to be Vandy, but if it was Vandy, he wouldn't be so godawful alone. Cursing himself, he turned up the volume and watched the show.

A disco beat, then a haggard woman was gobbling a donkey-sized dick while Donna Summer belted, "She Works Hard for the Money." Fade-out, logo, then Rhonda the Fox was taking on four guys at once, the Beach Boys wailing for her to help them. Blank frames, blurred logo, "This Land Is Your Land" on the sound track, Mondale and Ferraro doing a handshaking tour on the screen, intercut with a girl in a red, white and blue negligee giving head to a jig in an Uncle Sam costume.

No Vandy.

If you fuck whores, then all women start looking like whores.

If you love a woman, then all women start looking like her.

Rice kicked over the V.C.R. and ran out of the room and across Sunset to a phone booth. He dialed the Garcias' number; Joe answered on the first ring. All he got out was "Hello?" before Duane the Brain took over in force:

You want to come to New York, get away from your batshit brother and work a real musician gig?

You and Bobby want two-thirds of a hundred K foolproof, in and out Monday morning in six minutes?

You want to be a fucking *pachuco* for the rest of your life, or do you want out?

You get your brother to come with you to La Talpa tomorrow at noon. Tell him I'll apologize; tell him I need him.

The words stuck in his throat. Joe's final answer would always stick in his brain: "I'm your man, Duane. And don't worry about Bobby. He likes getting hit. In fact, he said you remind him of this priest he used to know."

"Thanks for sparing my face, Duane-o. The old Sharkman owes you for that. I lit a candle for you last night. Figured you was Protestant, but what the fuck."

Rice looked up to see Bobby Garcia sliding into the booth, his right hand held out. He shook it, glad that the restaurant was dark, so the greasy piece of sharkshit couldn't read the contempt on his face. Thinking, *Ice City*, he said, "Sorry, Bobby. I flipped out."

Bobby sat down across from him and dug into the bowl of nachos and salsa on the table. Between wolfish mouthfuls, he said, "No strain, no gain, no pain. Little brother's coming in a minute. You got another score?"

"Yeah. Straight in and out bank job."

Bobby whistled. "Righteous. Little Bro said a hundred big ones. That true?"

"If I'm lyin', I'm flyin'."

Bobby giggled and slithered a shark hand over the bowl of nachos. "Then you gotta have wings somewhere, 'cause your first two righteous big-time scores netted me and Little Bro about a dollar eighty-nine, and I'm startin' to feel like the bottom man in a Mongolian cluster fuck."

Rice took in a deep breath, hoping his voice would come out just right, giving Sharkshit the perfect amount of slack. "That was secondhand information I acted on. I was crazy to trust it. But we've hit twice. We're on a roll, and this one is all mine. I've had it in mind for a long time, I was just waiting for the right partners."

Bobby smirked. "I hope it ain't a roll into the gutter. I been there twice, and I ain't goin' for sloppy thirds."

"You'll like this one—it's *you*."

"Yeah? *Me?* Tall, dark and handsome? Hung like a mule?"

"No. Nasty, simple and out front. Easy to understand, so I know you'll eat it up."

Bobby giggled. "You said the magic word—eat. You know how to pick up chicks without saying a word? Sit at the bar and part your hair with your tongue."

"It's you, Bobby. So simple and low class that it's got class."

A waitress came up to the booth with menus; Rice grabbed them and said, "We'll order in a few minutes." When she walked away, Bobby said, "We shoulda hit a smorgasbord. The furburger buffet: all you can eat for sixty-nine clams." Rice felt a tide of slime wash over him. Then Joe Garcia was there, saying, "Duane, how's it hanging?"

Rice said, "Long and strong," and squinted across the booth to get a handle on how the tagalong was holding up. Not bad, he decided; scared, but probably cash flushed, and more scared of continuing a crime career with Sharkshit Bobby. A born follower about to trade leaders.

The waitress returned. The brothers ordered Carta Blanca; Rice another iced tea. When she brought the drinks, the three partners fell silent. Then Rice looked straight at the Garcias, knowing they'd go for the plan: bullshit, truth, the whole enchilada.

"Nifty little Cal Federal on Pico near the West L.A. freeway crisscross. One camera—we shoot it out. One plainclothes security man—a juicehead. Big payroll payouts on the twelfth and twenty-sixth of the month, so we hit the twelfth, this Monday. I've got one car pegged for the approach, another for the getaway—a family car right around the corner from the bank. The people are away on vacation, and I've got a master key for the doors and ignition. We go in wearing suits and beard-mustache disguises, carrying briefcases. Six tellers stations, two to a man. I know an abandoned garage in Hollyweird where we can stash the getaway sled. In, out, on the freeway by the time the fuzz show up. Three-way equal split. I've been casing this score for a long time, but I didn't know how stand-up you guys were. *Are you with me?*"

Bobby chugalugged his beer, reached into the bowl and crumbled the remains of the nachos, then placed his hands palms up on the table. Rice placed his right hand on top of them; Joe sealed the partnership agreement with both of his. Rice said, "You know how to dress and what to bring. Meet me at Melrose and Highland Monday morning at ten."

The partners withdrew their hands and stood up. Bobby squeezed out of the booth, walked over to the waitress and began a soft rendition of the *Jaws* theme. Joe looked at Rice, swallowed and said, "Was that for real about New York and the music gig?"

Rice smiled. "We leave on Wednesday. You stick with me after the job. We have to pick up my old lady, then we have to keep you away from Sharkshit over there. *Comprende?*"

"*Si, comprendo, mano.*" Joe put out his hand jailhouse style; Rice held it down in a square-john shake. "That lowrider shit is dead. You pull that stuff in New York, and they'll laugh you out of town."

13

Lloyd pulled up to the back entrance of the West L.A. Federal Building and honked his horn. Peter Kapek walked over to the car and got in. Expecting a rebuke for the Confrey approach, Lloyd was stunned when the junior G-man said, "Good work on the girlfriend. I got a good statement out of her. No positive I.D. on the white man, but Confrey and Eggers worked up a composite with an L.A.P.D. artist. It'll be distributed all points by tomorrow morning. Where are we going? And by the way, you look like shit."

Lloyd nosed the Matador out onto Wilshire. "Didn't you get the complete message? We're going to brace a suspected gun dealer. Luis Miguel Calderon, a.k.a. "Likable Louie," male Mexican, age thirty-nine, two convictions for receiving stolen goods, former youth gang member mellowed out into small-time businessman. He's got an auto parts shop in Silverlake, my old neighborhood. A snitch I trust says he's dealing army-issue .45s. And I look like shit because I've been doing police work all night."

Kapek laughed. "I like it! Learn anything?"

Lloyd shook his head. "Not really. I canvassed the Security Pacific area and Confrey's neighborhood; Brawley from Van Nuys Dicks couldn't spare any men. I got a big zero—no suspicious people or vehicles. I read every report on Hawley's and Issler's associates eight times—nothing bit me. Then I called a couple of media people and gave them the whole ball of wax. It goes to press and on the air Monday night, giving us exactly forty-eight hours to figure out a strategy. What's the matter, G-man? You're not doing your famous slow burn."

Kapek toyed with the knobs of the two-way radio. "Don't call me 'G-man,' it turns me on. I didn't rat you off on Confrey because I heard these homicide guys at Parker Center talking about you with awe, and I actually started to like you a little bit. Also, I got a good statement from Confrey. The rape guy turned out *not* to be a rape-o, more like a psycho muff diver. He did this rebop about being a shark, then went down on Chrissy's bush. I've computer-fed the info nationwide—nothing—and I've put it in a memo for L.A.P.D. roll calls—maybe we'll get a bite."

"A shark bite?"

"Very fucking amusing. We need a hard lead, Hopkins; this thing is *covered* from every paper angle. Our eyeball witnesses have checked every local and federal mug book—zero. The men checking out the victims' associates have got nothing, and I've got an agent going over Hawley's and Eggers' credit card slips with them—you know, all the places they rendezvoused with the girlfriends have got to be checked out. If nothing breaks by Monday, I'm planting people in the offices where Issler and Confrey work."

Lloyd nodded and said, "I've been kicking around an idea that might account for a connection between Hawley and Eggers and explain why the robbers have escalated their M.O. I'm thinking both these guys might be pilfering traveler's checks—at least Hawley. Here's the reconstruction. While they're casing the B. of A., the robbers see Hawley stealing the *green* traveler's checks, which from a distance look like cash. They think that money is left overnight in the tellers boxes—"

Kapek interrupted. "Hawley said the inside man wanted the bank checks—that he asked for them by name."

Lloyd shook his head. "That's Hawley the pilferer covering his ass, obscuring the robbers' reasons for hitting *his* bank. Here's my reasoning. The robbers have either seen Eggers pilfering similarly, or they figured, and this isn't likely, given their intelligence, that all banks leave loose cash out overnight.

So, after the low score on the traveler's checks, they figure that Eggers is just another check stealer, say to themselves 'Fuck that' and decide to make Eggers go for the vault. You like it?"

Grinning, Kapek said, "It floats. But what do we do about it?"

"Have your Bank Fraud Division people give you a crash course in check rip-off scams. Maybe they can tell us something we can use to squeeze Hawley and Eggers. I've got a hunch on this. I think that if these guys are pilferers, it's out of desperation—cash flow problems that they can't talk about. And *that* makes me think *vice*—gambling, dope, sex. Sex the least likely, because they've got the outside stuff going. I'm going to initiate inquiries with every vice squad in the Valley— maybe our boys are heavy in hock to bookies, or loan sharks, or they're into kinky shit we don't know about. If we get a bunch of vice dicks to pump their informants, we might get something."

Kapek elbowed Lloyd and said, "I like it! There's nothing on the traveler's checks, by the way, but on the cash flow problems, I'm going to peruse our boys' bank accounts, see what I get."

Lloyd took the words in silently and, as the old neighborhood drew closer, thought of his family. "You didn't rag me on the media goose," he said. "Come Monday night a lot of innocent people are going to be hurting. I figured a sensitive guy like you would be pissed."

Kapek flushed. "It was the right thing. I would have waited a day or so, then done it. I'm doing the family interviews, though, and *discreetly*."

"We're almost there, G-man. Any thoughts on this interview?"

"No, you?"

"Yeah. Let's test Likable Louie's fuse."

Lloyd pulled to the curb, then pointed to the white adobe building that housed Louie's One-Stop Pit Stop.

"No violence?" Kapek said.

"No violence."

"Then I like it."

They walked across the street and through the wide-open front door of the garage, into a small room filled with stacks of retread tires. A Chicano youth popping a pimple at a wall mirror gave them the fisheye, and Lloyd said, "Where's Louie?"

The youth gouged the zit a last time and reached for an intercom set mounted on the connecting door. Lloyd said, "Don't do that," and motioned for Kapek to walk ahead of him. The kid shrugged, and Kapek pushed through the door. Lloyd was right behind him, tingling at the thought of a razzle-dazzle interrogation.

The garage proper was huge, with pneumatic grease racks, sliding drawers full of auto parts, and a large drive-in space leading to a back entrance and work area. Lloyd and Kapek walked slowly, catching cop-wise squints from the mechanics working beneath the racks. A heavyset man glanced at them, and Lloyd recognized him from his R&I snapshot: Luis Calderon.

He walked over and smiled, revealing buck teeth and a fortune in dental gold. "Good afternoon, Officers. Looking for me?"

Lloyd flashed his badge. "Hopkins, L.A.P.D. This is Special Agent Kapek, F.B.I. We'd like to talk to you."

Calderon sighed. "Have I got a choice?"

Lloyd sighed back. "Yeah, you do. Here or Rampart Station."

"I've already seen it," Calderon said. "Let's go out back and get some air."

Catching an edge in his voice, Lloyd said, "No. Your office." Calderon sighed again and started walking toward the garage's street entrance. Lloyd tapped him on the shoulder. "No, Louie. Your *real* office, where you've got your desk and your files and your invoices."

Louie turned around and walked over to and up a flight of wooden stairs next to the tool bin. Lloyd let Kapek get between them, knowing the mechanic/hood's reaction to a fed roust was out of kilter. When Calderon opened the office door, he squeezed in ahead of him and quickly sized up the room. Soot-stained walls, paper-cluttered desk, refrigerator and a *Playboy* Playmate tacked to the wall, probably hiding a safe. Two phones on the desk, one red, one black; a clipboard holding notebook paper leaning against the red one. Nothing incriminating at first glance.

Calderon opened the refrigerator and took out a Coors, then sat down behind the desk. Popping the can, he said, "Topped out my parole, topped out my probation. Pay my taxes and don't associate with no criminal types. My only vice is brew. I'm a righteous sudser. If outfits were legal, I'd geez the shit. I'm a suds-guzzling motherfucker. I pour the shit on my Rice Krispies in the morning, and sometimes I even shave with it. I give my dog a brew chaser with his Alpo. If I was a fag, I'd squirt the shit up my ass. I am a righteous beerhound motherfucker. So how come you're coming on like storm troopers, when all the Rampart cops know Likable Louie likes to cooperate?"

Lloyd breathed the spiel in, savoring the tension that fueled it. He looked over at Kapek, who was chuckling with genuine amusement, and said, "I don't work out of Rampart, and I didn't come here to catch your Richard Pryor shtick. I could roust your workers for green cards and get myself a bonaroo immigration bust, and I'd love to run the numbers on your engine blocks. A third time receiving conviction is a nickel minimum. State time, Louie, and what you get up the ass there ain't Coors."

Louie Calderon sipped beer. Lloyd saw that his first salvo was on target, but not a wounder. Sensing that Kapek was being quiet out of real respect, he bored in: "You snitching for Rampart Dicks, Louie?"

Calderon smiled; Lloyd could almost feel the fat man's blood pressure chill out as he said, "It's well known that Likable Louie likes to cooperate."

Lloyd twisted a wooden chair around and sat down in it, facing Calderon. Smiling and hooking a thumb over his back at Kapek, he said, "Louie, that man over there is an F.B.I. Criminal Division agent. Why haven't you asked me about him?"

"Because unless he wants a boss transmission overhaul, I don't care if he stays, lays, prays or strays."

"How come you've got two phones, different colors?"

"The black phone's for business, the red phone's my hot line to the White House. Ronnie calls me up sometimes. We chase pussy together."

"Who's your connection at Rampart Dicks?"

"Who's your tailor? Your suit sucks."

The black phone rang. Calderon picked it up and spoke into it in Spanish. Lloyd raised his eyebrows at Kapek; the F.B.I. man said, "Not a word." Shaking his head, Lloyd watched Likable Louie talk a blue streak, then hang up and say, "Okay, let's see if I can scope this out. You need a favor, and someone at Rampart said I could help. You came on strong to test me, to see if I could be trusted. I'm tired of playing games. What do you need?"

Lloyd was reaching for his most disarming smile when the red phone rang. Louie picked up the receiver and said, "Yes," then nodded and wrote on the clipboard. Lloyd squinted and saw that the top sheet of paper was half covered with pencil scrawl.

Calderon said yes a final time and hung up. Lloyd looked at the veins in his neck and saw the signs of a slamming heart. "Who's your connection at Rampart Dicks?"

Louie's voice was hoarse; Lloyd could tell that he was getting genuinely befuddled. "Why you keep asking me that, man?"

Lloyd's third volley began with his most evil shitkicker glare. "I grew up in Silverlake. I was in the Dogtown Flats back when you were in the Alpines. My parents still live over on Griffith Park and St. Elmo, so I like things safe around here. Rampart does a pretty good job of keeping the peace, because they've got snitches like you to rat off the bad dudes that everybody hates. You get to hire wetbacks and turn over some stolen parts, and my mom and dad go to sleep safe at night. Right, Louie?"

"R-r-r-right," Louie stammered.

Lloyd stood up and pulled a .45 automatic from his shoulder holster. Holding it in front of Louie Calderon's trembling face, he said, "There's these three guys perving on women and taking out banks, and maybe they got their pieces from you. Here's the pitch: if you turned the pieces, you've got twenty-four hours to give me the names. If you didn't, you've got forty-eight hours to find out who did, and who he sold them to. If I don't hear from you in forty-eight one way or the other, I go to the commander of Rampart Dicks and snitch you off to him as the kingpin motherfucking gun dealer of L.A. County." He dropped his Robbery/Homicide business card on the desk and reholstered the gun. "Be cool, homeboy."

Back at the car, Kapek looked at Lloyd and said, "Jesus fucking Christ."

Lloyd unlocked the door and got in. "Meaning Calderon?"

Kapek took the passenger seat. "No, you. How much of that was bluff?"

"Everything but my threat. Calderon had that self-satisfied look, and he had a shitload of wetbacks working for him, and he didn't want us to see his office. My guess is that he's snitching dope dealers to the Rampart narks in exchange for immunity on the illegals. I know the squad commander at Rampart—he'll let minor shit slide for good information, but he's death on violent crime. If he finds out Louie's dealing guns, Louie's ass is fucking grass."

"But is he *our* gun dealer?"

"I don't know. The important thing is that he's scared. He's between Lieutenant Buddy "Bad Ass" Bagdessarian and me on one side, the robbers and getting a rat jacket on the other. We've got to put a twenty-four tail on him—your men—he's too hip to local cops. He's an old homeboy, a criminal with contacts, and he may damn well *not* be our gun dealer, but be able to put the finger on him, or he may snitch off the robbers straight out to save his ass with Buddy. Either way, we're set. How soon can you implement the surveillance?"

"As soon as you drop me off at Central Office. What are you going to do?"

Lloyd hit the ignition and gunned the car out onto Tomahawk Street. "Read all the paperwork again, then write up my ideas for Brawley at Van Nuys Dicks. Then I'm going to visit an old pal of mine. He's a superior court judge, and he's senile and a right-wing loony. He gets his rocks off issuing search-and-seizure warrants. I buy him a case of Scotch every Christmas, and he signs whatever I ask him for. Right before Louie's forty-eight are up, I'm going in his front door with a .12 gauge and due process to seize every scrap of paper he's got. You like it?"

Kapek was pale; his voice was shaky. "Jesus fucking Christ."

"You said that before. One other thing. I'm almost positive that the reason Calderon didn't want us in his office is the red phone. He's either taking bets or running a bootleg message service."

"What's that?"

"A two-way answering service. Mostly it's used by parole absconders and their families. He had a clipboard with writing on it next to the phone—messages for sure. Calderon's house is right next to the garage, and he's probably got someone there monitoring an extension all the time. Sometimes those numbers are legit Ma Bell handouts; sometimes illegal hookups that can't be traced. I want a tap on all Calderon's lines. That requires a federal warrant—your side of the street. Can you swing it?"

Kapek's color was returning, but a thin layer of sweat was creeping over his forehead. He wiped it off with his sleeve and said, "Monday at the earliest. Federal judges *all* go incommunicado on the weekends to avoid warrant hassles. You really want these guys, don't you?"

Lloyd smiled. "I'm probably getting stress-pensioned soon, against my will. I intend to go out in true hot-dog fashion." He pulled up in front of the downtown F.B.I. building, and Kapek got out. Highballing it to Parker Center, the junior G-man's pale face stayed fixed in his mind, and he knew he had taken over the investigation.

With twenty-eight sleepless hours behind him, Lloyd pushed *his* investigation for another twenty-four flat out.

At Parker Center he checked the "monicker" file for every nickname variation of "Shark," coming away with a large assortment of data pertaining to black youth gangs. Useless trivia. An R&I check of male Mexican registered sex offenders with a cunnilingus M.O. yielded seven names, but three of the men were currently in prison and the other four were in their fifties—way above Sally Issler's and Christine Confrey's "late twenties, early thirties" appraisal. The only remaining option was to add the "Shark" and oral sex abuse facts to the roll call reports and distribute the word to all L.A.P.D. informants.

Peter Kapek called in the early evening. Louie Calderon was under constant rolling surveillance. The agents would be keeping a detailed log on his movements and would be running vehicle and address checks on all persons he came into contact with. A team of agents was going over his record for possible armed robbery connections. The Likable Louie angle was covered, as were continuing probes into the recent pasts of Robert Hawley, Sally Issler, John Eggers and Christine Confrey. Come Monday, Channel 7 *Eyewitness News* would leak its "cautionary" report on the bank robbery/extortion gang, without mention of the sex assault facts. This would leave the families of the male victims open for interrogation on the investigation's "Big Question": *how did the robbers get the information on the two extramarital affairs?*

At home late that night, Lloyd phoned in the vice squad query he had mentioned to Kapek, then read the existing files and applied his thinking solely to that question. He came up with four logical answers:

Through connections to the victims' families;

Through connections to the victims' friends and acquaintances;

Through connections at the two banks;

Through the random factor: overheard conversations at meeting places such as bars, restaurants and other public gathering spots, and through informational sources that the four suspects have either consciously or unconsciously refused to reveal.

Knowing that the fourth "answer" was the most likely, Lloyd read through the case file two more times, then wrote out a memorandum stating his conclusions.

0330 hrs; 12/11/84.
To: S.A. Peter Kapek, Det. Lieut. S. Brawley.
Re: Hawley/Issler–Eggers/Confrey Investigation.

Gentlemen:

Having participated in every aspect of this investigation, and having read the case file a dozen times, I have come to one conclusion concerning the robbery gang's access to information on the four victims, one supported by sound suppositions based on existing facts. We know that Robert Hawley and John Eggers, both middle-aged bank managers, are as yet not connected to each other in any discernible personal or professional way. Exhaustive record searches have turned up no common denominators other than:

1. Identical professions;

2. Long-term marriages that appear to be flourishing despite the fact that both men are engaged in extramarital affairs;

3. The said extramarital affairs themselves, both involving women in their late twenties.

The same absence of connections exists between the two women involved. All our victims live and work in the San Fernando Valley, yet interrogations and cross-checks of credit card records show that these two sets of clandestine lovers have not even dined in the same restaurants or drunk in the same bars as each other, at any time in the course of their affairs. The odds of a criminal gang divining the existence of two such potentially lucrative and jeopardy-prone liaisons separately is preposterous. I think there is a viable Hawley/Issler–Eggers/Confrey link, one that the four principals are either willfully or subconsciously suppressing. I believe all four principals should be induced to undergo rigorous polygraph tests, and, should that fail to reveal the link, Pentothal and/or hypnosis questioning—radical investigatory measures that I think are justified in this case. Also, since the basic facts of this series of crimes will be aired and published by the media late tomorrow (released by me in the interest of a public safety precaution), I deem it advisable that the four principals be taken into custody and held without media access on Monday morning, in order to avoid repercussions deriving from familial reaction to exposure of the two affairs. I undertook the media release on my own authority, realizing the full implications. Both my newspaper and television contacts told me they would include a plea for information along with their coverage, and pass said information along to us immediately.

Respectfully,
Lloyd W. Hopkins,
#1114,
Robbery/Homicide
Division

Finishing, Lloyd looked out his kitchen window and saw that it was dawn. Feeling the family angle gouging at him, he walked through the downstairs of the house that he once shared with four women; the four rooms he had apportioned himself in their absence. Every step made him both more exhausted and more aware of the need to work. Finally he gave in to the need and slumped into the big leather chair where he used to sit with Penny.

No thoughts came, and neither did sleep. Staring at the telephone, hoping it would ring, supplied one minor brainstorm: Louie Calderon's phone number or numbers. Lloyd called the top supervisor at Bell and gave his name and badge number, then feverishly asked his question. The woman came back with a sadly unfeverish answer: Luis Calderon of 2192 Tomahawk St., L.A., had one house and one business phone—with the same number. The red phone was total bootleg.

More numbing sleeplessness followed, temporarily interrupted by a call from Peter Kapek. The first surveillance shift had just reported that Louie Calderon had left his pad only once, at 6:00 A.M. He walked to the corner and bought a case of beer. "Beer-guzzling motherfucker," Kapek said, promising to call with the next shift's report.

Lloyd shaved, showered and forced himself to eat a packet of cold luncheon meat, chased with a pint of milk and a handful of vitamins. Still unable to sleep, he checked the mailbox for the previous day's mail. There were three bills and a postcard from Penny, Fisherman's Wharf on the front, her perfect script on the back: Daddy—Hang in. Roger's dog peed on Mom's beloved carpet. Rog refused to pay for the cleaning. Mom's response: "Your father, despite his many faults, was housebroken and never cheap." Hang in, Daddy. Love Love Love—Penguin.

Now Lloyd's shot at blissful unconsciousness was broken up by an injection of hope. Feeling a second mental wind coming on, he dialed the home number of Judge Wilson D. Penzler, prepared to listen to a long right-wing rhapsody before making his warrant request. The judge's housekeeper answered, and said that His Honor was in Lake Tahoe and would be returning home and to the bench on Wednesday. Lloyd hung up, then picked up the receiver to call Buddy Bagdessarian at

Rampart Dicks and blow the whistle on Louie Calderon. His finger was descending on the first digit when caution struck. No, Buddy would blow the plan by going straight for Louie's throat. Better to give the beer guzzler some slack.

Daylight came and went. Lloyd remained fitfully awake, swinging on a brain tether of sharks, old neighborhood homeboy-crooks and his family. He was debating whether to turn on the lights or sit in darkness when the phone rang.

All he got out was "Speak" before Kapek came on the line. "Third shift just radioed. The beerhound, his wife and rug rats just took off. They're following cautiously. I also grabbed Calderon's jail jacket. The K.A.s are being checked out. What have *you* been doing?"

Lloyd tingled as the idea took hold. "Thinking. Gotta run, Peter. I'll call you tomorrow." He hung up and grabbed his burglar tools from the kitchen, then ran for his L.A.P.D. Burglar Mobile.

Likable Louie's One-Stop Pit Stop and the built-on adobe house were dark and silent as Lloyd parked on the opposite side of Tomahawk Street and got up his B&E guts. Pulling on surgical rubber gloves, he brought his previous visit to the garage to mind and thought of access routes. The house was probably too well secured; the street door too exposed. There was only the back way in.

Lloyd checked the contents of his burlap "burglar bag" and pulled out a battery-operated drill and an assortment of bits, a set of lock picks, a jimmy, a can of Mace for watchdog debilitation and a large five-cell flashlight. He dug in the backseat and found an old briefcase left by another officer, stuck his tools inside it, then walked down the alley that cut diagonally across Tomahawk Street.

A full moon allowed him a good view of the back entrance, and music blasting from adjoining houses took care of any noise he might make. Lloyd looked at the barbed-wire fence encircling the work area and resigned himself to getting cut;

he looked at the pulley-operated steel door and knew it was the window next to it or nothing.

Taking a deep breath, he tossed the briefcase over the fence and hoisted himself up the links. His right hand ached from his Frisco bookcase smashing, and he had to favor it all the way to the top. When he reached the barbed wire, he rolled into it, letting his jacket take the clawing until the last possible second, then hooking the strands with his index fingers, gouging his legs until he was free of sharp metal and there was nothing left but a twelve-foot drop. Then he pushed himself off with all his weight, landing feet first on a patch of oil slick blacktop.

No dog; no sounds of approach. Lloyd picked up the briefcase and took the flashlight from it, then walked to the window and compared its circumference to his own bulk. Deciding it would be a tight but makable squeeze, he smashed in the glass with the end of the flashlight and tossed in the briefcase. Then he elbowed himself through the hole, his jacket again taking the brunt of the damage, his legs getting another brief tearing. Coming down hands first into the garage, the smell of gas and motor oil assaulted him.

Still no dog; still nothing to indicate he had been spotted. Lloyd got to his feet and picked up the flashlight and briefcase, then took his bearings. As his eyes got used to the darkness, he picked out the stairway leading up to Louie Calderon's private office.

Lloyd tiptoed over and up the stairs, then tried the door. It was unlocked. He deep-breathed and pushed it open, then flicked on the flashlight and shined it in the direction of the desk. The beam illuminated the red phone and clipboard dead-on.

He walked to the desk, memorizing the exact positions of the invoices and beer cans on top of it, then took a pen and notepad from his back pocket and sat down in Louie Calderon's chair. Holding the flashlight in his left hand, he pushed aside a half-finished Coors and put down the pad in its place. Centering the beam right on top of the clipboard, the office around it went totally dark, and he did his transcribing in a tunnel of eye-grating light.

12/11—A.M.—Ramon V.—Call 629-8811 (mom & bro.) *before* you talk to P.O.

12/11—P.M.—Duane—Rhonda talked to friends in P.S., Stan Klein returning Monday night *late*, remember to call Mon. nite—H.(654-8996)—W.(658-4371)—wants $.

12/11—P.M.—Danny C.—Call home.

12/11—P.M.—Julio M.—Call home.

12/11—P.M.—George V.—Call Louise, Call P.O. No violation.

Completing the copy-over, Lloyd put the pad back in his pocket and returned the beer can to its proper place, pleased that it was a bootleg service rather than a bookie drop. He turned his flashlight toward the floor and retraced his steps downstairs, grabbing a box of baby moon hubcaps on his way to the front door, hoping to put the onus on punks out for a quick score. Driving home, he got his usual post-burglary shakes, followed by his usual post-B&E knowledge: *crime was a thrill.*

In his kitchen, Lloyd copied over the transcribed names and phone numbers for checking against Louie Calderon's K.A. file, then called up the three numbers he had gleaned.

The first one was a sad non-connection. Pretending to be a friend of "Ramon," Lloyd asked his mother about his whereabouts, learning that he had been cut loose from Chino on Friday and hadn't as yet contacted his parole officer or family. The woman was terrified that he was back in Silverlake and on smack.

The two numbers for "Rhonda" were even sadder—both recorded messages that boomed "prostitution" loud and clear: "Hi, this is Rhonda. If you've called for my business and your pleasure, or the converse, leave a message. Bye!"

"This is Silver Foxes. Beautiful women of every persuasion for every occasion. Please leave your name, customer number and wishes at the tone."

Lloyd put down the phone, then added the information to

his K.A. check-out list. The singsong lilt of the last message stayed with him as he turned out the lights and flopped down on the couch. While he waited for the sleep that he knew had to come, he toyed with the words. An exhaustion gibberish crept over him. He knew what was behind it: the occasions of *his* persuasion were over. The finality of the thought helped, and unconsciousness was just about there when he grabbed at an escape hatch: *an apocalypse could save him.* The thought was too scary to toy with. Lloyd slammed the hatch shut with every ounce of his will and slept dreamlessly.

14

Clockwork.

Rice looked at his watch as he nosed the '78 Malibu into the shade of a stand of trees by the freeway off-ramp. At 9:43 he'd glommed the car; at 9:56 he'd picked up the brothers, who were outfitted for bear and looking greedy. At 10:03 he stopped at a 7-11 on the edge of Hollywood for a last-minute acquisition—a brainstorm—and now, at 10:22, there was nothing left but to do it. He glanced at Bobby and Joe as he set the brake. Their suits fit, and their off-color facial hair made them look almost non-Mexican. Their briefcases were big and scuffed. It was all running perfect. "Now," he said.

They walked the half block to the corner of Pico and Westholme and waited for the light. When it turned green, Rice took the lead, striding ahead of the brothers. In front of the bank, he peered through the window and framed the scene inside: six tellers stations on the left, roped-off waiting line with no one standing in it, the execs at their desks in the carpeted area on the right. No armed guards; no sign of Gordon Meyers; the surveillance camera sweeping on its tripod above the doors. *Perfection.*

The brothers caught up, and Rice let them go through the doors first. When they were halfway to the teller area, he took a can of 7-11 shaving cream from his jacket pocket, shook it and fired a test spritz at the ground. When it hit the pavement, it hit *him*: when you look into his eyes, you'll know.

Rice pushed the doors open, wheeled and extended his right arm at the camera, missing his first spray, catching the lens on-center with the second. Coming off his toes, he saw that no one in the desk area had seen him, and that Joe and Bobby were dawdling by a cardboard display near the rear teller's station. He reached into his briefcase and pulled out his .45, then let the spray can drop to the floor. The man at the front desk looked up at the noise and saw the gun. Rice shouted, "Robbery! Everybody be real quiet or you're gonna be real dead!"

For a second, everything froze. Heads darted up behind the tellers' counter; the Garcias pulled out their .45s and moved into position, their briefcases held open. Then little gasps and flutters took over, and Rice saw everything go blackish red. Swallowing, he heard a scream from a woman staring at Joe Garcia's silencered piece; "Oh my Gods" were bombarding him from every corner of the bank. Swallowing what tasted like blood, he ran to Bobby, shoved his briefcase at him and said, "Three minutes. Fill it up."

Bobby flashed his shark grin and leveled his gun at the teller directly in front of him, hissing, "Feed the shark, mother-fucker, or you die." The man fumbled packets of currency into the briefcase, and Bobby shoved Rice's briefcase over to the next station, growling, "You, too, bitch—you fucking too." The woman dumped in whole cash and change drawers, and coins spilled over the counter onto the floor. When both tellers backed up and showed empty drawers, then ducked to their knees, Bobby slid down to the next station, catching a shot of Joe out of the corner of his eye. Little Bro had already hit three stations and was holding a shaky bead on the tellers. Tears and sweat were pouring off his face, soaking his phony beard. His face was as red as a baby's, and his lower lip was flapping so hard his whole head shook along with it. From somewhere in the bank Duane Rice was shouting, "Where's the fucking security boss!" sounding like a stone loony. Bobby maneuvered both briefcases and his piece too in front of the last teller, going wired when he saw it was a foxy young blonde.

"Where's the guard! Where's the fucking security man!"

Bobby heard Rice's shouts, then turned to scope out the blonde. She had her three drawers open and the money stacked on the counter. Bobby scooped it into the briefcase closest to him, tickling the girl's chin with his silencer as he clamped the case shut. "You like seafood, chiquita?" he said. "You like a nice juicy shark sausage? Go fine as wine with a nice blond furburger."

Rice saw the whole bank shake in front of his eyes. His voice sounded like it wasn't his, and the people cowering at their desks looked like scary red animals. He turned around so he wouldn't see them, and saw Sharkshit Bobby talking trash to a young woman teller. He was wondering whether to stop it when Gordon Meyers walked out of a door next to the vault.

And he knew.

Rice raised his .45; Meyers saw him and turned to run. Rice squeezed off three shots. The back of Meyers' white shirt exploded into crimson just as he felt the three silencer kicks. The dinged-out ding jailer crashed into an American flag on a pole and fell with it to the floor. The bank became one gigantic blast of noise, and through all of it, Rice heard a woman's voice: "Scum! Scum! Scum!"

Bobby turned around at the blonde's final epithet, and saw a dead man on the floor and Duane Rice and his brother gesturing for him to *move*. He turned to give the girl a *Jaws* theme good-bye, and caught a wad of spittle square in the face. Wiping it off, he saw her huge open mouth and knew that whatever she said would be the truth. He jabbed his .45 at her teeth and fired twice. The shots blew off the back of her head. Bobby saw blood and brains spatter the wall behind her as she was lifted off her feet. Recoil spun him around, and then Joe was there, grabbing the two briefcases and shoving him toward the doors.

Outside, Rice was standing on the sidewalk with the third briefcase, jamming a fresh clip into his piece. When the brothers crashed through the doors all sweat, tears and head-to-toe tremors, he shoved the briefcase at Joe and managed to get out, "Go around the corner to the car," from somewhere cool inside his own shakes. The Garcias *moved*, stumble-running, the three packages of money banging against their legs. Rice was about to follow when a siren came out of deep nowhere, and a black-and-white with cherry lights flashing zoomed down the sidewalk straight at him.

Rice made frantic flagging motions and fell to his knees as if wounded, holding the piece inside his right jacket pocket, knowing the silencer would cut down his range to close to nothing. When the patrol car decelerated and braked, he held his ground, knowing they had to have seen him; when it did a final fishtail, he counted to ten, got to his feet and pointed his .45 at the windshield.

The cops inside were less than four feet away and about to come out the doors with shotguns when he squeezed the trigger seven times, the gun at chest level. The windshield exploded, and Rice flung himself to the ground and rolled toward the passenger door, ejecting the spent clip, jamming in another. When both doors remained shut, he stood up, saw two blood-soaked blue uniforms and gasping faces and fired seven more times; all head shots. Blood and bone shrapnel sprayed his face, and in the distance he could hear other sirens screaming.

Suddenly he felt very calm and very much in control. He ran through the bank parking lot and down the alley that paralleled Graystone Drive, then vaulted a chain link fence, coming down into a cement backyard. The driveway led him out to the street, and there were Joe and Bobby, standing by the '81 Chevy Caprice. No neighbors; no nosy kids; no eyeball witnesses.

Rice walked across front lawns to the Chevy and unlocked the driver's-side door, then the passenger's. The brothers got in the back with the briefcases and huddled down without being told. Rice started the car and backed out, then drove slowly down Graystone to Westholme, then across Pico to the freeway. When they were headed north on the 405, the sudden screech of sirens became deafening. The fifty-foot freeway elevation gave him a perfect view of the bank and the street in front of it. It was bumper-to-bumper cop cars spilling shotgun-toting fuzz. Choppers were starting to fly in from the east. It looked like a war zone.

Rice drove cautiously in the middle lane; the challenge of holding down panic in an unfamiliar vehicle kept his mind off the past ten minutes. Moving out of the area, the cop noises subsided, except for occasional black-and-whites highballing it past in the opposite direction. Then when he hit Wilshire, it sounded like choppers and sirens were right there inside the car, and he remembered he wasn't alone.

The copter/siren noise was the combination of Joe Garcia sobbing and wheezing, and Bobby trying to talk. Rice thought of freeway roadblocks and pulled onto the Montana Avenue exit. He turned to look at the brothers, and saw that they were still on the floor, with their arms around each other, so he couldn't tell who was who. The sight was obscene, and the dried cop blood he felt on his face made it worse. Coming down onto a peaceful, noiseless street, he scrubbed his cheeks with his sleeve and said, "Act like fucking human beings and we'll walk from this."

Bobby untangled himself from his brother and the collection of briefcases. Rice checked the rearview and saw him lean into the backseat, then help Joe up. When he saw their unglued beards, he ripped off his own and sized them up for survival balls. Joe was twitching and sitting on his hands to control his shaking; Sharkshit looked like he was two seconds from a giggling fit that would last until his lungs blew. Knowing they were punk partners at best, he said, "Take off your beards, and your jackets and shirts. We're going to ditch the car, then go to my motel and chill out. Bobby, you do your shark act and you are one dead greaser."

Bobby winced. His voice was low, nothing like a giggle. "I had to, Duane. I knew what that bitch was gonna say, and only priests can say that to me." He started mumbling in Latin, then grabbed one of the briefcases off the floor. His garbled rosaries were hitting fever pitch as he reached in and pulled out a packet of hundreds and yanked the tab.

Black ink exploded from the wad of bills, sharp jets that hit Bobby in the face and deflected off his chest to cover the back windows. A second series of sprays burst over Joe, and he threw himself on top of the briefcase and smothered the residual jets with his body. Rice pulled to the curb and screamed, "Take off your shirts and roll down the windows!" and Bobby wiped ink from his eyes and ripped off his beard and starting pawing with it at the window beside him.

Leaning over into the backseat, Rice threw an awkward right fist at Bobby's face, a glancing blow that forced him to stop his scrubbing and reflexively flinch away, leaving the window handle exposed. Rice pushed himself toward it and cranked it down, just as Joe, his torso soaked jet black, lowered the opposite one. Hissing "*The back*," Rice struggled from his suitcoat and ripped off his white shirt. He passed them to Joe, who pushed them into the back window and let them absorb ink until they were saturated. When they were useless sopping rags, he pulled them away and let the remaining ink soak down into the top of the seat. Then he stripped to the waist and started pulling off his brother's clothes, murmuring, "Easy, Bobby. Easy. The watchdog is here."

Rice looked at the ink-streaked window and saw that it could pass for a bad "smoky tint" job; he looked at the Garcias and knew that the tagalong had bigger balls from the gate. "We're going to Hollyweird, homeboys," he said. "Just three bare-chested studs out for a ride."

A half hour later, Rice stopped in front of an abandoned welfare hotel on Cahuenga, two blocks from the Bowl Motel. He turned off the engine, got out and checked the trunk. No spare clothes, only a ratty-looking sleeping bag. He grabbed it, then shoved it through the side window at Joe Garcia, who was still baby-talking Bobby. "Wrap the briefcases up in this, and walk your brother down to my pad. Act like Chicano punks on the stroll and you won't get rousted. I'll take the money and catch up with you." He looked at the black film on their chests, then walked back to the garage that he hoped to fucking God was still deserted.

It was.

Rice cleared an entry path, kicking away mounds of empty T-bird bottles, and then walked to the car. Joe and Bobby were standing mutely beside it, the sleeping bag rolled erratically at their feet. Rice said, "Move," then backed the car into the garage and closed the rickety door on it.

Returning to the street, he started feeling good. Then he picked up the sleeping bag, and two dimes and a penny fell out of the folds and hit the pavement. Ahead of him, he saw the Garcias turn into the alley behind the motel. He tried to think of Vandy and the rescue mission, but the chump change on the ground wouldn't let him.

15

Driving out Wilshire to the West L.A. Federal Building, Lloyd knew that the street scene was somehow off, that something was missing. Passing the Winchell's Donut joint that the local cops favored, it hit him: he hadn't seen a black-and-white since Beverly Hills, and that one was B.H.P.D. Flipping on his two-way, the dispatcher told him why: "Code Four. Code Four. All patrol units at Pico and Westholme and bank area not directly involved in crowd control or house-to-house search resume normal patrol. Code Four. Code Four."

Lloyd attached his red light and turned on his siren, then hung a U-turn and sped to Pico and Westholme. "Bank" flashed "Them," and "house-to-house search" meant violence. When he was two blocks from the scene, he passed a string of patrol cars driving slowly north with their headlights on.

Feeling a wave of nausea, Lloyd floored the gas, then decelerated as Pico, a barricade of sawhorse detour signs and a streetful of nose-to-nose black-and-whites, appeared in his windshield. He braked and parked on the sidewalk, then ran the remaining block, pinning his badge to the front of his suit coat.

Two young officers with shotguns noticed him and stepped over a sawhorse, turning the muzzles of the .12 gauges downward when they saw his badge. Catching their red faces and rubber knees, Lloyd said what he already knew: "One of ours?"

The taller of the young cops answered him in a voice trying hard to be detached. "Two of ours, two dead inside the bank.

No suspects in custody. It happened forty-five minutes ago. What division are you—"

Lloyd pushed the officer aside and stepped over the detour sign, then walked around the corner to Pico, elbowing his way through the most crowded crime scene he had ever witnessed. Knots of plainclothes cops were huddled together, conferring over notepads, straining to hear each other above the radio crackle put out by dozens of official vehicles; young patrolmen were standing by their units looking fierce, scared and about to burst with rage. Cherry lights were still whirling, and the sidewalk was packed with forensic technicians carrying cameras and evidence kits. Shouted conversations were competing with the radio noise, and Lloyd picked out bits and pieces and knew it was *Them*.

" . . . guy inside said .45 autos, suppressors and—"

" . . . this spic was talking dirty to this teller and then just fucking offed her and—"

"One woman said one white, two Mexican, another said all white. This is the—"

In the distance, Lloyd could see the top of a forensic arc light reflecting a red shimmer. He shoved past a team of paramedics on the sidewalk directly in front of the bank, steeling himself when he saw a black-and-white sitting under the light, dried blood covering the back window.

A technician was standing beside the car, dusting a bullet clip; another S.I.D. man was squatting on the hood, his camera up against the shattered windshield, snapping pictures. Lloyd knew that he had to know, and walked over.

The remains of two young men were death frozen in the front seat. Every inch of their uniform navy blue was now the maroon of congealing blood. Both bore high-caliber entry wounds on their faces, and gaping, brain-oozing holes where the backs of their heads used to be. The driver had his service revolver unholstered on the seat beside him, and the other officer had his right hand on the butt of the unit's Remington pump, his index finger on the trigger at half pull.

Wiping tears from his eyes, Lloyd stumbled through the

"Official Crime Scene" rope in front of the bank's double glass doors. A technician dusting the door handles muttered, "Hey, you can't," and Lloyd grabbed him by the lapels and shoved him toward the sidewalk, then covered his hands with his coat sleeves and pushed the doors open. Inside the bank, a cordon of Detective Division brass saw him, then stepped aside, casting worried looks among themselves.

Standing on his tiptoes, Lloyd surveyed the bank's interior, straining to see something other than the plainclothes officers who were eclipsing almost the entire floor space. By craning his neck he could pick out an S.I.D. team marking the outline of a woman's body behind the tellers' counter, and another team in front of the counter vacuuming for trace elements. A deputy medical examiner was scooping the woman's brains off the wall and into a plastic bag, and at the back of the bank, near the vault, Peter Kapek and a half dozen feds were talking to distraught-looking people.

Lloyd threaded a path in Kapek's direction. More snatches of conversation hit him, a woman whimpering, "The tall Mexican was so scared and sweet-looking," a young cop in uniform telling another, "The security guy was a real wacko, he used to talk this weird shit to me. Hey, that's Lloyd Hopkins—you know, 'Crazy Lloyd.' "

Hearing his name, Lloyd swiveled and looked at the officers, who turned around and backed into a crowd of plainclothes-men. Again standing on his tiptoes for sight of Kapek, he saw the crowd part and create a space. A second later two M.E. assistants carrying a sheet-covered stretcher walked through it, and when he saw blood seeping through the white cotton, he walked over and yanked the sheet off.

Lloyd ignored the stretcher bearers' shocked exclamations and stared at the corpse of a middle-aged white man. His chest and stomach bore three large cavities circumscribed by burned and shredded tissue, obvious high-velocity exit wounds.

Shot in the back.

.45-caliber quality holes.

Them.

Before he could redrape the dead man, Lloyd felt a hard tap on his shoulder. When he turned around, Captain John McManus was standing there, legs spread, hands on hips, his face beet red, working toward purple. They locked eyes, and Lloyd knew that backing down was the only way to win. He raised his hands, and was groping for crow-eating words when McManus stepped forward and breathed in his face: "You fucking necrophile. I told you you weren't to involve yourself in any homicide investigations, collateral to your liaison assignment or otherwise. You're off that assignment as of now. This is a double cop killing, and I don't want trigger-happy vigilante shitheads like you anywhere near it. One word of protest, and I'll have Braverton suspend you. You meddle in this case and I'll have your badge and file on you for obstruction of justice. Now go home and wait for my call."

Lloyd shouldered the captain aside and pushed his way out to the sidewalk. A TV mini-cam crew was now inside the barricades, interviewing a group of Community Relations brass. Someone shouted, "That's Lloyd Hopkins, get him!" and suddenly a microphone was in his face. He yanked the mike out of the man's hand and hurled it in the direction of the patrol car cradling the wasted bodies of two young men, then ran through the crowd to his own official vehicle, with no intention of going home.

Too angry to think beyond *Them*, Lloyd drove to Louie Calderon's place, slamming the wheel when he saw federal surveillance vehicles stationed across the street and in the alley near the back service entrance. Parking down the block by a mom-and-pop market, he defused his tension by gripping the wheel until the strain numbed his brain and a semblance of calm hit, allowing him to answer his own questions rationally.

Roust Calderon? Probe, poke, threaten and scare the shit out of him? No—the Buddy Bagdessarian/warrant approach was still best.

What happened at the bank?—"This spic was talking dirty to this teller and then just fucking offed her"; "The tall

Mexican was so scared and sweet-looking." *Why was the man on the stretcher shot in the back? Did the Shark or the white man shoot the two cops?*

The only sane answer was insanity; the only strategy for now was to wait for Louie Calderon to leave, then trash his pad from top to bottom. The only easy question was whether or not to obey McManus.

No.

Lloyd settled in to wait, eyeing the surveillance unit parked a block in front of him. One hour, two, three, four. No movement except a stream of customers and mechanics leaving the garage. At dusk, he walked to the market and bought the evening editions of the *Times* and *Examiner*. The Pico Boulevard slaughter headlined both papers, and the *Times* featured the complete story of the first two robberies, complete with names, mention of the girlfriend angle and heavy speculation that the kidnap assaults were tied in to the stickup that had left four dead. The names of the two dead officers were omitted, and the bank victims were listed as Karleen Tuggle, twenty-six, and Gordon Meyers, forty-four, a recently retired L.A. County Sheriff's deputy and the bank's "Security Chief." California Federal was offering a $50,000 reward for information leading to the capture of the killer-robbers, and the L.A. City Council was putting up an additional $25,000. Predictably, Chief Gates announced "the biggest manhunt in Los Angeles history."

It all brought tears to Lloyd's eyes. He imagined himself squeezing Likable Louie's fat neck until either his brains or three names popped out. Then he saw Calderon walk out the garage door in the flesh and get into a Dodge van at curbside. When he drove off, the fed unit was a not-too-subtle three car lengths behind.

Lloyd started getting his B&E shakes and eyed the door of the house. Then the surveillance car from the alley pulled up. The driver got out, sat down on Calderon's front steps and lit a cigarette. Lloyd hit the wheel with his palms, sending shock waves up his bad hand. Kapek, hipped by McManus to his penchant for burglary, was safeguarding the investigation from hot-dog action. Feeling wasted, powerless and unaccountably exhausted, Lloyd drove home to think.

Going through the front door, he heard coughing coming from the direction of the living room. He drew his .38, pinned himself to the entrance foyer wall and moved down it, then hit the overhead light and stepped forward, his gun arm extended and braced with his left hand. When he saw who was sitting in his favorite leather chair, he said, "Jesus Christ."

"Don't act surprised," Captain Fred Gaffaney said. "You know why I'm here."

Lloyd reholstered his .38. "No, I don't."

"Address me as 'sir.'"

Lloyd studied the witch-hunter. Gaffaney looked colder than his deep-freeze norm; drained of everything human. "What are you doing here, Captain?"

Gaffaney fingered his cross and flag lapel pin and said in the most emotionless voice Lloyd had ever heard, "My son, Officer Steven D. Gaffaney, was shot and killed in the line of duty this morning. He was twenty-two. I saw his body. I saw his brains all over the backseat of his patrol unit, and half of his scalp hanging off his head. I forced myself to look, so I wouldn't back away from coming to you."

Standing motionless in the doorway, Lloyd saw where Gaffaney was going. For a microsecond, it seemed like salvation, then he gasped against the thought and said, "I swear to you I'll find them, and if it comes down to me or them, I'll take them out. But you're thinking execution, and I'm no killer."

Gaffaney took a manila folder from his jacket pocket and laid it on the end table beside him. "Yes, you are. I know a great deal about you. In the summer of '70, when you were on loan to Venice Vice, you befriended a young rookie who had never been with a woman. One night you borrowed a drunk wagon from Central Division and rousted a half dozen Venice hookers and brought them to the rookie's apartment. You made them a variety of offers: service the two of you, or suffer arrest for needle tracks, or outstanding warrants, or plain prostitution. They agreed to party, and you smoked marijuana with them, and fucked several of them, and the whores went away with a good deal of your money when you started feeling guilty. I have sworn depositions from three of those whores, Hopkins. I know you're trying to reconcile with your family. Think of how they'll feel when the *Big Orange Insider* runs the depositions on their front page."

Feeling the old shame settle near his heart, Lloyd said, "I've made amends to my family, and that story is ancient history—just another cheap notch on my rep. It's old stuff."

Gaffaney tapped the folder, then tapped his lapel pin. "Here's something you were probably too stoned to remember doing. After the whores left, you and that rookie had a long conversation about duty and courage. The young man doubted his own ability to kill in the line of duty, and you told him how in the Watts Riot you had killed an 'evil' fellow National Guardsman who had murdered a group of innocent blacks. I've checked your old unit's records. Your squad leader, Staff Sergeant Richard Beller, was presumed to have been killed in the riot, but his body was never found, and he was not seen skirmishing with any rioters. He was, however, on scout patrol with you on the night he disappeared. That rookie is now a lieutenant in Devonshire Division. He's a born-again Christian, and a protégé of mine. I have a sworn affidavit from him, detailing your activities that night in '70, repeating your conversation almost verbatim. Lieutenant Dayton has a brilliant memory. What's the matter, Hopkins? You're looking weak."

Transfixed by a nightmare flashback of Richard Beller's corpse, Lloyd trembled and tried to speak. His tongue and palate and brain refused to connect, and he shook even harder.

"So you see the position you're in," Gaffaney said. "I despise you, but you are the finest detective the Department has ever produced, and I need you." He pointed toward the dining room. "On your table are copies of the existing reports on the Pico-Westholme homicides. I understand the robbery is connected to two others you were working with the feds on, so that gives you an edge. I'm throwing all my clout into getting you assigned to the investigation, on your own autonomy. I'm sure I'll succeed. Whatever you need, from other reports to men for shitwork, you'll get—just call me. If you don't comply, I can guarantee your crucifixion in the form of a murder indictment."

Lloyd looked at his accuser and saw the faces of Richard Beller and the Hollywood Slaughterer superimposed over his mercilessly cold features. He tried to speak, but his brain was still jelly.

Gaffaney got up and walked past him to the front door. When his hand was on the latch, he said, "Get them and I'll have mercy. But they are not to be arrested. Kill them or bring them to me."

16

Now it was clockwork in a hurricane, staying icy in a heat wave determined to fry them to Cinder City. At 7:00, Rice gave the Garcias another check for survival balls. Bobby was quiet, sitting in a chair by the dresser, reading the Gideon Bible that came with the room. Joe was hanging drum-tight way inside himself, alternately staring at the walls and the non-inked 16K on the bed. Showered and dressed in Rice's own clothes, the tagalong looked like he had the juice to hold, the oldies but goodies he'd been softly humming for hours supplying him with the guts not to rabbit. At 7:10, for the second time that day, Rice said, "Now. Bobby, you stay here. Joe and I are going to pick up my old lady. When we get back, we'll split the money and split up. Sit still and be cool."

Bobby looked up from his Bible and made a weird gesture Rice figured was Catholic. Joe took his eyes from the stacks of money, and the tune he was humming jumped up three octaves. Rice recognized it as "Blueberry Hill," and said, "Come on, watchdog. Let's move."

They cruised down Highland in the Trans Am, then hung a right turn on Franklin and headed west toward the Mount Olympus development. Joe reached over to flip on the radio, and Rice touched his hand and said, "No. We'll buy a paper at the airport. *When we're free and clear*. Right now, you don't want to know."

Joe swallowed and returned to his humming. Rice openly scrutinized him. It looked like he was groping for words to go with the music.

164

At Fairfax, Rice swung over to the Strip and stopped at a stand of pay phones in a Texaco parking lot. Noting a newspaper rack beside the booths, he slipped in a quarter and nickel and forced himself to read the front page of the *Times*.

The headline screamed, "Four Killed in West L.A. Bank Stickup!" and the subheading read, "Robbery Linked to Two Others." Rice scanned the paragraphs that detailed their first two kidnap-heists, complete with the names of the victims and suspect descriptions provided by Christine Confrey, the bitch he'd saved from Sharkshit Bobby. Words jumped at him: "Largest manhunt in L.A. history"; "Stolen car by freeway off-ramp presumed to be approach vehicle, but no fingerprints discovered"; "$75,000 offered in combined reward money."

The bombshell was on page two: an artist's sketch of *him*, also courtesy of Chrissy Confrey. The resemblance was about three-quarters accurate, and Rice balled the paper up, then stepped into the booth and called Rhonda the Fox's home number.

"Hello?"

Rice breathed out in relief. "It's Duane. You want to get paid, with a little bonus for some extra info?"

"Have you found her?"

"Just about. We're flying to New York in a few days. I need the names of some music people—solid people, no cocaine sleazebags. Do you know people who know people there?"

After a long moment of silence, Rhonda said, "Sure. But listen, I'm booked straight through until tomorrow night late. Can you meet me outside Silver Foxes tomorrow night at twelve?"

"No sooner than that?"

"I have to ask around, and that takes time."

Rice said, "I'll be there," and hung up and walked back to the car. Joe swallowed a burst of song lyrics as he got in and peeled rubber up Fairfax toward the Hollywood Hills. When they were just north of Franklin, he pulled the Trans Am into a large vacant lot, wracking the undercarriage. Killing the headlights, he eased off the gas and let the car glide to a halt behind a long scrub hedge.

Turning off the ignition, Rice said, "Wait here," then got out and waded through the hedge. The Mount Olympus access road was right in front of him, and directly across it he could see Stan Klein's house, with no lights on and no Porsche in the driveway or on the street. Returning to the car, he unholstered his .45 and put it in the glove compartment, pulling out a push-button switchblade to replace it. "In and out, watchdog," he said. "You've got one job and one job only. Don't let me kill him."

They waited.

Rice sat perfectly still and stared at the access road, waiting for lights to show in number 14; Joe made music in his head. The night cooled and a light drizzle hit the windshield. Then, just after 1:00 A.M., the lights in the house went on.

Rice nudged Joe and handed him the knife, then pointed through the windshield at their target. Joe got out of the car and walked through the hedge, rubber-kneed, his hands in his jacket pockets to kill his tremors. Rice caught up with him. They crossed the blacktop, then Rice bolted up the steps and rang the buzzer.

Voices echoed within the house; Rice heard Vandy's, and knew from the tone that she was tired and cranky. Joe stood beside him, his eyes wide and panicky. Then the door was thrown open, and Stan Klein was standing there, flashing a shit-eating grin betrayed by tics around his temples. "Disco Duane and friend," he said. "When you get out?"

Rice sized Klein up. Red nose from too much coke, useless muscles from too much iron pumping, bullshit dope bravado fueling him for the confrontation. Stan Man shrugged, then faked a sigh. "I don't think she wants to see you, man."

Voice steady, Rice said, "She doesn't know what she wants. Go get her."

Klein sniffed back a noseful of mucus and pointed at Joe. "Who's this . . . Tonto? The strong silent sidekick? What's shakin', Kemo Sabe?"

Through the half-open door, Rice saw the stick skinny legs walking down a wrought-iron staircase. He moved straight toward the sight, pushing Klein backward. Joe was right behind him, sliding past Klein just as he muttered, "Hey, you can't—"

Her.

Rice saw Vandy at the foot of the staircase, wearing a pink crewneck and kelly green cords. She looked emaciated, but her face was pure waiflike beauty. Her voice was just a shadow of her old vibrato growl: "I don't want to go with you, Duane."

Rice stood still, afraid to move or say the wrong thing. Joe trembled with his hands in his pockets. Stan Klein walked over to an end table by the staircase and scooped up a mound of coke with a single-edged razor blade. Squatting, he snorted it, then laughed. "You heard the lady. She doesn't want to go with you."

Prepared to see red and hold it down, Rice moved his eyes back and forth from Vandy to Klein and *smelled* the bank before it all went haywire. Vandy nibbling her cuticles; Klein doing another snootful of coke. Vandy looking like the wasted little girls in concentration camp pictures. Then Joe Garcia's scared rabbit squeak: "Duane, he's got a gun."

Klein was standing by a row of Pac-Man machines near the living room entranceway, licking coke off his fingers and leveling a small automatic at Rice. "Come here, Annie," he said.

Vandy walked to Klein in jerky little-girl steps. He threw his left arm around her and nuzzled her cheek without relinquishing his bead on Rice. Keeping one eye on Joe, he said, "You were fucking comic relief for the whole crowd. Everybody used you. If you weren't such a boss car thief, we would have laughed you out of L.A. The biggest laugh was you making contacts to boost Annie's career, gonna make her a million-dollar rock video star. Dig this on your way to the door with Pancho: I'm gonna make Annie a rock vid star. She's gonna be the queen of porn vid first, then move up. I'm producing a flick with her and this guy I gotta pay by the inch, and I'm talking heavy double digits. Annie knows what's good for her career, and she's gonna do it, 'cause she knows I'm not a dumb shit dreamer like you."

No red, but the haywire stench ate at Rice's nostrils and made his eyes burn. "You ratted me off on my G.T.A. bust, motherfucker."

Klein bit at Vandy's ear, then looked directly at Rice and said, "No, Duaney-boy, I didn't. Annie did. She got busted for prostitution and talked her way out of a drug rehab by snitching you off. Romantic, huh?"

Now the red.

Rice made a slow, deliberate beeline toward the woman he loved and her destroyer. Vandy screamed; Klein squeezed the trigger. The gun jammed, and he pulled back the slide and ejected the chambered round, then slid in another and fired. The shot went wide, tearing into the wall by the staircase. Rice kept walking. Joe pinned himself to the Pac-Man machine farthest from Klein, and stared at the man he was supposed to watchdog, who *just kept walking*. Klein fired again; the shot hit the wall directly above Rice's head. He kept walking and was within point-blank range of his objective when Klein put the gun to Vandy's head, took a step backward with her and muttered, "No no no no no."

Rice halted; Joe fed himself a bomb-burst of music, pulled the switchblade from his pocket and jumped knife first, pushing the button just as Klein wheeled and aimed at him.

The pistol jammed; Vandy dropped to the floor. Joe caught Klein flush in the stomach and ripped upward with both hands. Blood spurted from his mouth, and Rice reached for the gun. Joe saw him aim it at Vandy and the dying man, and knew he was fixing to blow away the whole fucking world. He got to his feet and grabbed a portable TV from the top of the Pac-Man beside him. He swung it forward, and Rice turned and stepped into the blow, catching the plastic and glass missile head-on. He crumpled across Stan Klein's body, and Joe and Vandy ran.

17

Only repeated readings of the Pico-Westholme homicide files kept his mind off Watts in the summer of '65, and even then, the facts that were being imprinted in his mind stuck as self-accusation rather than indicators pointing to *Them*. Karleen Tuggle, Gordon Meyers, Officer Steven Gaffaney and Officer Paul Loweth were killed by .45 gunshots, the two patrolmen and Meyers by rounds fired from the same gun, Tuggle by shots from a different piece—solid ballistics confirmation. Three for the white man; one for the Shark.

And *he* had killed Richard Beller with the same type weapon.

Eyewitness accounts were hysterical, but cross-checking them allowed him to come up with a reconstruction: the robbers enter the bank, the white man shoots shaving cream on the surveillance camera. This means that unless the lens is cleared in two minutes, the silent alarm will go off. The Mexicans hit the tellers' stations, the Shark goes wacko at the sight of Karleen Tuggle, talks trash to her, she reacts and he blows her away. The white man is screaming for the "Security Boss." Gordon Meyers appears, then turns tail and runs, and he shoots him in the back.

The basics were covered: no eyewitnesses outside the bank; the '78 Malibu found by the freeway ramp, covered with glove prints, was reported stolen later that day by its owner, a rent-a-cop at a Burger King in Hollywood. Going on the assumption that the robbers lived in the Hollywood area, house-to-house checks were being initiated, the officers carrying the artist's sketch of the white man. Approach vehicle covered.

The escape vehicle was most likely an '81 Chevy Caprice belonging to a family around the corner from the bank. Neighbors reported it stolen three hours after the robbery. It was now the hottest car on the L.A. County Hot Sheet, and the object of an all-points bulletin. Lloyd shuddered. Any male seen driving that car was dead meat, and back in '59 he had paid for most of his Stanford tuition by clouting Chevys.

Them.

Me.

Looking out the window at his neglected front lawn, Lloyd thought of the new *Him*, Gordon Meyers. A team of L.A.P.D. dicks were checking out his personnel record for K.A.s and possible vengeance motives, and Gaffaney had included with his paperwork a hastily compiled addendum report on the man. As dawn crept up, signifying another sleepless night, Lloyd read the report for the fifth time.

> Gordon Michael Meyers, D.O.B. 1/15/40, L.A. Graduated high school in '58, joined sheriff's department in '64, during a manpower shortage wherein they lowered their entrance requirements to recruit men. After the mandatory eighteen-month jail training, assigned to Lenox Station. Assessed as being too ineffectual for street duty, reassigned as night jailer at county jail facility for nonviolent emotionally disturbed prisoners. Kept that assignment for seventeen and a half years, until his retirement. Unmarried, parents retired in Arizona. Address: 411 Seaglade, Redondo Beach.

The phone rang.

Lloyd jerked back in his chair; the shrill noise registered as a gunshot. Realizing it wasn't, he picked up the receiver and said, "Yes?"

The seething voice on the line was McManus': "You're back

on the investigation. Two heavy hitters pulled strings. Don't fuck up."

Lloyd hung up. A hideous thought crossed his mind: the condemned killer was being let out on parole. Getting to his feet and stretching, he ran mental itineraries: review the case with Kapek? No—this was *his*. Roust Calderon? No—Judge Penzler would be back in twenty-four hours to sign his warrant, and with Buddy Bagdessarian assisting they could squeeze Likable Louie to perfection. It was time to find out why Gordon Meyers was shot in the back. Another hideous thought made him wince. The .45 he had killed Richard Beller with was in his desk drawer, oiled, dum-dum loaded and encased in a shoulder rig.

Them.

Me.

Me or them.

Us.

Lloyd strapped on the weapon that had stood him through his baptism of fire, then went out to quash his murder indictment.

On Sepulveda southbound to Redondo Beach, he spotted a tail two car lengths in back of him. Decelerating and weaving into the slow lane, he saw that it was a Metro Division unmarked unit, distinguished from his own Matador by an olive-drab paint job and a giant whip antenna. Slowing to a crawl, he let the car come up on his bumper. When the driver applied the brakes, he stared in his rearview, fuming when he saw two classic Metro hot dogs in the front seat—burly, crew-cut white men in their mid-thirties wearing identical navy windbreakers: Gaffaney's or McManus' insurance against possible fuckups.

Lloyd gave the cops the finger and hung a hard right through a liquor store parking lot, fishtailing into the alley behind it. Seeing no cars or pedestrians, he punched the gas until the alley ended and angled off into a quiet residential street. He took the street at ninety, then slowed and zigzagged in a random pattern until he was within sight of the Redondo Beach Pier. Parking by a chowder stand, he looked around for the Metro unit. It was nowhere in sight. Exhilarated by the speed, Lloyd drove slowly to 411 Seaglade.

It was a garage apartment in the shadow of the pier. Lloyd parked and surveyed the front house. There was no car in the driveway, and the old white wood frame stood quiet in the early morning sunlight. No media vehicles were anywhere to be seen, and by squinting he could tell that there was no "Crime Scene" notice tacked to the door of 411. Knowing that McManus' "two heavy hitters" were Gaffaney and in all likelihood the Big Chief himself, he grabbed an evidence kit from the back seat, walked up the driveway and kicked the door in.

The burst of sunlight illuminated a dreary living room, spotlessly clean, but featuring mismatched sofa, chairs, coffee table and bookshelves. Lloyd stood in the doorway and made repeated eyeball circuits of the room, picking up a profusion of small details that spelled *loner*: expensive TV, the only wall adornments photographs of Meyers himself, alone in his sheriff's uniform and standing by himself holding a fishing reel and string of trout, no magazines or ashtrays or portable bar for guests.

Lloyd shut the door and walked into a small dining room, catching a first anomaly: all the living room furniture was squared off at right angles; here the table and chairs were haphazardly arranged. The kitchen was more loner confirmation: nothing but frozen dinners in the refrigerator, plates and dishes for one in the sink, a dozen bottles of cheap bourbon in the cupboard.

The bedroom was off to the side of the kitchen. Lloyd flicked on a wall light and tingled. Everything in the small rectangular space was immaculately clean and tidy, from the G.I. made-up bed to the perfectly aligned end table with an alarm clock dead in its middle. But the dresser had been pulled out, and the three scrapbooks stacked across it had been replaced unevenly, one upside down. The pad had been crawled.

Lloyd retraced his steps to the front door, opened his evidence kit and took out a vial of fingerprint powder and a print brush. Removing surgical rubber gloves from the kit, he put them on and limbered his fingers with a series of stretching exercises. Then he went to work to find out just how solitary Gordon Meyers was, and if the pad crawler knew his stuff.

He discovered that Meyers was a stone loner, and the crawler was a pro.

For two solid hours Lloyd dusted print-sustaining surfaces and compared fingerprint points under a magnifying glass. Concentrating on doors, doorknobs and doorjambs, he found overlap smudges and viable latents for thumb and index finger, all "grab" prints likely to have been made by a person walking through the apartment, opening and closing doors behind them. There were also smooth glove prints on the same surfaces, and on the living room bookshelves and the dust covers of the books there. All the left and right thumb and index prints matched to the tune of ten comparison points, and there were no conflicting latents to be found. Meyers and the man who searched his apartment.

For what?

Lloyd looked under the furniture, behind the books. Nothing. He checked the kitchen and dining room; nothing but cooking and eating utensils. The desk in Meyers' bedroom was nothing but a tidy or tidily rearranged collection of bankbooks, pens, pencils, paycheck stubs and I.R.S. forms, and his closet held nothing but L.A.S.D. uniforms and cheap civilian clothes.

Which left the scrapbooks.

Lloyd dusted the spines and held his magnifying glass and penlight on them to assess the results. Seeing smudged latents and what looked to be glove streaks, he began a page-by-page scrutiny of the books.

The first two books contained photographs of Gordon Meyers posing with various trophy fish, neatly mounted to the black paper in gummed edge-holders. Lloyd dusted three snapshots at random and got pristine glossy surfaces—no latents; no glove prints.

The third scrapbook was cop memorabilia—candid group shots of sheriff's deputies in uniform and Meyers himself with jail inmates in blue denim. Lloyd leafed through the book, going cold when he came to a page of snapshots with the corners poking out of their edge-holders, going colder when he saw that the opposite page held two empty photo squares.

Thinking, *check the back for writing, just like the crawler did,* Lloyd fumbled at the snapshot immediately in front of him. When his gloves made the task too unwieldy, he went *ice* cold, then dusted the crookedly replaced photos, coming away with a perfect left thumbprint on a snap of Meyers and another deputy. Holding his magnifying glass over it, he recalled comparison points from the left thumbs assumed to be Meyers'. This print was markedly different in whirls and ridges. Lloyd replaced the scrapbook, put the snapshot in an evidence envelope, packed up his kit and got the hell out of the tidy loner apartment.

Forty minutes later, Lloyd was at Parker Center, handing the powdered snapshot to Officer Artie Cranfield of S.I.D., saying, "Feed to the central source computer, the one with the D.M.V. and armed forces input. I'll be up in my office. If you score, get me a printout from R&I."

Artie laughed. "You're very authoritative today, Lloyd."

Lloyd's laugh was humorless. "I'm authorized on this, the big man himself. It's the cop killings, so please fucking hurry."

Artie took off at a jog, and Lloyd busied himself arranging the surveillance reports on Louie Calderon that littered his desk. Thoughts of calling Peter Kapek for an interagency confab crossed his mind, then he saw a memo propped up against his phone: Sgt. Hopkins—meet or call S.A. Kapek at downtown Fed bldg.—12/14—0940. He was debating whether to call or roll when Artie returned, breathless, and handed him a manila folder. "I ran the print. He's one of ours, Lloyd."

Lloyd shivered and thought: *Gaffaney*, then read through

the L.A.P.D. personnel file, holding a hand over the full-face and profile snaps that were clipped to the first page.

The file detailed the twelve-year police career of Metropolitan Division sergeant Wallace Dean Collins, age thirty-four. His record was impressive: Class A fitness reports and a number of citations for "Meritorious Service." Lloyd scanned the list of Collins' "special assignments." Surveillance detail, narco, vice decoy, then a transfer to Metro on the recommendation of Captain Frederick Gaffaney. Since his rookie days, Collins had partnered with Sergeant Kenneth R. Lohmann of Central Division, and there was an addendum memo from the Central personnel officer stating that Lohmann was also flagged for Metro duty—on the next available opening.

Lloyd took his hand from the snapshot and smiled. Collins was the driver of the car tailing him down Sepulveda. Looking at the fidgeting Artie Cranfield, he said, "How'd you get the file so fast?"

Artie shrugged. "I told the clerk at Personnel Records you had special clearance from Braverton and up. Why?"

Lloyd handed the file back. "Just curious. Take this back to Records, hold on to the photo and be very quiet about this, okay?"

"Quiet as the grave," Artie said.

Lloyd drove to the downtown Federal Building, thinking of angles to cutthroat Gaffaney and kill the murder indictment now being held over his head. As he pulled to the curb at Sixth and Union, the Metro unit sidled to a stop two car lengths in back of him, Collins at the wheel.

Getting out and slamming the door, Lloyd's thoughts moved from blackmail to a double suicide scene to blow Gaffaney's career along with his own. Then curiosity about Collins crawling Gordon Meyers' pad took over, and he ran upstairs to Kapek's office, rapped on the door and said in his most commanding tone, "Come on, G-man. We're going cruising."

"Where to?"

"A hot-dog rendezvous."

They drove east through downtown L.A., Lloyd silent, with one eye on the road and the other on the Metro unit riding their tail behind a slow-moving Cadillac. Kapek fingered his acne scars and stared at Lloyd, finally breaking the tense quiet. "I've been forcing myself to concentrate on the first two robberies exclusively, and I think I may have a hypothetical connection between Hawley and Eggers."

Lloyd's mind jerked away from the plan he was hatching. "What?"

"Listen: I checked out both men's bank accounts and got something weird. They both withdrew similar large amounts of cash, on the same dates—October seventeenth and November first. Two five-hundred-dollar withdrawals for Hawley, two six-hundred-buck shots for Eggers. Non sequitur stuff—both guys are strictly check writers. These withdrawals were from their individual accounts—not the joint accounts they share with their wives. What do you think?"

Lloyd whistled, then said, "Vice. I've already put in *my* Vice query, so you call the squad commanders and have them shake down their snitches for specific info. What happened on those dates? Bookies taking heavy action? Cockfights, dogfights? I don't buy Eggers or Hawley as dopers, but I could see Sally and Chrissy doing a few snootfuls of blow, with their sugar daddys footing the bill. By the way, how did the families react to the girlfriend bit? Any feedback on that?"

Kapek breathed out sadly. "Hawley's wife moved out. Eggers lost his job, because he lied to us about Confrey, and because the big boss at Security Pacific freaked when he heard about the dead cops and blamed Eggers. Eggers' wife is still up at Arrowhead, and he went up there to work it out. Both Hawley and Eggers are refusing to talk further to us, under attorney's orders."

Lloyd said, "Shit. I wrote out a memo requesting that they be held as material witnesses to avoid that, then all hell broke loose. By the way, we're being tailed. There's a Metro unit in back of us."

Kapek looked in the rearview. "Is that what this is all about? And what's 'Metro'?"

Passing out of downtown into the East L.A. industrial district, Lloyd said, "Metro is an L.A.P.D. special crimes unit, a diversified attack force. Gang fights in Watts? Send in Metro. Too much dope in schools? Metro shakes down bubble-gummers on their lunch hour. The unit is effective, but it's full of right-wing wackos. And what this is all about is me being watchdogged. We're going to the L.A. River and park. Follow me and do what I tell you."

Now Kapek was silent. Lloyd turned off Alameda and skirted the Brew 102 Brewery, then took the Water and Power Department road to the embankment that overlooked the bone-dry "river." The tail car remained fifty yards in back of them, and Lloyd slowed and parked at the embankment's edge. Checking the rearview a last time, he said, "I'm hoping they'll think we're meeting a snitch. Come on."

They walked down the concrete slope sideways, plaster debris crackling beneath their feet. When they reached the riverbed, Lloyd got his bearings and saw that the old maintenance shack was still there and still mounted on a cinderblock foundation to keep it from washing away during flood season. He pointed Kapek toward it, and they trudged over through an obstacle course of empty wine bottles and beer cans. When they were standing in the shade of the shack's corrugated tin door, Lloyd tilted his head sideways and caught sight of the two Metro cops peering over the edge of the embankment. "Stand here," he said. "Keep looking in the direction I take off in, and keep looking at your watch like you're expecting someone."

Kapek nodded, looking befuddled and slightly angry. Lloyd walked around the edge of the shack, then climbed the embankment on its opposite side, coming onto level ground behind a line of abandoned cars. Squatting low, he moved down the row to the end, then stood up, seeing nothing but a short patch of pavement between himself and the Metro unit, with Collins and his partner fifty yards away, still holding surveillance on Kapek.

Lloyd sprinted to the car and opened the driver's-side door. The two cops turned around at the noise and started running. Lloyd flipped open the glove compartment—nothing—then noticed an attaché case on the floorboard, "Sgt. K. R. Lohmann" stenciled on the front. He opened it and tore through blank report forms and plastic evidence bags, and was about to give up when his hands brushed a bag that held two glossy photographs. He fumbled the bag into his inside jacket pocket and backed out of the car just as Collins loomed in front of him.

With the open door between them, Collins halted, then approached on tiptoes. Lloyd saw his partner ten yards in back of him, looking scared. When Collins moved into a cautious streetfighter's stance, Lloyd slammed the door into his legs, knocking him backward onto the ground.

Collins got to his feet and started swinging blindly; Lloyd sidestepped the blows and brought him to his knees with a left to the solar plexus. Collins sucked air and held his stomach; Lloyd balled his right fist. The old pain was still there, so he swung a short left uppercut instead. Collins grabbed his nose and fell prone, his legs twitching. Lloyd stood over him and hissed, "Tell Captain Fred I don't need a backup."

The other cop was trembling beside the car. Lloyd stepped toward him, and he backed away. Then Peter Kapek walked over, stationing himself squarely between them. Shaking his head, he looked at Lloyd and said, "Don't you get tired of walking all over people? Aren't you a little old for this kind of shit?"

18

At first he thought it was an awful new kind of rage that took over his whole body, making him ache from head to toe and vomit and see double. Then he thought it was something even stranger—a defense mechanism put out by his brain to keep the truth from driving him where everything was bright red and skunk-stenched. A tagalong *puto* cold-cocked him and took off with his woman, and if he freaked out and went crazy he was stone fucking dead, because he was the most wanted man in L.A., bullet bait for every cop who breathed.

But confronting the truth and driving the Trans Am skillfully through the hottest part of town did nothing to kill the revolt inside his body, and he couldn't tell if he was *in* a hallucination or *was* the hallucination.

At dawn he'd awakened, sprawled across Stan Klein's body. It all came back, and he got to his feet, reeling, stumbling and puking, and ran outside to the car. Driving away, he started seeing double and pulled over behind the scrub hedge and passed out. When he came to, it was better, and he drove into downtown Hollywood on side streets. Then it got brutal.

Passing the Burger King on Highland, he saw cops handing out pieces of paper to customers; other cops were knocking on doors on Selma and De Longpre and the little cul-de-sacs north of the Boulevard. Cruising by the park two blocks from the Bowl Motel, he saw more cops distributing more paper, this time to the winos who used the park as a crash pad. The motel, Sharkshit Bobby and the money was right there, free of cops, but with the *feel* of a giant booby trap. Looking up at the palm trees that bordered the place, he started to see triple, then thought he saw snipers with elephant guns hiding inside the fronds. Attack dogs started to growl everywhere, then the sound became the whir of helicopter rotors.

When he saw a German shepherd behind the wheel of a Volkswagen, something snapped, and he laughed out loud and rubbed the blood-crusted bruise that covered the left side of his face. He drove to a pay phone and called Louie Calderon at the bootleg number, and Louie screamed that the fuzz had him pegged as the gun dealer, and there was a twenty-four-hour tail on his ass. He hadn't given up any names, but the heat was huge and Crazy Lloyd Hopkins himself had hassled him.

He'd hung up and made another circuit of Highland. More cops on the street; a group of plainclothesmen house-to-housing the block where he'd stashed the '81 Caprice. He was about to make a dash for Sharkshit and the money when he noticed a scattering of paper in the gutter. He pulled to the curb, got out and picked up the first sheet he came to. It was the sketch of himself he'd seen in the newspapers, with "White Male, Age 25–33, 5'10"–6'1", 150–180 lbs." written below it.

The Bowl Motel gave him a brief come-hither look, then blew up in his mind. Bobby had probably rabbited with the money or the cops were waiting there, trigger-happy and pumped up for glory. All he had left was Vandy.

Getting back in the Trans Am, it all came together.

Concussion.

Meet Rhonda at Silver Foxes at midnight, get *her* to make the run to the motel for the money. Promise her a big cut or nothing at all. Vandy was probably hiding out with her cocaine sleazebag friends. Force Rhonda to help find her.

Rice looked at his watch. 1:14, twelve hours since the cold-cock. A wave of nausea hit him, producing stomach cramps that shot up into his head and made his vision blur. Through the pain he got the most frightening idea of the whole horror-show past month:

Control the concussion so you can survive to get Vandy and a shot at the money and kill Joe Garcia.

Rice drove back to Stan Klein's villa and walked in the unlocked front door like he owned the place. Giving only a cursory glance to Stan Man's body and the dried lake of blood beside it, he ran upstairs to the bathroom, opened the medicine cabinet and read labels. Darvon, Placidil, Dexedrine, Percodan. He remembered a thousand Soledad bull sessions about dope and dry-swallowed two perks and three dexies. He thought of his boozehound parents walking out the door and never returning and almost retched, then walked into the bedroom and fell down on the bed. The soft surface made him think of Vandy, and when the drugs kicked in, easing his pain and juicing him with a new shaky energy, he wondered if she was worth killing for.

19

Lloyd turned on the light in his cubicle and saw that the papers on his desk had been sifted through. He looked for an inanimate object to hit, then remembered Kapek's "Aren't you a little old for this kind of shit?" and the junior G-man's disgusted good-bye when he dropped him off. Only Fred Gaffaney was worth violence, and he was much too potent to fuck with. Calmed by hatred of the Jesus freak, he took the plastic evidence Baggie from his pocket and studied the two photographs inside.

The snapshots were of Gordon Meyers and a young man, dressed in civilian clothes, seated at what looked like a restaurant or nightclub table. Meyers beamed broadly in both, but in one photo the young man was slack-jawed, as if caught by unpleasant surprise; in the other he held an arm up to cover his face.

Lloyd studied the face, knowing that he had seen the blunt cheekbones, close-set eyes and crew cut before. Then the resemblance hit him. He ran to the switchboard for a newspaper confirmation, and got it from a black-bordered photo on the second page of the *Times*: the young man in the snapshots was the late Officer Steven Gaffaney.

Lloyd smiled; the connection felt like aiming a crucifixion spike at Jesus Fred's heart. He ran back to his cubicle and dialed Dutch Peltz' number at Hollywood Station. When Dutch answered with "Peltz, talk," Lloyd said, "No time for amenities, Dutchman. I'm on the cop killings, and I need a favor."

"Name it."

"Dave Stevenson still the commander of West L.A. Station?"

"Yes."

"You still tight with him?"

"Yes."

"Good. Will you call him and ask him about Gaffaney, the dead rookie? Anything and everything, no departmental hype, the real skinny?"

Dutch said, "Call you back in ten minutes," and hung up. Lloyd waited by the phone, ready to pounce at the first ring. In eight minutes it went off, a siren shriek. He picked it up, and Dutch started talking:

"Stevenson called Gaffaney Junior a punk kid, a pain in the ass and a dummy, unquote. He was resented by his fellow officers because he used to preach religion to them and because he used to brag about his father and how his clout would let him climb the promotion ladder in record time. The kid was also a thief. He stole clerical supplies up the ying-yang and used to rip off ammo from the armory. Interesting, huh?"

Lloyd whistled. "Yeah. Did Stevenson report any of this? Did he—"

Dutch cut in. "Yes, he did. He reported the thefts to Intelligence Division, rather than I.A.D., because that's Gaffaney Senior's bailiwick. Dave clammed up then. I just called a friend at Intelligence. He's going to check into it for me on the Q.T. If he gets something, I'll let you know. What are you fishing for, Lloyd?"

"I don't know, Dutch. Do me another favor?"

"Shoot."

"Call the manager at Cal Federal and set up an interview for me in forty-five minutes. He's probably been besieged by cops, but tell him I'm new on the investigation, with new questions for him."

"You've got it. Get them, Lloyd."

Lloyd said, "I will," and hung up, knowing the statement was aimed at Fred Gaffaney more than *Them*.

* * *

The California Federal manager was a middle-aged black man named Wallace Tyrell. Lloyd introduced himself in the bank's desk area, then followed him back to his private office. Closing the door behind them, Tyrell said, "Captain Peltz mentioned new questions. What are they?"

Lloyd smiled and sat down in the one visitor's chair in the room. "Tell me about Gordon Meyers."

Positioning himself carefully in the swivel rocker behind his desk, Tyrell said, "That isn't a new question."

"Tell me anyway."

"As you wish. Meyers was only with the bank for a little over two weeks. I hired him because he was a retired police officer with a satisfactory record and because he accepted a low salary offer. Aside from that, I had him pegged as a garrulous, good-natured man, one with a fatherly interest in the young policemen in the area. He—"

Lloyd held up a hand. "Slow and easy on this, Mr. Tyrell. It's very important."

"As you wish. Meyers used to buttonhole the local officers at the coffee shop next door, apparently to trade war stories. I saw him doing it several times. It was obvious to me that the officers considered him a nuisance. Also, Meyers approached several policemen who had accounts here. Basically, he impressed me as a lonely, slightly desperate type of man."

"Yet you had no thoughts of firing him?"

"No. Hiring one man to be head of security saves money and avoids having an old pensioner with a gun hanging around, reminding customers of possible bank robberies. Meyers adequately handled vault and safe-deposit-box security *and* served as a guard—without a uniform. It was extremely cost-effective. As I said before, these aren't new questions you're asking me."

Staring hard at Tyrell, Lloyd said, "How's this for new? Were there any shortages of cash or safety-box valuables during the time Meyers worked here?"

Tyrell sighed and said, "That is a new question. Yes, two customers mentioned small amounts of jewelry missing from

their boxes. That happens sometimes, people are forgetful of
their transactions, but rarely twice in one week. If it happened
again, I was going to call the police."

"Did you suspect Meyers?"

"He was the only one *to* suspect. He was vault custodian;
part of his job was to insert the signature key when the
customer inserted their key—our boxes are double-locked. He
could have made wax impressions of some of the bottom
locks—his application résumé said he worked as a locksmith
before he joined the Sheriff's Department. Also, this is a busy
time for safety-box transactions—people withdrawing jewelry
for Christmas parties and cashing in bonds. If Meyers was
very careful, he would have had ample opportunity to pilfer."

"Have you told any of the other investigating officers this?"

"No. It didn't seem germane to the issue."

Lloyd stood up and shook hands with the bank manager.
"Thank you, Mr. Tyrell. I like your style."

"I work at it," Tyrell said.

Driving away from the bank, recent memories tumbled in
Lloyd's mind. During the pandemonium following the Pico-
Westholme bloodbath, he had heard one young patrolman tell
another: "The security guy was a real wacko. He used to talk
this weird shit to me." The cops had backed away when he
noticed them, but their faces were still in his memory vault,
now part of the blurred, but clearing focus of the Gaffaney
offshoot of the case. Checking his dashboard clock, he saw that
it was 3:40, twenty minutes until daywatch ended. Focusing
only on those faces, he drove to the West L.A. Station to make
them talk.

His timing was perfect.

The station parking lot was a flurry of activity, black-and-
whites going in and out, patrolmen walking back and forth,
carrying report notebooks and standard-issue shotguns. Standing by the locker room door, Lloyd scanned faces, drawing
puzzled return looks from the incoming officers. The flurry was

dying out when he saw the two from the bank approach with their gear.

Lloyd walked over to them, making a snap decision to play it straight but hard. When they saw him, the patrolmen averted their eyes almost in unison and continued on toward the locker room door. Lloyd cleared his throat as they passed him, then called out, "Come here, Officers."

The two young men turned around. Lloyd matched their faces to their name tags. The tall redheaded cop named Corcoran was the one who had made the remark at the bank; the other, a youth with glasses named Thompson, was the one he'd been talking to. Nodding at them, Lloyd said, "I'm on the bank homicides, gentlemen. Corcoran, you said, quote, 'The security guy was a real wacko. He used to talk this weird shit to me.' You told that to Thompson here. You can elaborate on the statement to me, or a team of I.A.D. bulls. Which would you prefer?"

Corcoran flushed, then answered, "No contest, Sergeant. I was gonna tell the squad room dicks, but it slipped my mind." He looked at Thompson. "Wasn't I, Tommy? You remember me telling you?"

"Th-that's right," Thompson stammered. "R-really, Sarge."

Lloyd said, "Talk. Omit nothing pertaining to the security man."

Corcoran spoke. "Tommy and I sort of had lunch with him twice, last week. He came over to our table, flashed his retirement badge from the Sheriff's and sat down, sort of uninvited. He started asking these weird questions. Should prostitution and weed be legalized? Didn't we think cops made the best whoremasters, because they knew the whore psyche so good? Didn't we think that the county could cut costs by legalizing weed and getting inmates up at Wayside to harvest it? Stone wacko. I th—"

Thompson cut in. "I couldn't believe this clown made twenty years as a cop. He came on like he was from outer space. But I knew he was leading up to something. Anyway, the second time he crashes our lunch, he tries to act real cool and asks us if we know any fences 'who work good with us.' Unbelievable! Like he thinks policemen and fences are good buddies."

Feeling his blurred focus gain another notch of clarity, Lloyd said, "Tell me about Steven Gaffaney. Don't be afraid to be candid."

A look passed between the partners, then Corcoran said, "Nobody on the daywatch could stand him. He was a religious crackpot and a freebie scrounger, always hitting the halfer restaurants and pocketing the check, leaving a quarter tip. I heard rumors that he stole stuff from the station and that his old man, some heavy-hitter captain, bribed instructors at the Academy to pass him through. Wh—"

Lloyd interrupted. "What's the source of that last rumor?"

Corcoran stared at the ground. "I heard the squad room lieutenant talking to Captain Stevenson. The skipper shushed him."

"How did Gaffaney and his partner get along?" Lloyd asked.

"Paul Loweth couldn't stand him," Thompson said. "When they got assigned together, Paul requested another partner, you know, because of a personality conflict. They even took separate code sevens, because Paul couldn't stand eating with Gaffaney."

Lloyd said, "Here's the crunch question. Did you ever see Gordon Meyers and Gaffaney together?"

Both officers nodded their heads affirmatively, and Corcoran said, "About four or five days before the killings I saw Meyers and Gaffaney at the coffee shop next to the bank, talking like old buddies. I didn't hear what they were talking about; Tommy and I sat down at the counter so the wacko wouldn't hassle us."

Bowing with a flourish, Lloyd said, "Thank you, gentlemen," then ran for his Matador and drove to 411 Seaglade.

Still no car in the driveway; still no activity around the front house; still no "Crime Scene" notice on the door of the garage apartment. Again Lloyd kicked the door in, this time splintering the wood around the lock. Knowing that the pad had already stood two professional prowlings, he went straight for the kitchen and opened drawers until he found a large, sawedged steak knife. Then he walked into the bedroom, upended the mattress and looked for telltale slits or stitchings. Finding a long seam of catgut near the headboard, he dug the knife in and ripped out stuffing until his blade hit a sharp object.

Lloyd withdrew the knife and stuck in his hand, touching a flat metal surface. His fingers pried it loose, and he pulled it out.

It was a fishing tackle box, rectangular-shaped, about two inches deep and unlocked. Lloyd lifted up the top. Inside were a half dozen Dieboldt "Security" keys, balls of molding wax, loose colored gemstones and a rolled sheaf of papers. Unrolling them and turning on the lamp by the bed, he smiled. No more blur—the Gaffaney offshoot of the case was now crystal clear.

The pages were an official L.A.P.D. form—a West L.A. Division daywatch car plan list, the names of the officers, their sector and unit numbers in one column, their assignment dates in another. The list detailed November-December 1984, and beside sector G-4, the names "T. Corcoran/J. Thompson" were crossed off, while the name "S. Gaffaney" bore exclamation points followed by question marks.

Lloyd stood up and put the form in his pocket, wondering why the old pursuit high wasn't there. Long moments passed before the reason came to him: Gaffaney Junior probably didn't have time to receive the stolen jewelry, or flat out resisted the temptation. The two nightclub snapshots were probably evidence of Meyers' second go-round at recruiting him. The kid was already pegged as a thief within the Department, second-generation kleptomania was not blackmail parity with first-generation murder, and the Gaffaney offshoot was probably coincidental to *Them*.

Them.

Lloyd thought of Louie Calderon, and of Judge Penzler, still luxuriating at Lake Tahoe. He thought of the blank warrants in his desk at Parker Center, and of the signatures he had forged on stolen payroll checks during college. Forgery to kill a murder indictment was easy parity, even more justified as a means to *Them*. One thought stuck in Lloyd's mind all the way to the Center: *Who were they?*

20

Dusk.

Joe Garcia looked at Anne Atwater Vanderlinden and wondered for the three thousandth time who she was. Crouched in the Griffith Park hideaway he'd discovered in high school, he watched her chain-smoke and stare at the lights popping on all over the L.A. Basin. She'd run with him, away from the lover he'd killed and the old lover chasing her, no tears, no show of fear until she ran out of cigarettes and threw a tantrum in front of a liquor store. Guts, shallowness or dope exhaustion?

She'd fallen asleep in his arms, and holding her made him feel strong, even though he knew he was a dead man. Was it her, or would any woman have done it for him?

They'd slept and talked on and off all day, and he filled her in on Bobby and the money, but not on the bank and dead cops. She took it in with a shrug, looking like a bored rich girl with no connection to dead men and blood money. Stupid, insensitive or just burned out?

Her weird little speeches didn't make figuring her out any easier. During the day she'd wake up, say things like "Duane and Stan had the same karma," or "Stan was a pragmatist, Duane just thought he was," or "Duane didn't understand my music, so it was easy to split from him," then doze off again. After a fifteen-hour crash course in closeness, all *he* knew was that *she* didn't know they were up someplace worse than the creek with *nada*.

Anne pointed to the lights going on in the Capitol Records Tower. "Stan was going to set me up with a producer there. Have you ever been in jail?"

"Yeah."

"I knew it. It's your clothes. You're wearing the kind of clothes Duane would wear if he was trying to fit in someplace he didn't belong."

Seeing a picture of himself drenched in ink, Joe said, "These are Duane's threads. You know we have to get out of here. We can't stay here forever."

"I know that. Clothes should reflect a person's early environment, then, as they put out karma, they transform what they wear. What did you wear when you were growing up? You know, prep like me, or mod, surfer, what?"

Joe watched Anne light a cigarette, then exhale and sniff the air like it could get her high in place of coke. He said, "This isn't the time to be talking fashion. We've got no car and no money, and a crazy man on our ass. I can't go by my pad or the motel, because *he'll* be there. But we have to move, and *I* have to eat."

Anne said, "I've got friends who can help us, and I can make money. Just answer my question."

"How? Peddling your pussy?"

"Don't say that! I can give sex and not sacrifice my karma! Don't say that!"

Joe put a hand on her arm and said, "Sssh. I'm sorry, but I am in *deep trouble*."

"Then answer my question."

Joe sighed. "I grew up dressing like a ridiculous Mexican gangster. Plaid Sir Guy shirts buttoned to the top when it was ninety-five degrees, bell-bottom khakis that dragged the ground, spit-shined navy shoes and an honor farm watch cap. It was a joke, and it had nothing to do with karma."

"Everything does."

"I killed a man last night. Aren't you scared?"

Anne sniffed the air. "I took a Dilaudid Black Beauty speedball just before it got bad with Stan and Duane, and I'm starting to crash. In about an hour I'll be *real* scared. You act like a tough guy, but you talk like you went to college. You're sort of a *phony*."

Only Bobby knew that about him.

Joe put his arms around Anne and whispered, "It's because of this song I can't write, and Bobby and Sir Guys and khakis and what I have to do, but I can't do any more. Does that make sense to you?"

Anne dry-sobbed into his chest. "No no no no no."

Joe whispered back, "You're just pretending not to know. You're a musician, so I know you know. Listen. I'll tell you exactly what we're going to do. We're going to walk down the Observatory Road to Vermont, then steal some rich preppy car. Then we're going to hit up these friends of yours and get some money and get the hell out of town. Say yes if you think we can do it."

Anne made a choking sound and nodded her head up and down. Joe looked out at the L.A. skyline and knew for the first time in his life that it was his—because now he could leave it behind.

21

Lloyd pulled up across from Likable Louie's One-Stop Pit Stop. Seeing no fed units, he grabbed his forged search warrant and Ithaca pump, ran across the street and knocked on the door of the built-on house. A feeling of being close grabbed him, and he flicked off the safety and jacked a shell into the chamber.

The door was opened cautiously, held to the frame by a long chain. A Mexican woman peered through the crack and said, "Luis not here. Police took him."

Lloyd saw copwise smarts. "You mean federal officers?" he said. "F.B.I.?"

"Luis hip to men watching him. These L.A. cops, green car, big antenna."

Lloyd shuddered. Metro had glommed the Calderon info. "When?" he asked.

"Half hour. I call lawyer."

Lloyd ran back to his car and lead-footed it the two miles to Rampart Station, hoping to find Lieutenant Buddy Bagdessarian or another detective familiar with Calderon. Parking in the lot, he saw no black-and-whites, only civilian cars, and knew that the station contingent was skeletal—probably because every available unit was aiding Hollywood Division in the cop-killer canvassing. Then he spotted an olive-drab Metro wagon parked crossways in the watch commander's space. The feeling of being close got claustrophobic, and he ran into the station full-tilt.

There was a single officer on duty at the front desk. Lloyd

eased his stride and approached slowly, knowing that the early evening station scene was way too quiet, way *off*. The desk officer grimaced when he saw him coming. He moved toward the intercom phone on the wall behind him, then changed his mind and mashed his hands together. Lloyd reached the desk and saw a cross and flag pin attached next to the man's badge. The abomination made his head reel. He was about to rip the insignia from the officer's chest when a muffled noise stopped him and made him perk his ears to identify it.

There was a short moment of silence, then the noise again. This time Lloyd knew it was a scream. He ran down a long corridor toward the echo, past the booking area and drunk tank to a half-open storage room door. Behind the door the screams melded with a barrage of other noises: retching, garbled obscenities, loud thuds. Lloyd forced himself to count to ten, an old strategy to resurrect cool. Then a brass-knuckled fist arced across the open door space, followed by a burst of blood. At seven, he attacked.

Collins and Lohmann looked up as the door crashed open; Louie Calderon, handcuffed behind his back to a chair, spat blood and flailed at the Metro cops with his legs. Lloyd moved straight in, both fists cocked and aimed shoulder-high. With no swinging room, he hurled jerky shots, catching Lohmann in the neck, Collins a glancing blow in the chest. Calderon toppled his chair to the floor; Collins tripped over him, missing a wide roundhouse right at Lloyd's head. Lloyd grabbed his wrist as the blow grazed his shoulder, bringing his knee up flush into Collins' abdomen. Louie Calderon moaned beneath the tangle of feet, and Lohmann lunged at Lloyd with two brass-coiled fists, his momentum sending them both back into the door. Then hands grabbed Lloyd from behind and pulled him out of the room, Lohmann still on top of him, trying to extricate himself. When the knuck wielder got untangled, Lloyd had a clear shot. He kicked Lohmann in the face and felt his nose crack.

Lloyd was hurled into the holding cell across the corridor. When the cross-and-flag officer got the door secured, he stood up, reached through the bars and tore off his badge. The polished oval hit the floor, and the officer picked it up, looked at Lloyd and hissed, "Satan."

Lloyd laughed in his face, then spat in his face. Collins yelled, "Get back to the fucking desk!" and the cross-and-flag man half-walked, half-ran down the corridor and out of sight. Lloyd watched Collins help his partner to his feet. Lohmann was blowing cartilage and bloody mucus out of both nostrils, spitting the overflow on the floor. Collins made him tilt his head backward; then, with one arm around his shoulders, he walked him toward the front of the station.

Louie Calderon was still on the storage room floor, twisted sideways in his chair. Lloyd watched him gasp and let out little sobs. His own breathing was almost back to normal when Collins returned, picked up the chair and placed a finger under Likable Louie's chin. "You're going to give me three names," he said. "A federal officer saw your little boy with a tranq gun. We know you're the dealer."

Calderon pulled his chin free. "Your mother's the dealer," he slurred. "She deals AIDS at a lesbian bar."

Collins hit him in the stomach, knocking the chair back to the floor. Calderon retched for breath, then started hyperventilating, thrashing with his feet, heaving with his shoulders. The chair buckled off the floor as he squirmed, and one by one the wooden slats on the backing snapped. Collins stood over Calderon until he got his wind and started shrieking, "Pig, pig, pig." Then he knelt beside him and said, "The three names."

Calderon took a long gasp of air and said, "Your mother, your partner's mother and Crazy Lloyd's mother. *Chinga su madres todos.* Lesbian pig three-way with niggers. *Puto! Puto! Puto!*"

Collins said, "Pig is a no-no," stuck his right thumb and forefinger behind Calderon's ear and squeezed the carotid artery. *"The three names."*

Lloyd squinted and saw Calderon's face start turning purple. He squeezed the bars, pushing harder and harder into them. It felt like he was the first part of a chain of pressure moving straight through the bars to the hot dog and his victim, and if he let up, he would never get to *Them*. Then, when Calderon's face looked like a plum about to burst, he saw what he was doing and screamed, "No!"

Startled, Collins withdrew the hold. He looked over at Lloyd, and Lloyd saw his own eyes burning into him. Knowing it couldn't be, he held his hands up in front of his face. Seeing nothing, he felt all his senses go into his ears and pick up whispers:

"The names. I'll maim you for life if you don't give them to me."

"No. No. Fuck you. No. Don't. Please don't."

"Think of your family. Think of your wife at Tehachapi, where she'll be on dope charges if you don't tell me."

"No. No. No. Please, please. No."

"The three names. Think of your kids in a cut-rate board-and-care home. Have you watched the news lately? Lot of sexual abuse in those places. *Give me the three names*."

"No. No. No."

"No? No? 'Yes,' or I get a dykey woman officer to skin search your wife for the narcotic substances that I know she'll find."

"No. No. N—"

"Tell me, Luis."

"No. They'll hurt me."

"They won't hurt you, but I will."

"No."

"Don't say no to me, say yes to me, or I'll hurt your family."

"Yes. Yes. Duane Rice. Bobby Garcia. Joe Garcia."

Them.

Lloyd closed his eyes and flashbacked: The "Duane/Rhonda" message on Calderon's bootleg message list; Christine Confrey's puzzled reaction to the mug shots of Duane Richard Rice, allegedly serving a year in county jail for G.T.A. He pressed himself into the bars, the better to see and listen.

Collins was squatting beside Calderon, unlocking the handcuffs that bound him to the chair. "There's lots of Bobby and Joe Garcias," he said. "Be more specific about them."

Likable Louie fumbled himself away from the chair, slowly stretching his arms and kneading his gouged wrists. "Bobby 'Boogaloo' Garcia, the ex-boxer. His brother Joe." His voice was filled with the self-disgust of the freshly turned snitch. Lloyd held his eyes shut to give the man back some of his dignity. He kept them shut until he felt a tap on his shoulder.

Collins was standing directly in front of the cell. Lloyd saw that his eyes were brown, not gray like his own, but that they were still somehow identical. "I'll have the desk officer let you out in a little while," he said. "But stay out of this, it's ours."

Lloyd couldn't think of anything to say. He stared at Collins as he walked back to the storage room and helped Calderon over to the holding cell next to his. Still too numb to talk, he heard the door being unlocked and locked again, followed by footsteps moving away from the blood-spattered corridor. Then, from beyond the periphery of his vision, Louie Calderon said, "Don't let them kill the kid. Bobby and Duane are hope-to-die trash, but the kid was just too weak to say no. Don't let them kill him."

22

Midway down Vermont to Los Feliz, Joe Garcia realized he didn't know how to steal a car. He'd heard nine million raps on hot-wiring and drilling steering columns, and that was it. Anne Vanderlinden walked beside him, talking gibberish about karma and the ritzy houses they were passing. Her voice was getting more and more feverish, and when streetlamp light caught her eyes, they glowed wide and loony.

Then Joe caught a blast of Bob Seger and the Silver Bullet Band and weaving headlights. He grabbed Anne just as a yellow Corvette cut a sharp left turn and screeched to a stop in the driveway next to them. A young man got out of the car and stumbled across the lawn and through the front door of a large Tudor house. Joe left Anne on the sidewalk and checked out the 'Vette. The keys were in the ignition. He looked at the house and saw window lights going on, then off. Now or never.

He walked back to Anne and shoved her toward the car. She got in the passenger side and started burrowing in the glove compartment. Joe slipped behind the wheel, trembling when he saw the shifter on the floor and realized that he didn't know how to drive a stick. Muttering "Fuck it," he remembered the way Bobby used to drive his old VW and watched Anne open up a prescription bottle and start shoving pills in her mouth. He found neutral; he depressed the clutch; he hit the ignition. Bob Seger boogied. Joe slammed the shifter into reverse and inched out of the driveway. Anne giggled, "Drive to the Strip and we'll call my friends!" and Joe ground his way through the gears, stalling the car twice, but finally working clutch and gearshift to the point where he could keep them going. The moment on the hillside came back, ten times as strong, and they fishtailed toward Hollywood.

23

Two-way radio crackle in the distance; helicopter searchlights swooping the motel at irregular intervals. Duane and Joe gone over twenty-four hours, probably dead. Twice the radio had screeched, " '81 Chevrolet Caprice."

Bobby "Boogaloo" Garcia knew they were coming for him. His hours of Bible reading and prayers had reaped *nada*. He was going to die alone, excommunicated, away from God and his brother, two .45 automatics and 16 grand in cash his only companions.

No one to mourn him;

No one to talk to on the night he finally figured it all out;

No chance to pay back his victims and slide into heaven on last-minute good deeds and acts of contrition;

No one to grant absolution for his sins.

At first, when he got it all down in his head, it made him feel peaceful. Then the choppers kept buzzing and flashing their lights, pissing off the old juiceheads boozing in the parking lot, who started jabbering and throwing their empty T-bird bottles at the wall. That made him mad, made him feel like going out defiant, even when he knew that defiance was his most heavy-duty sin. That was the funniest part of it. Half of him wanted to admit it and go out clean; the other half wanted to go out righteously defiant, because that's what he was for thirty-four years, and if he reversed his act now, it meant that he never existed at all.

Bullhorns barking from up the block; copter lights flooding the sky every five minutes; the winos wailing like nigger banshees. Finally Bobby decided to cover his bets. He pulled up his chair to directly in front of the door and placed the Bible on the right armrest, then loaded both .45s and unscrewed the silencers for better range. Sliding shells into both chambers, he sat down with the guns in his lap. When they kicked in the door, he'd know how to play it.

24

Three minutes after his cell door was opened by a station trustee, Lloyd was in a phone booth on Rampart and Temple, turning out his pockets for change.

His first call was to the Central Jail Records night line, where an information clerk told him that Duane Richard Rice, white male, D.O.B. 8/16/56, 6'0", 170, light brown hair, blue eyes, had been released on a sentence modification on November 30, after serving six months of a one-year sentence for grand theft auto. He had one previous conviction, for vehicular manslaughter, and had put in three years of a five-year sentence at the California Youth Authority Facility at Soledad. He was now on both state parole and county probation, and his last known address was 1164 South Barrington, West Los Angeles. Pressing, Lloyd asked the clerk what module Rice was housed in at the Main County Jail. After a moment spent checking other records, she came back on the line and said, "Twenty-seven hundred."

The Ding Tank—Gordon Meyers connection.

But *why*?

Lloyd called the Los Angeles County Probation Department and got an operator who put him through to a series of clerks, who finally put him through to the county's chief probation officer at home. The chief made a series of calls herself and buzzed Lloyd back at his pay phone with the word: Duane Richard Rice had not reported to his P.O. after his release from jail and had vacated his condo on South Barrington. He was now technically a parole and probation absconder, and a bench warrant for his arrest had been issued.

Hanging up, Lloyd tried to recall the phone numbers from Louie Calderon's message book. After a minute, they came to him: Rhonda, 654-8996; Silver Foxes, 658-4371.

He dialed Rhonda's number and got the beginning of a recorded message, then hung up and called Bell Telephone and made his demands. A supervisor gave him the information he wanted: Rhonda Morrell, 961 North Vista, West Hollywood; Silver Foxes, 1420 North Gardner. Lloyd smiled as he wrote it down. The addresses were only a few blocks apart. With his .45 unholstered on the seat beside him, he drove to West Hollywood.

961 North Vista was a modern building, with two stories of apartments around a cement courtyard. The directory by the front gate listed *R. Morrell* in Unit 20. Lloyd studied the numerical scheme and judged Rhonda's apartment to be on the first story, dead center. He walked over, the .45 pressed to his leg.

No lights were on, but he pressed the buzzer beneath the taped-on *Morrell* anyway, then stepped to the side. A full minute passed with no sounds issuing in response to his ring. No Rhonda.

Lloyd walked around to the parking space in the back of the building. The slot for Unit 20 was empty. Feeling itchy but *close*, he drove the three blocks to Silver Foxes.

Pulling up and surveying the lavender Spanish-style, Lloyd was surprised to see no neon beacons or other accoutrements of sleaze, only a quiet four-flat with lights coming from the left downstairs side. Again holding the .45 to his leg, he walked over to the lights and rang the bell next to the smiling fox emblem. Pressing himself against the wall beside the doorway, he held the gun next to his chest, prepared to wheel and fire.

Silence, then a whiney male voice muttering, "Oh shit," then footsteps approaching the door. When he heard inside locks being unlatched, Lloyd stepped out and leveled the .45 at midpoint in the doorway.

The door swung open, and a muscle-bound young man in a tight tank top stood there, frozen by the gun held only inches from him. "Police officer," Lloyd said. "Walk backward inside, turn around and place your hands on the wall above your head, then step back and spread your legs."

Biting his lip, the young man complied. Lloyd followed him into a stark white room and nudged the door shut with his toe, pressing the .45 to the back of his neck, frisking him with his left hand. The youth moaned when Lloyd brushed the insides of his thighs. Finding no concealed weaponry, Lloyd said, "How many other rooms?"

"Just the bathroom, sweetie. There's nobody here but us chickens. Are you a chicken hawk?"

Lloyd gave the room a quick once-over, catching tube furniture, white Plasticine desk, white walls hung with pictures of rock and rollers. "No banter," he said. "Go over and open the bathroom door, then come back here."

The young man walked over to the bathroom door and pushed it open, then returned and sat down on the white desk, one foot on the floor, one leg dangling in Lloyd's direction. "Like I said, 'No one here but us chickens.' My name's Tim. What's yours?"

Lloyd reholstered his .45 and said, "Son, I am the last person in the world you want to get cute with tonight. *The last*. I'm going to ask you some simple straight questions, and I want simple straight answers. Do you understand?"

Tim smiled coyly and tapped his heel against the desk. "Shoot, baby."

"First, do you know a man named Duane Rice? Late twenties, six feet, one seventy, light brown hair, blue eyes?"

"No, but he sounds cute. Is he your lover?"

Lloyd backhanded the young man, knocking him off the desk. He smiled and wiped a trickle of blood from his nose. Lloyd said, "I don't want to hurt you, but please Jesus God don't fuck with me. Not tonight."

Tim stood up. "Say 'pretty please' and I'll be a good Boy Scout and cooperate."

Penny and Janice moved through Lloyd's mind in precaution reflex, then Jesus Fred Gaffaney and Collins eclipsed them. He pushed Tim across the room and held him to the wall with a hand on his neck. "Pretty please talk, motherfucker, before I trash your worthless ass."

Tim made gurgling sounds until Lloyd released him and stepped back. Smiling, he rubbed his neck and sighed. "Rough play is one thing, hurting is another. You said 'pretty please,' so I'll be a good Scout and be nice. What do you want to know?"

The singsong words settled on Lloyd like fallout, and he wondered if this night would ever be over. "One of your whores," he said. "Rhonda Morrell. I picked up on one of her phone messages from Duane Rice. He was supposed to call her at home or here last night. The message mentioned someone named Stan Klein. What do you know about this?"

Tim moved to the desk and opened drawers, then pulled out a white Naugahyde binder and leafed through it. Holding the binder open, he said, "That's Rhonda. Isn't she foxy?"

Lloyd looked at the nude photographs. Rhonda Morrell was a beautiful brunet. He memorized her face, holding his eyes from the rest of her body. "Tell me about her. And about Rice and Klein."

Tim snapped the binder shut. "What's to tell? Rhonda is a real brain fox, wants to be a stockbroker. She's very much in demand with our clients. Rice and Klein I don't know about, although the way you described Rice, he sounds like this guy who came by last week, this guy Rhonda's got some kind of nonsex scene going with, you know, for money. Rhonda's a real money fox."

The "Wants $" in Calderon's message book popped into Lloyd's head. "Tell me about him—and Rhonda."

Tim wrapped his arms around himself. "Last week a man came in, looking for a fox. He didn't seem like Silver Foxes caliber, but I liked his style, so I fixed him up with Rhonda. He gave me a name, but I knew it was phony. Later on, Rhonda tells me she's helping the guy look for his girlfriend, for big bucks. In fact, she called this afternoon and told me she's supposed to meet him here tonight at midnight. She wanted me to hold him in case she's late."

Lloyd fingered the gun he had killed with, then looked at the clock on the wall. 10:49. In August of 1965 he had gone one-on-one with a .45-caliber killer; now he was coming full circle back to that point, to pay his dues for the event that had formed him. Shivering, he said, "Tim, do you believe in God?"

Tim shrugged. "I've never given it much thought."

"You should. He's a tricky bastard; you might dig him. Go home. I'm going to wait for Rhonda and her friend."

"Is this legal?"

"No. Go home. I'm sorry I hit you."

"I'm not," Tim said, and walked out the door.

Lloyd waited for ten minutes, then went out to his car and turned on his two-way. He listened for twenty minutes. The air was flooded with calls directing Hollywood Division units to the area near the Hollywood Bowl, but there was no mention of the hottest trio in L.A. history—Duane Rice, Bobby and Joe Garcia. Gaffaney and his hot dogs were sitting on the information. It was coming down to their outlaw vendetta, and his own. And when Rice fell into his hands at midnight, would he be able to press his advantage and take him out in cold blood?

Lloyd walked back to the Silver Foxes office to await Rhonda Morrell and then the moment. He sat down in an uncomfortable white chair and stared at the pictures on the white walls, unable to identify any of the rock and rollers by name. Checking the clock repeatedly, he hoped that Rhonda would be late, so he could take a post outside and back-shoot Duane Rice as he walked up to the door. God as an ironic bastard stuck in his mind. Taking out the Pico-Westholme cop killer would be considered the zenith of his career, not the desperately selfish survival tactic that it was.

At 11:42 there was a rapping on the door. Lloyd took out his .45 and tiptoed over and opened the door, startling Rhonda Morrell, who saw the gun and opened her mouth to scream.

Lloyd got her in a headlock with his free arm and pulled her inside, stifling her attempts to make noise. She bit at his jacket sleeve, and he kicked the door shut and whispered, "L.A.P.D. I'm here for Duane Rice, not you. I just want to ask you a few questions, then get you the hell out of here before he shows up. Now, I'm going to let you go, but you have to promise not to scream. Okay?"

Rhonda quit squirming and biting. Lloyd released her, and she twisted around and stood with her back to him, fluffing out her Afro. Turning back, she said in a perfectly composed voice, "He owes me a lot of money. If you arrest him, he won't be able to pay me."

Lloyd blurted, "Jesus," then mustered his thoughts and said, "There's a lot of reward money being offered for his capture. You talk to me, *fast*, and I'll see that you get it."

Rhonda smiled. "How much money?"

"Over seventy thousand," Lloyd said, stealing a glance at his watch. "Tim told me you're helping Rice look for his girlfriend. Tell me about that, and tell me about Stan Klein."

"You know a lot about it already."

"I don't know a fucking thing! Tell me, goddammit!"

Rhonda looked at the clock and said, "I guess this is trading up. Rice has a coke-whore girlfriend. I've been helping him look for her. I found out that she's been living with a sleazy entrepreneurial type, Stan Klein. I got—"

"What's the girlfriend's name?"

"Anne Vanderlinden. Duane called me Monday night, and we made a date to meet here at midnight. He said he and Vandy were flying to New York in a few days, and he needed the names of some music people. Apparently Vandy is a singer, and he wants to help her career. He promised me a bonus for that, and—"

"That was the last time you spoke to him?"

"No! He called me this afternoon, at home, to confirm our date. He sounded spacey, and he said that Vandy had left Stan Klein's place last night, with a *puto* Mexican, whatever that is.

Now he's promising me the moon if I help him find her again. He also said we have to pick up some money."

Lloyd stared at the clock, his mind suddenly blank. Rhonda fidgeted, plucking at her hair. Finally she pointed to the gun in Lloyd's hand. "Why have you got that out? Is Duane dangerous?"

Lloyd laughed. "Yeah, he's dangerous."

"I think he's basically sweet, with some rough edges. If he's so dangerous, where are all the other cops?"

"Never mind. You've got to get out of here."

"Wait. I read the papers today. They said there's seventy-five K in reward money out for the person who killed those people at the bank. You don't think Duane did that? He might be a thief, but he's not vicious."

Lloyd grabbed Rhonda's arm and pulled her toward the door. "Go home," he hissed. *"Get out of here now."*

"What about my money? How do I know I'll get it?" She paused, then looked in Lloyd's eyes and gasped, "You're going to kill him because he's a cop killer. I've read about that kind of thing. You can't fool me."

"Get the fuck out now, goddamn you."

There were footsteps on the walkway outside. Rhonda screamed, "Duane, run!" Lloyd froze, then threw himself prone when three shots blew the front picture window to bits. He grabbed Rhonda's legs and yanked her to the floor, then rolled to the demolished window and fired twice blindly, hoping to draw a return volley.

Two muzzle bursts lit up the lawn; the shots ricocheted around the white walls, ripping out jagged crisscrosses of wood. Lloyd aimed at the flashes of red and squeezed off five rounds, then ejected the spent clip and slipped in a fresh one. He took a deep breath of cordite, chambered the top round and charged out the window.

No dead man on the grass; Rhonda's screams echoing behind him. Lloyd ran up Gardner to Sunset. Rounding the corner, he heard a shot, and a plate-glass window two doors down exploded. Then he saw a crowd of people on the sidewalk scatter into doorways and out on the street. And there *he* was.

Lloyd watched the man weave through shrieking pedestrians, then dart past parked cars and start sprinting east on Sunset, out of his firing range. He sprinted full-out himself, closing the gap until he saw Rice stick his gun in the passenger window of a car stopped for the light at the next intersection. Then he ran and aimed at the same time, knots of late-night strollers making scared and startled sounds as they got out of his way. The running posture was awkward and cut down his speed, but he almost had a clear shot when Rice got in the car, and it took off against the light.

Then he heard approaching sirens, and it jolted him away from the escaping car and back to his own jeopardy. Rice would probably ditch the escape vehicle within blocks. "Shots fired" and the location would hit the air *huge* and goose Jesus Fred and his hot dogs into the area in force. Lloyd ran back to Silver Foxes and found Rhonda on the front lawn. He forced her into his car, but when he pulled out, he didn't know where they were going. He only knew he was terrified.

Rice knew that he had to ditch the car, or keep the car and kill the driver. Digging the barrel of his .45 harder into the old man's neck, he said, "Hang a left at the next corner and park."

The man obeyed, turning onto Formosa, double-parking. Grasping the wheel, he shut his eyes and began weeping. Rice snapped to a new plan: tie Pops up and leave him somewhere, take his money and roll. "You got rope in the trunk, motherfucker?"

The man nodded yes, and Rice grabbed the key from the ignition and walked back to the trunk. He was about to open it when the driver bolted and started running toward Sunset. He was almost there when a black-and-white pulled to the curb on the opposite side of the street two doors up from the car.

Pops *down* from him; the fuzz thirty yards *up*. Rice got back in the car, this time behind the wheel. His head throbbed, burned and crackled, but he got a message through all of it: *be calm*. He turned on the engine and put the Fairlane in drive, then started to accelerate. Then he heard the old man screaming, "Police! Police!" *behind* him; then the cop car *in front* of him turned on its cherry lights.

Time stood still, then zoomed back to Doheny Drive and the first time he had dope in his veins. Rice punched the gas just as the driver of the patrol car got out with his gun drawn. Caught in blinding headlight glare, he stood transfixed. Rice smashed the nose of his three-hundred horsepower battering ram into him at thirty-six miles per hour, catching him flush. The impact ripped off the grille and a chunk of the fender; the windshield went red, just like before. Rice drove blind, his foot held to the floor until wind whipped the crimson curtain from in front of his eyes, and real vision made him stop the car and get out and run.

25

Bobby heard the radio voices stop screeching about the '81 Chevy and the house-to-house searches that were zeroing in on him, and start barking, "Man down, Sunset and Formosa, man down! Man down!" Within seconds sirens were wailing *away from him*, and the choppers took off, leaving the Bowl Motel in darkness and silence. Knowing it was a stay of execution straight from God, he packed all the money into a supermarket bag and walked out the door, leaving the .45s and Bible behind on the chair.

Outside, the street was deserted and still, with no cars moving either way on Highland. Walking south, Bobby saw why: sawhorse roadblocks hung with flashing lights were stationed at all intersections, shutting off northbound traffic. Turning around, he could pick out other lighted blockades a block up, just past the motel. As he stared at the cordon, a group of plainclothes cops with shotguns entered the courtyard. God had shot him a split-second salvation.

Stepping over the sawhorse at the corner of Franklin, Bobby saw the church and sent up a prayer for it to be Catholic. His prayer was answered when the white adobe building was caught by headlights coming off a side street: "Saint Anselm's Catholic Church" in large black letters.

A light was burning in the window of the white adobe bungalow adjoining the church. Bobby ran to the beacon and rang the bell.

The man who opened the door was young, dressed in black clerical trousers and a polo shirt. Bobby grimaced when he saw the alligator on his chest and his new-wave haircut. Not Mexican and not Irish-looking; probably a social activist type. "Are you a priest?" he asked.

The man looked Bobby up and down. He stuck his hands in his pockets, and Bobby knew he was digging for chump change. "I don't want no handout," he said. "Money's the one thing I got big. I want to make a confession. You hear confessions?"

"Yes, weekday afternoons," the priest said. He reached into his front pocket, pulled out a pair of glasses and put them on. Bobby stood under his gaze, watching him pick up on his ink-stained arms and face and Duane Rice's shirt that hung on him like a tent. "Please, Father. Please."

The priest nodded and moved past Bobby onto the sidewalk, making beckoning motions. Bobby followed him over to the church. Unlocking the door, the priest turned on a light and walked inside. Bobby waited by the door and murmured Hail Marys, then bolted up the steps and anointed himself with holy water from the font by the back pew. As he genuflected toward the altar and made the sign of the Cross, the shopping bag slipped out of his arms. A wad of twenties dropped to the floor, and he stuffed them into his pockets and walked to the scrim of velvet curtains that separated the confessional booths from the church proper.

The priest was in the first booth. Bobby pulled the drapes aside, dropped the bag and knelt in front of the partition that shielded him from his confessor. The screen was slid open, and Bobby could see the priest's lips move as he said, "Are you ready to make your confession?"

Bobby cleared his throat and said, "Bless me, Father. My last confession was about five or six years ago, except I heard some confessions when I worked this religious scam. I faked being a priest, but I always tried to be fair with the suck—I mean the people I scammed. What I mean—"

Bobby leaned his head against the partition. When he saw that his lips were almost touching the lips of his confessor, he gasped and brought himself back into a ramrod-straight posture. Muttering Hail Marys under his breath, he got down what he wanted to say in the right order. When he heard the priest cough, he pressed his palms together and lowered his head, then began.

"I am guilty of many mortal sins. I worked this phone scam where I impersonated priests and ripped off money in God's name, and I pulled burglaries, and I fired off lots of low blows when I was a fighter. Sometimes I rubbed resin on my gloves between rounds, so I could fuck—so I would waste the guy's eyes when I went head-hunting. I robbed a bank, and I raped a woman, and I pulled evil sex shit on another woman, and I shot a woman and killed her, and—"

Bobby stopped when he heard the priest chanting Hail Marys. Slamming the partition with his palms, he shouted, "You listen to me, motherfucker! This is my fucking confession, not yours!"

Silence answered the outburst. Then the priest said, "Finish your confession and I'll tell you your penance."

The sternness in the kiddie-confessor's voice gave Bobby the juice to say *it*, the big stuff he finally figured out. "I got a brother," he said. "Younger than me. He's weak 'cause I made him weak. I committed a heinous mortal sin with him when we was kids, and I been trying to atone for it by looking after him ever since, when what I should have done was cut him loose years ago, so he could get balls on his own. I always felt guilty about hating him, 'cause I knew that riding herd on his ass was killin' *me*, too. See, I always figured that he *knew* what I did, but he was afraid to say it, 'cause of what it would make us. Then, dig, tonight I figured out that he just didn't remember, 'cause it was so long ago, which means that all this time I sp—"

The priest interrupted, his voice impatient and severe, like a confessor's voice should be. "Don't interpret. Tell me the sin."

Bobby said *it*, sounding to himself like an old TV judge handing down a life sentence. "When we was kids, I used to tie Little Bro up so I could go out and play. I came back one day and saw that he'd wet himself 'cause he couldn't get up. The whole bed was wet, and I got righteously turned on and pulled down his pants and touched him."

"And that is your heinous mortal sin? After all the other acts you confessed?"

Now Bobby heard *disgust*. "Don't *you* interpret, Father. They're my sins. *Mine*."

."Say the act of contrition and I'll give you your penance," the priest whispered.

Bobby bowed his head and forced the second part of his sentence out in an Anglo accent, like the old Irish sisters had taught him. "O my God, I am heartily sorry for having offended thee. I detest all my sins because I dread the loss of heaven and the pain of hell. But most of all because I have offended thee, O God, who are all good and deserving of all my love. I firmly resolve with the help of thy grace to confess my sins, do penance and amend my life. Amen. Well, Father?"

"I grant you absolution," the priest said. "Your penance is good deeds for the rest of your life. Begin soon, you have much to atone for. Go and sin no more."

Bobby heard his confessor slide through the curtains and walk out of the church. He gave him enough time to make it back to the rectory, then got to his feet and picked up the shopping bag, smiling at the weight. "Begin soon" rang in his ears. On wobbly legs, he obeyed.

The poor box was on the side wall near the rear pews, ironclad, but too small to hold sixteen K in penance bucks. Bobby started shoving cash in the slot anyway, big fistfuls of c-notes and twenties. Bills slipped out of his hands as he worked, and he was wondering whether to leave the whole bag by the altar when he heard strained breathing behind him. Looking over his shoulder, he saw Duane Rice standing just outside the door. His high school yearbook prophecy crossed his mind: *"Most likely not to survive,"* and suddenly Duane-o looked more like a priest than the *puto* with the alligator fag shirt.

Bobby dropped the bag and fell to his knees; Rice screwed the silencer onto his .45 and walked over. He picked up the bag and placed the gun to the Sharkman's temple; Bobby knew that *defiant* was the way to go splitsville. He got in a righteous giggle and "Duhn-duhn-duhn-duhn" before Rice blew his brains out.

26

Joe sat in a booth in Ben Frank's Coffee Shop, forcing himself to eat a cheeseburger platter. Through the tinted plate-glass window he watched Anne talk into a pay phone in the parking lot. He tried to read her lips, but she was too far away, and distant siren blare from the east kept distracting him. The food that he figured would calm him down didn't; the 'Vette, ditched on a side street two blocks away, had his prints all over the wheel and dashboard. The copter lights and sirens made the Hollywood/Strip border area feel like a war zone. The thrill of mastering the stick shift in a stolen car was dead, and Anne had now fed a dozen quarters to the phone, trying to connect with her "good music friends" who would "help them out." The black pimps at the next table were talking about a shootout on Gardner and barricades and cops with shotguns up by the Hollywood Bowl. One of them kept repeating, "Righteous fucking heat," and Joe knew he was digging it because the heat wasn't directed at him. Every word, every bit of noise, from the war sounds to waitresses clanking dishes, brought back Stan Klein's face just as he stuck in the knife. That was bad, but he knew it was only a delayed reaction, something like shock. What made it terrible was his music turning on him, "And death was a thrill on Suicide Hill" bopping in his brain along with pictures of the man he killed.

Joe felt his insides start to turn over. He jumped up, bumping the table, knocking his food on the floor. The pimps laughed when french fries flew onto a passing customer's legs, and Joe ran to the bathroom and vomited his meal into the sink. Holding the wall with one hand, he turned on the faucet and doused his head with cold water. His stomach heaved, and his chest expanded and contracted with short blasts of breath. He looked at himself in the mirror, then turned away when he saw Bobby just like *he* always looked after getting his ass kicked at the Olympic. Standing upright, he gave himself another dousing, then wiped his face with a paper towel and walked back into the restaurant.

A busboy was cleaning up the spillage by his table; the pimps snickered at him. Joe sidestepped the mess and ran out the door, the cashier yelling, "What about your check!" On the sidewalk, he looked for Anne. She wasn't by the pay phone, and she wasn't in the parking lot. Then he saw her across the street, upstaging a group of hookers with a pelvis-grinding boogie aimed at passing cars.

Joe started to jaywalk across Sunset; a Mercedes stretch limo pulled up in front of Anne, and she got in. The stretch hung an immediate right turn, and Joe ran, rounding the corner just in time to see it park halfway down the block. Walking over, he heard male sex grunts shooting out of the backseat. Then a disco tune smothered the groans, and the chauffeur got out and stood by the car, trying to look cool about the whole thing. With anger blotting out all traces of Stan Klein's death mask, Joe retreated to a dark front lawn to play watchdog.

The limo wobbled on its suspension for half an hour, the musical accompaniment going from disco to reggae. Joe moved back and forth between pins-and-needles alertness and nodding-out sleepiness. Total exhaustion was dropping over him when a door slammed, and Anne began skipping up to the Strip. When she passed him, Joe said, "You really rocked that stretch. Any bitch that can rock a Benz fender to fender has got to be a pro."

Anne squinted into the darkness. When Joe walked up to her, she said, "I told you I could give sex and not sacrifice my karma, and if you give sex for money you might as well do a good job. And I wasn't leaving you; I was coming back to B.F.'s."

Joe snickered, imitating the pimps at the coffee shop. "That's because you need a man to tell you what to do. Okay, I'll tell you what we're gonna do. How much did that scumbag in the Benz give you?"

"A c-note."

"Groovy. We're gonna use about seventy of it to check into that motel next to B.F.'s. You check us in, I'll follow you back. Dig?"

Anne did a nervous foot dance. "Now you're starting to *talk* like a tough guy—"

"People change."

"All right, but that trick just told me about this all-night open-house party at an exec producer's place. I used to trick regularly with the guy when I worked outcall. He's a video heavy, and he really liked me. I can get some money there, I know I can."

Joe shook his head. "First we're getting a flop. Come on."

Without a word, Anne led the way back to the Strip. Joe saw that she looked dejected, but was secretly glad he'd taken charge. From the rear of the Ben Frank's parking lot he watched her hit the motel office, pay the night clerk and glom a key, then walk around to the street and into the courtyard. When the clerk sighed and returned to his paperback, he followed.

She was waiting for him in the doorway of a downstairs unit, one hip cocked, one elbow resting on the doorjamb, looking like an evil little girl born to fuck. She smiled and shifted her weight; her preppy shirt fell away and revealed huge dark hollows across her stomach. Joe moved toward her to smash the pose and make her real.

Anne resisted the soft kisses on her neck and the softer hands that tried to stop her hips from gyrating. Holding herself rock still, she said, "Whores don't respond to kindness, whores rut."

Joe said, "Hush," slid his hands under her shirt and traced

soft circles on her back. Anne sighed, then caught herself and said, "Whores don't make love, whores do the dirty dog deed." Her own wordplay made her giggle and press her hands to her mouth, and Joe bit at her neck until she started to squeal uncontrollably. An upstairs voice called out, "Go, lovebirds, go!" and Anne began to cry. Joe didn't know what the tears meant, so he picked her up and carried her to the bed. Applause and catcalls rained down as he shut and bolted the door. When he turned around, Anne was naked and he was crying himself.

27

The smell of decomposing flesh hit him the second he walked in the door.

Lloyd turned to Rhonda Morrell and said, "Wait here," then shot a look at an arched entrance hall crowded with video equipment. Drawing his .45, he walked in the direction of the stench.

It was a dead man who matched Rhonda's description of Stan Klein. He was lying in the middle of a large living room filled with electrical equipment—V.C.R.s, TVs, computer terminals and video games. His corpse was drained of blood, the handle of a switchblade was extending from his stomach, and the carpet beneath him was caked thick with dried blood. A small caliber automatic was in his right hand. The knife wound spelled death by stabbing; the smell and body drainage indicated that the murder had taken place at least twenty-four hours prior. Lloyd held a handkerchief to his face and knew that this night would never be over.

He walked to Rhonda, still standing by the door. "Go identify the body. Try not to get hysterical."

"Is that what that awful smell is?"

"Smart girl."

"Am I under arrest?"

"I'm holding you as a material witness. Give me shit and I'll fabricate a felony to keep you off your back for years. You almost got me killed. Be grateful that I'm a sensitive cop."

Rhonda gave Lloyd a slow once-over. "You look spooky Really weirded out. When can I go home?"

"Later. Go identify the stiff."

Rhonda walked into the living room and let out a ladylike shriek; Lloyd found a phone in the entrance hall and dialed Hollywood Station. Dutch Peltz answered, "L.A.P.D.," and Lloyd could tell from his hollow tone that he was scared.

"It's Lloyd, Dutch. What is it?"

"*It's* fucking all coming down crazy," Dutch said. "There was a shootout on Sunset and Gardner. Both perpetrators got away, and one of them commandeered a car, then ran down one of my men with it. He died at Central Receiving. The killer escaped on foot, and the man whose car he commandeered I.D.'d him from the eyewitness sketch of the white bank robber. Two of my men raided his pad half an hour ago—the Bowl Motel on Highland. No one was there, but they found two .45 autos. Then, and I still can't believe it, there was a body found *inside a fucking church* three blocks from the motel and a half mile from the spot where the officer was hit and run. He was twenty-six, Lloyd. He had a wife and four kids and he's fucking dead!"

The news of the two dead men and Dutch's grief squeezed out Lloyd's last remaining calm. The night came down on him from all sides, and he started to weave on his feet, death stench assailing him from the living room, mass insanity over the phone line. Finally Dutch's "Lloyd! Lloyd! Lloyd, goddammit, are you there!" registered, and he was able to answer: "I don't know where the fuck I am. Listen, have any A.P.B.s been issued?"

"No. The white man signed into the motel under an obvious alias—John Smith."

Lloyd marshaled his thoughts, deciding not to add Stan Klein to the list of the night's dead. "Dutch, Fred Gaffaney and at least two of his Metro freaks are in this big, which is why no A.P.B.s have hit the air. They know, and I know, the names of the three robbers. They—"

"What!"

"Just listen, goddammit! I was one of the perps at the

shootout on Gardner. I thought I could take out the white man myself. I blew it, and he got away."

"What!"

"Don't grief me on that, goddamn you! It was the only way to do it. Have you I.D.'d the stiff at the church?"

His voice more hollow than Lloyd had ever heard it, Dutch said, "Everywhere you go there's nothing but shit. The dead man is Robert Ramon Garcia, male Mexican, age thirty-four. Is he one of the three?"

"Yes."

"Give me the two other names."

Lloyd signed his own murder indictment. "The white man is Duane Richard Rice, D.O.B. 8/16/56. The other Mexican is Joe Garcia, the dead man's brother. It's crazy out here, Dutch."

"I know it is. Largely due to you. Every single one of my men is on the streets, along with half the Rampart and Wilshire nightwatches. I've got two reservists running the station with me."

"You feel like helping me, or you feel like pouting?"

"I'll forget you said that. What do you need?"

"First, what did you get from Intelligence Division on Gaffaney?"

"Gaffaney's in deep shit in the Department," Dutch said. "Intelligence has him nailed as having bribed school officials to doctor up his son's records so he could secure an appointment to the Academy. Apparently the kid was a long-time petty thief with a lot of crazy religious beliefs. Also, Gaffaney is building up a huge interdepartmental power base—right-wing hot dogs from Metro, I.A.D. and various uniformed divisions. To what end, I don't know."

Lloyd let the information settle on him, then said, "I need a favor."

"You always need favors. I forgot to mention that right when all hell started breaking loose a guy came to the station looking for you, said he had info on the first two bank robberies. He read about you, and about the rewards, and he wants to talk. I was about to tell him to split, then one of my squad room dicks told me he had two armed robbery convictions. I've got him in a holding tank. Ask your favors quick; I want to broadcast those names."

"I want complete paper on the three names, plus Anne Vanderlinden, W.F., twenties," Lloyd said. "R&I, parole and probation department files, jail records. You've got the juice to shake the right people out of bed to get them, and you can send one of your reservists to make the run, then deliver them to my pad."

Now Dutch's voice was incredulous. "Don't you want to be on the street for this?"

Lloyd said, "No. It feels like I'm inches away from the biggest fuckup I've ever pulled, and if I hit the bricks I'll go nutso. This whole mess is so full of weird angles that if I don't figure them out I won't survive, and I just want to think. Hold that guy for me, I'll be at the station in fifteen minutes."

"What do you mean, 'you won't survive'?"

"No. Don't ask again."

Lloyd hung up and looked around for Rhonda. He found her smoking a cigarette by an open window, and said, "Come on. Don't mention Stan Klein to anybody, and you may still make a few bucks out of this."

"What are you talking about?"

"Survival."

"Whose survival?"

"That's the funny thing. I don't know."

Outside Hollywood Station, Lloyd handcuffed Rhonda to the steering column and said, "I'll be no more than half an hour. While I'm gone, think about Rice and his girlfriend, and where she'd go if she were scared."

"I think better without handcuffs."

"Too bad, I don't trust you, and with Rice on the loose you're in danger."

"That's a laugh. He didn't drag me all over town and handcuff me."

Lloyd slammed the car door and walked into the station. A uniformed reserve officer noticed him immediately, handed him a sheaf of papers and said, "Captain Peltz said to tell you that he's busy, but he sent the other reservist to get your paperwork. Here's a memo and the stats on that clown who wants to talk to you. He's in a holding cell."

Lloyd nodded and read the memo first:

> To: Det. Sgt. L. Hopkins, Rob/Hom
> From: Det. Lt. E. Hopper, West Valley Vice
>
> Sergeant—Regarding your inquiry as to vice activities of R. Hawley and J. Eggers, informers have reported that both men are long-time heavy gamblers known to utilize Valley area bookies. Hawley said to sporadically pay debts through "percentage arrangement" with blank bank checks (assumed by informant to be stolen). Different informant states that Eggers has also paid debts with blank check lots—"past six weeks or so."
>
> Hope this helps—Hopper.

Feeling *the* connection breathing down his neck, Lloyd turned to a rap sheet in Dutch's handwriting.

> Shondell Tyrone McCarver, M.N., 11/29/48. A.k.a. "Soul," a.k.a. "Daddy Soul," a.k.a. "Sweet Daddy Soul," a.k.a. "Soul King," a.k.a. "Sweet King of Soul." Conv: Poss. Dang. Drugs—(2)—6/12/68, 1/27/71. Armed Rbry—(2)—9/8/73, 7/31/77. Paroled 5/16/83—clean since—D.P.

Shaking his head, he looked at the officer and said, "Bad nigger?"

The reservist said, "More the jive type."

"Good. Crank the door in sixty seconds, then lock it again."

The officer about-faced and walked to the electrical panel, and Lloyd strode through the muster room to the jail area. Passing the framed photographs of Hollywood Division officers killed in the line of duty, he pictured another frame beside them and the station hung with black bunting. He knew he was pumping himself up with anger to fuel his interrogation, and that it wasn't working—at 2:00 a.m. on the longest night of his life, all he could drum up were the motions.

Except for some babbling from the drunk tank, the jail was quiet. Lloyd saw his man lying on the bottom bunk of a cell on the misdemeanor side of the catwalk. The door clanged open a second later, and the man shook himself awake and smiled. "I'm Sweet Daddy Soul, the patriarch of rock and roll," he said.

Lloyd stepped inside, and the door creaked shut behind him. Sizing up the man, he saw a good-natured jivehound who thought he was dangerous and might even be. "Not tonight, McCarver."

Shondell McCarver smoothed the lapels of his mohair suitcoat. "Another time, perhaps?"

Lloyd sat on the commode and took out a pen and notepad. "No. You said you've got information, and you've got a heist jacket, so I'll listen to you. But catch my interest quick."

"You know I want that reward money."

"You and everyone else. Talk."

"Some brothers I know said you was always good for some rapport."

"Cut the shit and get to it."

McCarver crossed his ankles and laced his fingers behind his head. "Guess they was wrong. How's this for starters: bet you don't know how the guys who pulled them kidnap heists snapped to the two girlfriends. That safe to say?"

Lloyd's exhaustion dropped; his head buzzed with the coming of a second mental wind. "You've got my interest. Keep talking."

"The heists was my idea," Shondell McCarver said. "Up till about two weeks ago I had a bouncer job going, a temporary gig every other week or so, two hundred scoots a night, work-ing for these people of the Eye-talian persuasion.

"The basic scene was this setup trying to re-create the sporting houses back in the old days, you know, like in New Orleans. For a c-note admission you get complimentary coke within reason, high-class whores, a shot at a few semi-pro ladies, crap game, high-stakes poker, old Ali fights on big-screen TV, fuck films, nude swimming, sauna. What—"

"Where?" Lloyd said.

"I'm getting to that," McCarver said, drawing out the words teasingly. "The spot was a big house in Topanga Can-yon. The two bank guys, Hawley and Eggers, brought their chicks to the parties. They—"

"How often were they held?"

"Every two weeks or so. Anyway, there was these mirrored bedrooms, you know, for romance. They was all rigged for sound, and one of my jobs was to listen for good info, like stock tips and the like. That's where I heard Hawley and Eggers talking to their bitches, and where I figured out Hawley was pilfering from his tellers boxes. Still got your interest, Mr. Po-liceman?"

Lloyd remembered Peter Kapek's mention of Hawley's and Eggers' large cash withdrawals. "Were parties thrown on October seventeenth and November first?"

McCarver laughed. "Sure were. I got a righteous memory for dates. How you know that?"

"Never mind, just keep talking."

"Anyhow, I heard Hawley run down his scam to his bitch. He told her that Greenbacks were left overnight at the tellers cages and—"

Lloyd interrupted: "Did you know that Greenbacks is a brand name of traveler's check?"

Slapping his knee, McCarver said, "Ain't that a riot? Shit. I read that in the paper, and it made me fuckin' glad I never got to utilize my plan. Anyhow, I think he's talkin' *cash*. He tells the bitch that he goes to the bank early on certain mornings, gloms the Greenbacks from the teller drawers, runs a transaction with a duplicate bankbook belonging to some senile old cooze with big bucks, doctors tally slips so that it balances out and looks like a cash withdrawal—to the cooze, who of course is Hawley boy.

"See, Hawley is scared, 'cause the scam only works if the cooze don't get hip to the missing bucks, and he's heard the old girl's relatives is about to have her declared noncompas mental and grab the fuckin' scoots. So Hawley is pouring his soul out to his bimbo, and, unbefuckingknowst to him—me."

Lloyd looked up from his notepad. "What about Eggers?"

McCarver said, "I'm getting to that. Anyhow, I concocted the plan that ultimately got utilized by them guys you're looking for. I staked out Hawley for days, watched him glom them Greenbacks, thinkin' they was cash, watched him do his number with the tally slips and bankbook and computer. I'm thinkin', 'Too bad there's only one of these scamsters,' when this bookie workin' the house tells me about Eggers bein' way behind on his vig. So I think, 'Gifts in a manger' and nudge the bookie to nudge Eggers into the scam that Hawley pulls. Then I start tailing Eggers, and damned if he didn't start pulling the same tricks. You dig?"

Lloyd said, "I dig. But you never saw Eggers with cash in his hands, right?"

"Right. His hands was out of sight when he did his rippin'. I just assumed that since he followed Hawley's procedure, it had to be cash."

"And it was about six weeks ago that you told the bookie to nudge Eggers?"

"Yeah. How'd you know that?"

"Never mind, keep going."

"Anyhow, I never told the Eye-talians about any of this, and I cased the kidnap part of the deal real good—the bitches' cribs, the managers' cribs, the whole shot. Then I got me a partner, then he decided to take off a liquor store and got busted. You follow so far?"

"I'm ahead of you," Lloyd said. "Wrap it up."

McCarver lit a cigarette, coughed and said, "Homeboy's a

righteous partner. A little on the impetuous side, but solid. Except that he's fat-mouth motherfucker, which ain't as bad as bein' a snitch, but still ain't good. When I read about my plan gettin' utilizized, I called Homeboy at Folsom, got through 'cause he got this cush orderly job. I said, 'Who the fuck you shoot your fat motherfuckin' mouth off to?' He says, 'Who, me?' I says, 'Yeah, you, motherfucker, 'cause whoever you blabbed to utilizized my plan, plus one other, and killed four people, includin' two cops, and there is seventy thou in reward bucks on that motherfucker's ass.'

"So . . . Homeboy tells me he talked to two paddy dudes in the High-Power Tank at the New County—Frank Ottens and Chick Geyer. I figure, righteous, those are cop killer motherfuckers. Then I back off and think, 'What if those dudes blabbed to someone else, and righteous third- or fourth- or fuckin' fifth-hand info was responsible for the utilizization of my plan?' So I call the jail, and they tell me Ottens and Geyer is still in High-Power fighting their beefs. So, big man, you find out who Ottens and Geyer blabbed to, and you find your fuckin' cop killer. Now, is that a righteous tip or a righteous tip?"

Lloyd stood up and stretched. What would have cracked the case twenty-four hours before was now stale bread. The High-Power Tank adjoined the Ding Tank, where Duane Rice was incarcerated until two weeks ago. Gordon Meyers was the night jailer there, and he had incurred Rice's wrath as a member of the overall robbery scheme or for some other reason—stale bread also, because Meyers was dead, and Rice was unlikely to live through the night. Everyone involved in the twisted mess was dead or marked for death, including himself. Thinking inexplicably of Louie Calderon's "The kid was just too scared to say no. Don't let them kill him," Lloyd looked at McCarver and said, "A righteously too late tip, but I'll give you some righteous advice: walk real soft around cops, because nothing's going to be the same with us anymore."

McCarver said, "What the fuck," and Lloyd walked out to his car and handcuffed witness. A crew of reservists were hanging black bunting on the front doors of the station as he drove away.

Pulling into his driveway a half hour later, Lloyd saw a stack of L.A. County interagency records sleeves beside his kitchen door. Killing the engine, he said to Rhonda, "You're staying with me until Rice is kill—I mean captured."

Rhonda rubbed her wrists. "What if I don't like the accommodations? You also mentioned money a while back."

Lloyd got out of the car and pointed to the door. "Later. I've got some reading to do. You sit tight while I do it, then we'll talk."

The records sleeves were thick and heavy with paper. Picking them up, Lloyd felt comforted by the bulk of the cop data. He unlocked the door, flicked on the light and motioned Rhonda inside. "Make yourself at home, anywhere downstairs."

"What about upstairs?"

"It's sealed off."

"Why?"

"Never mind."

"You're weird."

"Just sit tight, all right?"

Rhonda shrugged and started opening and closing the kitchen cabinets. Lloyd carried the sleeves into the living room and arrayed them on the coffee table, noting that the paperwork came from the L.A. County Department of Corrections, L.A. County Probation Department, County Parole Bureau and California State Adult Authority. The pages were not broken down by the names of his four suspects, and he had to first collate them into stacks—one for Duane Rice, one each for the Garcia brothers, one for Anne Vanderlinden. That accomplished, he broke them down by agency, with R&I rap sheets on top. Then, with the sounds of Rhonda's kitchen puttering barely denting his concentration, he sat back to read and think and scheme, hoping to pull cold facts into some kind of salvation.

Duane Richard Rice, quadruple cop killer, grew up in the Hawaiian Gardens Housing Project, graduated Bell High School, had a 136 I.Q. The first of his two arrests was for vehicular manslaughter. While working as a mechanic at a Beverly Hills sports car dealership, he lost control of a car he was test-driving and killed two pedestrians. He ran from the scene on foot, but turned himself in to the Beverly Hills police later that same night. Since Rice possessed no criminal record and no drugs or alcohol were involved, the judge offered a five-year prison sentence, then suspended it on the proviso that he perform one thousand hours of public service. Rice shouted obscenities at the judge, who retracted the suspension and sentenced him to five years in the California Youth Authority Facility at Soledad.

While at Soledad, Rice refused to participate in group or individual therapy, studied martial arts and worked in the facility's auto shop. He was not a disciplinary problem; he formed no discernible "close prison ties." He was not a member of the Aryan Brotherhood or other institutional race gangs and abstained from homosexual liaisons. Judged to be a "potential achiever, with high intelligence and the potential for developing into a highly motivated young adult," he was paroled after serving three years of his sentence.

Rice's parole officer considered him "withdrawn" and "potentially volatile," but was impressed with his hard work as foreman at a Midas Muffler franchise and his "complete eschewing of the criminal life-style." Thus, when Rice was subsequently arrested on one count of grand theft auto, the officer did not cite him for a parole violation, mentioning in a letter to the judge that "I believe this offender to be acting under psychological duress, deriving from his relationship with the woman with whom he was cohabitating."

Rice received a year in the county jail, was sent to the Malibu Fire Camp and evinced spectacular bravery during the Agoura brushfires. His parole officer and the judge who tried his case granted him a sentence reduction as a result of this "adjustment," and he was given three years formal county probation and released from custody.

Lloyd put the Rice records aside, and turned to the paper on the girlfriend.

Vanderlinden, Anne Atwater, white female, D.O.B. 4/21/58, Grosse Pointe, Michigan, had a file containing a scant three pages. She had been arrested twice for possession of marijuana, receiving small fines and suspended sentences, and three times for prostitution. She was given two years formal probation following her second conviction, and bought her way out of a probation violation on her third arrest by informing on a "suspected auto thief" to L.A.P.D. detectives. Shaking his head sadly, Lloyd checked the date of Anne Vanderlinden's dismissed charge against the date of Duane Rice's G.T.A. bust. Three days from the former to the latter; Vandy had snitched off the man who loved her.

The two remaining stacks of paper read like a travelogue on eerie fraternal bonding, with even eerier informational gaps. Robert Garcia, known during his losing boxing career as Bobby "Boogaloo" Garcia, the "Barrio Bleeder," had been a fight manager, the owner of a coin laundromat and a hot-dog stand, while his brother Joseph had his occupations listed as "asst. fight manager," "asst. laundry operator" and "fry cook." The brothers had been arrested only once, together, for one count of burglary, although they were suspected of having perpetrated others. Once convicted, they were sentenced to nine months county time together, and served it together, at Wayside Honor Rancho. At Wayside, the brothers' antithetical personalities rang out loud and clear. Lloyd read through a half dozen reports by correctional officers and learned that Robert Garcia was disciplined for attempting to bribe jailers into placing his brother in the "soft" tank where youthful inmates who might be subject to sexual abuse were housed, and, that once those bribes were rebuffed, he assaulted two prisoners who spoke jokingly of Joe as "prime butthole." Released from the disciplinary tank after ten days confinement, the Barrio Bleeder then beat up his own brother, telling a psychiatrist that he did it "so Little Bro would get a little bit tougher." When Bobby was again placed in solitary, Joe set his mattress on fire so that *he* would be placed on the disciplinary tier, within shouting distance of the brother who protected and abused him.

Those facts were eerie, but the absence of facts on the brothers' last five years was even stranger. Based on Christine Confrey's description and R&I stats, the late Robert Garcia was obviously the "Shark," yet he had no arrests for sex offenses, nor was a penchant for sexual deviation mentioned anywhere in his file. Both he and his brother were placed on formal probation after their kick-out from Wayside, and reported dutifully until their probationary term was concluded. Yet there was no mention of employment for either man. Only one fact made sense: listed as the Garcias' "known associate" was Luis Calderon. Lloyd thought the burgeoning fed investigation into Calderon right before the bank slaughter sent everything topsy-turvy. The connection was there, just waiting to be made.

But it wasn't, because there was a correctness, a sense of inevitability about this spiral of death. Lloyd shivered with the thought, then took the mental ball and ran with it, wrapping up the odds and ends of the case into a tight but anticlimactic package.

After killing the officer with the commandeered car, Rice traveled by foot to the vicinity of the Bowl Motel, came across Bobby Garcia on the street, where he could not safely take him out, then followed him to the church and killed him. Why? The reason was meaningless. Joe Garcia, the "tall," "sweet-looking" Mexican who bank witnesses said "didn't shoot anyone" was also the "*puto*" Mexican that Rice told Rhonda took off with his girlfriend from Stan Klein's pad. The only loose strand in the fabric was Klein. Rice was there to grab his woman, presumably armed with a silencered .45. Yet Klein was killed with a knife. Joe Garcia was there, too, but he did not read, sound, feel, or in any way play as a killer.

Again, Louie Calderon's words echoed: "Don't let them kill

him." Lloyd put down the paperwork and called out, "Rhonda, come here."

Rhonda walked in. "Time to talk money?" she said.

Nodding, Lloyd watched her sit down in Janice's favorite left-behind chair. "That's right. Questions and answers, but first there's this: if other police officers question you, you don't mention Stan Klein's name, or anything about this "*puto* Mexican" you told me about. Got it?"

"Got it, but why?"

"I'm not sure, it's just an ace in the hole I'm working with."

"What are you talking about?"

"Never mind. First question: when Rice called you today, did he mention this Mexican guy by name, or anything else about him, or where he thought he and Anne Vanderlinden might have gone?"

"That's easy: no, no and no. All he said was 'This *puto* Mexican took off with Vandy and you've got to help me find them.' "

"All right. You said Rice wanted you to pick up some money. Did he say where?"

"No."

"He just assumed that since you and Anne worked outcall together—"

"We didn't work Silver Foxes together. I've never met her. It's just that we move in some of the same circles, and know some of the same people, and we've both tricked with a lot of music industry biggies. Besides, Vandy isn't working Silver Foxes now. She quit two months ago, in October."

"How are you so sure of the date?"

"Well . . . I got Duane the information about Vandy and Stan Klein on my lonesome, and I thought if he paid for that, then maybe he'd pay me for a list of all the clients Vandy tricked with regularly, so last week, when I was in the office, I looked at her old file and made a list. I was going to sell it to Duane tonight, you know . . ."

"Exploit his jealousy?"

"I wouldn't call it that."

"Do you think if she were scared and broke she'd run to any of the men on the list?"

"I'd make book on it. There's one guy, a producer, who used to use Vandy for theme parties, paid her top dollar. He's a really good bet."

"How much for your silence and the list?"

Rhonda took a piece of paper from her bodice. "Duane's bought and paid for, right? I mean, you guys are going to kill him sooner or later, right?"

"Smart girl. How much?"

"An even thousand?"

Lloyd got his checkbook from the dining room table and wrote Rhonda Morrell a check for one thousand dollars. When he handed it to her, she smiled nervously and said, "Still want me to stick around?"

Lloyd looked away from the smile. "Get out," he said.

The door was opened and shut quietly, and high heels tapped toward the street. Lloyd picked up the piece of paper that Rhonda had left, saw a list of four names, addresses and phone numbers, then looked at *his* phone. He was reaching for it when an internal voice said "*Think*" and made him stop. Obeying, he sat down in Janice's chair, still warm from the Silver Fox.

He was doomed, because he could not kill Duane Rice in cold blood. Rice was doomed from all sides, and Jesus Fred Gaffaney was doomed within the Department. He would undoubtedly offer up his evidence on the Watts riot killing as a tactic to save himself—a legendary L.A.P.D. detective as youthful murderer was prime media meat, and the Department would pay heavily to stonewall the revelation. If the high brass capitulated, they would be looking to save face by every means possible, and *he* would be dismissed without the early pension deal now being offered, while Jesus Fred himself would keep his captaincy and get shunted to some safe, shithole outpost where a new generation of witch-hunters would keep him under wraps until his retirement or death. If Gaffaney went public with his information, as civilian or policeman, the grand jury would either indict him or not indict him, but either way, Janice and the girls would know, and his local celebrity would be exploited to full advantage.

Lloyd thought of the other victims: the families of the dead cops, Hawley and Eggers and their disintegrating marriages; Sally Issler and Chrissy Confrey, dropped like hot rocks amidst desperate declarations of future fidelity. The bank teller and her loved ones, and the shitload of harmless street people who were going to be bait for thousands of cops in an impotent rage, because three of their own got taken out, and there was nothing they could do about it.

Feeling *buried*, Lloyd thought of Watts and the fatuous idealism that had carried him through the riot and into the Job. He had convinced himself that he wanted to protect innocence, when he really wanted to crawl through sewers in search of adventure; he had sold himself a bill of goods about the just rule of law, when he really wanted to revel in the darkness he pretended to despise, with his family and women as safety buffers when the dark ate him up.

To take the edge of failure off his admissions, Lloyd tried to bring to mind the most tangible evidence of his success—the faces of innocents spared grief as a result of his hard-charger actions. None came, and he knew it was because their well-being was only a rationalization for his desire to plunder.

The last admission shined a spotlight on the survival plan that was forming in his mind all night. Lloyd laughed out loud when he realized he couldn't figure it out for one simple reason—he thought *he* was the one he wanted to save. Knowing now that he wasn't, he picked up the phone and punched a painfully familiar number.

"Hollywood Station, Captain Peltz speaking."

Dutch's voice was stretched thin, but it was not the grief-stricken voice of two hours before. Trying to sound panicky and apologetic, Lloyd said, "Dutchman, we're in deep shit."

"One of your rare dumb statements, Lloyd. What do you want?"

"Any response on the A.P.B.s yet?"

"No, but there's roadblocks and chopper patrols all over Hollywood, and we've got Rice's vehicle, a '78 Trans Am, purchased five days ago. It was parked a block from where you guys shot it out. If he's still in the area, he's dead meat. Did you get—"

"I gave you a wrong name, Dutch. Joe Garcia wasn't in on the heists or the killings. I can't go into it, but the third man is a guy named Klein. He's dead. Rice killed him yesterday."

Dutch's hollow voice returned in force: "Oh, Jesus God, *no*."

"Oh, Jesus God, *yes*. And listen: Gaffaney and his freaks had his name and package for hours before the bulletin was issued, and they don't give a fuck if he's innocent or—"

"Lloyd, all the stats on the robbers say one white man, two Mex—"

"Goddammit, listen! Rice is the white man, Bobby Garcia is Mexican, Klein, the other dead man, is tall and Latin-looking. And he's dead. All we've got is Rice on the loose, and he's a pro car thief and probably out of the area."

"How sure are you of all this?"

Lloyd tried to sound quietly outraged. "I'm the best, Dutch. We both know it, and I know Joe Garcia is innocent. Do you want to help me, or do you want one of your men to gun him down?"

A long silence came over the line. Lloyd imagined Dutch weighing the odds of innocent lives intersecting with trigger-happy cops. Finally he said, "Goddamn you, what do you want?"

A wrench hit Lloyd's stomach; he knew it came from manipulating his best friend with an outright lie. "Garcia is most likely running with Rice's girlfriend," he said. "A blond white woman in her mid-twenties. Gaffaney's hot dogs don't know about her, because I just found out about her myself. The Garcia brothers have got no family, and the one K.A. in their file is a gun dealer already in custody. I'm assuming they'll run to *her* friends. I've got a list of names and addresses of four likelies. I want surveillances on the four pads, experienced officers. Tell them to apprehend Garcia and the woman without force."

Another long silence, then Dutch's voice, cold and all business: "I'll implement it. I'll direct four unmarked units to the pads and have them hold tight until 0800, then I'll bring in a fresh shift when the daywatch comes on. We're talking *obvious* unmarked cars, though. There's no time to have the men come to the station for their civilian wheels. And I want a full report on this guy Klein—fast."

Lloyd picked up Rhonda's list and read it off slowly. "Marty Cutler, 1843 Gretna Green, Brentwood; Roll Your Own Productions, 4811 Altera Drive, Benedict Canyon. That has to be a house—it's all residential down there. Another no name address—Plastic Fantastic Rock and Roll, 2184 Hillcrest Drive, Trousdale Estates—that's also all residential. The last one is Tucker Wilson, 403 Mabery, Santa Monica Canyon. Got it?"

"Got it. These are all fat city addresses. Wh—"

"Rice's girlfriend is a class outcall hooker. These are former customers of hers. My source put an asterisk after the Trousdale address, and she said some 'exec producer' was an especially good bet. You take it from there."

"I will. What are you going to do?"

Lloyd said, "Figure out a way to cover a lot of asses," and hung up, looking at the door in front of him and the phone by his right hand. He knew that the door meant a trip to Stan Klein's house, wiping it free of possible Joe Garcia prints, then firing his .45 into Klein's body and retrieving the spent rounds. If the stiff moldered for a few more days, then the M.E. who performed the autopsy would not be able to determine whether the knife and gunshot wounds had occurred concurrently. The .45 quality holes and slugs straight through the body and floor to the probable dirt foundation would, when unfound, be attributed to the gun of Duane Richard Rice. It was an evidential starting point, and if maggots ate away Klein's face, a death picture could not be shown to the bank eyewitnesses. There might be no other Klein photos available, and Joe

Garcia's picture, most likely a six-year-old mugshot from his burglary bust, might not be recognized. If he could plea-bargain Louie Calderon into changing his testimony and make sure Joe Garcia got out of town without being busted *or* standing in a lineup, "Little Bro" might survive.

Still looking at the door, Lloyd knew that it meant ending the night earning McManus' "necrophile" tag, desecrating a corpse, then crawling in the dirt. It *had* to be done, but the more he stared at the door, the more it loomed as an ironclad barrier.

So he picked up the phone, hoping his wife's lover wouldn't be roused from sleep and answer. His hands trembled as he tapped the numbers, and when he got a tone he was sobbing.

After the third ring, a recorded message came on: "Hi, this is Janice Hopkins. The girls and I have taken our act on the road, but we should be returning before Christmas." There was a slight pause, then Penny's voice: " 'The woods are lovely, dark and deep.' Leave a message at the beep."

Unable to speak through his tears, Lloyd hung up and called the number again and again, until the repetition of the message lulled him past weeping, and he fell asleep with the phone in his hands.

28

With the bag of money clutched to his chest, Rice beat a footpath to Silver Foxes and the Trans Am, stumbling through dark backyards, scaling fences and rolling into a camouflage ball every time a chopper light came anywhere near him. Roadblocks on Sunset to his north and Fountain to his south fenced him in, and as he crouched low and sprinted across one residential street after another, he could see cars being searched on the wide expressways.

But here, in a womb of old houses with backyards and apartment buildings connected by block-long cement walls, he was invisible and safe. The cops expected him to be on wheels. In the three hours since blundering into Sharkshit Bobby and blowing him away he'd stuck to the dark like a night animal, working his way deeper into the danger zone, taking shelter in shadows and rest breaks every three blocks. His head still ached from the cold-cock and his vision shimmied when light hit his eyes, but the perk/dexie speedballs he'd eaten just before the one-on-one with the cop kept the pain down and juice in his system. He could still function, and when he got to his car, he could still drive.

And he could still think.

Coming out of a long driveway, Rice turned his brain into a map and calculated two blocks to Silver Foxes. If his luck was holding, his registration papers wouldn't have hit the D.M.V. computer, the fuzz wouldn't know the Trans Am was his, and the outcall office window he'd blown to bits would give him a shot at some kind of file on Vandy—and the rock sleazos she might have run to. If the office was under guard, he was still armed for pig with the .45.

The map thinking gave him a new jolt of juice. Getting itchy to *be* there, he loosened his grip on the bag in order to regrip it for a straight run at his target. When it felt lighter to his touch, he checked the bottom and saw a big hole. Sticking his hand in, he saw that more than half the money had fallen out.

Catching himself about to scream, Rice clutched the bag with all his strength and beelined, running across the street and sidewalk, back through another driveway and yard. Ignoring a copter light scanning only three houses away, he hurtled an ivy-covered chain fence and ran out to the street. He was about to keep going when a flash of lavender dented his wobbly vision and registered as *home*.

Rice let his eyes trawl Gardner Avenue for danger signs. There was no one on either side of the street, and no cop cars, marked or unmarked. Squinting at the whore building, he saw a black tarpaulin covering the demolished front window. Flipping an imaginary brain switch marked "caution," he placed the money bag on the ground and memorized its location, then took the .45 from his waistband. Catching his breath, he walked to Silver Foxes.

There were no lights on in the four-flat. Rice checked the luminous dial of his watch, saw that it was 3:40 and did a mental run-through: the whoremasters hobnobbing with the fuzz after the shooting, getting workmen to do a quick fix-up job until the window could be repaired properly, getting rid of the incriminating shit, then getting out. The thought of no files brought him to the point of screaming, and he ran to the tarpaulin, grabbed the right-side fastenings with both hands and pulled.

The tarp came loose and crashed to the lawn. Rice stepped in the window, found the wall light and turned it on.

The dispatch room was a bullet-wasted ruin, big chunks of white wall ripped out, the plastic desk dinged and cracked from ricochets. Remembering a Rolodex, Rice scanned the room unsuccessfully for it, then went through the desk drawers. Finding nothing but blank paper and rolls of film, he stood up to think and saw an old-fashioned filing cabinet just inside the bathroom door:

All three drawers were locked. Standing to one side, Rice closed the door on the barrel of his .45, so that just the silencer was inside the bathroom. He fired seven times at the cabinet, and soft plops went off like muffled thunder. The last shots reverberated off the metal surface and tore the door in half; through muzzle smoke he could see the cabinet on its side spilling manila folders.

Digging into them, Rice saw names typed on side tabs, and that the files had spilled out in close to alphabetical order. Tearing through the R's, S's and T's, he felt his bowels loosen. Then "Vanderlinden, Annie" was in his hands, and he didn't know if it was good or bad, so he turned off the light and ran with it out to the Trans Am.

But it wasn't there.

Land mines, booby traps, snipers and werewolf-faced dogs flashed through his mind, and he hit the ground like soldiers in the million old movies he'd seen on TV. Eating curb grass instead of dirt, he waited for machine-gun ack-ack and managed to slide Vandy's file into his pants along with his .45. When no attack came, he did a squat run over to the money bag and picked it up, then walked slowly toward the Fountain Avenue roadblock—the eye of his hurricane.

Staying in the shadows of front porches and shrubbery, he saw the cordon setup come into focus: north-south traffic on Gardner was blocked off, with two cops standing at the ready to pass innocent cars through and fire on ones that rabbited. East-west traffic on Fountain was being inspected the same way, but only at stoplights. Since the nearest lights were three blocks away on the east and two on the west, all he had to do was get south of Fountain, steal a car and *roll*.

Rice eyed the barricade and cops twenty yards away. The roadblocks had probably been set up right after he plowed the pig on Formosa. They were figuring him for a car thief and had zipped the area up tight as a drum. If they found Bobby

Sharkshit, a block off the Boulevard, they were probably knocking down doors up there. Sunset and Fountain were sealed, and probably Hollywood and Franklin. They would not have the men to hit the streets further south, and they probably figured he couldn't have made it that far anyway.

Rice swallowed and secured his only three possessions: the gun, the file and the paper bag of money. Feeling them bonded to him, he lowered himself to the ground and rolled off the corner house lawn to the sidewalk and into the street, a dark, pavement-eating dervish. Catching sight of the cops with their backs to him, he kept rolling, gravel digging into his cheeks and shredding the bag until a trail of cash drifted in his wake. He rolled until he hit the opposite sidewalk, then elbowed his way over the curb and rolled until soft grass kissed his gouged face. When he finally felt safe enough to stand up, he was on the beautiful front lawn of a beautiful little house, midway down a beautiful little block, with no barricade at its southern intersection and plenty of beautiful cars parked within stealing distance.

29

O n the doorstep of the big house, Anne smoothed Joe's shirt front and said, "You look like a *real* street person. I'll tell my friends you're a producer, that you're scouting Chicano groups in the Barrio. Just listen to the music, and you'll have a good time."

Punk rock boomed inside. Joe took a long look at the spectacular view: the Strip winding to the east, Beverly Hills below them, glow from swimming pools the only light. "I don't want to have a good time," he said. "We're down to twenty scoots, and we need a traveling stake. Just remember that."

Anne said, "You got it, tough guy," and put out her cigarette on an Astroturf mat embossed with "If You Don't Rock, Don't Knock." She took a deep breath, then started in on her signature boogie and pushed the door open.

Following a pace behind, Joe thought he'd been transported back to Lincoln Heights in the sixties, when the vatos and the hippies were waging war, and one side of North Broadway was bodegas and poolrooms, the other side a twenty-four-hour-a-day light show/love-in/dope-in. While Anne bebopped into the scene, he hung back and eyeballed for details to prove that it was '84, not '68, and he wasn't having a shock-induced acid flashback.

The whole downstairs was a pressed-together mass of people in costume—men in full-drape zoot suits and Nazi uniforms, women in gangster moll dresses and Girl Scout outfits. Groups of gangsters and molls slam-danced into Nazis and scouts, while colored lights blipped from the ceiling and different rock videos flashed on screens hung to the four walls. The refrain "Go down go down go down go down" blasted from quadrophonic speakers, and Joe felt his head reel as he scoped out Godzilla attacking Tokyo and Marlon Brando tooling on a Harley hog while caped musicians genuflected into his exhaust. The other screens were out of focus, but he could catch people in weird makeup fucking and sucking. A conga line of gangsters were facing off against a trio of goose-stepping Nazis, who were kicking molls and scouts out of their way in the direction of a circle of amyl nitrate sniffers. And preppy Anne cut a path through all of it, screeching, "Where's Mel? Where's Mel?"

Knowing she was stone '84, Joe stood on his tiptoes and followed her bobbing pink sweater, keeping his head down as he pushed past partyers, hoping they wouldn't see his face reflected in the lights and know how scared he was. At the far side of the room he saw Anne break free and talk to a guy in a butler's outfit, who pointed her down the hall. Slipping out of the crowd himself, he caught a glimpse of Anne entering a darkly lit room.

Joe walked toward the door. When he was just outside it, he heard Anne pleading: "Just two hundred, Mel. My squeeze and I have to leave L.A."

"You'll blow it on blow, Annie," a coarse male voice said. "And I thought you were with Stan K. I know for a fact he ain't hurting—I bought some vids off him last week."

"Stan and I broke up, Mel. It was sort of . . . quick. My new guy and I *have* to leave. You remember Duane?"

"Sure. Disco Duane the discount car king. Your squeeze before Klein before your current bimbo. You see a pattern there, sweetie?"

"Mel, he's crazy, and he's after me!"

"I don't blame him; you're a class act. Third class, but class nonetheless. Sweetie, if I give you money you'll just get coked and be broke again quicksville. There's complimentary outside. Have some."

Anne screeched, "I popped some strange stuff I found, and it's still on! I don't need blow, I need money!"

Mel laughed. "You've got to earn it."

"I know," Anne said. "I know."

Joe walked away from the door, wondering why he felt betrayed—Anne was a one-hour stand at best. Retreating toward the back of the house, the reason grabbed him by the balls. She's your witness. She saw you kill a man and steal a car and drive a stick shift. She doesn't know about you being dominated by Bobby. She thinks you're as bad-ass as Duane Rice.

Coming to a small room next to the kitchen, Joe looked in and saw a guy watching TV with the sound off. The guy was strumming an electric guitar while chortling at a beer ad, and Joe got another whiff of the bad old sixties. Then double stone '84 hit the TV, and he knew it was hallucinogenic.

Bobby was on the screen, wearing gloves and trunks, crouched in his "Boogaloo" stance. Joe ran to the TV and fumbled the volume dial; the guy put down the guitar and blurted, "Hey, man, I want it that way!" Joe got the sound on just as Bobby the boxer dissolved into a shot of paramedics carrying a sheet-covered stretcher out of a church.

" . . . and Garcia is the second person to be murdered in the Hollywood area tonight. His body was discovered inside a Catholic church on Las Palmas and Franklin, half a mile from the spot where an L.A.P.D. officer was hit and run by a man in a stolen car. Police spokesmen have said that there may be a link to Monday's West L.A. bank robbery that left four dead. Meanwhile, a massive—"

The TV blipped to another beer ad—"This one's for you, no matter what you're doing and you"—and Joe saw that the guitar guy had hit a remote-control button. "This one's for you!" rang out nonhallucinogenically, and he knew it was Bobby's epitaph. He grabbed the guitar from the guy's lap and stalked with it back to the party.

Gangsters, molls, Nazis and scouts were arranged in a circle in the middle of the living room. The video screens were blank, and the strobes were replaced by normal lighting. Mel's coarse voice rose from inside the circle: "Ladies and jelly beans, Little Annie Vandy, dirty, raunchy, coked-out and randy, does the too-hep dance of the dirty prep!"

Holding the guitar by the neck, Joe used the business end as a prod and poked his way into the circle. Anne was there, attempting to gyrate and pull off her sweater at the same time. Her eyes were glazed, and her whole body twitched. Mel, standing beside her in tennis whites, was snapping his fingers.

"This one's for you!" and the shot of Bobby in his leopard-skin trunks gave Joe the necessary guts. He roundhoused the guitar at Mel's head, knocking him into a line of zoot suiters and Nazis, then swung an overhand shot that grazed helmets and snap-brim fedoras before catching the host in the neck. Mel hit the floor, and the partygoers separated and moved backward. Joe saw that they weren't frightened or shocked, but that they were digging it, and that Anne was running for the door.

Holding the guitar/weapon by the tuning pegs, he stuck it out at arm's length and spun around and around on a tiny foot axis, moving into the crowd, assailing them with glancing blows that set off a chain reaction of shrieks, squeals and bursts of applause. As the partygoers gave him more and more space, the applause became thunderous. Joe felt a queasy vertigo, and realized that the sleazebags loved him.

Screaming "Bobby!" he hurled the guitar into the middle of them and ran out the door. Reeling across the lawn toward a speck of pink down the street, he thought he saw an unmarked fuzz car parked in the shadows. Feeling invulnerable, he flipped it the bird and ran until his preppy partner was only a few feet away. Slowing to a walk, he caught up with her and tapped her shoulder. When she turned and looked at him with Twilight Zone eyes, he gasped, "I ain't no fucking musician. I ain't no fucking rock and roll fool."

30

Sunlight on his face forced Lloyd awake. The telephone fell from his lap, and he bent over to pick it up. Remembering Dutch's promised surveillance deployment, he put the receiver to his ear and started to call the Hollywood Station number. Then three little clicks came over the line instead of a dial tone, and the phone fell from his hands.

Bugged.

Gaffaney.

Lloyd ran outside and looked up and down the block. There were no vans on the street, and no other vehicles large enough to hold a mobile bugging apparatus. The tap was stationary and had to originate in a nearby dwelling.

Eye trawling, Lloyd saw his familiar landscape of two-story houses and apartment buildings turn menacing. His own small Colonial seemed suddenly vulnerable, surrounded by potential monsters. Then the most likely monster caught his attention and made him wince: the old Spanish-style building next door, recently converted to condos.

Lloyd ran into the entrance vestibule and checked the mailboxes. Only one unit—7—was without a name. He walked down the hallway, feeling his rage escalating as the numbers increased, hoping for a flimsy door and another shot at Sergeant Wallace D. Collins. Finding a solid doorway with a Mickey Mouse lock, he took a credit card from his wallet, slipped it into the runner crack and jiggled the knob. The door opened, and he entered a musty apartment furnished with only a desk holding electrical equipment.

Calling out "Collins," Lloyd reached for his .45, then flinched at the simple reflex and what it meant. When no sounds answered his call, he moved to the desk and examined the setup.

It was a simple tapper to outside wires hookup, with a tape recorder attached to record calls. A red light glowed on the panel by the "Remote Receiver" button, and a green light and the number 12 flashed on and off under the switch marked "Messages Received." Shuddering, Lloyd pushed the "Rewind" button and watched the tape spool spin. When it stopped, he hit "Play." "Hollywood Station, Captain Peltz speaking" filled the empty room, bouncing off the walls like a deadpan death decree.

Lloyd pushed the "Off" button. Gaffaney and his freaks had word on the surveillances and had listened to him sob to the inanimate voices of his wife and favorite daughter, and there was nothing he could do to turn it around.

Turning off the recorder and pulling the plug on the bugging device made the powerless feeling worse. Lloyd walked home. The phone was ringing, and he picked up the receiver like it was something about to explode.

"Yes?"

"Dutch, Lloyd."

"And?"

"And you owe me a report, and that outcall place on Gardner was broken into last night. The files were gone through, and there's fresh large-caliber gunshot holes in the walls, and they had to have come from a silencered piece, because two of my men were stationed at a roadblock half a block away. A Ford LTD was reported stolen on the adjoining block, and there's no reports from the first surveillance shift. I just dispatched daywatch units to relieve them, so that's covered. *And*—"

Lloyd hung up. Listening to Dutch's angry litany had been

like watching two trains heading toward each other on the same track, both on locked-in automatic pilot. All he could do now was patrol the wreckage and hope for survivors.

31

Rice steered the LTD through the winding roads of Trousdale Estates. His vision was going blurry again, and he had to hold Vandy's file up to right in front of his eyes in order to read the address. Driving with one hand, he remembered his first three possibilities—big dark houses with fuzzmobiles parked across the street. If he hadn't given each pad a slow-around-the-block circuit, he'd be dead. This approach had to be just as cautious.

By squinting until tears came into his eyes, he was able to pick out Hillcrest. He tried to make his brain into a map like he did in Hollywood, then flashed that that only worked when you had some idea where you were. Slowing to a crawl, he squinted for street signs. There weren't any; Trousdale was strictly for people who knew where they were going. He was about to scrounge the glove compartment for a street atlas when an unmarked Matador passed him in the opposite direction.

So Plastic Fantastic had to be nearby. Rice drove slowly, watching the Matador hazily disappear in his rearview mirror. Straining to read house numbers was futile, making the blurring worse and causing head pounding and stomach cramps on top of it. Pulling to the curb, he got out and walked.

His legs were wobbly, but he was able to move in a straight line. Thinking in a straight line was harder, and he kept wondering why the cop car had split, giving him a clean shot.

Finally he gave up thinking and kept walking. The front lawns he was passing looked soft and cushiony, and every time the green shined through his tear blur he started to yawn. Reaching into his shirt pocket for the last of the speed, he saw that he'd already swallowed it, and snapped that squinting at addresses from the sidewalk was no better than from the car, and twice as dangerous. He was about to go back to the LTD when strangely dressed people started walking across an especially beautiful stretch of grass. He cut over to meet them, and they slid past him in a jet stream that reminded him of taillights on a freeway at night.

He grabbed at their shadows and spoke to what he could see of their faces: "Vandy Vanderlinden, you know her? You seen her?" He said it a dozen times, and got nothing but hoots and catcalls in return. Then the people were gone, and there was green grass in all directions. Rice heard breathing in front of him, and rubbed his eyes so he could see who he was talking to.

The absence of tears gave him back most of his sight, and his eyes honed in on two big men in Windbreakers. When he saw that they were aiming shotguns at him, he reached for the .45. The butts of their weapons crashed into his head just as he remembered he'd left his piece in the car.

He was on the main drag of Hawaiian Garbage, running red lights on a dare, trying to break his old night record of nine straight. Everything was dark red and very fast, and he knew he could go on forever. Everything was also very warm, getting warmer as the string of reds extended. Then everything went cold, and his eyes were forced open and someone was wiping water from his face. He knew he was standing, that he was being held upright. His old 20/20 snapped in on scrub bushes, dirt and a cement embankment that stank of chemicals. He knew immediately that he was at Suicide Hill.

A fuzz type in a cheapo suit stepped in front of him, blotting out his view of the terrain. The grip on his arms tightened. Rice saw a weird lapel pin on the fuzz type's jacket and a .357

Python in his right hand, and knew he was going to die. He tried to think up a suitable wisecrack, but "She was a stone heartbreaker" came out instead. *And I loved her* was about to come out, but three slugs from the magnum hit him first.

32

Lloyd waited in the third-floor attorney room of the Main County Jail. He had a perjury script in his jacket pocket, Stan Klein's rap sheet in one hand, Louie Calderon's arrest report in the other. Klein had two convictions for possession of marijuana back in the early seventies, and Likable Louie had been booked for assault on a police officer. So far, the survivor patrol was surviving—at least on the basis of planning strategies and circumstantial facts. And the more he looked at Klein's mug shot, the more he resembled Joe Garcia.

A jailer ushered Calderon into the room and pointed him toward the chair across the table from Lloyd. His face was bruised and stitched from the Metro beating, but he walked steadily, and his soft brown eyes were clear. He looked like a man capable of making smart snap decisions.

Lloyd stood up and stuck out his hand; Calderon sat down without grasping it. "What do you want?" he said.

Lloyd slid Stan Klein's mug shot over to him. "I want to save Joe Garcia's ass from the gas chamber and help you beat your assault beef. Do you know this man?"

Calderon glanced at the snapshot and shook his head. "No. Who is he?"

"He's the third member of the robbery gang. His name is Stan Klein, a.k.a. 'Stan Man.' He's taking the fall for Joe Garcia, and he's a longtime known associate of yours. *Comprende*, homeboy?"

Calderon narrowed his eyes. "He gonna lie down for a frame?"

Drawing a finger across his throat, Lloyd said, "He's dead. Have you made a statement to anyone here or back at Rampart?"

"No. I just kicked loose with the names. You should know—you were there. If this joker Klein is eighty-six, how you gonna make him for the heists? And what the fuck do you *want*?"

Savoring Likable Louie's wariness, Lloyd said, "Rice killed Klein. Bobby Garcia is dead, shot by Rice last night. Joe and Rice are still out there. Rice won't last much longer, but Joe's got a chance. Here's the pitch: I give you a little fact sheet on Klein, you memorize it. You shut your mouth until you get word that Rice is dead. I know he's a smart guy, but the heat is huge, and no cop is going to let him see due process. When he's dead, you talk to the D.A.'s investigators, who are going to start hounding your ass as soon as I submit my report to them. You tell them that you sold the hardware to Rice, and that he told you that he was forming a gang—him, Bobby Garcia and Klein. Got it?"

Calderon leaned forward. "What's in it for *me*, and what's in it for *you*?"

Leaning forward himself, Lloyd said, "Louie, there's a lot of dead people out there, and most of them are cops, and you supplied the guns that killed them. You're dead and buried. The feds have got your number, the regular L.A.P.D. and the freak cops have got it, I've got it. Bobby's dead, and Rice is as good as dead, and the D.A. is going to look for someone to crucify on this thing, and it's going to be you."

Pale now, Calderon plucked at his stitches until blood trickled out. When he saw what he was doing, he stopped and stammered, "Y-y-yeah, b-b-but what do you *want*?"

Lloyd said, "To see you and Joe get out of this alive. Here's the rest of the pitch. I've got a little scenario for you to memorize before you talk to the D.A. How you fingered Joe Garcia because he stiffed you on some burglary goods, stuff like that. You play it right, and the D.A. and his boys will buy your story. And I go to the D.A. and tell him how those Metro bulls beat the confession out of you, and I clean all the incriminating shit out of your pad, and I get Nate Steiner to defend you if you go to trial, which you probably won't, because the D.A. will not want me to testify in court against other officers. I'd lay three to one that if you cooperate with me, you'll walk."

Calderon slammed the tabletop with clenched fists. "Hopkins, nobody does something like that for nothing. What do you fucking *want*!"

Smiling, Lloyd took the survival script from his pocket and laid it on the table. "I don't want anything. If you're as smart as I think you are, you'll believe me."

He stood up and stuck out his hand, and this time Calderon grasped it and said, "Crazy Lloyd Hopkins, Jesus Christ."

Lloyd laughed. "I'm no savior. One more thing: have you got any idea where Joe would run to if he figured the heat was off?"

Likable Louie thought for a moment, then said, "The guitar shop on Temple and Beaudry. He's sort of an amateur musician, and sooner or later he'll show up there." He put the two pieces of paper in his shirt pocket and added, "Memorize, then flush."

Lloyd buzzed for the jailer to return. On his way out the door, he pointed a cocked-gun finger at Calderon and said, "Support your local police."

Now the shitwork.

Lloyd drove to the Western Costume Company and purchased a high-quality black wig and full beard, then drove to Stan Klein's Mount Olympus villa. A fresh morning newspaper indicated that the pad was untampered with since last night's prowling with Rhonda. Steeling himself with a deep breath and a handkerchief around his nose, he picked the lock and walked in. The smell was awful, but not overpowering. Lloyd gave the corpse a cursory glance, then donned gloves and went to work.

First he found the central heating and turned the temperature up to eighty-five, then he stripped to the waist and wiped all the downstairs touch and grab surfaces, visualizing the

Klein/Rice/Garcia/Vanderlinden confrontation all the while, finally deciding that musician Joe never made it to the upper floor. The heat and the increased odor of decomposition it created were oppressive, and he gave up his wiping after a peremptory run-through, leaving the video gadgets surrounding Klein's body alone.

With potential Garcia latents in all probability eliminated, Lloyd tossed the house for photographs of Stan Klein. Drenched in sweat, he opened drawers and tore through dressers; checked the bureaus in all three bedrooms. The upstairs yielded a half dozen Polaroids that looked recent, and the living room two framed portrait photos. Lloyd placed them by the banister, then took a pen and notebook paper from his jacket and jogged up to the master bedroom to write.

With the door shut and the air-conditioning on full, he wrote for three hours, detailing his investigation of the first two robbery/kidnaps, and Captain John McManus' assigning of him to the Pico-Westholme robbery/homicides. This account was factual. The rest of the report comprised a companion piece to his script for Louie Calderon, and stated how Calderon, under physical duress, gave the names Duane Rice, Bobby Garcia and Joe Garcia to Sergeants W. D. Collins and K. R. Lohmann, later partially recanting his statement to him, stating truthfully that Stanley Klein was the "third man," and that he had named Joe Garcia for revenge on an old criminal grievance. Omitting mention of Rhonda Morrell, he concluded by stating that he had discovered Stan Klein's body, and that a scrap of paper beside the corpse led him to Silver Foxes and his still unaccounted-for shootout with Duane Rice. Attributing his delay in reporting the body to a desire to "remain mobile and assist in the active investigation," Lloyd signed his name and badge number, then sent up a prayer for lackluster forensic technicians to aid him in his lies.

The smell was now unbearable.

Lloyd turned off the air-conditioning and heat, then went downstairs and put on his shirt and jacket. Seeing that the body had bloated at the stomach and that the cheeks had rotted through to the gums, he tossed the wig and mustache at the pile of video tapes, then found a plugged-in stereo and turned on the FM full blast. The noise covered the three desecration gunshots with ease, and he forced himself to look at the damage. As he hoped, the entry wounds got lost in the overall decomposition. Knowing he couldn't bear to crawl under the house for the expended rounds, Lloyd turned off the music and sent up another prayer—this one a general mercy plea. Then he got out, hyperventilating when fresh, sane air hit his lungs.

Now the loose ends.

Lloyd drove to Hollywood Station. In the parking lot, he put the report in an envelope and wrote *Captain Arthur F. Peltz* on the front, then left it with the desk officer, who told him that there was no word on the whereabouts of Duane Richard Rice, and that the dragnet was still in full force.

The funereal air of the station was claustrophobic. From a street pay phone, Lloyd called the office of Nathan Steiner, Attorney at Law, and asked for a ballpark figure on a murder one defense. Steiner's head clerk said 40K minimum. Hanging up, Lloyd figured that with a "police discount" he could swing it.

Now the scary part.

Lloyd fed all the change in his pockets to the phone and dialed Janice's Frisco number, grateful that the voices he would be speaking to wouldn't be able to answer back. Holding his breath, he heard, "Hi, this is Janice Hopkins. The girls and I have taken our act on the road, but we should be returning before Christmas," and "The woods are lovely dark and deep. Leave a message at the beep."

The beep went off. Lloyd let out his breath and said, "Take your act south before I do something crazy. You're all I've got left." Then he drove home and walked upstairs to the bedroom he had kept inviolate since his wife left him two years before. There, on a dust-covered bed, he fell asleep to wait for survival or oblivion.

33

Eight hours after executing his only son's executioner, Captain Fred Gaffaney sat down in his study and began the writing of his last will and testament.

The execution weapon rested on the desk beside him, and he breathed cordite residue as he put to paper his bequest: cash amounting to slightly over twenty thousand dollars, the house, its furnishings and his two cars to the Church of Jesus Christ, Christian. The magnum loomed at the corner of his vision, and he tried to recall Bible passages that dictated suicide excluding heaven and meeting the Savior. Verses came and went, but none stuck, and the .357 was still there. Finally he gave up trying and accepted the fact. Only Catholics bought suicide as an exclusionary sin, and they could not justify it with Biblical references. It was an acceptable out for a warrior Christian with nowhere else to go.

Looking over his words, Gaffaney saw that they took up only one yellow legal page. He had written accident reports ten times that long, and he didn't want to pull the trigger on a note of brevity. He thought he could perform the execution as a ritual that affirmed the rule of law, but when Lohmann and Collins tossed Duane Rice's body into its sewage bed grave, he knew that he had violated everything he believed in, and that that apostasy demanded the death sentence. Knowing also that the condemned deserved reflection before their sentence was carried out, he allowed himself the mercy of returning to Suicide Hill in the fall of '61.

He was a rookie then, working daywatch patrol out of East

Valley Division, twenty-six years old, with a wife and baby son. His beat included the Sepulveda V.A. Hospital, and half his duty time was spent ferrying sad old soldier boozehounds from the wine bars on Victory Boulevard back to their domiciles, the other half writing traffic citations. It was boring police work for a young man who knew only one thing about himself—that he was ambitious.

There was an old wino who kept escaping the domicile to get bombed on white port and pass out religious tracts to the teenaged gangsters who inhabited Suicide Hill at night. The local officers respected him, because he refused to accept welfare and stuck the V.A. with the full tab for his room and board. He was a tall, Germanic-looking man with haunting blue eyes, and the tracts he distributed emphasized a warrior Jesus Christ, who loved his followers fiercely and exhorted them to strike down evil wherever they saw it.

The wino was a brilliant storyteller, and the gangsters liked to get him juiced and incite him to tall tales. He always obliged, and he always weaved sermons into his stories, ending them with a handing out of leaflets emblazoned with a cross and a flag.

To Officer Fred Gaffaney, Irish Catholic atheist, the wino was a pathetic crackpot. He grudgingly followed the implicit division edict of never busting him for "plain drunk," but he would not listen to his stories for a second. Thus, when the wino approached him one afternoon with a feverish account of a bunch of Demon Dog members out to kill him, he turned a deaf ear, gave him fifty cents for a jug and told him to get back to the domicile.

A week later, the wino's body was found, scattered all over Suicide Hill. He had been drawn and quartered. The investigating detectives reconstructed his death as being caused by four motorcycles taking off simultaneously, each with one of his limbs tied to the rear axle. The M.E. reconstructed that he had been decapitated after his death, and Officer Fred Gaffaney reconstructed himself as a coward and did not come forward with his information on the Demon Dogs, because it would hinder his career.

The anonymous tip on the Dogs that he sent to Robbery/Homicide Division two torturous weeks after the killing did not lead them to the slayers or ease his conscience. The wino's blue eyes singed him in his sleep. Booze and illegally procured sleeping pills didn't help, and he could not talk about it to a single human being.

So he sought out God.

Returning to the old Catholic fold helped, but he could not take his wino/victim with him to the confessional. Liquor in concert with the Church helped a little more, but the blue eyes and "The Dogs got a contract out on me, Officer Fred, and you gotta help me!" were always a half step away, ready to pounce just when he thought everything was going to be all right.

The Job helped most of all, but still did not provide a panacea. He *served*, working long overtime hours, writing laborious reports on the most minor occurrences, afraid that any parcel of information left unreported would lead to spiritual catastrophe and death. A few superior officers regarded him as fanatical, but most considered him a model of police meticulousness. Spurred by constant encouragement, he climbed the ladder.

He became a sergeant and was assigned to the Detective Division, then passed the lieutenant's exam and went to Robbery/Homicide. The Church, the wino, and cross and flag nightmares simmered on his soul's back burner, pushed there by ambitiousness and a barrage of rationalizations—his drive for power was atonement; his stern rule over lax, libertine underlings was a sword thrust that would move the blue-eyed specter himself; encouraging of his son to become a policeman was evidence that the atonement would pass to a second generation of Gaffaneys. His wife's death of cancer gave a weight of grief to the guilt procession, and when he buried her he felt that the sad old storyteller had finally been put to rest

Then he met Lloyd Hopkins, and the out-of-control hot dog blew everything to hell.

He had, of course, been hearing about him for years, taking in accounts of his exploits with amazement and disgust, but never considering him worth knowing from the standpoints of career advancement or Robbery/Homicide efficacy. Then, assigned as supervisor of his sector, Thad Braverton gave him the word: "Hopkins is the best. Give him carte blanche."

The undercutting of his authority had rankled, but Crazy Lloyd's actions made it pall by comparison. Hopkins' life was one giant sword swipe at real and imagined evil; the terror and guilt and rage that burned in his eyes were laser beam incisions into that part of him where "Suicide Hill '61" was engraved like gang graffiti. He had to fight what Hopkins was, so he tracked down the cross and flag leaflets and was born again.

It worked.

He carried the wino's message; took comfort in its call to duty. He studied the Bible and prayed, and found fellow officers who believed as he did. They followed him, and when he passed the captain's exam and was flagged for the I.A.D. exec position, he knew that nothing could stop him from achieving a spellbinding selfhood preordained by God and a martyred madman twenty years dead.

Then Hopkins took out the "Hollywood Slaughterer." The boldness of his measures inspired awe among the men of the born-again officer corps, and had Hopkins walked into one of their prayer meetings, they would have genuflected before him as if the sex-crazed lunatic were Christ himself. His solving of the Havilland/Goff homicides a year later again brought the men to their figurative knees. He became a rival spiritual patriarch who was dangerous precisely because he did not covet spiritual power, and the means to his destruction had to be divinely sought and given.

Hours and hours were spent praying. He spoke to God of his hatred for Hopkins, and got small comfort. His strategy to upgrade his son's school records and gain his admission to the Academy worked, and Steven graduated and was assigned to West L.A. Division. Prayer and the appointment of a second-generation Gaffaney to the Department helped diffuse Hopkins' hold on his mind, as did the building up of the interdepartmental dirt files. Then his prayers were rewarded, and promptly backfired.

Lamar Dayton, a Devonshire Division lieutenant and long-time born-again, joined the corps and told him of whoremaster Hopkins and his Watts baptism of fire. Circumstantial verification of National Guard records made the final message ring clear: Hopkins, not himself, was the divinely gifted policeman/warrior, and what drove him was not God, but awful self-willed needs and desires—all mortal in nature.

Gaffaney stood up and looked at the clock above his desk. His stay of execution ruminations had consumed an hour, and were still not one hundred percent conclusive. He thought of things to be grateful for: he and Steven had been close in the days before his death, and Steve had confided that he had resisted the retired deputy's fencing imprecations, turning over a new leaf. That was comforting, as was the fact that he had not compounded his self-hatred by letting Hopkins perform the execution.

"Hopkins" and "Execution" filled in the missing percentage points, and extended the stay of sentence to the indeterminate near future. Gaffaney looked at the magnum and suddenly knew why he had stolen his death weapon from an L.A.P.D. source. Only Lloyd Hopkins would be crazy enough and bold enough to follow the gun to its source and back to him, regardless of the consequences and devil take the hindmost. He had taken the magnum from a Wilshire Division evidence room in full view of a half dozen officers because he wanted to sacrifice himself to the man he most admired and envied.

Thinking of "Suicide Hill '61" and mercy, Gaffaney carried his three armfuls of files into the bathroom and dumped them in the tub, then walked downstairs and grabbed a bottle of bourbon off the bar. Returning upstairs with it, he doused the pile of paper and dropped a match on top. His hold on scores of men went up in flames, and he waited until all the data was obliterated before turning on the shower. The fire hissed, sizzled and died, and Gaffaney walked back to the den to wait for his executioner.

34

Awakening from eighteen hours of dreamless sleep, Lloyd rolled off the dusty bed and walked to the window to see if it was night or day.

Creeping sunlight from the eastern horizon told him it was dawn, and the paperboy hurling the *Times* at the front door told him that it was neither survival nor oblivion, simply time to get on with it. After shaving, showering and dressing in his favorite sport coat/slacks combo, Lloyd sat at the dining room table and wrote out a declaration that two weeks before he would have considered incomprehensible.

Gentlemen:

This letter constitutes my formal resignation from the Los Angeles Police Department. It is tendered with regret, but not under a state of emotional duress. The reasons for my resignation are threefold: I wish to devote a good deal of time to my family; I have incurred the enmity of several high-ranking officers; and events of the recent past have convinced me that my effectiveness as a homicide investigator is drastically diminished. It is my wish to be assigned to either clerking or nonfield supervisory duties until my twenty-year anniversary comes up next October. I am grateful for the Department's offer of early retirement with full pension, but feel it would be dishonorable to accept it without serving the required twenty years.

Respectfully, Lloyd W. Hopkins

Bracing himself for the outside world, Lloyd put the resignation letter in his pocket and walked to the door, hoping the *Times* would carry news of one man's death and another man's safe passage. Throwing the door open, the headline beamed up at him: "'Suicide Hill' Suicide Ends Four-Day Murder Spree."

Leaning into the doorway, Lloyd let the subheading of "Cop Killer–Robber Takes Own Life at Fabled Youth Gang Meeting Ground" sink in. Then, with his brain screaming first "Gaffaney," then "No!" he read the entire account:

Los Angeles, December 15

The Los Angeles Police Department announced today that the greatest manhunt in L.A. history has ended with the suicide of multiple murderer Duane Richard Rice, the mastermind behind Monday's West Los Angeles bank robbery that left four dead.

Rice, twenty-eight, a career criminal with convictions for vehicular manslaughter and grand theft auto, is believed also to be responsible for Tuesday night's hit-and-run murder of L.A.P.D. officer Edward Qualter and the fatal shootings of the gang's two other members, Robert Garcia and Stanley Klein, bringing the total of his victims to seven.

At a late night press conference at Parker Center, L.A.P.D. Chief of Detectives Thad Braverton explained how the cooperation of an anonymous associate of the gang gave police the means to reconstruct the reign of terror:

"It was a classic case of a falling out among thieves," the Chief said. "Rice, Garcia and Klein were the perpetrators of two well-planned robbery/hostage forays in the Valley the week preceding the Pico-Westholme bank robbery, which we view now as having been undertaken by Rice partially out of a desire for revenge—one of the bank employees, Gordon Meyers, a former Los Angeles County deputy sheriff, was his jailer during a recent incarceration."

Braverton went on: "We do not know precisely *why* Rice wanted revenge, but *that* he did is a safe assumption. Our witness in custody is the man who sold the robbery gang their guns, and he, a long-term associate of the three men, states that distrust ran deep among them. The other men also possess criminal records—Garcia for burglary, Klein for possession of narcotics. Klein was also heavily involved in video pornography. Circumstantially, we believe that Rice shot and killed both Garcia and Klein, his motive being a desire to keep their share of the money from the Pico-Westholme robbery. There is also an evidential corroboration for this—our chief ballistics officer, Arthur Cranfield, has examined the .45-caliber slugs taken from the bodies of Garcia, Klein and Rice, and he states *conclusively* that they came from the Colt army-issue .45 found in Duane Rice's hand when patrolmen discovered his body lying in the Sepulveda Wash."

Lloyd scanned the rest of the article, a hyperbolic spiel about tragedy, law and order, and the forthcoming L.A.P.D. funerals. The total picture bombarded him as a patchwork of victory and defeat, survival and denial. His report to Dutch, the forensic subterfuge at Stan Klein's pad and Louie Calderon's testimony had been, if not actually believed, accepted in the spirit of letting sleeping dogs lie. But the Duane Rice "suicide" was preposterous. On Tuesday night Dutch had said that two .45s were recovered at the Bowl Motel, while his own gun had supplied the Stan Klein "death" shots. If Rice had been killed with his own piece, which was doubtful, because he never would have relinquished it—he didn't pull the trigger himself.

Lloyd felt a queasy rage overtake him. Rice had deserved to die; he had contemplated his cold-blooded murder himself. And the man who most likely killed him held a death sentence over his own head. Running red lights and siren to Parker Center, he couldn't believe he was crazy enough to take the both of them out in one fell swoop.

The Central Crime Lab was bustling with technicians. Lloyd found Artie Cranfield in his usual workday posture, hunched over a double-plated ballistics microscope. Knowing that nothing short of an air raid would force Artie's head up, he said, "Tell me the real dope on Klein and Rice. What's Braverton stonewalling?"

Artie came up smiling. "Hello, Lloyd. Would you repeat that?"

Lloyd smiled and cleared his throat; Artie said, "Not here," and pointed to his office. Lloyd walked in, and five minutes later Artie joined him. Shutting the door, he said, "Straight business?"

Nodding affirmatively, Lloyd said, "A bunch of fixes are in. I found Klein's body, D.O.A. knifing. I fired three shots from my .45 into his stiff, so I know that 'same gun' stuff in the papers is bullshit. Did you process the evidence on Rice?"

Artie gave his four walls a furtive look, then said, "I was there at the autopsy. The M.E. handed me three spent .357s, dug them out of Rice's chest. The rear of the jackets were nicked, right where the firing pin would make contact. Very distinctive, and very familiar. I checked ballistics bulletins going back eighteen months. Bingo! Matchup to an old unsolved in Wilshire Division, street shooting, gun found and held by the Wilshire Dicks, you know, to lean on possible shooters with."

Taking the stats in, Lloyd got the feel of a wild card or big wrong move. "Your conclusions, Artie?"

"Do I look dumb? One of our guys zapped the cop-killing cocksucker. Anyway, I called John McManus and told him what I found, and he said, 'Keep it zipped, Officer.' A half hour later Big Thad shows up, hands me three .45 spents and says, 'Garcia, Klein, Rice, case closed. Capice?' Since I intend to collect my pension, I said, 'Yes, sir.' So you keep it zipped. Capice, Lloydy?"

A Technicolor movie of Louie Calderon guzzling beer and Joe Garcia strumming a guitar surrounded by hula girls passed through Lloyd's mind's eye. He resisted an impulse to grab Artie in a bear hug, then said, "Do *I* look dumb?"

"No," Artie said, "just slaphappy."

"Well put. I need a favor."

"You always need favors."

"Well put. I've got a long stakeout coming up. Processed any speed lately?"

"Black beauties?"

"Music to my ears. I've got a phone call to make. I'll see you in five minutes."

While Artie made the speed run, Lloyd called Wilshire Detectives. His old friend Pete Ehrlich's answer to his question made wild card/big wrong move a *big* understatement:

At 9:30 Wednesday morning, Captain Fred Gaffaney appeared in the Wilshire squad room, looking uncharacteristically nervous. He cracked several uncharacteristic dirty jokes with officers on duty there, then demanded the key to the evidence room, got it, and rummaged through the lockers until he found a .357 Python, sealed in an evidence bag that also contained a dozen loose shells. Offering no explanation for his actions, he spurned Ehrlich's condolences for the loss of his son and walked out of the squad room, shaking from head to foot.

When Artie returned with five biphetamine capsules, Lloyd had gotten *his* shaking under control. After dropping his resignation letter off with Thad Braverton's secretary, he drove to Temple and Beaudry. Finding an ace stakeout spot across from the guitar shop, he swallowed a black beauty and settled in to await his hand-picked survivor. Soon an amphetamine symphony was ringing in his head:

Gaffaney.

Hopkins.

Two killers doing the doomsday tango.

35

"**U**nfucking real!"

Joe balled up the newspaper, took a bead on the bright blue sky and hurled the missile of good news straight at the sun. Street passersby turned to stare at him, and he shouted, "I got a fucking guardian angel!" and let the ball fall into his hands. Running with it like a halfback with a hot short pass, he headed straight for the motel and Anne.

She was sitting up in bed, smoking, when he came through the door and smoothed the headline out on the sheet in front of her. "Read it," he said. "Bad news and good news, but mostly righteously *good*!"

Anne put out her cigarette and read the front page; Joe sat on the edge of the bed, wondering how the fuzz had got it so wrong and why Rice offed himself there. Watching Anne read, his old song obsession did a brief boogie reprise: " . . . and death was a thrill on Suicide Hill."

Anne turned to the second page, and Joe got curious about how she'd react to the story on her old boyfriend and his death. He'd had her on decreasing coke use for two days now, and she was probably as close to being a normal woman as she ever would be. Would she have the soul to grieve for the crazy motherfucker?

Putting down the newspaper, Anne lit another cigarette and said, "Wow, I thought Duane was just a car thief. I think that stuff about Stan being a bank robber is phony, though. I think we were together on Monday when that bank was robbed."

Joe couldn't tell if she was being cagey or straight. "You

were probably stoned," he said. "He probably split for the heist, then came back."

Anne shrugged and blew smoke rings, then said, "Wrong, baby, but who cares? Also, the paper says Duane *shot* Stan. That's wrong. I was there. Duane stabbed him."

Joe tingled at her mistaken certainty—it meant he could ditch her with a free mind. "Cops screw up sometimes," he said. "Or they work things around to fit the evidence they got. Sweetie, what do you want to *do*?"

"You mean in general? And about us?"

"Right."

Anne blew a string of perfect rings and said, "I like you as a boyfriend, but you're too uptight about dope, and too macho. When we first got together, you weren't so bad, but the more I get to know you, the more stern you get, like you think violence and manhood are synonymous or something. But basically, I want to be with you, and I want to get back into music. I think we're a wave. We last as long as we last."

Joe bent over and cupped her breasts. "What about Rice? He righteously loved you."

Anne caressed the hands caressing her. "He was a stone loser. And you know what's sad? Karmacally he betrayed himself, because he said suicide was for cowards. That's sad. How much of Mel's money have we got left?"

Thinking R.I.P. Duane Rice, Joe said, "We're almost broke, but I've got a buddy holding a guitar of mine, and we can get at least three bills for it. So let's move."

"Is it okay to be out on the streets?"

"I think so. We got some kind of weird guardian angel, and I want to see if the old neighborhood still looks the same."

36

At twilight, just when the long stint of surveillance was starting to drive him batshit, his survivor walked up to the guitar shop window, a skinny blond woman in tow. From a distance they looked like a down-at-the-heels couple—modest dreamers in rumpled clothes peering into the glass in search of a dream fix. Letting them enter the shop, Lloyd hoped they wouldn't do anything to blow the impression.

When they walked back out a minute later, he was there on the sidewalk, waiting. Joe Garcia looked into his eyes and knew; Anne Atwater Vanderlinden looked at Joe and got the picture secondhand. Lloyd stepped back toward the curb and put up his hands in surrender. "Peace, homeboy," he said. "I'm on your side."

Anne moved to Joe's side as he stared at Lloyd; the tense three-way silence stretched until Lloyd put down his hands, and Joe said, "What do you want?"

"People keep asking me that," Lloyd said, "and it's getting old. You read the papers today?"

Joe put an arm around Anne. She nuzzled into his chest and said, "Maybe he's the guard—"

"He's a fucking cop!" Joe blurted. Seeing a woman pushing a baby carriage past them, he lowered his voice. "Crazy Lloyd Hopkins, big fucking deal. You don't scare me, man."

Lloyd smiled. Garcia looked like a thirty-year-old teenager trying to impress a high school chick and get a date for the Junior Prom. Given what he'd been through in the past two weeks, the impression was astounding.

The silence hit again, broken this time by Joe's broad smirk. Smirking back, Lloyd hooked a finger at the strangest armed robber he'd ever seen. Joe walked over, and Lloyd draped an arm around his shoulders and whispered, "Don't be a dumb taco bender. Let Klein take the fall and get the fuck out of L.A. before something goes wrong. And don't ask me what I want again, or I may have to kick your ass."

Joe twisted free. "I killed Stan Klein, man. I righteously killed him."

The proud statement hit Lloyd between the eyes as truth, and he started sensing juice behind the ancient teenager's bravado. "I believe you. Tell your old lady we're going for a little ride."

The last of the mechanics were leaving when they pulled up across the street from Likable Louie's One-Stop Pit Stop. Lloyd let them finish locking up and gave them time to get down to Sunset, then took a crowbar from the trunk, ran over and pried the garage door open. Flicking on the overhead lights, the first thing he saw was low-rider perfection.

It was a mint-condition '54 Chevy ragger, candy-apple sapphire blue, canary yellow top, continental kit, tuck-and-roll upholstery. Lloyd checked the dashboard and grinned. The key was in the ignition.

"Bonaroo, man! Fine as fucking wine!"

Lloyd turned around and saw Joe stroking the Chevy's rear fender skirts. Anne Vanderlinden stood behind him, smoking a cigarette and eyeing a tool bin loaded with portable TVs. Tapping Joe's shoulder, Lloyd said, "Are you legit with the greaser act, or are you just trying to impress me?"

Joe started polishing the car with his sleeve. "I don't know. I *righteously* don't know."

"What *do* you know?"

"That I righteously know what I don't want to be. Listen, I got a question."

"Shoot, but nothing about what's going down. All you need

to know is get the hell out. There's loose ends all over the place."

Joe fingered the Chevy's pinstriping. "Why'd Rice kill himself at Suicide Hill? What was he thinking of?"

Lloyd shrugged. "I don't know."

Anne was by the tool bin, fiddling with the dials of the TV sets. Joe could tell that she was dope-itchy, looking for something to do with her hands. Moving his eyes back and forth between his maybe girlfriend and his guardian angel, he said, "Hopkins, what's with that place? I mean, you're a cop, you must have heard the stories. It started out with this dude Fritz Hill, right? Back in the forties? He was a righteous hardball and the Hill was named after him?"

Lloyd looked out at the street, getting nervous because he was a civilian now, with no official sanctions for breaking and entering. "I think most of the story is bullshit," he said. "What I've heard is that back in the fifties and sixties there was an old snitch who used to hang out by the Sepulveda Wash. He pretended to be a religious loony, so the local cops and the punks who partied there would think he was harmless. He ratted off shitloads of gangsters to the juvie dicks downtown, and he got a snitch jacket and got snuffed. He was a German guy, and his name was Fritz something. What's the matter, homeboy? You look sad."

"Not sad," Joe said. "Relieved, maybe."

"The keys are in the ignition. Can you drive a stick?"

"Can niggers dance?"

"Only to soul music. Grab some of those TVs and split."

Joe loaded the trunk and backseat with portable Sonys. Anne stood and watched, chain-smoking and shivering. When the Chevy was filled to capacity, he led her over to the passenger's-side door and lovingly eased her in, then returned to Lloyd. Sticking out his hand jailhouse style, he said, "Thanks. And tell Louie I'll pay him off someday."

Lloyd corrected the shake in mid-grasp. "My pleasure. And don't worry about Louie, he owes me. Where are you going?"

"I don't know."

Lloyd smiled and said, "Go there fast," then dropped Joe's hand and watched him walk to his chariot. The strangest armed robber of all time hit the gas with a flourish and crunched the Chevy's gears backing out of the garage, sideswiping parked cars as he headed south on Tomahawk Street. Lloyd turned off the light and shut the door, brushing B&E splinters from his hands. When he got to his Matador, he had a clear view of Sunset. The Chevy was fishtailing it eastbound, and Anne Atwater Vanderlinden was standing under a streetlamp, dancing with her thumb out.

Tango time.

Lloyd took an inventory of his person, punching the seat when he saw that he had forgotten both his newly resurrected .45 and his standard .38 snub nose. The only piece in the car was the .12 gauge mounted to the dash, and it was too obtrusive—overkill all the way. He had to go to the house first and grab a weapon; to show up unarmed for the dance would be suicidal.

He drove home slowly, the amphetamine keeping him hyper-alert, fear of the confrontation making him dawdle in the slow lane. Turning onto his block, he began composing epitaphs for himself and Jesus Fred. Then he saw the moving van in his driveway, its headlights illuminating Janice's Persian carpet, rolled up against the side door. Antiques were arranged on the lawn like welcome beacons, along with piles of Penny's books.

Mine.

Home.

Yes.

Lloyd gasped and punched the accelerator. The homecoming dissolved like a mirage, and new bursts of death prose kept it pushed down to where it couldn't maim him; couldn't destroy his resolve. Then, with miles of obituaries behind him, he pulled up in front of Captain Frederick T. Gaffaney's house and let it hurt, letting his old hot-dog persona take over from there.

Mine.

Home.

Him or me.

Lloyd grabbed the shotgun and flipped off the safety, then pumped in a shell and walked over to the house. The downstairs was dark, but dim lights glowed from behind curtained windows on the second floor. Giving the door handle a test jiggle, Lloyd felt it click and give. He pushed the door open and moved inside.

The smell of stale cigarette smoke and whiskey filled the living room. Lloyd padded forward in the darkness, the odor getting stronger as a staircase came into shadowy view. Tiptoeing up it, he heard coughing, and when he got to the second-floor landing, he saw diffused light glinting off empty liquor bottles strewn across the hallway. Holding the Ithaca at port arms, he pressed himself to the wall back first and scissor-walked toward the light source.

It was a bathroom, giving off a different odor—that of charred paper. Stepping in, Lloyd saw that the smell emanated from the soggy mounds of blackened folders that filled the bathtub. Poking the barrel of his shotgun at the top of the pile, a layer of soot crumbled, and he was able to pick out the stenciled words: *Confidential–Need to Know Basis*. A cross and flag logo was imprinted below it.

A sudden burst of coughing forced Lloyd to wheel and aim. Seeing nothing but the bathroom walls, he traced the racking sound down the hall to a half-open door with total dark behind it. He raised his right foot to kick; the door flew open and harsh light blinded him. He threw the Ithaca up into firing position, and when his vision cleared, he saw that he was muzzle to muzzle with Fred Gaffaney and a cocked magnum.

"Freeze, asshole."

Lloyd didn't recognize the voice, and could hardly recognize the man it belonged to. This was a high-ranking witch-hunter of booze breath, slept-in clothes and frazzled nerve ends; a born-again with a three-day beard and a shaky finger on a trigger at half pull. A doomsday apparition.

"Freeze, asshole."

The second warning came across as hideous self-parody. Lloyd lowered his shotgun, and Gaffaney eased down the hammer of the .357. The two weapons fell to rest at their bearers' sides simultaneously, and Lloyd said, "What are we going to do about this, Captain?"

Stepping back into the study, Gaffaney waved his gun at the framed L.A.P.D. group shots on the walls. "I'm not a captain anymore, Sergeant," he said, his voice regaining its authority. "I resigned this morning. You outrank me. I did it to make it easy for you."

Lloyd propped the Ithaca up against the doorjamb, keeping it within grabbing range. "I'm not a sergeant anymore. I asked to top out my twenty, but they'll never go for it. We're both civilians. That make it easier for *you*?"

Gaffaney looked at a picture of his wife pinning lieutenant's bars to his collar. "My resignation was accepted, yours was shelved. Braverton told me this afternoon. He wants you around. He wants you around because he loves you."

Lloyd kept his eyes on the magnum that Gaffaney dangled by a finger. "Captain, we're both down the—"

"Don't call me that, goddamn you!"

"We're both down the river! We killed men in cold blood, and the Department has got the fix in on yours, and you've got the fix in on mine, and all I want to do is seal the jackets on both deals and go home to my family. That's as easy as I can make it."

Gaffaney's raw-nerved features went lax; his voice went blank. "You didn't come to arrest me?"

The evidence room charade clicked in as a deliberate big wrong move. Lloyd let his fingers brush the .12 gauge. "I thought I could do it, but I can't. How about it? Your indictment for mine, then I get out of here before something crazy happens."

Gaffaney started shaking his head. His arms shook involuntarily, as if his entire body were trying to shout his denial. The

.357 dropped to the floor just as he found his voice. "No. No. No. No. No, no, no, no—"

Lloyd made a grab for the magnum. He got it in his hands before Gaffaney could make a move, and had the cylinder emptied just as the string of no's trailed into a weirdly lucid monotone. " . . . I didn't come this far for you to betray me."

Lloyd slipped the shells into his pocket and tossed the revolver back on the floor, then picked up the Ithaca and ejected the round in the chamber. When the carpet was littered with neutralized weaponry, he said, "Why me?"

The witch-hunter's monotone took on resonance. "Because I was good, but you're the best. Because you were a punk civilian when you killed that man in Watts, while I was a high-ranking police officer when I committed murder. Because the Department will never let me be prosecuted, because justice in this affair must be total." Gaffaney paused, then said, "Because I love you."

Lloyd moved backward until he bumped the wall. "You're insane if you think I'm going to kill you. I'd let you hang me for Richard Beller before I'd do that."

With a ghastly smile as segue, Fred Gaffaney said, "We both learned the gift of sacrifice late, Lloyd. That happens with selfish men like ourselves. I'm only sorry that our sacrifices have to conflict. Now tell me in light of this if I'm insane:

"From the tap on your phone I surmised that you wanted to frame a dead man for Joe Garcia's part in the robberies and killings. I held on to the information. Then this afternoon, when I read the paper and saw what you had gotten away with, I sent Sergeants Collins and Lohmann to check up on Klein. He was involved in the filming of pornographic movies on the dates of the three robberies, in full view of a dozen witnesses. He cannot be connected in any way to Luis Calderon, and a friend of mine in S.I.D. said that he died of knife wounds. He has in his possession a switchblade whose edges perfectly match a biopsied section of Klein's abdomen. The handle has Joe Garcia's thumbprint on it."

"No," Lloyd said in his own doomsday drone. "No, no, no, no, no."

Gaffaney said, "Yes," and started ticking off points. "Klein's alibi witnesses won't come forth, for fear of their involvement in porno coming to light, but questioning the Pico-Westholme eyewitnesses with Klein's and Joe Garcia's mugshots should get some interesting feedback, and Calderon could never get by a persistent grand jury. Collins and Lohmann have Duane Rice's .45, taken from the car he was in when they apprehended him. That will contradict Braverton's fix. Had enough?"

"You filthy cocksucker," Lloyd hissed.

Gaffaney spoke softly, as a loving parent would to a child. "I know your guilt, and I know you have to expiate it, and I know Garcia is convenient for that. But if we don't follow through on the investigation, then it means as policemen we mean nothing."

Lloyd imitated Gaffaney's lucid lunatic whisper. "Captain, between us we've been hot dogging for over forty years. Joe Garcia is a drop in the bucket compared to all the railroad jobs we've pulled, *all the laws we've broken*. You're giving me a song and dance about the law to pump me up to kill you? *You are stone fucking insane*."

Running his fingers over the wall photos, Fred Gaffaney said, "I heard a human interest story on the radio today. A bunch of high school kids found some of the robbery money strewn throughout their neighborhood, some inked, some not. They didn't turn it over to the proper authorities, of course; they descended on the Strip and tried to spend it as fast as they could. An off-duty sheriff's deputy saw a boy trying to change an inked twenty and got him to talk, but by the time a search team was dispatched to the area where the money was found, not a single dollar bill could be located. You see the kind of world we live in?"

Lloyd picked up the .357 and began loading it. "It's a pretty lackluster parable, Captain. Tell it to Collins and Lohmann. It'll get them jazzed up to do some serious ass-kicking. Have you gone forward with your information on Garcia? Anyone beside you and your boys know?"

"No, not yet."

"Why did you burn your files?"

"I'm not a policeman anymore. I don't deserve to lead, and none of my followers are capable of leading. Th . . . that's finished."

Snapping the cylinder, Lloyd said, "I did what I could. Garcia's got wheels and a head start, more than he would have had without me. You got anything to say?"

Gaffaney frowned. "Rice said, 'She was a stone heart-breaker.' What do you think he meant?"

"I don't know, Captain. For the record, you did the right thing. He killed your son."

Gaffaney reached out and touched Lloyd's arm; Lloyd batted his hand away and said, "What do *you* have to say?"

"Nothing," Gaffaney said. "I have nothing."

Lloyd placed the gun in the hands of his old enemy. "Then go out like a soldier, but don't take anyone else with you."

"You won't?"

Lloyd said no and walked down the hall to the bathroom. He was clenching the edge of the tub, staring at the cross and flag logo, when he heard the shot. His hands jerked up, ripping out jagged chunks of porcelain, and then there was a second shot, and another and still another. He ran back to the study and found Gaffaney on his knees, holding the gun and an armful of framed photographs to his chest. He was muttering, "I've got nothing. I've got nothing."

Lloyd helped him to his feet. The mementos he was grasping made the embrace cumbersome, but he was able to get his arms around the sobbing man anyway. The simple act felt like mercy for all their lost ones, all their stone heartbreakers.

MORE MYSTERIOUS PLEASURES

HAROLD ADAMS
The Carl Wilcox mystery series
MURDER	#501	$3.95
PAINT THE TOWN RED	#601	$3.95
THE MISSING MOON	#602	$3.95
THE NAKED LIAR	#420	$3.95
THE FOURTH WIDOW	#502	$3.50
THE BARBED WIRE NOOSE	#603	$3.95

TED ALLBEURY
THE SEEDS OF TREASON	#604	$3.95

ERIC AMBLER
HERE LIES: AN AUTOBIOGRAPHY	#701	$8.95

ROBERT BARNARD
A TALENT TO DECEIVE: AN APPRECIATION OF AGATHA CHRISTIE	#702	$8.95

EARL DERR BIGGERS
The Charlie Chan mystery series
THE HOUSE WITHOUT A KEY	#421	$3.95
THE CHINESE PARROT	#503	$3.95
BEHIND THAT CURTAIN	#504	$3.95
THE BLACK CAMEL	#505	$3.95
CHARLIE CHAN CARRIES ON	#506	$3.95
KEEPER OF THE KEYS	#605	$3.95

JAMES M. CAIN
THE ENCHANTED ISLE	#415	$3.95
CLOUD NINE	#507	$3.95

ROBERT CAMPBELL
IN LA-LA LAND WE TRUST	#508	$3.95

CHRIS WILTZ
The Neal Rafferty mystery series
A DIAMOND BEFORE YOU DIE   #645 $3.95

CORNELL WOOLRICH/LAWRENCE BLOCK
INTO THE NIGHT   #646 $3.95

■■■■■■■■■■■■■■■■■■■■■■■■■■■■■■■■■■■■